Public Enemies

Jess Money

PUBLISHED BY FINCHVILLE PUBLISHING

A division of Finchville Entertainment, Inc.
www.finchvillepublishing.com
info@finchvillepublishing.com
PublicEnemiesBook.com

Cover design by Candescent Press
www.candescentpress.com
Cover Photo: Keith Lamond

Library of Congress Cataloging-in-Publication Data Applied for
ISBN 978-0-9912650-2-2 (paperback)

Revised Third Edition March 2014

Acknowledgements

The wonderfully talented, gracious, and supportive editor Hillel Black, without whose guidance the finished work might not be worth reading.

Editor Madeline Adelstein, for nudging me in the right direction early on.

Writer Christiana Miller, whose knowledge and advice about the modern publishing environment saved me on too many occasions to count.

Agent Peter Riva, who encouraged me to write this book, and pointed me to the editors I needed to successfully do so.

Dedication

To my late father, James Money,
Who set an example of courage and integrity.

To the late, wonderful Nance Mitchell,
Without whose friendship and support I would
never have had the opportunity to write this book.

To Mark Iwasykiw,
Friends come no better than this man.
And he doubles as a damn good story advisor.

To Lori,
The extraordinary woman who passed through my
life for only a moment, but changed me forever.

Author's Notes

The battle at Point Pleasant in 1774 actually took place, essentially as described.

DAS, the Domain Awareness System, is real. It is an "integrated intelligence solution" created by the NYPD in partnership with Microsoft and offered for sale to other government entities beginning in 2012. DAS combines surveillance footage from government cameras, private security networks, and automated license plate readers with information in government and private databases. Images captured by DAS can be integrated with facial recognition and pattern recognition software to identify specific individuals and their associations with other persons, groups, or organization. DAS in New York City is monitored in a Command-and-Control Center staffed by both the NYPD and representatives of private "stakeholders" such as banks and financial institutions.

The article mentioned on page 71 about the hacking vulnerabilities of private surveillance systems such as those used by hotels, stores, parking structures, etc., was published in 2013.

The Main Core database of persons considered domestic threats to the government is also real. According to figures from reliable sources, including testimony to Congress, it contains at least eight million people and is added to on a consistent basis.

Public Enemies

April

Chapter 1: Linn Cove

Senator Arlen Stowe's motto was, "If it's not a jet, it's not an airplane." Deathly afraid of heights, the Chair of the Senate Finance Committee knew just enough about flying to lack faith in turbo-prop commuter planes destined to encounter thunderstorms, thermal drafts, and clear air turbulence. Even on commercial jetliners he sat on the aisle, or preferably in the center section, just to avoid any possibility of looking down.

Speed, however, was another issue. The senator loved to drive fast, especially on curvy roads where he could fantasize about being a famous race driver. Stowe's family, on the other hand, would rather have taken flight in a battle-damaged WWII bomber than ride across the street with Arlen at the wheel. This worked out well for everyone when it came time to make the annual pilgrimage from Stowe's home in Virginia to the family farm near Ashville, North Carolina for his mother's birthday. His wife and kids flew on ahead, and the senator followed later by car.

The only practical route was the Blue Ridge Mountain Highway, a road not conducive to those in a hurry. The maximum posted speed limit along its entire twisting, curving 470-mile length was 45 mph. However, car and weather permitting, in some places a driver like Stowe who was so inclined could go a lot faster. As was his custom, Stowe spent the early evening with his mistress and started his drive around nine. This gave him a chance to race through the really curvy stretches of the highway by slicing over into oncoming lanes in the safety of darkness, where the glow of on-coming headlights gave him plenty of time to ease off the throttle and get back into his own lane.

The crown jewel of the Blue Ridge Mountain Highway was

the Linn Cove Viaduct, a span that seemed to hang in space on concrete pillars as it curved in and out around Grandfather Mountain. Driving over it had been described as "feeling like a soaring flight around the edge of the world," the operative word being feeling. Like many people with a fear of heights, Stowe wasn't bothered as long as he didn't have to look down, and as he expertly lined up his approach into the viaduct's first curve, he certainly didn't intend to do any real soaring. His instructor at the high performance driving school in Phoenix would have been proud as Stowe's muscular imported luxury sedan cut the apex of the first curve perfectly and came out flat, glued to the road, holding a perfect line. Attacking the apex of the second curve, the car dipped across the centerline into the on-coming lane, which should have been empty.

But it wasn't.

The Senator hadn't counted on a vehicle coming the opposite direction without lights, especially not a beefy six-wheel Chevy Cheyenne pick-up with a massive steel off-road front bumper. After two-dozen practice runs with the truck's lights on, The Man at the wheel had the truck in exactly the right spot at exactly the right time. Small sensors behind the front bumper picked up the first glimmer from Stowe's headlights and triggered an electrical relay that activated the truck's four regular headlights, four quartz-iodide off-road running lamps on the bumper, and four large Halogen lamps on the roll bar behind the cab.

Instantly blinded by over a thousand candlepower, Stowe instinctively yanked the wheel to the right. The car slammed into the guardrail head-on. Its crush package worked perfectly, absorbing energy exactly as it was designed to do. But the combination of speed, weight, and angle of impact was irresistible and the guardrails failed.

The viaduct was built with a double height guardrail for a

reason. Its graceful curves and the picturesque beauty of the setting belied the fact that its support pillars rose sixty-five feet, and below them the mountain fell off at a very steep angle. If a car went off the viaduct, its occupants could forget about being saved by seat belts and air bags. Even if the car landed upright, the impact would be such that the best their family could hope for was maybe an open casket at the funeral.

Stowe's family would not be so lucky. His gleaming silver status symbol vaulted off into space nose down and then gracefully, almost in slow motion, momentum carried the car the rest of the way over. It landed upside down one-hundred-and-fifty feet below, dead center on a granite outcropping. The impact blew open all four doors and collapsed the roof down until the backs of the leather bucket seats broke. Stowe's family could have put coffin rails on the car and buried him in it.

Back up on the highway, the truck's extra lights went off and it kept going at the same steady speed.

A few minutes later a local veterinarian, responding to an emergency involving a mare in labor, spotted the missing guardrail and notified authorities. Law enforcement officials on the scene quickly agreed that it was virtually impossible to accidentally drive off the Linn Cove Viaduct. Over the years a number of drivers had scraped or bounced off the guardrail, and a few trucks had even smacked it pretty hard after hitting black ice in the winter. But nobody had ever gone Evel Knievel off the viaduct. Nobody. Not ever.

When bad things mysteriously happened to powerful and important people, phones in Washington started ringing. The Director of Homeland Security, Elliot Hoover, and Director Louis Bartholomew of the FBI agreed that if the Rasputin of the Senate had just died in an accident that local authorities deemed suspicious, the federal government needed to have somebody look into it. Right away. Pronto.

That somebody was Senior Special Agent Darren Medlin and his Special Assignments Section Bravo. At thirty-six the youngest head of an SAS unit, Medlin -- known around the Bureau as Doc because his mentor, legendary Agent John O'Neil, had dubbed him "the cure for tough cases" -- had a core staff of only three agents. The stated rationale was that by virtue of being based at the FBI's D.C. headquarters Doc had access to temporary manpower and resources that SAS teams in other regions didn't. But it was an open secret around the Bureau that Bravo was deliberately understaffed so that the Director could more easily keep O'Neil's star protégé on a short leash.

Doc never let the situation bother him. As far as he was concerned, if other SAS teams had more permanent staff, it just proved they needed more help. He could get along just fine with the handpicked trio he dubbed the Blessed Trinity because he was "blessed to have them." Special Agent Kenny Johnson, a burly ex-marine nearing mandatory retirement age, functioned as Doc's alter ego. Agents Kelli Randleman, an attractive lipstick lesbian with a droll sense of humor, and Scott Rennick were young, energetic, versatile, and proven. Both were likely to head SAS units of their own someday.

Just before sunrise a pair of FBI choppers landed at a park Visitors Center not far from the crash site. Doc and his Blessed Trinity rode to the scene in a Park Service Chevy Tahoe. A handpicked FBI forensics team that Doc dubbed his "whiz techs" followed in a Suburban.

The highway was a state road, but the Blue Ridge National Park was federal land. To their credit, both the park rangers and the North Carolina state troopers on the scene were more interested in following good police procedures than in fighting a jurisdictional turf war. While the troopers diverted traffic, park service personnel cordoned off the hillside from the wreck site down to the service road at the bottom of the mountain. Considering the formidable terrain challenges, Doc's whiz techs could not have hoped to work a more pristine and well-preserved scene.

When Bravo got to the site, the head Park Ranger didn't have to ask who was in charge. Doc radiated command presence. Of course, standing six-six and a tapered two hundred-thirty pounds certainly didn't hurt.

The first thing Doc wanted to know was, "What was the senator doing on this road at this hour?"

"According to the manager of Stowe's field office in Lynchburg, he was on his way to Ashville to celebrate his mother's ninety-third birthday on the family farm."

"Driving? Why didn't he fly?"

"Evidently the senator really hated flying in small planes."

Doc looked out over the crash scene below. *Wonder how he liked flying in his car?* "So he was going down there to celebrate alone? What about the rest of the family?"

"Oh, they flew in earlier today," deadpanned the Head Ranger.

While state officials brought in a crane, a shipping container was rushed to the nearest local airport on an Air National Guard C-130 cargo plane, then trucked to the site. Doc's whiz techs went over the car carefully before it was sent back to Quantico on the same C-130. Except for being sealed with heavy sheet plastic and tape, the car traveled the same way it had been found: upside down, with Stowe's remains still inside.

With the car out of the way, Park Rangers strung climbing ropes and safety harnesses. Each whiz tech paired up with a ranger and the teams scoured the hillside to retrieve the guardrails and anything that might have fallen off the car in flight.

Chapter 2: Point Pleasant

Nobody paid any attention to The Man sitting quietly near the Point Pleasant Battlefield National Monument. This was good. His ability to blend in and not stand out had served him well, and would be crucial in the coming months.

The tiny park was quiet this morning, as it always was. Only the faint murmur of early morning traffic on the Ohio River Bridge intruded on the silence. The Man with the soft brown eyes was grateful for the tranquility. He had come to this small town at the junction of the Kanawha and Ohio rivers to make a big decision.

Point Pleasant National Park commemorated a battle no one except local residents knew about. Contrary to popular history, the Revolutionary War didn't start with the Battle at Lexington Green and "the shot heard 'round the world." The shots that started the American Revolution were fired here.

Anticipating that revolution was brewing in the colonies, Lord Dunsmore, the Crown Governor of Virginia, devised a scheme for Shawnee and Mingo Indians, working with British redcoats, to lure the colonial militia into an ambush. Unfortunately for Lord Dunsmore, militia Colonel Andrew Lewis suspected as much and secretly fortified his position on the Point Pleasant bluffs. After a day of bloody fighting, Col. Lewis turned the tide by sending two companies around to attack Dunsmore's forces from behind. Two-hundred-and-thirty British and Indians died. The date was October 10, 1774, six months before the events at Lexington.

It wasn't until 1908 that Congress finally recognized the Battle of Point Pleasant as an official battle of the American Revolution. Even then, its dedication as a National Park was misleading. The entire site was no larger than the football stadium at an average suburban high school. And by that time the story of Lexington, and the tourist dollars that go with it, was firmly rooted in American tradition.

The Man already knew the story of Point Pleasant well. His ancestors, brothers John and Edsell, commanded the two companies sent to flank the British and Indian forces. Faded letters in an old family Bible described the battle, and how each of the brothers, who went on to serve as captains throughout the Revolutionary War, had killed and scalped British officers.

The Man knew that the militia who fought at Point Pleasant had been brave and committed men. *Was he that kind of man? Was it delusional for one ordinary citizen to think he could change the country?* More importantly, he pondered the advice of Abbie Hoffman: "The first duty of a revolutionary is to get away with it." *Was his goal to escape identification a fantasy? Was it really possible, in an age where personal privacy and anonymity were relics of the past, to attempt action on such a grand scale, and yet remain anonymous, unidentified?*

Identification meant either death or life in prison. Death didn't scare him nearly as much now as it had when he was younger, but the possibility of permanent incarceration was out of the question. He would never allow himself to be subjected to the Special Procedures wing at the Federal SuperMax Prison in Colorado, with each cell in its own soundproof chamber, the silence broken only by the maddening buzz of fluorescent lamps overhead. There was also the issue of collateral blowback to consider. *What price would his children and grandchildren pay for his sins?*

His ideas were not new. He'd just assembled and organized them. But if he managed to present those ideas in a way that inspired the public, the resulting movement could create a new national agenda. Once things got that far, anything was possible. On the other hand, *What if he failed?* Until recently, The Man had followed the laws of both God and man. He had served his country with distinction, worked diligently, raised two fine children, and remained faithful to his wife throughout forty-one years of marriage. But would God forgive his recent actions, and what he was planning to do?

In addition to Senator Stowe, Admiral Copeland was also dead now, week-old fish food at the bottom of the sea. They had been tests, of The Man's ability to plan and execute missions, and of his conscience. So far, so good on all counts. Both attacks had come off without a hitch and The Man felt no regret, no fear, and no guilt. But these events had also been carefully staged to look like accidents. What The Man intended to do next would be overt, deliberate, in-your-face. If he went ahead, there would be no turning back.

Everything was ready. All the pieces were in place, all the weapons and safe houses secured, all the preparations complete. Only the final decision remained.

As the sun climbed higher in the morning sky, The Man made up his mind. The spirit of his ancestors spoke to him. They knew that he was declaring war only on the oligarchs and the plutocracy, not the country. At least he could say he tried. And if Hell was what God had in mind for him, then he would just have to settle for the consolation of knowing that he had sent a lot of other people there first to keep him company.

Chapter 3: Out There

New York screenwriter William Goldman coined the phrase "out there" to describe the Hollywood movie business. But Hollywood being as much a state of mind as an industry or a geographic territory, in earlier times "out there" included Palm Springs. That was no longer the case. Current celebrities and industry players preferred to cavort at The Palms in Vegas, and similar trendy places in South Beach, Aspen, or Mexico. Now home to stuffy old money and retired snowbirds escaping cold Midwest winters, Palm Springs continued to offer two things: superb golfing, and privacy. It remained a perfect environment for those who liked to take their swings and have their conversations in private. Men like Senator Dominic Trammello and former Attorney General Luis Navarro.

The Man gazed through the 20X scope and marveled as Trammello and Navarro walked up the seventh fairway. The two supposedly fierce partisan foes from opposing parties were having such a good time, which was only natural since there was no substantive difference between them. Both men were confirmed liars with complete disdain for the intelligence and the needs of the public. Both viewed corruption as their right, an entitlement accorded their status and positions. Their only differences involved whose campaign contributors were rewarded. And, of course, how much was in it for each of them, personally. This golf outing symbolized the symbiotic relationship between them. One created a scandal. The other benefited from it.

At the start of former President Lyman's administration, Attorney General Navarro had been a key player in Lyman's plan of illegal domestic wiretaps, surveillance, and blackmailing of political rivals. Eventually, voter backlash against the incompetence and corruption of the Lyman regime swept the opposition party into power in both houses. As new Chairman of the Senate Judiciary Committee, Trammello's television face time increased ten-fold. He made the most of it, loudly venting outrage over, "the despicable actions of Navarro and others in the Lyman administration." It sounded so good, so righteous, and so indignant. And it was all such bullshit.

What Trammello actually cared about was preventing the release of files Navarro had copied before resigning from the Justice Department. Although the public justification for the illegal spying program was the war on terrorism, at least half the motivation lay in uncovering dirt about political rivals. It paid off better than Lyman and his administration, also nicknamed the Lyman Organized Crime Family, had dared hope. Lyman's Black Files contained damaging information, from the merely embarrassing to the clearly criminal, on every member of either party.

The Black File copies Navarro had in his possession documented millions of dollars in bribes by defense contractors and drug companies to Trammello to kill unfavorable legislation. There was also the issue of the seven ghost employees on Trammello's staff payroll, whose federal paychecks were laundered back to Trammello through dummy accounts. But this paled next to the videos of the senator's summer vacations in Latin America and Thailand. Each started with a doctor certifying the virginity of young girls about fourteen or fifteen. That was followed by sessions lasting as long as a week in which the Senator beat, raped and sodomized the girls, forced them into sex acts with each other, and generally debased them in every way that didn't necessitate the use of animals. If those tapes ever got out, Dominic Trammello would go to jail until his corpse rotted.

At his far-away perch, The Man knew nothing about Navarro's Black Files or Senator Trammello's depravity. Nor did he know what corrupt new enterprise they were discussing. Not that it mattered. He already had plenty of good reasons -- well known to anyone who followed politics seriously -- to kill both men. And this morning the conditions for doing so could not have been better. The flag hung limp on the flagstick. Even the occasional faint wisp of wind was straight down The Man's line of sight and wouldn't affect his aim.

Navarro's third shot landed just past the hole, under the crest of the green, and rolled back to within nine feet, leaving a very makeable putt for a golfer of his ability.

The Senator uttered an insincere "Nice shot," then stood over his ball. Following through on his swing, Trammello never noticed the slight wind from the bullet as it passed a few feet to his left. Nor did he hear the shot. At the sniper's nest, the silencer adapted from a motorcycle muffler reduced the usual booming WHOMP! of the .50 cal Barrett sniper rifle to a soft moan. Nine hundred yards away at the point of impact, there was no sound.

Navarro landed flat on his back with a thump and wheezed as the air left his lungs. At first, the Senator thought his partner had suffered a heart attack, but after taking a couple of steps closer, Trammello knew better. There was a black hole in the middle of Navarro's sternum. Behind him, blood and bits of flesh fanned out on the grass in a V-shaped pattern.

To his credit, the Senator reacted quickly and didn't freeze as many would in a similar circumstance. He was almost to the golf cart when a bullet vaporized his left knee, effectively separating his lower leg from the rest of his body. Writhing in agony, Trammello dragged himself to a sitting position against the golf cart.

Through the scope, The Man saw the most startled look on the senator's face, as if to say, "Why me? What did I do?" Clearly he had no idea why someone would want to kill him.

Trammello's self-delusional arrogance infuriated The Man. Instead of finishing off the Senator with a headshot, The Man let him suffer. Even if the Senator didn't bleed out before help arrived, cyanide coating on the bullet guaranteed that he would foam at the mouth and die long before he ever got to a hospital.

The Man carefully wiped the gun with pads pre-soaked in bleach to remove any DNA. To prevent the accidental transfer of genetic material from one area of the gun to another, each portion was wiped with its own separate pad. First came the eyepiece of the scope, then the cheek rest, followed by the stock and then the barrel. Since his trigger finger was the only part of either hand not protected by latex gloves, the trigger and trigger guard assembly got a double cleaning. He moved quickly but carefully, methodically. The Man shoved the gun deep into a dark crack between two large boulders and carefully covered it with dead brush.

The hill was small and The Man went back down the back of it briskly but carefully, not risking a fall that might leave DNA evidence or cause visible injuries. At the base of the hill a nondescript older model Chevy van waited in the shadows behind a clump of Joshua trees. The Man carefully stripped off his disposable painter's overalls and put them in a waiting shopping bag along with the gloves and his shoes. Only after he got into the car, closed the door, and slipped on his driving moccasins did The Man remove the bandana covering his hair.

By the time the bodies were discovered, The Man was cruising down a side road at a speed that wouldn't attract attention. A few miles later he pulled in behind an abandoned service station, one of many left by the consolidation of the oil companies over the past two decades. The shopping bag went into a waiting drum half-full of hydrochloric acid. After quickly wiping down the drum to remove any fingerprints or trace DNA, The Man returned to the van. A mile-and-a-half later, he was heading east on U.S. Highway 10 with the cruise control set.

Chapter 4: A Bigger Boat

In addition to the Stowe case, Bravo was also looking into the mysterious disappearance of Admiral Farris Copeland off his sailboat, which had run aground on the Carolina coast a few days before Stowe's death. In some ways, the Admiral's case was even more disturbing. As the former head of the NSA and later the CIA, Copeland had, literally, a world of enemies, foreign and also domestic. This last issue had prompted Doc to warn Director Bartholomew not to put him on the case "if you're afraid where it might lead."

Although both cases had officially been ruled accidents, Bravo was still quietly trying to find any possible common link between them. That's why Doc and the Blessed Trinity, along with a few other agents pulled in for the investigation, were assembled in the conference room when Doc's phone rang. He listened for a minute, said "Yes, sir," then hung up and briefed the staff on the shootings in Palm Springs, which were being combined with the Stowe-Copeland investigation.

Doc immediately detailed his Supervising Assistant, Grace McCallister, to send out an ENN message. Created after 9-11, the Emergency Notification Network alerts top federal and state officials about national security situations. The mayors and chief law enforcement officers in the one hundred largest cities were also on the network. Brief text messages, followed by a more detailed recorded phone message, shot out simultaneously to just under four thousand officials and key aides.

Just as Grace left the room, the conference room phone rang. The Palm Springs Police Chief was on the horn. Doc put him on the speaker.

The Chief added nothing to the little they knew so far, but

judging by his recap of the actions already being taken by his department, the Riverside County Sheriff's Office, and the CHP, it sounded like the locals were on top of things. He concluded with, "I assume you'll be sending a team from D.C.?"

Doc had already decided to let SAS Gloria in Los Angeles do the legwork. "Actually, a team from L.A. is coming out. Agent-in-Charge is Jack Rose."

"We'll give 'em all the assistance we can. If it helps your peace of mind any, the Bureau personnel out of L.A. that I've worked with in the past were pretty professional, not the type who had their head up their ass." What the Chief was really saying was, "We're pretty good and we're pretty professional, and I don't have my head up my ass, so don't send folks out here to lord it over us."

"Thanks, Chief. That's good to know."

Getchen Polamalu, one of Doc's favorite agents that he pulled in whenever a case required extra manpower, didn't have to be told to get Jack Rose, already en route to Palm Springs by chopper, on the speakerphone.

"Hi, Jack."

"Hi, Doc. Been expecting your call."

"Just wanted you to know I didn't pull rank. Giving me the case was the Director's call."

"Yeah, sure," Rose joked with mock sarcasm. "Same ol', same ol'. I do the work, you steal the credit."

"Not telling you how to run your investigation," which he was, "but I think this might turn out to be a *locus* case," meaning a case where the evidence was primarily or exclusively circumstantial and the lynchpin was being able to put the suspect in the area around the time the crime occurred. "As I understand it, our Domain Awareness network penetration in that area is pretty hit-and-miss so we'll need supplemental video from every surveillance camera within a fifty-mile radius of Palm Springs, and for another fifty miles beyond that in both directions along Interstate 10. That means every ATM, convenience store, gas station, bank, hotel, shopping mall, industrial park, public storage facility, you name it. Get video from all the CHP and local police dashboard cams as well. A single license plate might break the whole case. Pull in all the manpower you need. Borrow from the San Diego, Vegas, and Phoenix offices if you need to. Interview every employee who's been on duty since midnight last night at any gas station or convenience store. And get copies of all their credit card transactions."

"You want fries with that?"

"Yeah, with extra ketchup and a large chocolate shake. And do me a favor? Check the parking lots at both Ontario and Palm Springs airports. They photograph license plates as a control check to prevent employees from skimming cash. Also interview all California and Arizona state border control agents that have been on duty since yesterday morning. See if they remember anyone or anything even the slightest bit out of the ordinary. If they do, have them identify the people and vehicles on their videotapes."

"That's two favors."

"Hey, treat me nice, I'll make sure they spell your name right when we crack this case. Agent Randleman will be your primary contact."

"Hi, Kelli."

"Hi, Jack."

Doc told Rose to, "Coordinate with Ed and Ginger. And good luck."

Rose signed off with, "Copy that."

Ed and Ginger Bridges were Doc's technology lifesavers. A husband-and-wife team of computer experts, they had every aspect of information management down so cold that they designed and maintained the separate computer system used by all the SAS teams. Sometimes, just to entertain other agents or upstage the boneheads down in the Bureau's MIS/IT office, they gave demonstrations on how to locate and extract data from the FBI's hopelessly antiquated regular computer system. Ed supervised all database search functions and oversaw analysis of video or audio evidence. It would be his job to crosscheck the avalanche of incoming video. Ginger's forte was evidence intake. Cataloging and tracking mountains of evidence as it came in was not only crucial to solving cases, it was critical to establishing a legally airtight chain-of-custody. Evidence that a judge wouldn't allow into court wasn't evidence.

Doc ended the meeting with one final admonition. "What's most important in a case like this is: Keep. An. Open. Mind. Think logically, but creatively. This is the Federal Bureau of Investigation, not the Federal Bureau of Assumption."

After everyone else left the room, Doc asked Kenny, "So, whattya think?"

Kenny looked around their current workspace, the tiny Operations Center C, and said, "I think we're gonna need a bigger boat."

Chapter 5: The Wrong Coast

If California was the Left Coast, then to The Man the east coast was the Wrong Coast. Almost everything that was wrong with the country emanated from the two east coast power centers, New York and Washington. The Man called it, "the true axis of evil." And nobody exemplified the corrupt linkage between the two cities more than SEC Chairman Lloyd Beber.

Except for his three thousand dollar blue pinstriped suits, Beber matched Boss Hog from the original Dukes of Hazzard TV series to a T. Short and round, Beber was as smooth and bald down the middle of his head as a billiard ball. He was also the regulator who didn't regulate. Instead, for every fraudulent deal, Beber got a kickback, a bribe, or a slice of the IPO. Every time a company settled an "enforcement action" for pennies on the dollar while "neither admitting nor denying wrongdoing," Beber got a percentage of the amount the firm saved by not having to pay a heftier fine or full restitution. The payoffs went through a network of offshore accounts, dummy companies and, in some instances, briefcases full of cash. For three decades this kind of deal had been standard procedure for previous SEC chairmen, but Beber took it to a new level. Why settle for a limited term when you can remain in office forever, like J. Edgar Hoover at the FBI? Following J. Edgar's playbook, Beber included a lot of important elected officials in his dirty deals, then kept the evidence as insurance against ever being replaced.

While Beber knew where all these transactional bodies were buried, even he didn't know that the man sitting to his right on the rostrum, Senator Howard "Woody" Shorewood, had a real dead body buried in his backyard.

Twenty-six years earlier, Doug Hardin was the bagman in a pay-off to Shorewood from Silverstein-Goetz, the world's most powerful bank. In return for $450,000 in small bills, Woody was supposed to guarantee that a bill the banking industry -- and Silverstein-Goetz in particular -- did not want to pass would die in committee. In those days, four-hundred-and-fifty large was big money, so when Shorewood couldn't deliver, Hardin was dispatched to Woody's vacation home in the Catskills to retrieve the bank's investment. Woody shot Hardin in the head, then buried his body in concrete under an oversized granite birdbath in the garden. That night Linda, Woody's wife, followed while he ditched Hardin's Buick Le Sabre in the Hudson River.

Five days later a pair of detectives looking into Hardin's disappearance came out to the house. Linda served them homemade lemonade and carrot cake. While they snacked on the patio not ten feet from the birdbath, Woody claimed that Hardin had never showed up. The Senator said he'd called several times but always got Hardin's answering machine. Linda Shorewood not only corroborated her husband's story, she offered the detectives leftovers from the Saturday night dinner Hardin missed. The cops politely declined, drove back to the office, and verified a series of messages from the Shorewood house to Hardin's home and office on the days following his disappearance.

The cops knew that every day hundreds of people went missing. Some had accidents or met with foul play, but many simply took off to start over again. With nothing to go on, they tossed Hardin's file in with all the other unsolved missing-persons cases and forgot about it.

The CEO of Silverstein-Goetz didn't know what to believe. Having ordered several hits himself, he had no problem believing that Shorewood might have killed Hardin, or had someone else do it. On the other hand, Hardin had a shady past involving the kind of people who settled old scores Hoffa-style. Also, besides a well-documented drinking problem, Hardin wasn't in the best of health. Maybe he had just gotten sloshed or had a heart attack and went off the road someplace. Years later, some hiker or hunter would find the car, Hardin's skeleton behind the wheel like a grisly Halloween prank. Then again, Hardin wasn't getting any younger. Perhaps he'd decided to retire in some banana republic with $450K in lieu of an imitation gold watch and a grand a month from Social Security. Ultimately, the CEO wrote off the matter as an expensive lesson. But from then until the CEO retired nine years later, Silverstein-Goetz was conspicuously absent from the list of Shorewood's campaign contributors.

Back in California, The Man pulled off Interstate 10 where he knew he could tap into the free wi-fi service a chain hotel that catered to business travelers provided for its guests. He opened his MacBookPro and was soon viewing surveillance video from locations around the Marriott Marquis Hotel on Seventh Avenue in the heart of New York. At the moment nothing of importance was happening, but The Man wouldn't have to wait long.

Inside the Marriott's main ballroom, guests at a luncheon sponsored by the Wall Street Journal were finishing off the chocolate éclair dessert course when one of Woody's Senate aides and a plainclothes officer from the NYPD's High-Profile Security Detail appeared and huddled with the Senator. SEC Chairman Beber sensed that something was up and waddled over to find out what.

Farther down the dais, Beber's assistant also picked up the vibe. Easing out of his chair, he slid over and joined the conference. Beber motioned to the hallway, and said something to the Senator, who nodded. While Beber and Woody strolled casually out into the hallway, Beber's assistant and Shorewood's Senate aide stayed, pretending to make small talk. Once out of sight in the hallway, Shorewood and the SEC Chairman hustled down the service elevator and out through the kitchen. They were in their respective cars by the time Beber's assistant stepped to the podium. He got as far as naming Navarro and Trammello and the word "shot" before everyone reached for their phones and the stampede was on. Every exit door in the room flew open.

Most of those attending the conference had limos or town cars waiting in the Marriott's block-long private driveway. A few younger execs, still too low on the food chain to rate car service, dashed out into Seventh Avenue and threw themselves in front of the first cab that came by, empty or not. More than one passenger made a quick $50 to bail out and find another taxi.

Senator Trammello's Judiciary Committee had co-jurisdiction with the Senate Banking and Finance Committee over bills affecting Wall Street. Every analyst, investor, stockbroker, banker, hedge fund exec, financial planner, and pension fund manager at the luncheon instantly shared the same concerns that Shorewood, Beber, and the President now grappled with: How might the elevation of a new chairman change things? How would the financial markets react to news of the attack? What sectors of the economy could be hit hard? Which might benefit? What effect would an elevated terror alert status have on travel, shipping, energy prices, food stocks, short-term savings, gold prices, and interest rate policy? The people who guessed right for their companies, their clients, or themselves would be winners. Those who guessed wrong could be broke, or out of a job. Or worse, God forbid, both.

Whenever he was in Manhattan, Shorewood always used the same limo, a gray Cadillac owned and operated by a driver named Ron Fincher who lived out on Long Island. Most of Fincher's day-to-day work came from contracting out as an independent owner-driver for a limo service. But whenever Shorewood was in town, Ron worked directly and exclusively for the Senator, 24/7. The fact that the $3,500 a day fee was on the taxpayer's dime didn't bother Woody in the least.

Fincher's limo appeared in the lower left quadrant of The Man's computer screen. He zoomed in close to confirm the license number, then dialed a number from his pre-paid disposable cell phone.

Twenty-nine hundred miles away in New York, detonators wired to an identical disposable cell phone set off two pounds of M-118 Flex-X. A moldable plastic explosive of the PETN family that packed sixty percent more wallop than TNT, Flex-X came in strips three inches wide, twelve inches long, and a quarter-inch thick weighing a half-pound. Two sheets together weighed a mere pound, and made a package only a half-inch thick.

It was generally accepted that New York limo drivers lived and died with their private clientele. People who requested a driver by name, or by-passed the limo service and booked with a driver directly, were the difference for a driver between just scratching out a living and being able to send their kids to private schools. In this instance, a private client truly was a life or death matter. Ron the Driver and Howard the Senator, chauffeur and client, died together, instantaneously. Sitting directly over the blast area, Shorewood's body was shredded into a half-dozen pieces. Traveling at the speed of sound, the concussion turned Ron's brains to jelly even before his body was scorched by the flash fire. Later the coroner found his eyeballs stuck to the trim molding above the windshield.

Beber's midnight blue Mercedes 600S limo was a half-block behind Shorewood's, and Beber's driver immediately stood on the brakes. Seventh Avenue was one-way, but that didn't stop the former Secret Service agent behind the wheel from throwing the car in reverse and burning rubber backwards, going against traffic, which fortunately was lighter than usual.

SEC Chairman Beber's body may have been round, but his instinct for self-preservation was stiletto-sharp. A little voice told him to get out of the car. Fast. "Stop the car! Beber barked. "Stop the car!"

The Benz lurched to a halt. Beber threw the door open. For such a roly-poly little man, he moved with surprising quickness and was already half out of the car when an explosion blew him into the door with such force that the top of the door cut off his head. It landed on the canvas awning over a bagel shop eighty feet away. The rest of his three hundred-and-forty pounds remained stuck in the opening where the window had been.

Back in California, The Man resumed his trip but eventually turned off onto a side road. As in Palm Springs minutes earlier, he had just handed out more justice in New York than he realized. He knew nothing about Doug Hardin's body buried under Shorewood's birdbath. But even if he had, it wouldn't have made any difference. Like Trammello and Navarro, Beber and Shorewood had been targeted for bigger crimes and far greater sins.

An hour later, after zigzagging on various dirt roads, The Man was back on the highway again, but this time in Arizona, having by-passed the California and Arizona Border Inspection Stations. "Not a bad day's work," he said to himself.

Chapter 6: MICE

Kenny was right. They did need a bigger boat. The investigation was now a National Emergency Threat case that would involve thousands of agents, including several hundred working directly out of a central Ops Center. Doc got instant authorization to move Bravo and the initial corps of agents from the Stowe-Copeland case into the Bureau's biggest boat, Operations Center D, unofficially referred to by agents as the Mother of All Op Centers.

Doc immediately had to move from the threat of a lone assassin to dealing with an organized group capable of executing classic ambush strategy on a new transcontinental scale: a first attack that lured others into a second, even more deadly ambush. He wondered if the next few minutes would bring news of more attacks. New York was a lot closer than L.A. and with two bombs as well as potentially hundreds of witnesses the situation demanded maximum supervision to Doc's standards. "Scott, you're going to New York." His superb organizational skills would be invaluable at what was sure to be a complicated crime scene. "Take our best whiz techs and two teams from the Explosives Division, one for each car. Bill and his team," he said, referring to SAS Alpha in New York, "will work under you. Assert authority over the entire operation. These are federal crimes. If any locals get in the way or hold back anything, step on them. Take Price, Castaldo, and Lanigan with you."

Castaldo spoke Spanish, Price knew enough Russian and Ukrainian to get by, and Lanigan had taken three years of night school Italian while working two John Gotti cases. They gave the team a solid base in the languages that were most likely to be helpful in the Big Apple. Except Arabic, of course. But until he knew exactly what he was dealing with, Doc couldn't afford to spare the one member of his current staff who spoke Arabic and Farsi. Several Alpha agents in New York spoke one or both. Doc hated having to rely on anyone outside his own team, but for the time being, this would have to do. Besides, so far nothing about the attacks hinted at an Islamic connection.

Doc and Kenny quickly settled in front of a wall of television monitors inside OCD's separate, glass-enclosed A/V control room. Neither was surprised that ABC News hit the air first with live reports from the scene in New York. Good Morning America broadcast from a street level studio on Times Square where Broadway intersects diagonally with Seventh Ave at 44th Street. The Marriott Marquis was barely a block away, and clearly visible from the street outside the studio.

At least two ABC mini-cam crews were operating around the scene in Manhattan. That meant the network was cutting from one camera feed to another, selecting what, and more importantly, what not, to show. Kenny immediately called NSA and had intercepts of all ABC's satellite uplink feeds routed to the control room. Trained eyes could learn a lot from raw, unedited footage and Doc wanted as much of it he could get right at his fingertips. It could have long-term evidentiary value, but for now he and Kenny were more interested in possible immediate leads and impressions.

In Palm Springs, reporters were kept off the grounds of the Mission Hills country club, and TV news choppers were ordered so far back from the scene that nothing worth watching came in from there. Meanwhile, Grace scanned all reports from both sites and boiled down any relevant info into bullet-point Status Memos. As soon as Doc or Kenny initialed each one, a copy went to the Director. At the same time, other agents under Kenny's direction wore out the phones, filling up Bravo's roster with additional agents and specialists. Within hours the team went from a mere eighteen people to over two hundred. As information and possible leads poured in from California and New York, hundreds of other agents across the country were put to good use.

Unfortunately, good use didn't translate to good news.

The Man had done a good job of hiding the Barrett and it took a long ground search to find the weapon. Doc was a little surprised that the gun had been left behind. A Barrett was not an easy weapon to acquire. They were expensive and so few were sold legally that Doc wasn't aware of a single case where the seller couldn't positively identify the buyer in mug shots, a line-up, or the courtroom.

On those rare occasions when a Barrett became available in the black market, the price generally ran ten grand or more. Ammunition wasn't cheap or easy to come by either. Each six inch-long round cost about five dollars, and even most big gun stores had to special order the stuff. On the other hand, ditching the gun reminded Doc of the mob hit man motto, "Use it, then lose it." This added another unsettling scenario to the list of possibilities: rather than being ideologically motivated, what if these were professional hits? Mob killers usually work up-close. They rarely resort to long-distance surgical methods of killing. Yet the possibility couldn't be ruled out. This opened up a new set of problems. More angles to investigate meant more possible dead-end leads to run down.

The serial number of the Barrett traced back to a sporting goods store in Antigo, a small town in upper Wisconsin. Antigo's only claim to fame, if it had one, was being the home of medic John Bradley, immortalized in the famous WWII photo of the flag raising on Iwo Jima. The Clint Eastwood movie Flags Of Our

Fathers was based on a book written by Bradley's son.

The sporting goods store in question had gone out of business eight months earlier, strangled by competition from big-box retailers and on-line sources. According to the police report, shortly before the store folded somebody disabled the alarm system, broke in, and took the Barrett. In a strange twist, whoever broke in left behind no prints, hairs, fibers, or DNA but he did leave three thousand dollars in cash, the gun's listed sale price. The money was all in used bills of various denominations and a trace of the serial numbers led nowhere.

This was, however, good news. Doc could now eliminate the hired hit man theory. A pro certainly wouldn't have left payment behind. He also now had insight into the mindset of the assassins. This was about pure class warfare, little guys against the big boys. The group thought nothing of blowing away the head of NYSE, but wouldn't consider stealing from the sole proprietor of a small business. The bad news was that whoever stole the Barrett took nothing else except 120 rounds of ammo, leaving over a hundred other guns behind. This meant that potential suspects couldn't be linked to the Palm Springs shootings through possession of other items taken from the store. Doc concluded that his adversaries were taking every possible precaution, not only to avoid being identified and caught, but being convicted if they were. Equally frightening, it was safe to assume that the group had reliable access to other weapons.

By late afternoon, Scott reported that the bombers had gone to great lengths to confine casualties to the intended targets and their drivers. Half the Flex-X was placed on each side of the car against the inside of the frame rails, causing the blasts to collide and rebound off the street below, concentrating the killing effect inside the car. Because the blasts partially canceled each other out, injuries to bystanders were fewer and less severe than they would have been with a conventional car bomb. Of the sixteen people injured, none required overnight hospitalization.

After Scott signed off, Kenny noted, "Looks like they want to minimize the body count. Whatever their goal is, collateral damage is evidently bad for public relations."

Doc was thinking the same thing. His initial suspicions now confirmed, he immediately notified the Director that this new terror campaign almost certainly did not have an Islamic connection.

For three days, lots of information came in but the investigation went nowhere. Each bomb had been set off by dual cell phones, a primary and a backup, taped behind the rear bumper of each car. Separate wires connected each phone to both halves of the Flex-X charge, insuring that even if one phone failed, the entire charge would go off. The phones were wired to the frame, making the car a giant antenna. There was no telling exactly how long the bombs were in place; it had been weeks since either car was serviced.

Enough was recovered to trace the phones, but Doc suspected that as with the Barrett sniper rifle, they would probably not trace back to the user. He was right. The trail only went as far as a distributor in Los Angeles who sold them for cash as part of a bulk sale to a free-lance reseller who operated out of the back of a van. In between supplying local gangs and drug dealers, the free-lancer worked the major local swap meets at the Rose Bowl, Orange County Fairgrounds, and various drive-ins. He had no memory of the buyer, and even less interest in trying to remember.

Unlike bombs hooked to a car's electrical system or detonated by timers, the ones used to kill Shorewood and Beber had to be manually detonated. Beber's Mercedes limo was unusual enough even by New York standards that it would have been easy to identify from a distance. The rented limo carrying Shorewood, on the other hand, was virtually indistinguishable from hundreds of others in Manhattan, including several dozen waiting at the Marriott for other VIPs attending the conference. No evidence was found to indicate that it had been fitted with a GPS tracking device or homing beacon. Therefore the bomber or an accomplice either had to have been in line of sight position to see the Senator get into his car, or to identify the car by its license plate. But Doc thought, *Surely the bombers were aware that the entire Times Square area, indeed all of mid-town Manhattan, as well as the Marriott's external and internal security cameras, were part of the Domain Awareness System? Anyone sophisticated enough to plan this attack had to know they would be captured on video, right?*

The likely source of the explosives used in the bombs was a distributor in Amarillo, Texas, who shipped a lot of it to South America for use in mining operations. Four months earlier, thirty pounds of Flex-X had turned up unaccounted for during a surprise ATF audit. Nobody knew exactly when it went missing and if it had been stolen, pilfered by an employee, or sold out the back door under the table. Until now there had even been speculation that it might be a paperwork error. Perhaps a clerk had simply forgotten to list it among other items on a bill of sale or shipping manifest.

Agents turned up the pressure on all of the company's current or former employees and customers, but Doc wasn't sanguine about the prospects. He was pretty sure that the Flex-X had been stolen by the same people who hit the sporting goods store in Wisconsin. People good enough to bypass the distributor's alarm system, heist the material, and depart without leaving a trace. That the missing material had cost the distributor a year's suspension of its ATF Dealers Permit, and nearly put the company out of business, was of little consolation. Even if the bomber had used some of it in tests, that still left a lot of the stuff in the wrong hands.

While he waited for the mountain of DAS video to be analyzed and witness interviews verified, two questions dominated Doc's thoughts: *Who was he dealing with? What do they want?* He turned to MICE, an acronym for the four reasons a person could be induced to spy against their own country. The same motivations generally applied to terrorists.

> Money
> Ideology
> Coercion
> Ego

In this case, Doc was confident that he could ignore money. If this were some kind of an elaborate extortion scheme, like the D.C. sniper case, catching the perps would be relative child's play. He also ruled out coercion. He couldn't imagine that anyone with the skills to carry out sophisticated attacks of such magnitude also harbored a secret damning enough to make them act under pressure from someone else. That left ideology and ego. Of the two, Doc prayed that the driving force was ideology. At some point ideologues were compelled to proclaim their cause and unveil a list of demands, which inevitably led to their downfall. For two decades the Unabomber was a ghost. Then he released his manifesto to the Baltimore Sun and was captured within weeks.

What Doc needed now was a manifesto from those responsible for the attacks. *Please, God, let it be soon. Give me a manifesto and we'll solve this case in a heartbeat.*

Doc's wish was about to come true. His prediction, however, was not even close.

Chapter 7: The Feral Beast

The Man considered his crusade a marketing challenge. He wasn't selling violence and assassination; he was selling reform. The attacks in Palm Springs and New York were merely commercials, like showing a broken down car to demonstrate what happens when people don't change their oil. Now it was time to see if there were a market for his product, and if anyone was willing to invest in the enterprise of reform.

In planning his media campaign, The Man kept in mind former British Prime Minister Tony Blair's description of the media as "a feral beast" which operated on the premise that the audience needed to be arrested, held, and have their emotions engaged through stories with impact. The Man was determined to feed the feral beast plenty of stories with impact, but he had no illusions. His attacks would get lots of coverage, but finding the right vehicle for his real message would be much more difficult.

The television networks and most newspapers were owned by a small handful of mega-conglomerates subject to substantial government regulation. This vulnerability to various forms of government retaliation, and fear of backlash from big advertisers, kept many stories out of the news. What did get reported was shaded, and watered-down. Omitting inconvenient facts and vital context created the misconception that both sides of an issue were equally valid. Minor differences and superficial manufactured controversies were emphasized at the expense of substantive discussion.

Lust for access to officials for exclusive scoops and breathless reports of breaking news led the mainstream media into "access journalism," where journalists were co-opted, absorbed into the cocoon of the political and economic elite, isolated from the lives and problems of ordinary people. Anything that challenged the current system was a threat to reporters' status as insiders. Any proposal for real meaningful change had to be marginalized and ridiculed as radical, fringe, impractical or unachievable. The media went from watchdog to lapdog. Journalists became mere stenographers who transcribed official statements and repackaged them as news.

Among reformers this gave birth to the slogan, "The revolution will not be televised." In The Man's case, that was appropriate. Since his goals were based on principles considered archaic by the media glitterati, it was fitting that corporate television would have to take a back seat to the old fashioned medium of AM radio, where Paine had stumbled across the solution to his problem while driving past Baltimore during an early recon mission.

Crystal Clear Nights With Crystal Dickerson aired on WHYY, a rare locally-owned independent radio station. With ruthless competition from huge networks on one side and satellite radio on the other, independents like WHYY survived only by blending niche programming with strong local news and cheap payrolls, which meant lots of young talent desperately striving to make their mark.

Just a few years out of the University of Texas with a degree in Broadcasting, Crystal could have used her stunning looks to get into television from the get-go. Station managers tended to be mostly male, and would go with a gorgeous babe nearly every time. But that also meant starting in a small outpost market like Cedar Rapids or Flagstaff. Crystal wanted to be in a major market for the cosmopolitan atmosphere. Besides, too many small-market station managers couldn't or wouldn't keep their hands in check. WHYY, on the other hand, felt like a great place to hone her skills and perfect her style. When the right television opportunity arose, she would be ready. Until then, she wasn't about to make the move to television only to be pigeonholed as just another hot, news-reading bimbo.

Crystal's relentless principled focus on issues, and her refusal to manufacture outrage or discuss contrived controversies just for the sake of ratings, attracted The Man's attention. Her principles also explained why Crystal Clear Nights languished in radio's purgatory, weeknights from nine to midnight. The show would have been in the graveyard shift from midnight to six a.m. except the station broadcast recorded programming in that slot. The station manager probably wouldn't have kept her on the air at all but "the old man," station owner Charles McTige, adored her.

Coming out of a commercial break on the Monday after the New York and California attacks, Crystal's engineer and call screener, Sam Brooks, cut in on her headset. "Line six. Be prepared. Could be Looney-Toons."

Crystal glanced over at the message board which identified the caller on line six as Tom, listening to streaming audio on the show's website. She wasn't really too surprised by Sam's warning. Talk radio was a magnet for weirdoes and whack-jobs. The later the time slot the stranger the callers. "So what's his trip?"

"Says he knows who carried out the attacks and why."

"Oh, one of *those* callers, huh?"

"Maybe, but I don't think so. Those callers don't usually demonstrate that they're using a voice synthesizer."

Crystal immediately punched button number six and said, "Hello, welcome to another Crystal Clear Night."

"Hi, Crystal, thanks for taking my call." The Man's SpySource VCPRO-1 voice changer with four sliders to control tone, timbre, reverberation, and pitch delivered a voice so natural that The Man sounded perfectly normal.

"And your name is Tom, is that correct?"

"Yes. Tom. Thomas Paine."

Crystal rolled her eyes at the mention of the famous Founding Father, but on the other side of the glass in the control room, Sam started a back-up tape on the auxiliary recording system.

Crystal got straight to the point. "Well, Tom, my call screener says you claim to know who's responsible for these terrorist attacks."

For The Man, now calling himself Thomas Paine, this was it, the moment of no return. He paused, took a deep breath, and announced, "The American Insurgency."

"The American Insurgency?"

"Yes."

"This is some kind of group?"

"It's an organization."

"Okay, organization. And you're a member of this organization?"

"Yes."

"Just so I'm clear, you say that this organization is responsible for the killing of Luis Navarro and Senator Trammello in California, and the bombings that killed Senator Shorewood and Chairman Beber. Is that correct?"

"We also killed Senator Stowe and Admiral Copeland."

"I see." She paused for a moment. "You know, Tom, we get a lot of calls from people who make claims that are hard to verify. Have anything to back-up what you've said?"

"The scum in California were shot with bullets coated in cyanide. The New York bombs were each rigged with two cell phone detonators, a primary and a back-up."

Crystal took a deep breath. She couldn't recall any mention of how many cell phones were used in the New York bombings, but she was dead certain the FBI hadn't said anything about the Palm Springs sniper using cyanide. If this guy was on the level, she was on the phone with a real terrorist, a stone cold assassin. "Okay, we'll check into that. Now, how many people are in your organization?"

"Enough."

Damn! Crystal really hoped to get a number out of him. "Okay, how did you learn to plan and carry out these attacks? It's not the kind of thing you can sign up for as an extension course at the local community college."

"Nice try." Paine wasn't about to gratuitously give the FBI any clues.

"Well then, why did you murder six distinguished men in cold blood?"

"The only thing distinguished about these men was their arrogance, corruption, and abuse of power. They were traitors and crooks who manipulated the public system for private benefit. These men didn't just think they were above the law, they *were* above the law. Above the Constitution. They were key actors in a fascist takeover of America."

The words fascist and fascism were often tossed around and misapplied by people who didn't know what they actually meant. Crystal wanted to know if Tom was one of those people. "What's your definition of fascism?"

Paine surprised her. "Mussolini defined fascism as the perfect marriage of business and government. That's the America of today. Government doesn't regulate business, business regulates the government. The elite have robbed the country blind, turned the American Dream into the Impossible Dream, destroyed the middle class, and created a fictitious economy that wages war on ordinary everyday Americans."

Crystal leapt at the chance to explore the question of vigilante justice. Maybe it would produce some clues about the caller. "But that doesn't give you the right to murder people."

"You tell me what the alternative is."

"Isn't punishment up to the justice system?"

"What justice system? You mean the one with one set of laws for the top one percent -- who never get punished -- and another set for everybody else. That's a legal system, but it's sure not a justice system."

This exchange had quickly become more than Crystal was prepared for, and she wanted time to regroup. "Tom, we've gotta stop for a word from our sponsors. Hang on, and I'll come back to you right after the break, okay?"

"No, I think that's enough for tonight."

Tonight? Was he planning to call her again?

"You can find out more at AmericanInsurgency.org. Have a good night." With that, Paine clicked off his disposal prepaid cell phone and the line went dead. It was ten-seventeen p.m. Eastern Time.

Crystal told the audience, "Stick around, I'll be right back," and the show went to a commercial.

Sam immediately came over her headset. "Wow."

"Wow is right. Think he's the real deal?"

He nodded, and she asked, "You call the FBI?"

"On their way. I'll have that website up on your screen any second."

"Good. Thanks." She glanced over at the callboard, which was lit up like Las Vegas on the 4th of July. "Sam, throw in a couple of extra station promos, please? I need a minute.

Sam nodded.

Crystal leaned back in her chair. *Heavy stuff. But why call her? Why not somebody big, somebody who's syndicated all over the country?*

Twenty-five hundred miles away in Scottsdale, Arizona, Paine parked behind a carwash that offered free wi-fi access. The die was cast; he was now the focus of probably the biggest domestic manhunt since John Wilkes Booth. Nothing could change that, so the thing to do now was fire up his MacBookPro and monitor the reactions to his call. Just as he had planned, the story dominated the late night television news shows. As more and more stories mentioned the American Insurgency, its website hit counter just kept climbing and climbing.

Chapter 8: Manifesto

Doc was drying off in the locker room after a late-night workout in the bureau's Hoover Building D.C. headquarters gym when Kenny notified him of Paine's call. Doc threw on a set of sweats and rushed upstairs.

Snatching up a legal pad, Doc joined Kenny who was staring up at the big video screens along the north wall. There it was, every page of the AI website, including the manifesto Doc had been hoping for so fervently.

Except it wasn't at all what he had expected.

MANIFESTO

Reform, or Revolution

"In a time of universal deceit, telling the truth is a revolutionary act." George Orwell
America has become its corporations, not its citizens.

America's Longest War is America's Institutional War On Us!

For the past thirty years our institutions have waged war on our citizens. Congress, Courts, State and Local Governments, Stockbrokers, Bankers, Lobbyists, Lawyers, Multi-National Global Corporations, and most of all, Presidents, have waged war on America's poor and middle class:

With promises that turned out to be lies.
With pensions and health care benefits that vanished.
With treaties that took away our jobs.
With security that took away our privacy.
With laws and decrees that took away our rights.
With no prosecution of the rich, and harsh prosecution of all others.

The American Dream has been replaced by the American Delusion.

The great nation that once was America is no more. That America vanished because accountability vanished.

Without accountability --
We've become a hated Empire overseas...
And a Fascist Oligarchy at home.

Without accountability --
Corporations make the decisions
Special Interests get the representation.
We pay price in taxes, blood, and loss of freedom.

Without accountability, there is no justice.
And when there is no justice, there is no freedom.

Democracy = Accountability and Equal Justice for All

It's not too late. America can be saved.

It's time for the Second American Revolution.

It's time for a Crusade For Reform and Accountability.

We, the people, are responsible for the actions of our
government.
We, the people, are responsible for how it operates, and
what it has become.
We, the people, must replace Government of the
Corrupt, by the Corrupt, for the Corrupt
With Government of the People, by the People, for the
People.

Our Founding Fathers correctly believed that all power
derives from the people. To preserve and protect the
basic rights of the people, and to insure that government
always had the true consent of the governed, they built

safeguards into the Constitution. But they could not have anticipated or imagined how the political class of the last half-century would undermine, circumvent, and ignore those safeguards. Never before have the American people been so victimized, and never has the American public witnessed such disdain for the rule of law.

The actions of former President Walker Lyman and his replacement, President Welch, prove that it's not just Presidents and those that serve them who are above the law. An entire class of corrupt financial fraudsters can burn the economy to the ground without fear of prosecution. This shamelessly discredits the sacrifice of Americans who fought and died for the cause of liberty, democracy, freedom, and justice _for all_. It cannot, must not, and will not continue.

Our Ultimatum: Bring Democracy Back to America.
Restore the Rule of Law.
Your Choice: Reform or Revolution

We demand:

- Criminal prosecution of the Wall Street banksters and financial Masters of the Universe who stole our homes and our retirement, bankrupted the economy, and destroyed our future.

- A Constitutional Convention to enact the Second Bill of Rights amendments presented here.

- That all States and voting territories conduct a special election by which the voters shall have the opportunity to ratify these proposed Amendments.

If we can't have Constitutional justice, we'll have our own justice.

Until the Second Bill of Rights is enacted the American Insurgency will continue operations against those who lead, implement, or facilitate the Institutional War Against Americans.

Signed: **Thomas Paine**

Following the Manifesto were seven proposed constitutional amendments titled The Second Bill of Rights - Part I. "The Right to Good and Open Government" proposed to give any citizen legal standing to sue government agencies to enforce laws, required all legislative and government business that didn't deal with national security to be conducted in open, public sessions, and severely limited government use of the state secrets claim to block civil trials or criminal investigations.

The second amendment created a virtually ironclad press shield law, permitted public broadcast of all court proceedings, and set limits on ownership of media to would break up the concentration of power vested in a few corporations. A "Limits on the Power of the Executive" amendment proposed removing the President's ability to pardon members of his administration and prohibited the use of Presidential signing statements to invalidate portions of laws.

The remaining four amendments provided for the creation and funding of a permanent office of Special Counsel to investigate corruption, full public funding for all elections, limited the terms of Congressmen, Senators, and judges, and perhaps most shockingly, mandated the use of neutral computer programs to draw compact, unified, legislative districts without respect to the racial, ethnic, or party affiliation of residents.

Doc was stunned. This was wildly different from anything the Bureau or the country had dealt with in the past. This wasn't just radical or inflammatory, it was incendiary. "*Hooh-lee* shit," he muttered.

"Yep," Kenny replied, "This guy just moved the goalposts."

Chapter 9: BOG

Until Paine's call, the worst fear the FBI had was an Islamic BOG, a "Bunch of Guys" sitting around someone's apartment, inspired by Al Qaeda but operating entirely on their own. On the plus side, at least a search for Islamic BOGs could be narrowed down by looking for people who practiced Islam or came from countries where it was the dominant religion.

The occasional domestic BOGs the FBI had dealt with in the past were distinguished by racist philosophies well outside the political mainstream, and ludicrous extremist goals that were impossible to achieve. The Bureau had plenty of agents capable of infiltrating these groups, so busting them was often easier than going after Islamic terror cells.

The insurgency behind this Manifesto presented a unique challenge, far more profound -- and therefore far scarier -- than that presented by previous domestic BOGs. AI wanted to change the operational relationship between government and the governed. At first glance AI's actions -- which Doc dubbed "Equal Opportunity Terrorism" -- appeared to be carried out by a BOG without distinguishing racial, ethnic, geographical, linguistic, or religious characteristics. Its members could be anybody, from an airline pilot to the guy in the garden department at Home Depot.

By 11:30 p.m. everyone who had been called in from home was back in OCD. Since Doc didn't get the kind of manifesto he had expected, it was critical to extract maximum information from the one he did receive. Thus, even though Dr. John Herren and his profilers on the Document Analysis Team in the Behavioral Science Department would pick over the contents looking for the smallest, most minute clues, right now everyone focused on scribbling their own critical first impressions. Something spotted tonight might help decipher and exploit other clues unearthed far down the road.

For a long time, nobody in the main room spoke. Finally someone muttered, "Nuts. Flat ass nuts. Out of their fucking minds." Others immediately chimed in with, "insane" and "crazy."

"Crazy?" Doc bellowed. *Had everyone failed to grasp the danger of what they were seeing?* It had certainly leapt right out at him, as plain as day.

Kenny thought, *Listen up, boys and girls. The Doctor is about to get educational.*

Doc stepped up on a low stage under the wall of video screens. "Crazy? You want crazy? Read Mein Kampf. *That* was crazy. Chock full of really lunatic ideas. But it didn't stop Germany from rallying behind Hitler, did it? Crazy? Christ Almighty, I wish this was crazy! Crazy would make our job a whole lot easier." Pointing up at the screens he said, "This isn't crazy; this is *dangerous*." He paused for a moment. "Anybody know why?"

Doc stared out over the room, waiting for someone to speak up. He saw the light go on behind a few faces, but nobody was confident enough to speak up. "I'll tell you why," he said, "Because it's fair. Look up there and tell me what doesn't seem fair. Show me something -- other than a self-appointed right to kill people -- that's going to strike the average American as wrong. Find one thing that doesn't sound, that doesn't feel, quote/unquote, 'patriotic'."

Moving down to the screens displaying the Manifesto's Second Bill of Rights he asked, "You think these wouldn't pass if the public got a chance to vote? Somebody -- anybody -- wanna make a case for that?"

The room was silent.

Doc's blunt manner sometimes got him into trouble, but at times like this, it also helped him paint a clear picture. "Just so everybody understands, just so nobody underestimates what we're up against, let me spell it out for you: A coupla' hundred years ago, the guy who wrote this might have helped draft the Declaration of Independence and the Constitution. And judging by how effectively this group carries out attacks to back up its rhetoric, I fucking guarantee you that whoever plans their field operations would have been on George Washington's General Staff, right up there shoulder to shoulder with the Marquis de la Fayette and General Von Steuben."

The room remained quiet until Agent White broke the silence. "Boss, you make it sound like these guys are patriots."

"Absolutely not. Patriots don't attack their country. They defend it. Patriots use the democratic process. Legitimate grievances don't justify illegal actions. The end does not justify the means."

Rookie agent Melody Ganz spoke up. Ganz was on temporary assignment to Bravo after her gorgeous legs caught Kelli Randleman's attention early on in the Copeland investigation. Although basically straight, Melody had experimented a little in college and saw nothing wrong with switch-hitting if it got her out of the Bureau's dreadful backwater office in Jacksonville, South Carolina. "Isn't it counterproductive, even a little dangerous," Ganz asked, "to admit that the people we're after appear to be acting for the right reasons?"

"We will never admit that to anybody outside this room," Doc replied. "But in here, we damn well better admit it to ourselves." Doc sat back against a table. "Stopping whoever wrote this will be damn hard. If we don't understand his motivations and his appeal, if we don't understand which people may give him shelter or support, and why..." His voice trailed off.

Scott asked, "Him? Singular? One guy?"

"The guy who wrote this is Job One. See this line, The Second American Revolution," he said, using a laser pointer. "That isn't a statement of fact, it's a prayer, one that he hopes will be answered. But political movements don't pop up and take root overnight. They take time. He's gotta know that. This isn't the Thomas Jefferson of the new millennium. He's our very own little Che Guevara. And just like Che, my gut tells me that he's got no line of succession, nobody to take over and carry on if he goes down. We can't afford to give him time to develop a successor-in-waiting. This guy is the head of the beast. Kill the head and the body will die with it."

Even agents who had worked with Doc on other cases were a little taken aback by this description of their mission. Finally, Kelli asked, "Is it okay if we just arrest him?" Her kidding tone of voice disguised hope for a serious answer.

"Sure, if we can. But I don't expect this guy to run up the white flag. He calls himself Tom Paine, but I think we must operate on the assumption that he's prepared to be another Patrick Henry and go down for the cause."

After listening in the back of the room, Dr. Herren waited until Doc was in his office to voice his disagreement privately. "Good analysis, Doc, but I disagree with one point. If our mystery author is cornered, I think he'll surrender. What better way to keep his cause alive than a long, drawn-out public trial with the media reporting daily from the courthouse steps? Every day would be another forum for his ideas, another opportunity to put the system on trial."

"Hope you're right, Professor. I'd love to interrogate this guy."

Over at the White House, President Welch and his key advisors huddled with Secretary Hoover and Attorney General Godfrey. To them, the Manifesto was goddamn radioactive. And like anything radioactive, it had to be contained. By any means necessary.

Life as they knew it could be at stake.

Chapter 10: Division of Labor

Doc didn't see anything to gain by interviewing Crystal Dickerson in person. It was unlikely that she could add to what they'd learn from analyzing the show tape. He did, however, send agents Price, O'Leary, and White over to the station along with a team of whiz-techs with electronic gear so that if "Caller Tom" called again, the trap-and-trace equipment would be ready to go. NSA would trace the call using its communications intercept capabilities but Doc also wanted old-fashioned hard trace technology directly under his control in place as a backup.

Before he left to brief Director Bartholomew, Doc ordered Gretchen Polamalu to use as many agents as necessary to run a background check on Dickerson. "As deep as you can and as wide as you can. I wanna know everything there is to know about this woman, all the way back to who spanked her on the ass in the delivery room."

Scott couldn't resist adding, "Especially anyone who spanked her on the ass since then."

"Surveillance?" Gretchen asked.

"Electronic and physical. Full black. Twenty-four/seven, we never close." Full black meant that a covert entry team had to get into Crystal's condo, install bugs and cameras, and get out again before she got home, all without leaving a trace. Gretchen made a note to have the entry team coordinate with the agents interviewing Crystal to make sure they didn't cut it too close.

On Doc's way out the door to brief the Director, Kelli stopped him just long enough to deliver some bad news. Research on ownership of the AI website was still in progress, but as far as they could tell from a quick Google search, the term "American insurgency" had been coined years earlier by former Republican House Speaker Newt Gingrich to describe people opposed to former President Bush's occupation of Iraq.

Paine had timed his call so that it would dominate the late evening local news as well as the twenty-four hour cable news channels. Naturally, all of the news networks wanted Crystal for an interview. Immediately after signing off she hurried over to the make-up room used by the news staff for sister-station WHYY-TV. Sam had sweet-talked the make-up girl into sticking around. A little face powder, fresh lipstick in just the right shade, an eye shadow tune-up, and Crystal was ready for a live interview with CNN that lasted a full five minutes. In an era when ten-second sound bites were standard and news features rarely ran more than ninety seconds, eight minutes was an exceptionally long interview, even by cable standards. Of course, Crystal had turned out to be what was known in the business as a "good get."

Out in Los Angeles three of the biggest agents who handled TV newscasters recognized opportunity when it knocked. Each quickly called and left a message for Crystal, "to talk about her future." All three, a divorced guy in his fifties, a married guy in his thirties, and the married mother of two who had just turned forty, also shared a second ambition. Even if they didn't sign Crystal as a client, they each desperately wanted a chance to fuck her. The female agent also fantasized about being fucked *by her*.

After the CNN interview Crystal took the time to remove the heavy TV makeup before going into the station's conference room to be interviewed by Agent O'Leary. On the way home she played back three voicemail messages. Her boyfriend, Dennis Witherall, was mostly curious about the interview he assumed she had given the FBI.

Her mother said, "You handled it well. I'm proud of you. Call when you can."

Younger sister Janet simply said, "Way to go, sis."

Just because her family and three agents out in Hollywood were all excited didn't mean Crystal could afford to do the same. Not if she was going to get any sleep, that is. The Today Show had booked a live interview from her living room at 7:12 a.m. That meant she had to be up no later than six to be ready for the camera crew scheduled to arrive at six-thirty. It was already a little after three a.m. when she walked into her modest condo located in an aging suburb midway between Baltimore and D.C. After a quick shower she set the alarm, left a voice-mail message on her attorney Liz Fielding's New York office number, put everything else out of her mind, and was asleep by three-thirty.

Doc left Professor Herren's Document Analysis Team to labor over the Manifesto unmolested. Their work was already hard enough. At best his presence would be a distraction; at worst it might corrupt the process and distort conclusions. Instead, Doc decided to perform his own analysis of the Manifesto, to see how his conclusions might match or differ from those reached by DAT. Maybe one would catch something the other missed. More importantly, it might help him get inside the mind of his quarry.

Although highly computer literate, Doc was still "a paper guy." His mind worked best when he could spread things out and leisurely scan everything at once, like looking over loose pieces of an unfinished jigsaw puzzle. Somewhere deep in the wiring of his brain, the circuits sorted and re-sorted all the little pieces until they created a mosaic that made sense. Doc looked at the printed pages of the Manifesto and amendments spread out in front of him on the table. "Tell me a story," he said.

Pretty soon, they did. And it surprised him.

From the moment he saw the AI website, Doc's over-riding concern had been the portion intended to incite and justify vigilante action. But as he delved more deeply into the text, he soon realized that nothing in the rest of the material seemed to violate any criminal statute. All the ideas and criticisms about the state of government had already been expressed at one time or another by people with some prominence and credibility in political circles. People who were certainly not terrorists.

To test his conclusion, Doc woke up Ray Riggins, one of his old law professors. Riggins also concluded that, except for the portions advocating vigilante violence, the contents of the Manifesto provided no basis for criminal charges. This was an enormous problem. With no proof that either Stowe or Copeland had actually been murdered, if the author of the Manifesto could not be prosecuted for what it contained, the government would have to connect Paine to at least one of the attacks in Palm Springs or New York. Since days had passed between the attacks and posting of the Manifesto, Paine could argue that he had not been involved in the killings and simply composed the Manifesto after the fact to exploit the situation.

It also might not be possible to prove that the person who called Crystal Clear Nights was the same person who authored the Manifesto. "Caller Tom" might claim that he had simply discovered the AI website and decided to use it to taunt authorities. He could also claim that the information he'd given about the attacks were simply educated guesses. Without hard evidence to the contrary, in a courtroom these were not entirely specious arguments, and as far as Doc knew at the time, might even be true. Both "Caller Tom" and the Tom Paine who signed the Manifesto could simply be clever opportunists, and not the real quarry. No matter how Doc sliced it, at this point it didn't look like the government would have the luxury of convicting anyone for the Manifesto because it couldn't prove that they had committed murder.

Agent O'Leary called in to report that Crystal Dickerson seemed completely mystified as to why Paine had called her show. Then Kelli reported that the American Insurgency domain had been registered a few months earlier on behalf of an obviously fictitious "Clint Gore" by the host company as part of a package deal that included tech support and maximum traffic capacity for five years. The registration fee had been paid by money order. Since money orders, like checks, were imaged and then shredded, there was no physical document left to check for fingerprints. Doc suspected that it didn't matter anyway, and he was right. Paine had purchased the money order at a check-cashing place near skid row in Houston, and had the clerk put the money order in an envelope before handing it over. Neither Paine's fingerprints nor his DNA would have been anywhere on it.

Kelli also reported that the host company had received the web pages on a CD via a Fed Ex shipment paid for in cash. The Pasadena, California return address on the FedEx shipment turned out to be a former home for unwed mothers that had been closed for several years. So far, only a little more than a tenth of the website's allotted capacity was in use. This made Doc wonder about how much more was still to come, and what it would contain. The AI home page clearly stated that it was set up without cookies, which meant that the site kept no records of who accessed it. As if that wasn't enough bad news, Kelli warned Doc that her report had a punch line, and he wasn't going to like it: The website host was in Caracas, Venezuela.

Venezuela and the U.S. had not exactly been on the best of terms for quite some time. Failing to orchestrate the overthrow of both the current and the former democratically elected Venezuelan presidents had put a serious strain on diplomatic relations. It was a move smart enough to make Doc mutter, "Gotta' give the guy credit. This cocksucker is good."

Citing her lack of experience in such matters, Kelli told Doc that he'd have to be the judge of that.

Chapter 11: Capitol Nightmare

Paine's call to Crystal's show created a wildfire of interest. By the time she sat down for her Today Show interview, traffic had crashed the AI website. The White House greeted the news with mixed reactions. *Thank God it's down!* collided with *Damn! Way too many people visited that site.* Determined not to let Paine post any additional dangerous political blasphemy, President Welch vowed to do everything he could to keep the site from being resurrected. If you can't kill the messenger, at least kill any new messages. His plan was simple: prevent the site from going back up. If that failed, have NSA and compliant Internet Service Providers block access to the site in the U.S. and as many foreign countries as possible. The strategy had plenty of support. Politicians and business leaders across the country were united by the hope that the AI website would disappear forever. Given a chance, many elected officials would have gladly volunteered to drive a stake in the heart of the demon behind this website and its Manifesto.

The verdict on Crystal's Today Show appearance was unanimous: a winner. Considering her lack of sleep, even Crystal thought she had performed well. Key execs at NBC thought she was superb, and Paine felt vindicated in selecting her as his media contact.

In Beverly Hills, all three agents loved what they saw, and called again, stressing how important it was to strike while the iron was hot. They all wanted to fly back to discuss her next career move. Crystal responded that it was more important to her not to exploit a national security crisis. Each agent said they understood completely. And would call back in twenty-four hours. Crystal then gave each agent the name and New York number of her old college friend, attorney Liz Fielding, and said that for the time being, "Liz Fielding will be fielding," any calls involving her professional future. Crystal marveled at how each time the deliberate pun went right over the head of the agent on the other end of the call without so much as a chuckle or a comment. It was a safe bet that someone a bit less self-absorbed would guide her future. Maybe she should just let Liz do it. Fielding practiced entertainment and intellectual property law at a pretty big law firm and perhaps landing Crystal as a client would help her make partner.

The reforms popularized overnight as "The Manifesto Amendments" presented terrifying problems, the most obvious of which was that the public would perceive Paine as a political Robin Hood, riding around the country with his merry men taking from the powerful and giving to the powerless.

The process by which Paine specified the amendments were to be enacted and ratified was even more frightening. The Constitution could be amended if an amendment passed by a two-thirds vote of both houses of Congress was then ratified by three-fourths of the states. A second method allowed two-thirds of the states to pass resolutions requiring Congress call a Constitutional Convention. This method had never been used because it scared the shit out of everybody. Once a convention started, everything was on the table. Delegates could stray as far as they wanted from the issues that prompted the convention to be called in the first place, could change anything in the existing Constitution, even write a whole new constitution. Given the political strife and economic turmoil of the past three decades, for politicians the chilling prospect of a Constitutional Convention was surpassed only by how Paine specified the Amendments were to be ratified. Amendments normally had to be ratified by three-fourths of the states, either through act of the legislature, or by a state convention. The Manifesto demanded that the states submit the amendments to the voters, making the electorate of each state a "convention of the whole." It was settled constitutional law that once voters approved a measure, only voters could repeal it. Using a public vote to ratify a Constitutional amendment had never been tested in court, but if the Manifesto Amendments got all the way to the ratification stage, no court was likely to stand in the way. By demanding a state-by-state public vote, Paine sought to prevent politicians from gaming the system. Legislatures couldn't later rescind ratification.

Congress' natural response was to hold a massive bi-partisan press conference on the capitol steps. The event was impressive mainly for the security in place. Every Secret Service agent, U.S. Marshall, Capitol policeman, and DC cop not absolutely needed someplace else was on hand. SWAT teams and bomb squads stood by. Snipers deployed atop any building with a line of sight view. So many helicopters circled overhead that House Speaker Leon Rembert had them pulled back to keep from drowning out the press conference itself.

When the whirr of the choppers faded, Rembert offered the obligatory condolences to the families of those "noble and dedicated public servants who have been savagely murdered by enemies of freedom and democracy." Senate Majority Leader David Ardmore lauded what he said was, "a united, unshakeable, bipartisan response to the horrific actions of a small group of domestic terrorists." A parade of leaders from both parties followed, each repeating the same refrain: condolences to the families, disgust at the violent nature of the attacks, exaggeration (if not outright invention) of the laudable qualities of the martyred victims, and pledges to see that justice was done.

There was a concerted effort by the participants to avoid addressing the specific reforms demanded by the Manifesto Amendments, and the mainstream press generally played its role by not pressing the issue. The closest anyone came to talking about the subject was Ardmore's admonishment that, "Amending the Constitution is a sacred process that must be reserved for use only on rare occasions, and even then after the utmost careful deliberation." The implication was that even if the Manifesto did contain a few ideas worth considering, the members of Congress -- public servants whose only interest was the good of country -- could be trusted to enact the necessary legislation. Ardmore closed by saying, "Congress will not, under any circumstances consider, much less pass, any amendments until the people responsible for these heinous acts are captured and dealt with appropriately. Congress will remain steadfast. Terrorists will not deter us from doing the nation's business in a timely, fair, open, and efficient manner. We will not be intimidated by the threat of violence."

Watching on TV at home, Tom Paine lifted a Coors Light and asked, "Wanna bet?"

As the AI web hosting company in Caracas hustled to add more servers and bandwidth, Welch begged Venezuelan President Antonio Marquez to shut down the AI website. Marquez declined, and later held a press conference outside the offices of the web hosting company where he proudly announced that, thanks to help from the Venezuelan government, the American Insurgency website was back on-line, available for all the world to see. "As a proud example of democracy, Venezuela will never interfere with the sanctity of free speech, and the United States government should consider giving the same freedoms and protection to its people."

Watching in his office Doc said, "Ouch."

At home, Paine laughed. Things were going even better than he'd planned.

Chapter 12: Need To Know

Despite the NSA's best efforts, blocking access to the AI website proved impossible. Alert computer geeks, some with affiliations to Wikileaks or the hacker collective Anonymous, realized that AmericanInsurgency.org might have a short life span and downloaded the contents before the site crashed. By the time the country awoke for breakfast, the cat was forever out of the bag. Clone sites appeared everywhere. Excerpts were debated on personal web pages, blogs, and social networking sites. Key slogans shot back-and-forth in emails and text messages. By noon, it was impossible to go anywhere except a casino, a whorehouse, or a crack den where the Manifesto wasn't the center of discussion.

Professor Herren and his DAT corps of profilers, linguists, and experts in the psychology of visual design had three assignments:

First, profile the author of the Manifesto. Just in case his gut instinct about a single author was wrong, Doc ordered the team to look for anything that indicated multiple writers, including clues that might point to a female accomplice: a wife, girlfriend, even a mother or sister. DAT also had to consider the possibility that someone other than the writer, perhaps a person with graphic design experience, did the website layout.

Second, profile the people who carried out the attacks, including any clues about how they might have been recruited.

Third, determine the likelihood that the author actively participated in the attacks. Did Paine like to get his hands dirty, did he relish the adrenaline rush of being where the action was? Or was he the chicken-shit type who preferred to distance himself from the dirty work?

Herren's crew made good progress on all three assignments, in part because they didn't have to deal with certain elements usually associated with their work. Unlike the fictional Hannibal Lecter, most real serial killers, mass murderers, and homicidal self-appointed messiahs were not particularly articulate. As writers they were usually pedestrian at best. Many covered the same ground repetitively, while others contradicted themselves, even in the same document. Almost without exception, their goals were delusional and any demands they made were impossible to satisfy, which came as no surprise, considering they were all whackos. Although mass murderers and serial killers suffered various individual forms of psychosis with long medical names, shrinks in the FBI Behavioral Science Department referred to them collectively under the catch-all acronym SMF: Sick MotherFuckers.

The fact that the Manifesto differed from anything in previous cases also made it somewhat easier to analyze. Both its language and objectives were extremely clear. Vocabulary, sentence structure, thought progression, grammar, and punctuation were painstakingly dissected. Linguists on the team listened to the text read aloud for hints about the age, race, education, or regional background of the author. Visual elements like font selection, spacing, organization of the layout, and color choices underwent equally rigorous analysis.

When the Document Analysis Team finished its work, Doc convened Bravo's core agents. As Professor Herren explained DAT's conclusions, Gretchen Polamalu noted the key points on the long whiteboard that stretched across the far end of the conference room. Gretchen had a form of speed printing that was easy to read, and Doc teasingly referred to her as, "our blackboard monitor."

According to Herren, "Paine is almost certainly a white male at least forty-five years old, but more likely in his late-fifties to perhaps seventy. He's well educated and well read. He was raised with a strong sense of personal integrity and taught to draw clear differences between right and wrong. For most of his life he had a strong, perhaps overly idealistic belief in the fundamental fairness of our government, our political parties, and our justice system. In that sense he has a rigid personality. At some point those views changed. He couldn't reconcile his traditional concepts of right and wrong with the inequality of our real-world legal and political systems as they operate today. He feels betrayed, and this led to the great paradox: he now believes that murder -- assassination -- is the way to fix the system. He sees this not as criminal or immoral but as principled patriotism."

Giving presentations to groups always made the Professor a little tense and he took a sip of water. "Although the first two attacks were committed in the Carolinas, nothing indicates that he was raised or now lives in that area, or anywhere in the south for that matter. Judging from speech patterns it is our judgment that he was raised and lived the majority of his life in the western states. That said, he may have traveled or lived in the Carolinas for a short period of time, or perhaps was stationed at one of the many military bases in the area."

Herren paused for another sip of water. "Paine is neither a psychopath nor a sociopath. He's a big thinker, but not a narcissist. If anything, he considers himself a humble man, a common man, who believes that officials have a sacred duty. When leaders let him down by their actions, it just adds to his feelings of betrayal."

Herren put down his prepared notes and moved to the whiteboard where Gretchen had already posted four headings. The first, What Paine Claims, listed the key elements of his call to Crystal's radio show.

The next, What We Know About Paine, prompted Kelli to ad-lib "Not much."

She was right. At this point the only undeniable hard fact they had was that a pissed-off citizen had called Crystal's show using a voice synthesizer. They couldn't even be sure if the caller was, in fact, connected in any way to the American Insurgency website, or that the creator of the website was involved with the attacks. They couldn't yet dismiss the possibility that someone involved with the attacks decided to claim false credit for the website to throw off the investigation.

Doc reminded everyone that, "Paine took credit for killing Stowe and Copeland but we still can't prove that either one of them was actually murdered. It could just be another attempt to muddy the waters and throw us off-track."

One thing they did know for sure was that the author of the Manifesto was committed to game-changing political reform. If the same man was responsible for the attacks, he was careful, skilled, deliberate, and methodical.

After the last entry about the caller, "Forceful/Blunt/ Sarcastic," Gretchen added, "Related to Doc?"

"Probably," he deadpanned. It got a good laugh, but there was no denying the similarities.

Under What We Think We Know About Paine/AI, Doc stressed that this list contained only things, "we *think* we know." Nothing was set in concrete. Despite the arguments Doc had offered during their initial examination of the Manifesto, some Bravo agents were still not convinced that Paine and his followers weren't loony-toons.

There was also disagreement about whether AI was non-partisan in its selection of targets. Many felt that two Democrats, Trammello and Shorewood, on a list of otherwise Republican victims wasn't enough to support a non-partisan conclusion. Kenny pointed out that maybe Paine included Democrats merely because it doubled the number of high-priority targets to be protected. Protecting an expanded target pool inevitably diluted the level of protection afforded any one target, making all of them more vulnerable. Others argued that the Republican victims were just as likely to be decoys to point the investigation, and protection efforts, away from Democrats, whom many voters also blamed for selling out to big business and the financial industry.

Some agents weren't ready to accept the idea that Paine and his followers held traditional values. That determination depended on whether they defined traditional as revolting against an unjust government, as the Founding Fathers had, or if it meant working within the political system, as Americans had done for more than two centuries. While everyone agreed that there was no current evidence of a racist agenda, future attacks or future communications could reveal one. Gretchen postulated that maybe this was just a very cagey white supremacist group hoping to seduce the public before revealing its true goals and intentions.

Most of the white board was set aside for the last two headings, What It Would Help To Know About Paine, and What It Would Help To Know About AI. Ascertaining the exact source of Paine's anger was pivotal. Was he inspired by events that had befallen others, as Tim McVeigh and Terry Nicolls were, or was this a personal vendetta prompted by something that happened to him or his immediate family?

While these were all valid avenues of investigation, eventually Doc turned the discussion to questions of command, control, and logistics. How big was AI? How many followers did Paine have? How were they recruited? What was the common connection? Were the members all male, or were women involved? Was everybody concentrated in one location, or were they dispersed? If the members were dispersed, how were they organized, as individual lone-wolf agents or in cells? Did local agents or cells operate under a centralized command, or as autonomous units?

Was it a hybrid structure, defaulting to local autonomous command or a pre-established plan of operations if the centralized command was taken down?

How did AI select targets and perform reconnaissance? How was intel communicated and converted into a plan of operation? Was the mode of attack determined by the capabilities of local personnel, or were people transported to match the desired method? The Barrett and the Flex-X were stolen. Was robbery the only way AI obtained materiel? What about black market purchases in the criminal underground? Did they use dummy buyers with fake or stolen I.D. to buy from legitimate sources? If so, how did they pay without arousing suspicion and yet not leave a money trail?

AI's array of combat, high-tech, public relations, and communications skills meant there were too many possibilities to draw any conclusions. Somehow Doc had to narrow the focus. His best hope was that somebody would recognize elements of the Manifesto and provide a lead to the identity of Paine or one of his disciples.

Drawing on the lesson learned in the Unabomber case, Doc wanted the Bureau to make a television appeal asking anyone who had previously run across the specific package of ideas or key phrases in the Manifesto to come forward.

President Welch vetoed the idea. Even if the Manifesto was already a worldwide subject of discussion, Welch wasn't about to further publicize it. Doc marveled at how easy it must be for the man who enjoyed the world's best personal security to make that decision. Secretary Hoover, who also enjoyed superb security at government expense, didn't want it to appear that so far DHS and the FBI had nothing to go on.

Given no other choice, Doc assigned hundreds of agents to doggedly call newspaper publishers, bloggers, magazine and book editors, and universities asking them to search for possible pre-existing sources of the Manifesto elements. Scott sent another team of agents combing through websites that offered help with term papers, book reports, and college theses, including sites that helped teachers catch students who plagiarized previous authors. The process could take days, even weeks, and still not produce the results that a TV appeal would. Until then, Doc couldn't do much except wait for a tip, a traceable update to the AI website or most likely, the next attack.

Chapter 13: Breakthrough

Doc needed a break in the case, and he got one from a most unlikely source.

Something about the Caracas press conference bothered Kenny, but he couldn't put his finger on it. So while Doc and the rest of the team tried to figure out ways to solve the questions on the whiteboard, Kenny slipped into the control room and ran video of the press conference over and over until he found what he was looking for. Bringing up the rear of the Marquez motorcade was a Cadillac Escalade, stolen months earlier in Del Ray Beach, Florida, from his attorney brother John. The new owner hadn't even bothered to change the personalized "JOHN LAW" Florida license plates.

Kenny wasn't that surprised that his brother's car had popped up in Venezuela, which the L.A. Times had described as a criminal paradise. But the video suddenly reminded him of an article from Wired magazine forwarded by a former agent now working in private security. "Damn!" he muttered as he reached for the phone to call Bill Ramundo, head of SAS Alpha in New York.

An hour later Big Bill called back on an encrypted landline. While he waited for Kenny to answer, Ramundo couldn't help but notice the irony of the view out his window -- of Thomas Paine Park, located right across the street from Federal Plaza.

Doc listened in as Kenny took the call, then dialed the Director to say he was coming up. "Come on," he told Kenny. "Time to say your prayers." It was code for "going to the Director's office," also known as the Chapel.

Agent Johnson wasn't so sure this was such a good idea. "Aw, do I have to?"

Doc was amazed at what the ex-Marine was, or wasn't, afraid of. First man through a barricaded door? Kenny Johnson was the guy. Brief VIPS? Not so much. Doc brushed aside Kenny's concerns. He deserved the spotlight for turning up a crucial lead.

Prior to 9-11, the Director of the FBI held court in an expansive top floor corner office with a panoramic view typical of chief executive suites. After the Twin Towers came down his new office was a windowless personal panic room on an interior corridor three floors down from the roof. The floor, ceiling, and walls were eight-inches thick, featuring multiple layers of bulletproof Kevlar, plywood, anodized titanium, high-density foam, and fireproof Nomex, the material used in NASA space suits. All were sandwiched between a double-walled shell of one inch thick chrome-moly steel plates welded to both the inside and the outside of a steel I-beam frame. It even had an emergency oxygen system. The shell was not attached to anything so if the entire building ever went down, the pod would maintain its structural integrity and fall independently. Similar pods around town protected the Secretary of State, the Director of Homeland Security, the head of the CIA, and the Attorney General. This pod became known as the Chapel because one of Bartholomew's predecessors often got down on his knees and prayed at times of crisis.

Although surprised to see Kenny, Director Bartholomew was much more interested in the news than the messenger. DHS Secretary Hoover and Attorney General Goddard, patched in via videophone, also focused on the report and couldn't care less who delivered it. Doc let Kenny explain how watching the press conference had suggested how one person could pull off both a sniper attack in California and target-specific bombings in

New York less than thirty minutes later by using surveillance cameras. Not just any surveillance cameras. The NYPD's own DAS system.

Many of the cameras that fed into the DAS system belonged to private businesses such as retail stores, hotels, office buildings, and pay parking structures. As the Wired article noted, these systems were highly vulnerable to hacking due to the way the manufacturer configured them for easy remote monitoring over the Internet. Once in, a hacker could select from various cameras, independently manipulate focus, and even change the direction of some cameras. A back check of the system showed hacker penetration of multiple sources. Paine had turned the watchers into the watched.

Attorney General Godfrey immediately wanted to know, "Agent Medlin, how difficult -- how much technical expertise was required -- to perform this hack?"

"My whiz techs say, on the scale of one to ten, about a two-and-a-half," replied Doc. "Didn't have to be a skilled hacker, just determined to learn and spend a little time in hacker chat rooms."

Godfrey's next question was, "What's the best way to use this to our advantage?"

Doc then unveiled his plan.

Godfrey and DHS Secretary Hoover gave their blessings, and their videophone connections immediately went black.

On their way back to OCD, Doc stopped and instructed Dr. Herren to focus his profilers and the Document Analysis Team on a solitary suspect, "a Twenty-first century Renaissance Assassin" as he put it.

Doc assembled the core members of Bravo, told them that what they were about to hear was not to leave the room, and let Kenny do show-and-tell a second time. For Doc, recognition for good work wasn't only the right thing, it was a good leadership principle. Even so, Doc was bothered. A little voice in Doc's head kept saying, _You shoulda figured this out._ Jealousy didn't nag at Doc, worry did. Failing to suspect that a single killer might have hacked surveillance systems to facilitate the attacks wasn't just missing the basket; to him it was missing the entire backboard. _What else had he missed? Or might miss in the future?_ Just to be safe, Doc sent out a directive to every domestic Bureau field office to backcheck the DAS network feeder systems in their areas.

The discovery of the surveillance system hack confirmed that Paine was someone special. Doc wondered, _Was he up to the job of catching this guy before he had a chance to build a following and a real insurgency developed?_ For the first time ever, doubt crept into his mind. _Had Melody Ganz stumbled on to something?_ By admitting that Paine's goals and motivations had merit, _had Doc revealed something that even he didn't realize?_ Then he thought again about his plan. It reminded him of a story his mother used to tell about an old lady who heard a burglar and came down stairs calling, "Here, kitty-kitty," with a twelve-gauge shotgun cocked and ready. _Here, kitty-kitty,_ he thought, _the doctor will see you now._

Chapter 14: Reunion

The twenty-four hours from Paine's surprise call on Thursday night through the end of Friday's show was a hectic but exciting period for Crystal. Her best friend and former college roommate, Liz Fielding, suggested Crystal come to New York for the weekend to address some business matters that Liz felt were best discussed in person.

Saturday morning Crystal slept in, then hopped on Amtrak for the Big Apple. Liz had a driver and town car pick her up at the station. Unknown to Crystal, she was followed by an FBI surveillance team that linked up with local agents from SAS Alpha. High overhead a chopper made sure the tail did not lose contact in traffic.

The car and driver had been assigned to Liz Fielding for the weekend, so Crystal left her suitcase in the trunk when they arrived. A security guard in the lobby called ahead as she rode up to the thirty-fourth floor.

Liz was waiting when the elevator opened. "Hi, Crissy," she said as they embraced.

"Hi, Liz. You look terrific."

Liz led the way down a long hallway into a small, windowless conference room. "Nice view," Crystal quipped as she sat down.

"The lack of scenery is more than made up for by the security benefits. No view, no eavesdropping. With windows, anyone could aim an infrared beam at the glass and pick up every word. The walls and door are double insulated. The room is swept for bugs every day by our in-house security personnel."

"Every day?"

"Yep. Including this morning." Elizabeth Marie Fielding was a natural blonde, but she definitely wasn't a dumb one. Looking

Crystal in the eye, she said, "Crissy, as your attorney, everything you tell me is bound by attorney-client privilege and can never be revealed without your permission. So as your attorney I need to know, up front: do you have any idea who this Tom Paine is, or why he decided to call your show?"

Crystal shook her head. "No, absolutely none. I don't even know how he found my show. I'm not exactly a household name."

"Judging from the calls I've been getting, before this is over you may be the next Oprah."

Crystal chuckled. "Yeah, right."

"You think I'm kidding? Crissy, darling, I'm as serious as a heart attack. And to prove it, here's a representation agreement. Read it, then we'll go over any questions you have." The agreement was about ten pages long. Crystal flipped directly to the signature page, and reached for her pen, only to be told, "No. It doesn't work that way. You read every word."

"If I can't trust you, then who can I trust?"

Liz' eyes twinkled and she flashed a devilish smirk. "Who said you could trust me?" She reached for the door and said, "I'll be back in a few minutes. In the meantime, read that but don't sign it yet."

"Well, you're certainly all business today."

"Damn right. Tonight I'll be your friend, but today I'm your attorney."

Twenty minutes later Liz came back and quizzed Crystal to make sure she understood the agreement. Only then did Liz instruct her to initial every page of both copies, then sign and date the last page of each. The paperwork finished, Liz ran down a list of the offers that were coming in from agents in Hollywood, book publishers, movie producers, and others referred to her office by the station management at WHYY. Liz agreed with Crystal's position that career discussions were best put off until Paine was apprehended. From a tactical perspective, there wasn't enough to be gained by negotiating deals now, and doing so might open her up to charges of trying to cash-in on a national emergency. Signing a deal now might even cause Paine to stop calling her.

When they finished, Liz hit a button on the conference table. The door opened and Mark Ritter entered carrying a briefcase. "Mark, meet our newest client, Crystal Dickerson." As they shook hands, Liz explained that Ritter was head of security for the firm and had some items for her.

"This," said Ritter, handing over a CD, "contains the encryption program that we use for all non-voice electronic communications including IM's and texting." Ritter then showed her how to connect a scrambler to mobile devices. "From now on, if you need to contact Liz or anyone else here at the firm for anything other than simple messages like 'Please call me' use the scrambler or send an encrypted message. Oh, and even with the scrambler, don't call from indoors. Assume that your office and home are bugged, or that they have an infrared mic aimed at the window of any room you're in. Both defeat the purpose of a scrambler for voice communication. So what you do is, you go outside, turn around and face the exterior wall of the building, preferably in a corner. That way the vibrations from your voice bounce off the walls and get all jumbled up. No way an infrared mic can decipher the gibberish. Any questions?"

"Yes. Is all this really necessary?"

"I'll let Ms. Fielding answer that." Turning to Liz, Ritter asked, "Will there be anything else?"

"No, that covers it. Thanks for coming in on a Saturday."

"No problem. Any excuse to get away from the wife is always welcome." With that, Ritter snapped the briefcase closed and left the room.

It was Crystal's turn to fix Liz with a serious look. "Really, Liz, is all this necessary?"

"Afraid it is. Face it: right now you're probably the only connection -- possibly the only lead -- the FBI has to this Tom Paine. That means you're being rat-checked."

"Rat-checked?"

"It's an FBI term, left over from the Watergate days, like rat-fucking. Means gnawing through every aspect of someone's life looking for dirt. I have no doubt that the FBI is digging into the lives of your family and everyone you have ever known. Me, my family, associates, clients, our whole firm is under scrutiny. Assume that all correspondence and communications are being intercepted. Assume that your office, your car, and every room of your house are bugged. Are you seeing anyone?"

"Not really."

"Okay, let me rephrase that: Do you have a fuck buddy?" Liz was a liberated woman with a raging sex drive. During their college days, she once revealed that she hadn't gone without sex in one form or another for more than a week since the age of fifteen. That wasn't to say she was promiscuous. More often than not "BOB," her Battery Operated Boyfriend, had to, as she put it, *fill-in* for the real thing. Liz didn't pass judgment on other women, and figured every woman was entitled to all the sex she wanted. Right now she just needed to know how much sex her best friend was having and with whom.

"There is someone I get together with, periodically."

"Married?" asked Fielding.

"God, no."

"Position of prominence, politically sensitive job?"

"Kinda."

"Well, when you get back, you have to warn him that he's being rat-checked. Liz could tell from the look on Crystal's face that this probably wasn't going to be a pleasant conversation. She scooped up her copy of the contract and said, "Okay, now that

I've ruined your afternoon, let's hope I can salvage the rest of your visit."

Crystal and Liz spent a pleasant afternoon shopping and capped off the day with dinner at the Tribeca Grill. Liz didn't have much trouble spotting what she guessed was Crystal's FBI tail. The next morning they ate breakfast at the Plaza Hotel and then Liz dropped Crystal off for the ride back to Baltimore. From the train Crystal called Dennis Witherall, who agreed to meet her at the Baltimore Amtrak station.

By the time Crystal arrived back in Baltimore the weather had turned ugly, with lightning and heavy thundershowers propelled by strong winds. But that didn't prevent Witherall from looking perfect. The thirty year-old Dartmouth grad always looked perfect. Dennis Witherall in an overcoat under an umbrella was like watching a London Fog ad come to life. The scion of a prominent Baltimore family, Witherall toiled as an assistant to Baltimore councilman Jack Rein to establish the connections and profile he needed to run for the state legislature, the first stop on his plans for higher office.

Witherall met Crystal in the station lobby. Not sure how the conversation would go, she suggested a light lunch, someplace where the atmosphere would be more relaxed. He declined, claiming that he had to get to a family function. They ended up in his BMW in the Amtrak lot. The first thing he wanted to know was, "What were you doing in New York?"

"Meeting with my lawyer. Look, there are some things we need to discuss --."

"I'll say. At least you coulda given me a heads up. Do you have any idea what kind of situation you've put me in? The FBI came to the office yesterday to interview me, and Councilman Rein. Of course, until then Jack had no idea that we were, you know, together."

Crystal tried to explain. "That's what we need to talk about. Honestly, until my lawyer told me what to expect I had no idea that the FBI would go checking into all my friends and associates."

"Honestly, you're that naive? You're contacted by a terrorist and it doesn't occur to you that the FBI is going to check out your associates?"

Stung by his attitude, Crystal fired back. "I guess I could say the same. Shouldn't you have anticipated this? Shouldn't you have warned me?"

"Oh, that's rich. Don't try to put this on me," he snapped.

With any hope that he might offer support or sympathy now out the window, Crystal paused for a second and then said, "I guess we should put our relationship on hold until this thing is resolved."

"Oh, really? You think?"

Crystal considered passing along Liz' warning that his home, office, and car might be bugged but decided not to reward his sarcasm. She calmly opened the door, stepped out, and walked off without a word or a backward look.

Chapter 15: Bait & Switch

Doc's plan was simple: have Attorney General Godfrey use Crystal's show to reveal that there was no insurgency and that the attacks were the work of one man, then pounce with a trace when Paine called to dispute Godfrey's claim. That Paine would use a prepaid cell was a given. But prepaid cells were untraceable only in the sense that the number couldn't be linked to the name of a user. The location of the call was still traceable -- if the caller could be kept on the line long enough. And here, geography presented the big challenge.

Usually when law enforcement traced a call they were working a relatively small, defined area. But being able to react fast enough to apprehend Paine would require synchronized pre-arranged cooperation by every law enforcement agency in the country, from big metropolitan police departments to rural constables. Getting that cooperation, and keeping it secret from the media, was a real challenge. Nevertheless, over a four-day period thousands of local and federal law enforcement agencies were alerted and put on standby, ready to swoop down on the location of Paine's call. And not a whisper leaked to the press. This level of cooperation might turn out to be Doc's primary advantage. If Paine relied too much on calling from a distant location and underestimated the speed of the local response, he might just stay on the phone long enough to be cornered.

Senior Agent Kelli Randleman had briefed Crystal and Engineer Sam on the plan, but Doc met with Crystal an hour before the show to go over everything one last time. The meeting turned out to be a bit of a shock to both of them.

Doc knew from her dossier that Crystal was attractive, but to him all attractive female media types were automatically phony, glitzy, artificial careerists, the "bubble-headed bleach blonde" type Don Henley sang about in *Dirty Laundry*. In person he immediately realized that Crystal was striking, yet something about her was also real, and authentic.

Crystal wasn't exactly thrilled about meeting the person responsible for rat-checking her on the remote chance that she might somehow be part of Paine's insurgency. She also expected the head of the FBI's top special unit to be in his late-forties to late-fifties, not his mid-thirties. And she was really struck by how he filled the doorway to her office.

Kelli handled the introductions. "Ms. Dickerson, this is Senior Special Agent Darren Medlin. Most people call him 'Doc'. Boss, Miss Crystal Dickerson."

When Crystal stood up to shake hands the heels on her calf-length boots made her 6'1," still almost six inches short of eye-to-eye. His were deep blue, hers jet black like her hair.

After the polite but formal handshakes, Doc said, "I understand you go by Crissy?"

Not willing to let Mr. Federal Bureau of Invading Privacy plant himself on comfortable ground Crystal replied, "You can call me Miss Dickerson."

When they sat down, Doc thought that Crystal was remarkably relaxed for someone about to play what could be a pivotal role in the biggest national security case since 9-11. "You don't seem to be nervous about this."

"No reason to be. I'm just going to do my show. You're the one under all the pressure." She paused, "If he takes the bait and calls, that is." When Doc got to a list of questions he wanted her to ask, Crystal said, "Look, this is my show. I know how to do my job. If I can work these questions in, fine. But if the opportunity doesn't arise naturally, I'm not going to force it."

Doc couldn't get a read on her. Some media personalities refused to cooperate with law enforcement on the grounds that it compromised their journalistic credibility and independence. Others were okay supplying limited cooperation, such as publishing communications like the Zodiac's cryptograms or the Unabomer's manifesto, if it might help prevent further bloodshed or capture the bad guys. This was an extremely high profile situation, and if Dickerson played a role in Paine's capture, she was sure to get a hefty career boost. Whatever her motivations, she didn't seem to have any qualms about helping Doc trap his quarry, as long as it was on her terms.

For Crystal, those terms were *whatever gets the FBI out of my life*.

The show started off smoothly enough. Crystal spent the first half-hour promoting A.G. Godfrey's appearance and recapping the other news of the day. Coming out of the bottom of the hour break, Crystal introduced the Attorney General and welcomed him to the show.

"Thank you, Crystal, It's a pleasure to be here."

She got straight to the point. "I understand there's been a significant development in the investigation?"

"Yes. I'm happy to announce that the FBI has conclusively determined that there is no organization behind these attacks. They are all the work of one man."

Crystal asked, "How can one man carry out nearly simultaneous attacks in Palm Springs and New York? How is that even possible?"

"I can't reveal specifics about sources and methods, or the advanced technology that led us to make this determination, but the person we're after is not as clever as he thinks he is."

"By the 'person we're after', you mean the man who called my show, the man who identified himself as Tom Paine?"

"It's an insult to call the man responsible for these crimes by the name of a true American patriot," replied Godfrey. "It demeans the true heroism of the original Tom Paine. However, until such time as we determine his true identity, the suspect will be identified as our new Public Enemy Number One, 'using the alias Tom Paine'. The government has posted a tax-free reward of $2 million for information leading to his capture. But make no mistake about it; like anyone who acts outside the law, regardless of what he chooses to call himself, this man is no patriot, no crusader --" Godfrey immediately wanted to call back his words, but just like a bullet, once fired it was too late.

In the control booth, Doc and Kenny shook their heads. From that moment on, the man they were after was no longer a generic terrorist, or even just Tom Paine. Now he would also be "The Crusader," a title implying righteousness, even purity or nobility. At the control board screening callers, Engineer Sam heard Doc mutter, "Your tax dollars at work."

Crystal's very first caller compounded the gaffe by stringing together in one phrase, "This new Crusader Tom Paine Public Enemy #1 guy..."

Godfrey's claim that the insurgency was only one man didn't motivate Paine in the least. Until the government explained how it had arrived at that conclusion, to him it was just a meaningless assertion. But listening on the webcast Paine thought "The Crusader" had such a nice ring to it that he called to thank the AG.

Sam put the call right through.

"So how do I know that this is the real Tom Paine?" asked Crystal.

"In a few minutes I'm going to post six more Amendments for the Second Bill Of Rights on our website," Paine replied. "That should be proof enough."

Doc felt an immediate surge of cautious optimism. The website update would give the NSA and his whiz techs a second opportunity to track Paine's location.

At the same moment, Crystal pounced. "Our website? The Attorney General says there isn't any 'our' or 'we,' that you're out there all alone."

"If it comforts the feds to think that, far be it from me to argue. Eventually one of us will be proven correct. Besides," he added, "if I'm just one man, why is everybody so concerned?"

"Because you're a killer, Public Enemy Number One."

"The real public enemies are the members of Congress, the administration, law enforcement, and the lobbyists who've enabled the rich and the corporations to get away with stealing this country blind, destroying the rule of law, and crushing the middle class. People like the Attorney General are enemies of justice and democracy. People like him have made a mockery of our legal system and a shambles of our economy. We should change his title to Criminal General. Instead of Commander-In-Chief, the President is the Criminal-In-Chief."

Godfrey manufactured the appearance of great indignation over hearing the President called Criminal-In-Chief. "It's disgraceful and insulting." Beyond that, Godfrey was in no mood to discuss Paine's accusations.

Crystal tried to keep Paine on the line by asking him to summarize the new Manifesto Amendments.

Paine declined, but thanked the agitated Godfrey for naming him a crusader. "Yes," he said, "I am leading a crusade to restore democracy and accountability to the American political system." Paine promised to call back again and hung up.

A few minutes later Doc learned that updating of the AI website was in progress and that NSA had pinpointed the location as a mall in Hawthorne, California, a small suburb just southeast of the L.A. airport. Doc allowed himself to hope. *Maybe we've got that sumbitch.*

A $10 million white elephant, the Hawthorne Mall was a testimonial to the ineptitude of the redevelopment process. Financed by city-issued bonds, it opened to much hoopla, but gang shootouts in the food court, muggings in the restrooms, and rapes in the parking structure were the kind of shopping experience that quickly cooled public ardor. After a few years of steady decline, it finally closed entirely. In 2001 the northern section was converted into offices for the L.A. County Welfare Department's Fraud Division. It had been child's play for Paine to tap into the electrical system for power, and hijack a connection to the welfare office's Internet service.

Hawthorne P.D. SWAT and a SWAT unit from the nearby L.A. Sheriff's Lennox station advanced on the target location from opposite directions. SWAT has always had its own lingo, like the codes little boys devised to keep girls out of their tree houses. SWAT units never entered a location, they always "made entry." Hawthorne SWAT "made entry" from the front of what had been, at one time, a Victoria's Secret. The Sheriff's SWAT unit deployed in the delivery service corridor behind the store. Inching around abandoned display racks and dusty counters, Hawthorne SWAT converged on the faint light coming from the back room. The SWAT Commander clicked his radio twice to signal the Sheriff's SWAT unit, then heaved a flash grenade into the back room which had once held countless sexy panties and push-up bras. As soon as the grenade exploded, Hawthorne SWAT burst into the storeroom, then called "Clear," signaling the Sheriff's unit that it was okay to enter.

The two SWAT units, eleven officers in all, stood in a big circle around their prisoner, an older version Dell desktop. The screen read: "Thanks for using GoToMyPC.com."

Chapter 16: Getting To Know You

Once efforts to trace Paine's call and the website update proved futile, Doc decided to put Crystal Dickerson under a protective detail. He wasn't going to let anything happen to his only link to Paine.

Already furious over being rat-checked and put under constant intrusive surveillance, Crystal was naturally less than thrilled that henceforth she would be escorted everywhere.

Tonight, while her Chevy Cruze followed behind with an agent at the wheel, she got a ride home in Doc's personal mobile command center van. It wasn't one of those cramped affairs loaded with hardware often seen in movies. All Special Assignment Sections had those, and one followed Doc around whenever it was needed. Instead, his personal office on wheels was laid out for comfort and practicality, with just enough stuff, as he called it, to keep him in contact and provide critical video. Its biggest asset was a large fold-down table, for his incessant doodling and note making.

Doc steered Crystal to a pair of executive office chairs in the back. Kenny settled into the seat across from the driver and closed the sliding door behind the cab. The sense of privacy would help make the conversation seem less like the interrogation that it was.

After apologizing for the inconvenience of the protective detail, Doc offered her a glass of Merlot from the van's little refrigerator. Doc did not smoke or drink, but he kept beer, wine, and cigarettes on hand. Getting a suspect drunk to obtain information was illegal and would get a case tossed out of court. But Doc had learned that when working with nervous witnesses or potential informants in the field, offering a friendly beer, a calming glass of wine, or even just a cigarette could be the difference between a productive interview and one that went nowhere. It was an unorthodox and sometimes risky tactic, but his job was to take risks and use unorthodox methods to solve tough cases.

Crystal knew the wine was an attempt to soften her up, but she accepted anyway. When he opted for a Diet Sprite she asked. "So, you don't drink when you're interrogating the enemy?"

"One, I don't think of you as the enemy. Two, this is not an interrogation. And three, I quit drinking way before I even thought of joining the Bureau."

"Why?"

"Because when I drank, I knew no fear, felt no pain, and had no sense."

It sounded to her like a bad combination, and she said so.

Doc needed to find out what made Paine select Crystal as his media vehicle. He hoped for the kind of clue that only she could reveal, perhaps even unconsciously. If she and Paine had a connection of some sort, or had met at some point in the past, without her even realizing it, she could propel the investigation ahead. He let her sit quietly and sip her Merlot. When he thought she was as relaxed as she was going to get, he asked, "So, Ms. Dickerson, tell me about yourself."

"Why? You already know all there is to know about me." Curious to find out just exactly how much the FBI did know, or was willing to admit, she added provocatively, "All the way back to the name of the first boy I ever kissed."

"Kissed, no. Slept with? That would be Steven Mitchell. The summer before your senior year of high school. You gave it up to him on your second date."

"Gave it up? My, what a charming description of a girl's first romantic experience."

Doc was undeterred. Making a provocative statement to someone under interrogation was a proven technique that sometimes produced clues or unearthed other helpful information. "Like I said, you gave it up to him on your second date, and apparently have never regretted it. He was a good guy, always treated you with respect. He put it to you every chance he could until the two of you went off to different colleges."

Crystal didn't know what to think. The bluntness of "gave it up" and "put it to you" clashed with the "good guy, treated you with respect" part.

"By the way, he's doing fine. Good job, married, faithful to his wife, has a little boy, and another on the way. Wasn't real happy we brought your name up, though. Says thinking about you again makes him feel sorta like he's cheating on his wife. Like I said, a good guy."

Crystal took another sip of wine. "Good. I'm glad for him."

"So," Doc asked, "Did you learn anything about Mr. Paine from his call tonight?"

"Why ask me? You've got professionals analyzing every millisecond of the show tape."

"I want your impressions. I want to find out why he wants to connect with you. I don't think he just picked your name out of a hat."

Crystal thought before answering. "Well, he can handle pressure. When he got mad his voice didn't change pitch. And he remained articulate, didn't lose any command of the language. Those are hard things to do. Trust me."

"I do. Tell me more." He added teasingly, "Come on, give it up."

She shot him a sideways glance, sort of a playful reproach, and took refuge in another sip from her glass.

Doc glanced out the side window and saw that they were pulling into her condo complex. "About his anger? You get any sense of his motivations, what might have triggered him to act?"

Crystal didn't know why exactly, but she felt uncomfortable, and almost didn't answer. "His anger is an expression of pain. I think at heart he's a warm guy who's been hurt in some terrible way, and he's suffering through some deep pain. Could be from loss, could be from disappointment."

"Warm? Strange way to describe a serial assassin."

"Hey, you wanted my opinion."

The van stopped in front of her building. Kenny got out and opened the sliding door. Crystal was just about to step out when Doc asked the big question, "Why do you think he picked you to call?"

She turned and answered with a perfect dead pan, "Isn't it obvious? He hopes if he's nice to me, I'll give it up to him."

Before Doc could react she was out the door and headed up the walk to her condo, escorted by two agents.

Doc watched as the security detail followed her into the elevator. Those agents would remain outside her third floor condo until morning. Two other agents positioned their car near a wall in a location that offered a perfect view of her condo and some protection against anyone coming up from behind. Other agents were already in place, well out of sight, keeping the complex under round-the-clock surveillance. Crystal wasn't just under protection; she was also bait.

Riding up in the elevator, Crystal also wondered why she had described Paine as "warm at heart." What was it about him that made her feel that way? After all, Agent Medlin was right; it was a strange way to describe an assassin.

On the drive back to the office, Doc admitted to himself that Crystal rattled him. She was *one helluva package*. He didn't get the kind of manifesto he wanted from Paine, and now she confronted him with more problems he didn't need. Good reason to keep his distance and not get distracted from his J-O-B.

Chapter 17: Project Aquarium

Doc sat down in the OCD Control Room and told Ed Bridges, "We gotta stop chasing this guy."

Ed leaned back in his chair. "Meaning?"

"Cut him off at the pass. Identify a pool of possible suspects and then work our way through them 'til we find who we're lookin' for."

Bridges had an idea where Doc was going. Everything pointed to Paine having a military background. Unfortunately, twenty-five million Americans had served in the military. Subtracting current members of the Armed Services still left a massive, unwieldy Suspect Pool. "Sounds... ambitious," he said, understating the problem.

"Yeah, but I think we can cut it down to a manageable size. Look at these new amendments, this so-called Economic Bill of Rights. The first mandates a return to domestic manufacturing. The second is about universal single-payer health care. The third calls for guaranteeing pensions, the fourth expands union collective bargaining rights, and the fifth protects veterans from benefit reductions. Let's suppose that whatever motivates this guy is tied to these issues. Let's say he's a veteran with a blue collar or a lower-level white-collar job. The economy tanks, he's out on the bricks. No job, no health care, and his pension goes south. Maybe he was part of a union, but it wasn't strong enough to protect him. Or maybe he thinks a union could have saved his ass. We use this to narrow the field."

Doc pushed a piece of paper across the table.

Ed put his elbows on the table and read down a list of search criteria, then leaned back in his chair again. "I take that back. This is way beyond ambitious."

"But you can do it, right?"

"Yeah, sure. The hard part will be trying to do anything with the results."

Doc stood up. "Let me worry about that."

As Doc reached for the door, Ed asked, "Hey, boss, whatta we call this file?"

Doc thought for a moment and said, "Aquarium. Project Aquarium."

As Bridges set up the new file, he thought about the coming investigation: *Thank God I'm not a field agent.*

The terrain around the Palm Springs sniper's nest indicated that The Crusader was somewhat physically fit. Thus Bridges eliminated the people in the Veteran's Administration and other databases who were seventy or older, along with everybody under twenty-five. A guy in his early twenties would be impulsive and reckless, like Tim McVeigh and the Boston Marathon bomb brothers. Paine was patient and methodical, traits that take time to develop. Eliminating the upper and lower ends of the age scale brought the file down to just over 21,400,000 people.

Next Bridges created a separate file of ninety thousand people licensed to sell, transport, or use explosives, or holding a Federal firearms dealer's license. To that he added 1,962,000 people whose bankrupt private pension plans had been taken over by the federal government's Pension Benefit Guaranty Corporation. Typically the PBGC only paid about half of what pensioners would have received if their company pension program hadn't gone belly up.

Bridges merged the names in the second file with those in the military file and then deleted the dupes and all women. Swiped credit card transactions, airline and cruise ship manifests, Amtrak records, and passport scans eliminated anyone more than 200 miles from Palm Springs at the time of the shootings. Cellphone and landline phone records eliminated more people outside the

200-mile radius. Eliminating those in custody in a federal, state, or county facility, and anyone who had been hospitalized at the time reduced the file even further. To get to the final number, Ed purged the list against the Social Security Death Index.

While Bridges crunched data, Doc had Kelli send out an alert to every law enforcement agency nationwide. "Tell them we're going to need their full fuckin' cooperation to track down, interview and eliminate a shitload of potential suspects."

Kelli dutifully scribbled down and repeated back, "Full fuckin' cooperation...shitload of potential suspects...Got it."

When Bridges walked through OCD's vast open bullpen a few hours later, Bravo's core agents instinctively followed him to the conference room.

As soon as everyone settled in, Doc asked, "So, what'd we get?"

"Net number of possible suspects is 204,706. Two-Oh-Four, Seven-Oh-Six."

The number dwarfed any previous investigation, but Doc was unfazed. "We'll break 'em down into three groups. Level One, top priority, is anyone with experience in special ops, intel or counterintelligence, and combat engineers or others with demolition experience. Scott, we take those. Up close and personal."

Scott grinned. "Piece of cake."

Doc turned to Agent Randleman. "Kelli, Level Two is anyone not in Level One who has actual combat experience, in country, under fire. Include anyone not in Level One with a background in engineering, high-tech, or transport security. Farm those out to Secret Service, DEA, and ATF. Borrow investigators from the Defense Department who do background checks on DOD civilian workers and defense contractor employees."

He swiveled around to the other side. "Gretchen, Level Three is everyone else. They go to local police and sheriffs. Tell 'em, every detective they've got drops whatever else they're doing, and starts running these guys down. If they whine about manpower, tell 'em to use some of those lard-assed veterans who think police work is rearranging their desk drawers. Anybody gives you static, threaten to issue a press release about how that department is too busy to help, including the names of everybody who gave you shit." Doc surveyed the room. "Any questions? Anything to add?"

Kenny suggested that, "Just to be on the safe side, we should take anybody in Level Two or Level Three who's current or retired law enforcement."

Doc agreed. "It'd be just our luck, this guy's a cop and the local PD won't give him a second thought."

Doc's viable, proactive plan to identify Paine went out the window when Attorney General Godfrey ordered him to apply the Suspect Pool criteria to the FEMA Main Core database. Doc protested that Main Core was a joke -- bloated, flawed, imprecise -- and that a number of his search criteria weren't applicable to it. Told, "to use whatever is applicable," he rode back down in the elevator mumbling, "Mindless fucking morons. Dumbest fucking smart people I've ever seen."

Originally created by J. Edgar Hoover as an "index of suspicious persons," Main Core was expanded by Col. Oliver North under Reagan, then mushroomed after 9-11 to eight million people, eight million "threats to the government" -- academics, labor leaders, civil rights activists, anti-war protestors, bloggers and other potential "subversives," from Neo-Nazis to gay rights activists. Doc saw it as a stupid creation of fools with lots of power and paranoia but no common sense. He couldn't imagine it ever being put to effective use, and nothing demonstrated Main Core's deficiencies more than the results it produced when the Suspect Pool ballooned to over 1,296,000 people. Doc laughed. *Find Paine using this bullshit? We'd have better luck finding Amelia Earhart.*

Paine was once again a step ahead. Knowing that the FBI would use the Economic Bill of Rights to create a suspect profile and then run that profile through every database at their disposal, including Main Core, he had already taken the appropriate steps to insulate himself from the search pool. The civil rights violations and disruption of law-abiding peoples' lives that would inevitably result from using Main Core would lead to repercussions that he intended to exploit to the fullest. Until then, he was content to wait a few weeks and watch the fun.

May

Chapter 18: Blowback

Among the Main Core suspects were vets with severe PTSD who had three things in common: a hair-trigger temper (the clinical term was "free floating hostility"), nightmare flashbacks, and paranoia. Although they tried desperately to forget what they had seen or done in the military, none forgot what they had *learned* in the military. When investigators confronted enough of these vets, bad things were sure to happen. And did.

Awakened from a drunken stupor by an early morning knock on his dilapidated trailer in rural Arkansas, a hallucinating Vietnam vet mistook the lady cop in her dark blue uniform for a Viet Cong and emptied his .45 at her through the trailer door. Her bulletproof vest stopped the rounds from penetrating but she died from blunt force trauma to the heart.

A young former Marine, haunted by memories of the house-to-house combat in Fallujah, was pulled over on his motorcycle by a Nevada Highway Patrolman. The Marine couldn't understand why he was being stopped and questioned without having broken any traffic laws. One thing led to another, there was a scuffle, and the officer ended up dead, killed with his own gun. Chased down an hour later when he crashed his bike in the parking lot of a strip mall, the kid wounded a deputy sheriff, took two rounds from other officers, then stumbled into a coffee shop where he apologized for disturbing the terrified customers and blew his brains out.

Outside Dayton, Ohio, a detective coached out of retirement to interview "persons of interest" tracked down another PTSD vet in a dive bar. Hard-nosed but not very bright, the detective insisted on interrupting the vet's pool game to get his questions answered. The soldier, a veteran of the 10th Mountain Division in Afghanistan, clocked the detective upside the head with the fat end of his cue stick. Blood streaming from his temple, the cop opened fire. With his dying breath the vet plunged the sharp end of the pool cue into the cop's eye, killing him instantly.

There were also cases of mistaken identity or mistaken intentions. In Stockton, a man whose house was foreclosed on by the bank thought the deputies ambling up the front walk were there to evict him. Seized by panic and despair, he fired two rounds from his father's WWII souvenir M1 Garand, killing one officer and wounding the other. During a six-hour standoff the man turned off the pilot light for the stove and the water heater, and opened the gas valves all the way. When SWAT fired tear gas into the house, it blew up like something in a Hollywood action film. At first the FBI thought they had found The Crusader, but a subsequent investigation ruled him out.

Some people on the list were hard-core criminals, including members of notorious motorcycle gangs and organized crime syndicates of various racial and ethnic composition. Over two hundred attempted interviews resulted in either gun battles or high-speed chases that left six innocent bystanders, five peace officers, and seventeen suspects dead. In other cases, the person the investigator came to interview no longer lived at that address, but the current occupant had a good reason to panic when cops appeared at the door. Officers stumbled onto dope houses, meth labs, mountains of stolen goods and counterfeit merchandise, illegal alien smuggling dens, stolen car chop shops, unlicensed health clinics, dog and cock fighting operations, high school sex parties, and more than a few extra-marital affairs, including two involving students with teachers.

Things finally came to a head when a young agent insisted on pulling a suspect, Nelson Varrick, out of a client presentation at a major San Francisco ad agency. The reason Varrick's name surfaced in the suspect pool was that there was no record of his activities during the weeks before and after the Palm Springs attack. The simple explanation was that Varrick and his wife were on vacation, sailing their forty-foot sloop around the vast Pacific. Varrick had no choice but to explain to his boss -- and the prospective client -- that for some cockamamie reason the FBI thought he might be The Crusader. Unnerved, the client bolted. The agency panicked and fired Varrick. Incensed, he filed a wrongful termination suit against the agency. This made the local news, which caused his wife's employer, a ritzy private school, to panic and fire her. The ACLU stepped in and filed a class-action civil rights suit against the Justice Department, with the FBI as co-defendant. Lawyers from coast to coast, including prominent university law professors, got in on the act. Within days, movie stars were speaking out and donating money to defense funds. Famous musicians competed for the chance to hold benefit concerts.

Chapter 19: Dangerous Pastimes

Muskie fishing season started on the upper Michigan peninsula at sunrise on May 15th, which this year fell on a Friday. As was their annual custom, Tim Brantley and Aaron Goodman, former CEO and CFO, respectively, of bankrupt BlueStar Airlines, started the day before. Both men detested the very concept of laws and regulations, which they felt only applied to the little people. Why not? Laws and regulations hadn't kept them from looting hundreds of millions from BlueStar. Stockholders lost their entire investment. Newer employees with 401(k) plans had their retirement savings wiped out. Retired employees found their pensions slashed. Forced by FAA regulations to retire at age sixty, former pilots who had counted on BlueStar's health care until they reached Medicare age found themselves out in the cold. After cheating thousands of stockholders and employees, cheating to hunt a premiere North American fresh water game fish was nothing. Except this year, the muskies had a friend.

Using a.30-06 Remington hunting rifle with a six-power scope and homemade silencer Paine shot Goodman first, then Brantley, both in the gut just below the belly button. Despite all the recent attacks, they were still taken by surprise. Paine saw the same *Why me?* lack of comprehension on their faces that he had seen on Trammello's face in Palm Springs.

Paine dispatched Goodman with a hollow-point round that blew the back of his head off. Paine took his time with Brantley. By the time the kill shot shattered his spine, Brantley wanted to die. *Anything to stop the pain.* It was a feeling many of his former employees knew well.

After hiking a mile up a rocky streambed, Paine buried the rifle in a shallow trench hidden far back under a cliff overhang. Although the rifle was untraceable, Paine wanted the FBI to spend years checking other bullets of the same caliber, looking vainly for a match. Three miles later Paine reached another of his nondescript work cars, an old Chevy Malibu parked well off the highway in a grove of trees. There he sanitized his hands and face, changed clothes, and bagged his hunting outfit. After disposing of it at another pre-selected site, he paid a video visit Out There to Anaheim Hills in sunny Southern California.

No myth was ever greater than the one that America supported its people in uniform. For reasons from bureaucratic indifference and ineptitude to insider war profiteering, from the Civil War through the War on Terror, American soldiers consistently went into battle without the best available weapons and equipment. The treatment veterans received after discharge was even worse. Over the last hundred years the only promise made to service personnel that had been kept in full, without later being rescinded or watered down, was the WWII G.I. bill, which proved fortuitous. Otherwise, many WWII vets recalled to service for Korea would have probably refused to report.

John Ronda personified the callous attitude of many in the Veteran's Administration. Concealing the deplorable conditions at VA hospitals, falsifying statistics on wait times for medical and psych services, and burying reports on the number of PTSD cases was SOP for Ronda and his minions. But Ronda took things a step farther, awarding a lucrative VA contract to a private firm, then promptly leaving the VA for a job, at more than a million a year plus perks, at the same firm.

Thanks to Paine and the marvels of modern technology, Ronda didn't live to enjoy much of his newfound wealth. Having broken ninety for the first time ever, his scorecard was on the passenger's seat when his Lexus made a wide comfortable left turn out of the country club. The car was only eleven feet from the six-pound Flex-X shaped charge hidden in the landscaping when the explosion blew the passenger's side door through the car and out the driver's side, shearing off the passenger's seat, the center console, and the steering wheel. Like Lloyd Beber in New York, Ronda was decapitated, his deformed head stuck to the mangled roof while his body and the driver's seat ended up in the far northbound lane surrounded by debris. Miraculously, the scorecard survived intact.

This time Paine had hacked into the country club's surveillance system.

Brantley and Goodman weren't reported missing until early Thursday evening, too late to start a search. By the time the bodies were found Friday morning, Paine had reached his next destination, in D.C. His target would be the true cancer of the political system: K Street.

Chapter 20: The Quinella

Doc immediately recognized that the sniper attack in the Michigan woods and the bomb attack on John Ronda in California simply reversed the west-to-east pattern of the attacks in New York and Palm Springs. A little voice told him that the weekend festivities might not be over yet so he decided to let SAS Gloria in Los Angeles and Charley in Chicago handle the on-site investigations. Doc's instincts were correct. Just after nine p.m. Sunday night, word came in of another attack, in suburban Falls Church, Virginia. The victims were former White House Press Secretary Stan Speakes and his wife, Linda.

Minutes later Crystal's quiet evening at home was interrupted by a knock on the door. An agent from her protective detail said that Doc wanted her brought to the site of Paine's first local attack.

Doc marched Crystal by the elbow past the yellow crime scene tape to Speake's car and pulled back the plastic sheet. Hundreds of nails and small ball bearings had turned the bodies into unrecognizable hamburger. Linda Speakes was so shredded that her stomach contents oozed out across the floorboard. Crystal was stunned. She'd never imagined that a human body could absorb that much damage. The sickening sweet aroma of blood and stomach contents caused a sudden wave of nausea.

Doc moved close, his head right next to hers. "Don't you dare puke. You don't get off that easy. Hold on to that churning in your stomach. Take a deep breath. And every time you're tempted to think of this Tom Paine as a patriot, you remember this smell." Doc paused for a moment. "A block from home. One block. Their kids heard the explosion. Thank God that a fifteen year-old babysitter was smart enough to keep those kids in the house or else they would have seen this. Maybe you'd like to tell them about it, describe it in detail?"

"Why are you blaming me?"

Doc was out of line, and he knew it, but his anger and frustration needed some outlet. There was no telling what he might have said next, but his phone rang. "Shit! He's struck again." Doc told Crystal's protective detail to follow, then took off in his van with Kenny, lights flashing and siren blaring.

On K Street, D.C.'s famed "Lobbyshop Row," the two luxury office buildings that formerly housed the firms of Morris-Savage-Beck, and Craig/Thompson were now mounds of burning rubble. Windows were blown out in a two-block radius, and flaming debris had set several nearby buildings on fire.

Doc immediately wanted a body count.

"Two people working on some project at Craig/Thompson are presumed gone," said the Fire Captain in charge. "But it could take up to a week to dig out the bodies." A dozen people in other buildings were being treated, but none with life-threatening injuries. DCPD and FBI bomb squads were already on the scene. Otherwise, "that's all we've got at the moment."

The agent driving Crystal from the Speakes' murder pulled into a gas station long enough for her to toss her cookies and wash her mouth out with a Diet Sprite from a vending machine. By the time they reached K Street, Crystal was back in professional journalistic mode and ready to see the destruction up close.

"Your boyfriend's been busy," Doc said, when she joined him near what remained of the M-S-B building. "Five attacks in three days. He just hit the quinella."

"Let's hope he's not going for the Pick Six," Kenny added wryly. He couldn't tell which the site reminded him of more: a miniature 9-11, or Oklahoma City on a larger scale?

Chapter 21: Enablers

Review of video from D.C.'s Domain Awareness System showed that on Saturday morning a rental truck stolen from a location in Pennsylvania had delivered a pallet of file cabinets, presumably containing the bomb, to the M-S-B loading dock. A man who might be Paine was caught on tape walking away from the truck at the Craig/Thompson building. The basic physical identifiers -- medium height and build, indeterminate age -- were of no use, and because the suspect had worn a wide-brimmed hat, sunglasses, and what was probably a fake beard there were no facial features for facial recognition comparison.

DAS captured the suspect a number of times driving an old maroon Impala but finally lost track when he got far enough west into rural Virginia. The license plate traced back to a postal service employee in Maryland, but his Impala had body damage on one quarter-panel and a Postal Service parking permit decal on the windshield, neither of which showed up on the DAS video. Doc suspected that Paine had made a duplicate license plate, probably using one of the new plastic-injection 3-D printers now available to the public. Doc immediately assigned agents to trace all sales and thefts of these machines. A nationwide BOLO -- Be On the Look Out -- went out for the Impala, but Doc was pretty sure that it was already well hidden, possibly at the bottom of a river or lake someplace, and wouldn't be found for years, if ever.

Doc didn't particularly like being summoned to the White House to brief the President, the VP, Department of Homeland Security Secretary Hoover, Attorney General Godfrey, and the President's Chief of Staff, Zak Wooten. FBI Director Bartholomew was also there, but he didn't count. The Director knew what the Bureau could and couldn't do. The others were pure political types, under siege from the ruling elite. Striking at elected officials who were merely replaceable puppets was bad enough, but attacking lobbyists struck at the puppeteers. President Welch and the others wanted results, and reality be damned. Like truth, to them reality was a fungible concept. They just wanted a solution. Unfortunately, Doc couldn't suddenly pull a one out of a hat.

President Welch wanted to know if Agent Medlin was still certain that he was dealing with only one man. Doc said yes and Bartholomew concurred.

"Great. Just fucking great," the President muttered. "My presidency is being held hostage by a single deranged serial killer."

Doc leaned forward. "Exactly, Mr. President. A lone wolf who targets public officials and business leaders instead of little boys or prostitutes." It flashed through Doc's mind that to some people, politicians and public officials *were* prostitutes.

"So what next?" Godfrey wanted to know. "Anything out of Main Core?"

"Not yet, but we're crosschecking everything we have from the latest attacks against the Suspect Pool, and against evidence from the earlier attacks. Since this Dickerson woman is our only link, I'm camping out in her studio every night to personally monitor her next conversation with Paine while my tech people conduct our trace efforts."

"Efforts which so far haven't met with much success," Hoover noted.

"Paine can't stay one step ahead forever. There are only so many tricks he can use, and each time we improve our countermeasures. Eventually he'll make a mistake and I'll run him to ground. He's a man, not a ghost." The only problem with that statement was that sometimes Doc felt like he really was chasing a ghost.

In some ways, he was.

Paine called Crystal the very next night. Her first question was, "Why murder a former White House Press Secretary?"

"Press Secretary? You mean Propaganda Minister, don't you?"

Crystal ignored the bait. "What about his wife? Any regrets about killing an innocent woman, and leaving three kids without parents?"

Paine scoffed. "Innocent? What makes you think she was innocent? Time was, women were the moral backbone of this country. They had integrity and they valued it in a man. When Hugh Sloan had to testify during Watergate, his wife vowed to leave him if he lied. Nowadays it's different. Linda Speakes knew the kind of man she married, what kind of work he did."

"Sometimes you just can't help who you fall in love with."

"Principle has to trump love. Otherwise, it's not principle. If you can love that kind of man, you're just as bad as he is."

"Doesn't change the fact that you left three young kids without parents."

"Maybe now they'll grow up in a home where the adults set a better example."

Crystal thought that was awfully cold, and wanted to push the innocent victim angle. "Okay, what about the people killed on K Street? Don't they fall under the definition of innocent victims?"

"Hell, no. All Hitler needed was obedient little Nazis to carry out orders. There is no difference between people who work at a lobbying firm that coordinates fascist corporate control of our government and the Nazi minions who ran the Third Reich."

"Oh, come on. You can't believe that. You can't equate a couple of mid-level employees at an office in Washington with --"

Paine interrupted. "They were writing legislation! Legislation that Congress was going to adopt. Congress doesn't write laws any more, the special interests do. Congress is just a rubber stamp. They were enablers, helping the fascist train keep running down the tracks. The truly powerful are too well insulated from justice and accountability. We have to target the enablers.

Corporations and governments don't do bad things; people who work for corporations and governments do bad things. It's not just a job; it's a conscious moral decision. People decide to earn their living morally, or immorally. Victimizers are not victims."

"And you get to make that determination."

"Somebody has to." Paine suddenly changed the subject. "Why don't I take questions from your audience while the FBI tries tracing this call?"

Crystal glanced at Doc in the control room. Her talking to a serial killer fugitive was surreal enough, but the idea of average Americans doing it boggled the mind. Nevertheless, once Doc nodded "okay" Crystal said, "Sure, Tom, why not. Let's go to Cliff, listening on the Internet in Pasadena, California."

While Paine took five calls, all sympathetic to his goals if not his methods, Doc's whiz techs traced the location of his call to another taxpayer-financed municipal boondoggle, a nearly vacant city-owned office building in Hershey, Pennsylvania. Doc watched the raid over a live satellite feed from the Hershey P.D. SWAT Commander's helmet cam. The only thing they found in the vacant office on the third floor was an electronic device, about the size of a VCR, connected to two phone jacks in the wall.

Everyone at Operations Center D immediately recognized the device as a remote call diverter that relayed calls from one phone number to another. Doc didn't know if it was merely ironic or intentional, but it was the exact same model the FBI used to provide undercover officers with a check-in number that didn't trace back to the Bureau. Somewhere, someplace, Paine was calling into the diverter from a prepaid cell. A check of the building's telephone closet revealed a splice into two lines belonging to a CPA on the ground floor.

Watching the raid via a video camera hidden behind an air conditioning vent, Paine signed off with an ominous reference to several exciting new features on the American Insurgency website.

Chapter 22: High Anxiety

The idea that their corrupt work made them targets spooked many lobbying firm employees. Some quit. Those who could work from home started doing so. Many applied for jobs in other cities or in lower profile professions.

If the latest attacks weren't enough to push fear among the elite and their enablers to new heights, three new AI website sections definitely finished the job. Do Your Part -- branded "a recruiting poster for domestic jihadists!" by President Welch -- encouraged "local patriots" to carry out attacks. The Operational Doctrine section, with the motto "Their Pain Is Democracy's Gain," explained how to select and recon targets, determine the best methods of attack, obtain weapons or fabricate explosives, and execute a mission without getting caught or leaving trace evidence. The most troublesome, Name That Target, invited people to draft indictments outlining the alleged crimes or offenses of potential targets. Each week the top three vote getters would join the Public Enemies "To Do" list.

Professor Herren and his Document Analysis Team went over AI's Operational Doctrine and came up with three possibilities. "One, he's got experience in a crime lab somewhere, or maybe as a homicide detective. Two, he's done some serious research on modern forensics."

"And the third?" asked Doc.

Herren grimaced. "He's a spook." He hesitated, then added, "Hope I'm wrong about that."

He wasn't the only one. A deranged ex-CIA agent gone rogue was a staple premise of books and movies, but a real world version ranked as truly a worst-case scenario. It was hard enough stopping amateur terrorists who got most of their knowledge off the Internet. Chasing someone with years of professional U.S. government training would be a true nightmare.

Meanwhile, the call diverter was traced to a shipment of two-dozen picked up months earlier at a private mailbox in Cabo San Lucas, Mexico during Spring Break, when the city was awash in gringos. Besides complicating efforts to trace future calls, the call diverters meant the Task Force had to go back and check more than a hundred thousand people in the Suspect Pool who had originally been ruled out from previous attacks because calls made from their home or office numbers placed them at different locations.

For Paine's crusade to succeed, scaring lobbyists in D.C. or banksters in New York wasn't enough. A critical mass of people on a national level had to support AI's goals, if not its methods. Without public support, Paine differed from a common criminal only in his motives. Attorney General Godfrey wasn't about to let the latest AI website updates seduce that support. JGod upped the price on Paine's head to $5 million and announced that anyone who nominated a target on the AI website would be charged with conspiracy to commit murder, providing material support for terrorism, and treason.

Godfrey's threat deterred a lot of people, but not everyone. Name That Target got plenty of nominees. The depth and ferocity of public loathing for elected officials and business leaders shocked even Paine. Thanks to the surprising number of "indictments" alleging corruption at the state and local level, the panic and fear that had gripped D.C. and New York rocketed across the country. Since not every nominee was charged with a capital offense, for lesser crimes Name That Target offered the public the chance to vote on less severe punishments ranging from having a home, car, or business vandalized to kneecapping. Overnight, the by-products of terrorism -- fear, suspicion, and obsession with constant vigilance -- descended like an ominous cloud everywhere. Orders for armored limousines and SUVs soared. Security companies were swamped with orders for bulletproof glass and Kevlar curtains in offices and conference rooms.

Working through the bloated Project Aquarium suspect pool had been slow going, but at least some progress was being made. Now, with Name That Target nominees multiplying daily, law enforcement agencies everywhere were inundated with demands for protection from public officials and prominent private citizens. After staffing the new security details, most police and sheriff's departments didn't have enough personnel to meet basic crime-response obligations, much less track down Project Aquarium suspects. At the same time, city councils and county boards were subjected to heated criticism as ordinary citizens vented justifiable anger that local officials were being guarded at the expense of overall community safety.

Worse, as far as Doc was concerned, many of the investigators he had borrowed from other federal agencies to comb through his high-priority Aquarium suspects were called back to protect officials at their respective agencies. Efforts to outsource the investigation of Aquarium suspects also failed because private security firms were overwhelmed. Competition for retirees with law enforcement, national security, or military experience drove up the demand to the point that the nation's two largest private paramilitary security firms, Overlord and Praetorian, recalled personnel from posts in Middle East and other flashpoints around the world. That didn't sit well with the State Department folks whose safety now depended on the overextended resources of the Diplomatic Security Service.

The sudden influx of paramilitary private security types unsettled many police chiefs, not to mention a large segment of the public. Trained and conditioned for service in war zones, it was only a matter of time before one of them over-reacted or misread a situation and mowed down innocent bystanders. Rather than risk antagonizing the elite who employed these heavily armed security forces, many sheriffs and police chiefs opted to cross their fingers, hope for the best, and look the other way.

All of these factors combined to multiply the pressure Doc was under. Everyone wanted Paine caught or killed. Now. Today, in time for the evening news. Doc had a sign on his desk, "Frustration is not having anyone to blame but yourself." Not this time. His only solution, narrowing down the Suspect Pool, was hamstrung by a manpower shortage. He wondered: *Had Paine foreseen how things would mushroom out of hand? Or was he just lucky?*

Kenny also felt the pressure. If Doc failed and was yanked off the case, Kenny would probably walk the plank as well. Just because he had already accrued the maximum retirement benefits didn't mean that Senior Special Agent Johnson was ready to pack it in. He hated to lose as much as Doc did, and shared Doc's frustration at not having the resources to do the job right.

At the White House, President Welch wondered: *how could this happen?* With FISA, The Patriot Act, the Protect America Act, and the NDAA, it wasn't supposed to be like this. *I've got complete access to every phone call, email, and letter sent or received by anyone in the United States. I've got access to every internet search, website visit, financial, medical, educational, or library record, and every hotel, motel, airline, train, or bus reservation. With all this, the federal government can't prevent a campaign of public support for a revolution?!*

The sad truth was, NSA's electronic surveillance programs relied on Key Word Filters to scan for word combinations: bomb, assassin, target, revolution, etc. AI increased key word traffic until the data ballooned to unmanageable proportions. The analysis of communications flagged by the scan programs was now running weeks behind. The President considered having NSA divert resources from monitoring Islamic web traffic, but was warned against it. The danger that some Islamic terrorist group would use AI as a diversion for another domestic attack was simply too great. The last thing the FBI needed was the confusion that would result if Al Qaeda staged an attack and deflected the blame onto AI.

For Paine, everything was going according to plan, and since there didn't seem to be anything that government and law enforcement could do to stop it, he decided to stretch the playing field.

Chapter 23: Model Behavior

Following his pattern of multiple attacks in quick succession, Paine killed Supreme Court Justice Kurt Parsons in Northern California and CallCom CEO John Sorkin four days later in Austin, Texas. Both attacks featured a new weapon, radio-controlled model airplanes, high-end versions with four-foot wingspans intended for serious hobbyists. Each packed a quarter-pound of PETN with an impact fuse on the nose of the plane. The Parsons bomb flew right through the open French doors of his sunny breakfast nook before it splattered the Justice and his huevos rancheros all over the faux-painted walls and Spanish tile floor. Sorkin had the convertible top down on his Porsche Super Carrera when the dive-bomber landed in the passenger's seat.

Parsons earned the distinction of being the only Supreme Court Justice ever assassinated. In a lesser way, Sorkin's death was also historic. He held the patents for most of the world's automated voice-mail menu systems. Ninety percent of callers who heard, "Press 1 for Sales, Press 2 for Tech Support, Press 3 to Fuck Yourself," heard it from one of Sorkin's devices, which had come to symbolize the indifference of remote and unreachable corporations. Once someone identified him by name for dominating the market in these despised instruments of the devil, Sorkin quickly became a top nominee in Name That Target balloting. It was a distinction he dismissed. The idea that anyone might actually kill him seemed too outlandish to be real. Then again, Sorkin never had to personally deal with the feeling of impotence his systems inflicted on people. He had assistants for that.

Kenny monitored SAS Frank in San Francisco and Delta in

Dallas as they investigated the two attacks. Trace analysis confirmed that the explosive was from the same Amarillo robbery as that used in earlier attacks, so at least Doc could continue operating on the single terrorist theory. Remnants of the planes traced back to a shipment of six stolen a year earlier. The prospect of more flying bombs out there gave potential targets more to guard against, and more to fear.

Meanwhile, the last Manifesto Amendments went up on the AI website, but there was no coinciding call to Crystal. Doc wondered if this possibly signaled an end to Paine's calls.

The first of Paine's new proposed amendments extended the right of public initiative and referendum to all states, and created a mechanism for national initiatives and referendums. Another mandated airtight fenced border security, a prohibition on granting amnesty to illegal aliens, and the exclusive use of English as the national language for all official documents, including ballots. But it was his last amendment that rocked the debate. Unlike the others, which targeted government, this one took direct aim at the public. The suggestion of universal national service ignited a firestorm.

The idea that everyone, male and female, must serve the country was anathema to many young people who had grown up feeling entitled to all the benefits of American citizenship and prosperity without any reciprocal obligation. They and their parents felt that serving in the military was strictly to be outsourced to the poor and minorities. It certainly wasn't something for young adults from better backgrounds.

The military also went crazy over the idea. The Pentagon enthusiastically favored an all-volunteer military because it consisted of people predisposed toward an authoritarian disciplinary environment, or those from lower socio-economic circumstances that didn't have a choice. As Vietnam demonstrated, when the vast majority of those going in harm's way were draftees, both the public and the troops were guaranteed to resist unnecessary wars or, as the President now contemplated, the imposition of domestic martial law.

While Doc consulted with the Professor Herren's team to see if these new amendments held any additional clues to Paine's identity, all available new DAS data was scanned with facial recognition software in hopes of spotting someone who had also been in the vicinity of an earlier attack. Every license picked up on a plate reader from police cars, meter maids, tollbooths, and freeway cameras was compared against those from previous attacks. Airline, hotel, motel, and rental car receipts were checked. Anyone in the Project Aquarium Suspect Pool in the vicinity of a new attack shot to the top of the suspect list, and stayed there until they could be definitively eliminated. None of these efforts bore fruit.

Finally, Doc and Kenny came to the only logical conclusion: Paine was, as they said in the spy business, "traveling blank" -- staying only in safe houses, never flying, frequently changing from one nondescript, legally registered car to another, and never using the same car for two attacks. Carrying his own food and using fuel caches hidden at strategic points along pre-planned travel routes allowed him to avoid gas stations and fast food places with their ubiquitous security cameras. Usually traveling in this manner requires a support network, which was exactly the impression Paine hoped to convey. However, with enough planning it could be carried out by one man.

To minimize the chances of being tripped up like Tim McVeigh by a simple traffic stop, Doc and Kenny further surmised that the appropriate weapons were probably hidden close to the location of each attack and then retrieved only at the last minute.

They were right on all counts. This was exactly how Paine was operating, and it left them with virtually nothing to go on.

Chapter 24: Tipping Point

Despite Paine's insistence on calling it an insurrection, he was really fostering revolution, and revolutions have always tended to take unexpected turns. This one was no different. Ironically, it was the death of Sorkin, not Justice Parsons, that marked the tipping point in Paine's crusade for reform. As a caller to Crystal's show said, "Anybody who whacks the guy what invented that voice mail thingy can't be all bad." The fact that a person's death could be grist for a joke said a lot about the hostility many everyday people felt toward rapacious corporations.

Watching Crystal's webcast when the comment was made, Missouri Gov. Cliff Brand, a man with a finely tuned political sense, had an epiphany. He saw the Chinese symbol for crisis, the character for danger above the character for opportunity. Sensing a populist revolt brewing, Gov. Brand decided to seize the moment and see if he could turn crisis into opportunity.

After he consulted with his wife, of course.

The next morning Brand addressed the press on the steps of the Missouri state capitol. Normal procedure was for the media and leaders of the legislature to receive advance copies of his speech. This time everyone except his wife was in the dark. "To quote that great Missourian, President Harry Truman, in this state the buck stops here. While I deplore and reject the violent tactics employed by The Crusader, I find no element of the proposed Manifesto Amendments that is not a valid subject for serious legislative debate and national political discussion. Although I have serious misgivings about holding a Constitutional convention, I hereby ask the legislature to pass a resolution calling on Congress to either convene such a convention, or to pass these amendments and forward them on to the individual states for possible ratification."

Paine, watching coverage of the announcement, almost couldn't believe it. A mainstream politician, the governor of a heartland state no less, had just embraced public debate of the Manifesto Amendments. Paine's insurgency had reached a watershed moment.

Brand knew his action would be unpopular with other politicians but the venom of the first day's invective stunned him. Criticism immediately rained down like a Niagara of piss.

Leaders of both parties in the legislature quickly distanced themselves from the governor's action. A few fellow governors begged off with diplomatic responses about it being "each governor's responsibility to act in the best interests of their state," but elected officials almost everywhere disagreed vehemently with Brand's action. The outcry from Washington was deafening. As the first crack in the establishment's resistance to the Manifesto Amendments, Brand had become a twenty-first century Benedict Arnold, and mere condemnation was not sufficient. He had to be punished, made an example of for all to see.

President Welch announced that he was, "greatly disappointed by the governor's actions, which reveal a lack of courage and leadership in the face of terrorism." After Congressional leaders finished excoriating Brand for the C-Span cameras, bills were introduced to reduce or eliminate funds for numerous projects and programs in Missouri. The bills, targeting everything from agricultural programs and bridge repairs to the cancellation of control tower upgrades at the St. Louis airport, had full bipartisan support, with co-sponsors from both the Democratic and Republican wings of the corporate money party.

Brand's most ferocious critic was Gov. Norm Gilligan of

neighboring Illinois, a state infamous for continuous, never-ending corruption on a grand scale. "The only way Illinois will ever call for a Constitutional Convention, or ratify any of these amendments," Gilligan thundered, "is over my dead body." Gilligan had reason to worry. The last thing he needed was a breeze from the west blowing a reform virus across the Mississippi river into the Illinois capitol of Springfield. In office for less than a year, he hadn't had a chance to fully line his pockets yet. Millions in bribes, kickbacks, lucrative stock options run through blind accounts in offshore banks, and illegal campaign contributions were still out there for the taking. Not to mention the regular blowjobs and threesomes provided by secretaries and office assistants who worked for the more powerful state lobbyists.

Just as Brand began to feel as if Judas had received less condemnation, things changed. To give the Missouri legislature time to hold hearings, Paine posted a notice on the AI website ordering his followers "to immediately suspend action against any Missouri official or person, at any level of government or business, for one month." Suddenly many in the legislature saw the wisdom of debating the Manifesto Amendments. After all, *a few hearings and a little discussion couldn't hurt, now could they?*

Later that evening another, an even more significant turn of events took place.

When his pension vanished along with the company's other assets, lifelong Enron employee Joseph Kuri was forced to move from Houston to Illinois and live in his daughter's basement guestroom. For the seventy-six year-old Kuri, Gov. Gilligan's condemnation of Brand was the last straw. Joe put on his one good suit and took a cab to a hotel where Gilligan was holding a fund-raiser.

Kuri sat quietly in the lobby, pretending to watch the Bulls game on TV. Gov. Gilligan's security detail never gave him a second look, which was not surprising. Even with the hysteria caused by The Crusader, the governor's security detail was still primarily a plum patronage position. Having an influential rabbi in the state police hierarchy still outweighed considerations of training and professional competence.

As Gilligan and his entourage exited the ballroom, Kuri calmly rose from his seat. Nobody noticed that as his right hand came off the arm of the chair it settled around the handle of a Colt Model 1911 .45 caliber semi-automatic, a souvenir of his father's service in North Africa during WWII.

"Congratulations, Governor," Kuri called out.

Thinking it was a voter or perhaps someone from the fundraiser, Gilligan turned. The first shot caught him just below the heart. He lived just long to hear, "We'll get that Constitutional Convention now, just the way you wanted it."

Kuri finished Gilligan off with a head shot, dropped the gun, and raised his hands before any of the stiffs on the governor's security detail managed to draw their weapons.

When Kuri arrived for booking at the Cook County Jail he shouted to the waiting camera crews, "I did my part. I did my part." It was an unmistakable reference to the AI website's "Do Your Part" section. After the cops finished searching his daughter's house, a stream of neighbors fought their way through the media mob to offer support. Many expressed condolences that Kuri had been caught. Their consensus: *Joe should have used a hunting rifle and fired from long distance.*

Paine called Crystal's show but stayed on the line only long enough to surprise her by denouncing Kuri's methods as, "impulsive and amateurish, signifying rage and frustration more than a rational commitment to political reform. Actions of this type," he said, "allow the media and the political elite to characterize the insurgency as nothing more than disgruntled kooks and whacked-out nut jobs." Paine emphasized that AI's Operational Doctrine stressed careful planning and a successful escape by unknown assailants who would never be identified, captured, or put on trial. "We don't want our supporters to endure punishment and retribution."

Crystal asked Doc on the ride home, "You think he's sincere -- about not wanting his followers to get caught?"

"He doesn't give a shit about his followers. It's purely a tactical consideration. The more assassins we have to chase, the less effort goes into catching him." Doc wasn't about to admit that the more Paine's followers escaped identification, the more effective AI's terror campaign became. Instead, he added, "Paine cares only about winning over enough disciples to get his one line, his footnote, in the history books."

Crystal flashed on the word *disciples* and filed it away for future use. "Gee, I thought those amendments are what might get him in the history books."

"Not gonna happen."

"What, the amendments or the history books?"

"Both." Doc wished he was as confident about that as he tried to sound, but Crystal was part of the media, and he didn't dare admit that Paine had any chance of success. With the action by Gov. Brand and the killing of Gov. Gilligan, Doc felt things starting to tip.

The next day Kuri's neighbors set up the Joe Kuri Defense Fund on PayPal and donations poured in. A team of prominent attorneys agreed to represent Kuri. Although public opinion ran 2-1 against Kuri's assassination of Gov. Gilligan, polls showed widespread support for Governor Brand's actions.

Meanwhile, in the "Boot Hill" section of the AI website, Governor Gilligan got his own tombstone, the first that didn't belong to one of Paine's personal victims. Now the questions were: *Would other states follow Missouri's lead? And would others follow Kuri's lead and join in the terror?*

"One of us," Doc muttered to Kenny, "is going to be disappointed."

It wasn't going to be Paine.

Chapter 25: Public Discourse

Prior to Gov. Brand's press conference, media coverage of the insurgency had focused on the fruitless search for The Crusader and ignored any substantive exploration of the actual merits of the Manifesto Amendments. This was no accident. Discussion of the proposed reforms was a debate the elite couldn't win; their position was indefensible. Until Brand broke ranks, the effort had succeeded. Widespread public support for the amendments had remained below the surface, praying for a mainstream political figure to convey legitimacy. Now the authorities could no longer classify public support for the amendments as de facto support of terrorism. Literally overnight the political and media landscape changed.

Two days after Governor Brand's press conference Paine called and challenged Crystal. "Now that Missouri will debate the merits of the Manifesto Amendments, don't you think someone in the media ought to do the same? You know, someone like you."

Crystal realized he was right and decided on the spot to accept the challenge.

Listening in the engineer's booth, Doc nearly went ballistic.

Doc was still seething when Crystal signed off at the end of her show. "Are you nuts?! I can't believe you're going to provide a forum for the ideas of a terrorist whose entire known following consists of exactly one deranged old man."

"And one apparently quite sane governor," she corrected him.

"Brand's off his rocker, too." Doc didn't really feel that way, but he also didn't dare reveal what he really thought.

The following night Crystal told her listeners, "Next week I'm going to devote one night to each of the five sections of the first Manifesto Amendment. The week after that I'll pick another amendment. I may not go in order because some amendments interest me more than others and after all," she added playfully, "it *is* my show." She promised to address, "any truly newsworthy developments," of the day, but in general was going to leave the discussion of "diversionary news" to others. "Think of the next few weeks as a summer school civics class at the Dickerson University of the Air."

As Crystal's producer as well as her engineer, Sam Brooks discovered that what she had in mind was not going to be easy. So far, the establishment had quietly tolerated her show. Now it attacked with a vengeance. The developments in Missouri were a thousand miles away and could be dismissed as happening in Hicksville. Crystal broadcast from uncomfortably close to the D.C. Beltway, *in their own damn backyard!* Her prominence as Paine's media vehicle gave her a rapidly growing national webcast and podcast audience. Legitimizing the Amendments by discussing their merits was a direct affront to the establishment, and a further extension of the American Insurgency itself. Like the proverbial shit that runs downhill, pressure cascaded down from the White House, Capitol Hill, and state capitols to potential show guests. Publishers told their roster of authors to stay off her show. Pundits favored by the mainstream media caved when ordered by corporate bosses not to appear as guests. Threats from big alumni donors were passed along by university presidents to professors and department heads. Political consultants and campaign experts didn't have to be pressured; they knew where their bread was buttered.

Dependent on advertising from the very corporations that stood to lose if the Manifesto Amendments ever passed, prominent political bloggers also declined. The only mainstream figure that agreed to appear on the show during the coming week was Gov. Brand.

For Doc, the only potential silver lining to Crystal's plan was that it might induce Paine to call. Every call was a calculated gamble. No matter how many tricks Paine used, eventually his luck would run out.

Hoping to speed up that process, Doc's whiz-techs developed and distributed to FBI field offices a Rapid Forward Trace technology package that local agents could quickly connect to the call forwarding devices Paine was using. If Paine called often enough, and if he lingered just a few seconds too long on a single call, an RFT device might track down his true location.

Even with this new tool in his arsenal, Doc still didn't much like the idea of Crystal giving Paine's ideas a forum, and told her so. Several times.

At first she ignored him. Finally she said, "Lemme guess? Your theory is that if you can capture or kill The Crusader, the quote brilliant mastermind unquote, then his disciples will realize that they, too, can be caught, and will fold up the tent? Once the romantic notion of the insurgency fades, support for the amendments will evaporate?"

"If broadcasting doesn't work out, you should consider a career with the Bureau," he shot back.

"No thanks. But hey, if discussing these amendments bothers you so much, why don't you just catch him?"

Later that night during a break in the show Kelli bumped into Doc in the hallway outside the control booth. "Just under FYI, Ms. Dickerson asked me the other day if we had bugs and cameras in her condo."

"And you said?"

"That I didn't know and couldn't tell her if I did."

"What are we getting out so far?"

"Aside from video that would get a civilian arrested as a Peeping Tom? Nothing except strictly personal stuff with family and a few friends. Every time she talks to her lawyer she goes outside and faces the wall with that encrypted phone."

Doc nodded and went back into the control room.

Crystal and Sam weren't the only ones having trouble organizing a balanced discussion of the Manifesto Amendments. Key staffers of the Missouri General Assembly faced no shortage of officials, lobbyists, and bureaucrats eager to testify against the evils of the Amendments. Many of those against the public campaign financing amendment and the redistricting amendment were leaders of self-described progressive, environmental and public interest groups, including pubic employee and teachers unions. Although these amendments would drastically reduce the clout of the rich and corporations, banning private campaign contributions would also slash the influence of these other groups, and even threaten their existence. The thought of losing their privileged position and having to get a real job was no less horrifying to leaders of progressive groups than it was to kingpin corporate lobbyists.

A big part of the problem in finding qualified experts to testify in favor of the various Amendments was the perceived need to rely on experts in the first place. To find ardent, eloquent proponents of the Amendments all these staffers needed to do was contact the authors of various Letters to the Editors and blog reader comments in the St. Louis Post-Dispatch, the Kansas City Star, and other in-state media. Contrary to a popular conceit among the political and media class, many members of the general public could present clear, cogent arguments and string together coherent sentences.

June

Chapter 26: Good Government

Gospel among the political establishment was that voters harbored little interest in the fine points of policy, and that the details of legislation appealed only to nerdy policy wonks. But the public, a lot smarter and a great deal more pissed off than politicians realized, took to discussing the amendments the way hungry lions take to a fresh kill.

Discussion of the "Good Government" amendment made Crystal realize how little she knew about the holes in the nation's governmental structure. Court rulings that the public had no right to the expectation of good government, and that unless a person could prove they had been personally affected, they couldn't sue to challenge a law, or force government to enforce one, came as a shock.

Those opposed to the Amendment presented two primary arguments: First, government must be run by professionals and shouldn't be micro-managed by the public. Second, giving citizens automatic standing to sue would overwhelm the courts and force government entities to squander valuable time and money in court rather than doing their job. Most of Crystal's callers kept hammering away using the simple, persuasive prepared rebuttals on the AI website: If government entities did their jobs there would be no need for a flood of citizen lawsuits. Callers repeatedly stressed what most of the public knew, and virtually all in government wanted to ignore: for reasons ranging from a lack of resources to a lack of courage, many laws on the books were never enforced, especially against the economically powerful and politically influential.

Crystal arrived for Tuesday's production meeting just in time to watch a news conference from East Lansing, Michigan, announcing formation of the Manifesto Party. The party's Interim Executive Director, retired United Auto Workers executive Ellis Brown, had strong, handsome features and a body like a chocolate-colored refrigerator, no fat or flab, just wide and thick from the knees to the neck.

According to Brown, party activists had filed papers that morning to register the party in Michigan, Ohio, and Indiana. Applications were available on the party's website for anyone wanting to form a chapter in other states. The party's Mission Statement listed only one goal: passage of the Manifesto Amendments by a Constitutional Convention and ratification by the public.

Asked about supporting candidates for office Brown replied, "We can't prevent anyone from running as a Manifesto Party candidate, but the party will not endorse, fund, or otherwise support candidates at any level. Some sincere amendment supporters may wish to run for office, but in general candidates can't be counted on once elected. The Manifesto Amendments are principles for governing, and we're not going to let personalities distract us from enshrining those principles in the Constitution. The party is not about personalities and it is not going to be a vehicle for opportunists."

The history of third parties was such that formation of the Manifesto Party in an out-of-the-way place like East Lansing didn't rate much attention by the mainstream press. The political establishment largely ignored the announcement.

Until Ellis Brown made a guest call to Crystal Clear Nights.

After a brief recap of the party's formation Brown announced that, "In Indiana we will immediately start putting pressure on the state legislature to pass a Constitutional Convention

Resolution. But Ohio and Michigan permit public initiatives, so rather than relying on any grudging benevolence of the legislature, tomorrow morning we'll file the required paperwork to circulate initiatives."

All over the country, junior-level political staffers assigned to monitor Crystal's show fumbled their white wine spritzers, spit their coffee, or choked on chicken wings. *How many states permit public initiatives?* The answer was nineteen, including Missouri.

Listening at home, Gov. Brand and his wife chuckled. The possibility of someone pushing the Amendments using an initiative had factored heavily into his decision to propose that Missouri adopt a Constitutional Convention Resolution. *Don't get run over, get out in front.*

The number of state resolutions required to convene a Constitutional Convention was thirty-four. The realization that initiatives could bypass the legislature in more than half of those states added a disturbing new dimension to the equation, one that sent shivers down the spines of the political class. It didn't take a genius to figure out that pressure to pass convention resolutions would focus on legislatures in states *without* the public initiative process. And that pressure would likely manifest itself in dangerous and unpleasant ways.

At his Nebraska safe house, Paine opened a light beer. Like Gov. Brand, Paine knew that using initiatives to pass convention resolutions was bound to come up, but had deliberately left mention of initiatives off the AI website. It was better for the public to have some pride of authorship in building the movement. Until that morning, Paine hadn't known that Ellis Brown existed. Now the man had his admiration, and it was time to offer a toast. "To Ellis Brown, the Manifesto Party, and state initiatives, for they are beautiful things."

Tuesday may have been bad, but Wednesday was really not a good day for the ruling class. In a glorious accident of uncoordinated synchronization and pure serendipity, Paine got more than he could have hoped for, even in his wildest dreams: within a period of less than two hours, two different Public Enemy targets were killed by snipers firing from long range.

The first attack came at six a.m. outside Atlanta. Jonathan Bayard Smith, Chairman and CEO of one of the nation's most profitable HMO's, was killed as he fished along the shore of his private lake. The bullet shattered his spine. Former patients, having been given the shaft by his company's tricky policy wording and deliberate denial of legitimate claims, thought it only fitting that he'd gotten it just like they did: *In the back.*

Ninety minutes later Alston Kondracke, CEO of the mammoth hedge fund International Capital Partners, was shot through the head as he talked with his wife under the portico of the their stately Connecticut mansion. Given the distances involved and the compressed time frame, even if Paine had carried out one of the attacks, there was now at least one more assassin in the equation.

The immediate assumption was that the attacks represented a coordinated operation, either by a single cell or by multiple cells working together. Doc reminded everyone that, as movie mogul Peter Guber was fond of saying, "Assumption is the mother of all fuckups." But that begged the question: Could the two attacks be a random coincidence? The odds were astronomically long. However, Doc pointed out that the term "stranger than fiction" was invented for a reason. "We have to pursue both possibilities; coordinated group action, or two lone wolves on the prowl the same day."

Although the cases would never be solved, the attacks were the work of lone assassins acting independently. The timing was purely coincidental. Aside from Paine, the most surprised people on the planet were the shooters themselves, who also shared another secret; both had started planning their attack before Joe Kuri shot Gov. Gilligan.

Attorney General Godfrey denounced the killers of Smith and Kondracke as, "detestable misguided copycats."

Paine shouted back at his TV, "Patriots, you asshole."

In his office, Doc muttered, "Not copycats, disciples."

JGod posted rewards of $2 million for each shooter, and raised the price on Paine's head to $10 million. He also fired jibes at Gov. Brand and Crystal, calling the new attacks, "a tragic example of what happens when certain elected officials and media types elect to give an aura of legitimacy to terrorists."

Unfortunately for the establishment, there was more bad news. On Thursday, Maine and Vermont moved to enact convention resolutions. Legislators in both states had good reason to act. With sparse populations and correspondingly small law enforcement agencies, both states had oversized legislatures: 180 members in Vermont, 185 in Maine. This was a lot of legislators for a limited number of state police officers and local constables to guard. Passing convention resolutions was an easy way for the legislators to protect themselves, and look good to their constituents at the same time. Both states were promptly rewarded with designation as Action-Free zones on the AI website.

On Friday, Lanny Roven, CEO of Western Continental Communications, was shot while on the treadmill in his private gym atop the company's downtown Seattle headquarters. A major Democratic fundraising bundler, Roven had also been the first telecom CEO to endorse the government's warrantless wiretapping domestic surveillance of law-abiding citizens, but thanks to immunity granted by Congress, he escaped prosecution. He could not, however, escape the high-velocity round that hit him right in the heart. Some joked that hitting a target as small as Roven's heart from three hundred yards away was clear evidence of either superior marksmanship or divine intervention.

Was the shooter a new disciple, or a second attack by one of the shooters that took out Kondracke and Smith? Hoping for the latter, Bravo set to work looking for travel records, credit card receipts, or DAS footage that would place the same individual or vehicle in both the Seattle area and the vicinity of either earlier shooting.

While Kenny dubbed the three killings in three days the Trifecta, the AI website posted "Congratulations to our New England, Rocky Mountain, and Dixie Chapters."

Whether or not AI had any real chapters, or just individual fringe followers, was widely debated, but there was no denying that AI's Boot Hill now featured three more tombstones.

Chapter 27: Further Consideration

In the wake of the Trifecta shootings, traffic on the AI website declined significantly. Voting in the weekly Name That Target poll fell to almost nothing. The reality that participating on the website could lead to the murder of real people caused many AI supporters to rethink the entire subject of revolution, no matter how much reform it might bring.

Paine was not surprised. *What did they think would happen? There is no such thing as a bloodless revolution.*

The Trifecta killings changed things for Crystal as well. Some callers now criticized her decision to discuss the Manifesto Amendments. They accused her of encouraging violence, and being an accessory to the most recent deaths. People frightened by the proposed reforms went even farther and made a number of what the FBI considered viable threats. For the first time, Crystal began to think that having a protective detail wasn't such a bad idea after all.

Investigation of the three new attacks confirmed Doc's worry that there wouldn't be many clues. The shooters had evidently followed AI's operational instructions to the letter. Each used a homemade silencer and fired from medium distance, in the Connecticut and Atlanta cases, less than two hundred yards. The rifles left behind were cleaned with bleach, removing any trace DNA. All three were untraceable. Two, a .308 bolt-action 1903 Springfield and a 7.62 mm bolt-action German Mauser, were war souvenirs that had never been registered. The registered owner of the third weapon, a lever-action Marlin .30-06, had died in 1987, and his wife ten years later. The three surviving daughters vaguely remembered the gun, but hadn't seen it in decades and had no idea what became of it. Their best guess was that at some point their father either sold the rifle or traded it, possibly for some tool for his basement workshop. Attempts to track the ammunition also proved futile.

There were no eyewitnesses to the shootings, and no reports of suspicious vehicles near any of the three locations. The only forensic evidence investigators recovered were a few strands of torn cloth at the Connecticut site, and few boot prints near the Atlanta shooting. The cloth was a common type used in cheap plaid shirts sold by many discount retailers. Doc was pretty sure that the boots worn by the Atlanta sniper had been carefully disposed of and would never be recovered or traced.

A number of people were identified as having been in Seattle and the general vicinity of one of the earlier shootings, but each one had a legitimate reason for being in both places, and a solid alibi for the time of the actual attacks.

Missouri ended the week by passing its Constitutional Convention Resolution. The vote was unanimous; nobody wanted to be on record opposing it. Within minutes after the bill passed, AI's temporary suspension on attacks in Missouri was made permanent.

Sitting in Doc's office with the other key members of the team, Scott asked, "Given all the kooks and crazies that are out there, is it possible that without any real command structure, and without personally knowing any of his followers, this Crusader guy can command enough allegiance, just on his status alone, to put entire states off-limits, and have the order stick?"

"Well, aren't you full of happy thoughts," replied Doc. The possibility was frightening.

As passage of the Missouri convention resolution replaced discussion of the Trifecta attacks, the tone of Crystal's show slowly returned to normal. Hoping that Paine might finally call to gloat over the Trifecta, Doc again observed Friday's show from the control booth. He should have gone straight home. Paine was content to let a very good week come to a quiet end, and all that Doc heard were impassioned arguments in favor of the Good Government amendment. The idea that Congress and state legislatures could no longer exempt themselves from the laws and regulations they imposed on the public was sweet music to callers. The amendment provision that everything that was illegal also had to be a crime with a specified punishment enjoyed rabid support. What good was a law if there was no punishment attached for breaking it? Everyone called bullshit on that idea.

The discussion was so one-sided that Paine didn't even listen to the last hour of the show.

Chapter 28: Executive Power

The developments in Missouri, Maine, and Vermont, coupled with the launch of the Manifesto Party and the state initiative movements, proved that the threat of insurgency could change the political dynamic. Suddenly the Manifesto Party website was inundated. Chapters and initiative drives were announced in California and Florida. But people didn't just flock to the new party's website. Traffic on the AI website also rebounded. Particularly distressing to lawmakers was the big increase in Name That Target nominations. Public interest and participation in the movement was undeniably back on the upswing.

Monday night Crystal moved on to the next amendment, Limitations On The Power Of The Executive.

> *No President may pardon, commute, parole or grant other reprieve from sentence to any person serving, or who has served, as President or Vice President or who has served or advised, in an official or unofficial capacity, any branch of the Executive or any presidential administration or campaign.*

Crystal expected this provision to have strong support among her listeners, and she was not mistaken. The public clearly understood the effect this amendment would have on those down the chain of command charged with carrying out illegal actions. Not a single caller thought the amendment should be rejected, and the only suggestions involved adding more categories of people who could not be pardoned.

Tuesday Crystal awoke to discover her kitchen floor awash in soapy water from a broken dishwasher. All she had time to do was mop up the mess with bath towels that she left piled in the sink. She was still fretting about the situation when Doc showed up just before airtime. Normally he didn't arrive until after the show started.

"You're early," she said.

"Just couldn't stay away." It was the truth, concealed behind his deadpan delivery. "How's your day going?"

"Not well," she responded.

"How so?"

"My dishwasher died and I haven't been able to find anyone who can fix it at a time that fits my schedule."

Doc thought to himself, *There is a God.* "A guy I know runs an appliance repair service. If you like, I can get him to handle it for you."

"A twofer, huh? Fix my dishwasher and install more bugs at the same time?"

"There are no devices in your apartment."

"You had them taken out?"

"Yes."

The admission stunned her. For a moment she was unsure what to make of it. *Had he really had them taken out? If so, why? And would he really admit it?*

"And if I wanted to put new ones in, I wouldn't need a ruse to do it. Now, do you want me to call him or not?"

She hesitated for a moment, then nodded and said, "Thank you."

"No problem." Doc called Bob The Appliance Guy, explained the situation, and handed her the phone to work out the appointment time.

By Wednesday new Manifesto Party chapters had been announced in Arizona, Idaho, Washington, and Illinois. In

Chicago, the Illinois chapter director made it clear that despite the legislature's recent promise to consider a convention resolution, "If the cretins down in Springfield try to play parliamentary games with the resolution, we'll mount an initiative drive." Chapters in Virginia and Arkansas were announced later that afternoon.

Arkansas, which allowed initiatives, raised the specter of yet another state where the legislature was helpless to prevent a convention resolution. Virginia posed a different type of threat. Smack dab in D.C.'s back door, it did not permit public initiatives. But having the Manifesto Party apply traditional pressure on its General Assembly while the insurgency went after public officials might be too much for the Virginia legislature to resist.

Thursday night was ripe with irony. While Crystal's audience discussed the amendment limiting presidential authority, over in the Oval Office President Welch hatched plans to break all previous boundaries of presidential authority. It was no accident that Doc and Director Bartholomew were not aware of this meeting. Stopping The Crusader still remained a priority for them, but for the President a more dangerous threat now loomed. The Manifesto Party gave the insurgency a legitimate political arm with the terrifying potential to become the first third-party movement with wide centrist appeal. This could bring about true reform, which was simply not a permissible outcome.

What the President intended was an illegal, unconstitutional plan to secretly infiltrate and destroy the Manifesto Party. Welch wanted to marry the private operations force of Watergate with the off-books financing element of the Iran-Contra operation. Unlike Iran-Contra, which needed to generate large amounts of cash to purchase weapons, this operation could get by on a lot less money. The Secretary of the Treasury suggested using drug money seized by the DEA that was turned over to the Treasury Department via the Secret Service to be burned. It wouldn't be hard for the Secret Service to phony up paperwork to cover the diversion of millions.

Attorney General Godfrey suggested naming the unit the Special Observations Group. "Observation implies that all they are supposed to do is observe. If the existence of the operation ever leaks out, we'll claim that any unlawful activity was a result of excessive zeal by rogue elements."

The SOG designation added an element of unintentional irony. No one recognized that Special Observations Group was also the name of the secret unit that carried out the infamous Phoenix Program of torture and assassination during the Vietnam War. This new unit would operate out of vacant office space in an unmarked government office building in nearby Virginia. The Secretary of the Treasury would inform the General Services Administration that the space was being used for an undercover Secret Service counterfeiting investigation. NSA would provide wiretapping, eavesdropping, and satellite surveillance capabilities. Attorney General Godfrey would supply National Security Letters to obtain bank and other records that might not be otherwise available without a warrant. SOG would report to Godfrey, who would keep the Vice President and the President in the loop.

Now all they needed was a man to lead the Special Observations Group, and JGod knew just the right guy. He made a call on his personal disposable cell and set up a breakfast meeting at his house for seven a.m.

The next morning Tony Gilman slipped into Godfrey's house in Georgetown through the back alley at exactly one minute before seven. Retired from the Secret Service after leading the Presidential Protection Unit for President Lyman, Gilman had been effective in keeping Lyman's many affairs hidden from the press and the First Lady. Godfrey felt he could count on Gilman's talent, discretion and loyalty, not to mention his ruthlessness when a situation called for it.

Godfrey outlined the plan. Gilman agreed to lead it, but only if he could use men he knew personally in supervisory positions. For street work at the local level, Gilman wanted people who had flunked the psych exam or background check for jobs in law enforcement, particularly people with a rigid religious upbringing who could easily become true believers in the cause. When the time came, they'd be perfect agent provocateurs. They were also likely to keep their mouths shut, reject plea deals, and view taking the fall for bad deeds as a heroic act of patriotic martyrdom.

The Attorney General agreed to have the Department of Homeland Security collect records of rejected applicants from local, state, and federal agencies. The cover story was that these people were being crosschecked against The Crusader suspect database, and against unspecified clues in the recent Trifecta attacks.

Chapter 29: Special Counsel

By now everyone high in the political and corporate establishment saw themselves as a potential target of the insurgency, and rightly so. They, in turn, increased the pressure on the President to do something, just as long as it was cosmetic and didn't involve real reform. Prosecuting former President Lyman for crimes committed while in office was a perfect way to placate both the public and the political class, far better than squaring off with the bankers and other corporate leaders who pulled the real strings of power. From Welch's perspective, however, this was the last thing he wanted to do. Ever since Gerald Ford sold out the country by pardoning Richard Nixon, the core premise of American politics had been that the President was above the law. Going after a former President for crimes committed in office threatened the foundations on which presidential aspirations rested. The idea of limiting the power of the most powerful man on earth was inimical to the Unitary Executive theory of the president as a quasi-benevolent dictator.

While A.G. Godfrey sat around with the President and his closest advisors discussing possible ploys to placate the political establishment and quell rising public criticism without actually doing anything, the Assistant U.S. Attorney in Dallas held a press conference and lobbed a grenade into the conversation.

Angela Boone was just starting her career but already aspired to someday occupy the Oval Office. An attractive brunette with an M.A from Stanford, a PhD from Princeton, and a law degree from Harvard, she was perfect Presidential material: ruthless ambition masked by polite charm and good looks. She was also gutsy and creative. It required real inspiration and guts to assert geographic jurisdictional authority to prosecute crimes Lyman committed while at his vacation home in Texas. Boone announced a list of over thirty people, including Lyman himself, she had subpoenaed to testify before a Special Grand Jury.

President Welch was livid. "That fucking bitch!" he railed, almost spitting out the words.

The Attorney General was even more upset. "You cocksucking cunt!" he bellowed. JGod had good reason to be pissed. Although Assistant U.S. Attorneys served at the pleasure of the President, the day-to-day reality was that "that cocksucking cunt" worked for Godfrey, in his Justice Department.

Boone's action not only tied the administration's hands and foreclosed other options the president was considering, it made her virtually immune from termination. With the sudden momentum of the American Insurgency, the public was wound up as tight as a drum and wanted somebody, somewhere, held accountable. *The more the merrier, and the higher up the better.* Boone was aiming about as high as you could go. Firing her might be the spark that sent the whole country up in flames. Until her Special Grand Jury finished its work, as long as she wasn't caught having sex with a horse, Angela Boone was untouchable. Neither Godfrey nor Welch dared fire her. Or have her taken out. No accident, no robbery or mugging gone wrong, no sudden, previously unknown medical condition would be accepted by the public as a cause of death.

"God help me," the President said quietly to himself, "Don't let her slip and break her neck in the bathtub."

If Boone's Grand Jury indicted Lyman, and if the indictment wasn't thrown out by the courts somewhere along the way, President Welch could be forced to either issue pardons or live with this bitch all the way through Lyman's trial. The legal wrangling over issues like executive privilege and sovereign immunity would take years, keeping the issue alive throughout Welch's second term.

Caught by surprise like everyone else, Crystal devoted Monday's show to discussing the possible ramifications of the events in Dallas. After the show, Doc walked her out to the parking lot where the protective detail waited. As usual, Doc's demeanor was a mask, hiding whatever he was thinking, and that was beginning to annoy Crystal. She wanted to know more about him almost as much as she wanted to know more about Tom Paine.

"Surprised Paine didn't call tonight?" she asked.

"Probably too busy celebrating. He must be ecstatic."

Paine had spent the evening celebrating. It was his youngest grandson's eighth birthday. When the little fellow blew out the candles, Paine thought to himself, *Dunno what you wished for, tiger, but I got one of my wishes today.*

The next night Paine joined Crystal's debate of the proposed amendment to establish a permanent Office of Special Counsel. "Government is a crime scene," he said, "Judging by the number of criminals it houses, Congress should be a prison, with a permanent Special Counsel as the warden."

One caller suggested that if public campaign financing was enacted, a Special Prosecutor wouldn't be needed because most corruption stemmed from campaign contributions.

"The culture of corruption is now so deeply ingrained," Paine countered, "that the payoffs would simply shift from campaign contributions to straight bribes, kickbacks, and providing high-class hookers in exchange for votes."

Most other callers agreed that government was in such a terminal state of corruption that a permanent Special Counsel was necessary. Although the discussion kept Paine on the line longer than ever before, Doc's whiz-techs were unable to complete the trace.

Once again Doc decided to accompany Crystal home in his van while her protective detail followed.

Crystal asked what he thought of the Special Counsel idea.

"My opinion is neither pertinent nor relevant. And it wouldn't be appropriate for me to discuss it with a member of the press."

"A couple of weeks ago you didn't mind giving me your opinion after the Kuri shooting."

"That was a mistake."

"Well, we can't have that, can we?"

"Not with you."

She thought for a minute. "You know, Doc, this is getting a bit old. Could you please just think of me as a normal person, and not just strictly as a member of the media?"

"That wouldn't be a good idea."

"Why not? What are you afraid of? Scared you'll slip and reveal some big secret?"

"Exactly."

Something in his tone of voice caught her attention. *What big secret could he possibly reveal?* Then it hit her. "I think you just did."

"Let's just drop the subject, okay?"

That was fine with her. At the moment she wasn't sure how to handle the situation. She definitely needed to sleep on it, which would prove harder than she thought.

After tossing and turning for almost an hour, Crissy faced up to the problem and retrieved her Trojan Twister vibrator from the nightstand. She hadn't had any relief since the breakup with Dennis Witherall, and raging desire suddenly surfaced. Maybe it was the freedom she felt now that the bugs and cameras had been removed from her condo.

After a couple of minutes she gave up trying to exclude Doc from her fantasy. He had a flat stomach, which made her wonder if he had six-pack abs. Was he circumcised? In her experience cut penises were not only prettier but they got harder, rock-hard. She realized that she'd never once caught him looking at anything except her face, never caught him stealing a sideways glance down her blouse or checking out her ass. Sure, he was a trained agent, skilled in hiding things, but still, he must have some kind of superior self-control. Halfway into the long fantasy her mind was spinning, her body decided it wasn't going to wait. She came hard and immediately shut off the Twister. Pulling it out triggered another spasm, and rolling over to sleep on her stomach set off one final convulsion.

Miles away on the other side of D.C., Doc was also dealing with fantasies. Crystal was dangerous, compelling in a way that he'd never experienced before. He felt himself being pulled toward personal and professional shipwreck. His normally disciplined steel-trap mind couldn't suppress the images that kept popping into his mind. The scary part was, they didn't involve sex. He tried to think of her in that way, but couldn't. It wasn't that he didn't want to have sex with her; it was just that he couldn't imagine it, couldn't conjure up a make-believe scenario of what it would be like. Maybe it was a defense mechanism, a way to keep him from getting in over his head, a way to avoid thinking about something that would probably never happen. But he was already in over his head. When Doc couldn't imagine her naked, but could easily fantasize about how she'd look in a wedding dress, he knew he was in serious trouble.

The next morning in Los Angeles, another game-changing event took place. Seventy-seven year-old Cece Rayfield, heir to the Wainright-Rayfield Industries fortune, held a news conference in the driveway of her Bel Air estate. Her father, Edward Rayfield, started out as a union machinist at Wainright in the early 1930's and worked his way up from the shop floor to partner and CEO.

A man far ahead of his time, when Rayfield moved over to the management side he operated on the premise that, "whatever is good for the union has to be good for the company, and whatever is good for the company also has to be good for its employees." He was one of the first in southern California's booming defense industry to institute employee profit-sharing and stock ownership plans on top of traditional guaranteed defined-benefit pensions. Having gained great respect for the women who worked in the company's plants during WWII, he let those who wanted to keep their jobs when the war was over do so. He raised Cece in the business and after his death she spent ten years as CEO. Now it was time to spend some of her $850 million in net worth for a good cause.

Rayfield announced a donation of $1 million to each of the Manifesto Party initiative drives in California, Michigan, and Ohio. She also pledged to donate another $5 mil for initiative drives in other states. The money came with only one condition: in the hiring of paid signature gatherers, priority was to be given to laid-off workers whose unemployment benefits had expired.

Watching the press conference, Crystal said to herself, "I bet Doc is really gonna love this."

Rayfield's announcement wasn't the only bad news of the day.

Leaders of the North Dakota Legislative Assembly were caught between a rock and a hard place. If they didn't pass a convention resolution, a Manifesto Party chapter was sure to crop up and start an initiative drive to place one on the ballot. Then the state Senate Majority Leader had a brainstorm: Why not put a measure on the ballot and let the public decide if the legislature should pass a convention resolution? The carefully crafted measure wouldn't specify when the legislature had to pass the resolution. They could drag out the process at least two years, to the end of the next legislative session, and maybe longer. The governor concurred, and announced that the measure would be on the next ballot.

By late afternoon, South Dakota and Montana announced plans to follow North Dakota's lead. Farther south, new Manifesto Party chapters and initiative drives were announced in Nebraska and Oklahoma.

Chapter 30: Estrogen Warriors

Doc needed time to get a handle on his personal issues and almost skipped Crystal's next show. But the developments in the Dakotas and the plains states might prompt Paine to call, and Doc didn't want to miss a chance to personally coordinate the trace.

Crystal stopped him in the hallway just before the show and asked, "Can I speak to you for a minute?"

He really didn't want to, but nodded yes anyway.

She led him out the side door into the parking lot. "I realize that the FBI has strict rules about agents not getting involved with witnesses, which compromises investigations and raises all sorts of credibility issues in court. And I'm very flattered that you might be attracted to me. But we're never going to be involved with each other. Not now, not in the future, not even when the case is over." The last part was probably a lie, but she needed to tell it to herself as much as him. "I'm not going to sleep my way to success, or let it appear that I did. Nor am I going to sleep my way to disaster, like that newscaster in L.A. who lost her career for sleeping with the mayor."

"Understandable."

"Thank you. So, from now on, unless you tell me very specifically that something is on the record, I'm not going to use it on the show. In fact, I'm not going to repeat it to anyone, except possibly my attorney, and that's covered by attorney-client privilege. You have my word on that."

Doc thought for a moment. The not getting involved part was good news. At least it resolved half his problem. "So what do you hope to gain?"

"Insight. I've been thrust into the middle of events and I have no idea why. There are things I need help understanding, not just for my job, but for my sanity. You always want to know what I think about Tom Paine, and why he picked my show. I want those answers as much as you do. This hasn't been all fun and games, you know?"

"Well, you gotta admit, it has been good for your career."

"But it's cost me a lot as well. I have *no* personal life. I never dreamed I'd be under continuous government surveillance."

Doc knew that she had a point.

She paused a second, then asked, "So, deal?"

"I'll think about it."

About that same moment in Portland, Oregon, an attractive woman in her 30's wearing a blonde wig and a stylish wide-brimmed hat entered the elegant lobby of the historic Benson Hotel. The woman parked her small, wheeled suitcase next to a table in a corner of the hotel lounge and ordered a white wine spritzer. When nobody was looking she poured most of the drink in a flower planter and sat back with the nearly empty glass for her quarry.

Chris Bennett, a nightly regular, arrived at his usual time and noticed her immediately. Bennett ordered a Johnny Walker Red on the rocks and inventoried her in the mirror: stylish gray women's business suit, tight lilac colored silk blouse that buttoned down the front stretched over a nice rack, and dark blue closed-toe pumps with three-inch heels. The image screamed sales rep on the make, so he sauntered over. "Hi, I'm Chris."

"Jennifer. Jennifer Carnes," she answered, using the name she'd created by combining the first and last names of the two girls she hated most in high school.

"Can I get the lovely Jennifer another...?"

"White wine spritzer."

The cocksure Bennett stood quietly until the drink arrived

before he slid into the chair next to her and asked, "So what brings you to Portland?"

She fed him a story about being a sales rep for a lingerie company.

"I'm going to resist the urge to make some witty comment about seeing you model the line. You've probably already heard all the good ones."

"Yes, I probably have. But it's always good to find a man who can resist urges."

"Resisting urges is my specialty," he replied.

Carnes carried on the charade by asking Bennett what he did. While he embellished his current job title and accomplishments, Jenny thought about his previous job, as a Regional VP for Countrywide Financial. Listening to Bennett prattle on about himself, it wasn't hard for her to visualize him teaching his staff how to steer buyers like her sister and brother-in-law into adjustable rate mortgages that reset after a few years at three or four times the initial low teaser rates.

After some small talk Bennett suggested they get a bite. Leaning close to read the appetizer menu, she gave him a perfect view of her firm 34C tits supported in a white demi-cup front-hook bra. After a brief discussion they decided to split a shrimp cocktail and an order of chicken quesadilla. For dessert he hoped to put his dick between her tits.

There was an NFL exhibition game on the lounge TV. Eventually the crowd got rowdy enough to give Bennett a plausible opening. "Perhaps we should go someplace quieter."

Five minutes later they were in a room on the fourth floor. Minutes after that his fingers were inside her. He couldn't believe how wet she was. Neither could she. She'd had never set out to seduce a man before, and it was far more of a turn-on than she expected. Carnes imagined herself as a spy, seducing an enemy. Bennett was sure this was going to be the best fuck of his life. She was sure it was going to be the last. Neither was disappointed. After fingering her to orgasm he mounted her and began a steady rhythmic thrusting. A couple of minutes later she locked her legs around his hips and said "Put me on top...without slipping out."

Poor Chris Bennett wasn't in the same shape he'd been in during his halcyon days as a player on the club scene. He thought he was going to throw his back out or break his dick, but he managed to maneuver into a sitting position, swivel around, and ease down on his back without slipping out of her. *God, this is my lucky night.*

Carnes rode him ferociously until he couldn't hold back any longer. He hadn't come that hard since high school, and barely stayed awake long enough to leave a wake-up call. After mumbling, "God, you were great," he drifted off to sleep.

Jenny slipped her watch into bed and snuggled it against her side, the alarm set on vibrate.

Four hours later the alarm went off. Carnes eased out of the bed, and after a quick stop in the bathroom to pee she tiptoed over and removed a large knitting needle from her suitcase. Bennett, asleep on his right side, his hands tucked up under his chin, made it so easy she almost felt sorry for him. Then, just as she'd practiced at home on cantaloupes, with one firm stroke she drove the needle straight through Chris Bennett's left ear and out the right one. His eyes snapped wide open and his body went into convulsions. Bennett's brain died the instant the knitting needle punched through the cerebral cortex, but it took his body several minutes to catch up. Dispassionately watching his body go through its death throes, Carnes wondered if her sister and two nieces had convulsed the same way.

When her brother-in-law shot them as they slept in their beds in the house with the mortgage from Countrywide that was now in foreclosure.

Just before he put the gun in his own mouth.

Methodically following memorized procedures, Carnes slipped into an exercise outfit and running shoes, pushed her hair up under a shower cap, and slipped on latex surgical gloves. The bedspread went into the tub first, then the blanket. Each was given a thorough hot rinse under the shower. The top sheet and both pillowcases got folded neatly and placed in a green plastic trash bag. On the off chance that one of her pubic hairs might be tangled up with Bennett's, she shaved him clean with an electric hair clipper and used a small brush to sweep all the clippings into a pile on the bottom sheet. Getting the sheet out from under his dead body took more effort than she had anticipated, and the stench didn't make things any easier. There was very little blood on the pillowcase under Bennett's head but the bottom sheet and the mattress were soaked with rancid-smelling urine released when his muscles relaxed. *Thank God for gloves* she thought as she stuffed the sheet into a trash bag.

Their foreplay had left some of her epithelial skin cells on his clothes, so they went into the trash bag as well, along with the used condom. The trash bag then went into a large gym bag she'd brought folded up in the suitcase. Her clothes from the night before went into the suitcase, and out came a portable Dirt Devil vacuum that she ran over the mattress, the pillows, and the floor around the bed. Then came the bleach, double-bagged in large, heavy-duty freezer bags to prevent the odor from seeping into her clothes. She unscrewed the drain covers in the sink and the bathtub, cleaned them thoroughly, then flushed the pipes with a solution of warm water and bleach, followed by Liquid Drano. More bleach went into the tub of hot water where she left the bedspread and the blanket to soak.

After a final inventory of the room to make sure she hadn't missed anything, she poured the last of the bleach over Bennett's body and the mattress. To disperse the odor she set the air conditioning unit along the wall to the Outside Air setting and turned the fan on HIGH.

At 4:18 a.m. the hallway surveillance camera recorded her leaving the room head down in a hooded sweatshirt. She bypassed the elevator and went down the fire stairs, making sure to wipe the door handle. An outside security camera captured her from behind, walking away through a side exit, head still down. Carnes cut diagonally through Bryant Park to a parking lot on the corner of SW Allen and 10th Avenue. She stopped on the long drive home beside the Umpqua River to dispose of the evidence. Having been careful the night before to keep her head down, there were no clear shots of her face on the hotel's lobby, elevator, or hallway cameras. As far as authorities were concerned, she had appeared out of nowhere and then vanished.

That same night in ritzy Darien, Connecticut, Benjamin Nasitir, the American-born son of an Israeli mother and a Lebanese Christian father, hosted a private dinner. CEO of Silverstein-Goetz, the world's most powerful bank, Nasitir had gathered his peers from other megabanks to suggest that they finance a personal militia. Operating on the premise that events prevented are better than events contained, Nasitir wanted a pro-active private strike force. He named it Project Backfire. While he assumed that government infiltrators would target Manifesto movement leadership, Project Backfire would aim at its foot soldiers. It was understood that Backfire would operate without restraint and employ all necessary methods, including murder, to achieve its objectives. If Paine wanted to play outside the rules, so be it. Benjamin Nasitir would gladly fight fire with fire. And he knew just the person to fan the flames: a former staff attorney in the U.S. Attorney's Office for the Southern District of New York named Michelle Patisse.

Patisse had abruptly left the DOJ for a cushy corporate counsel gig and a seven-figure signing bonus at the prestigious New York firm of Bachmann, Royster, & Uecker. Her sudden departure derailed a multi-billion dollar government fraud case that was just about to go to trial, with Patisse as lead prosecutor -- and her new employer as defense counsel. It was typical of Patisse, who lived not just to defeat opponents, but to eviscerate them. However, where most people of this type craved the spotlight, Patisse patterned herself after the mob bosses of old, who knew the benefits of anonymity and preferred to remain in the shadows. Her elevation to partner at BRU was never announced. Her name never went on the door or the firm's letterhead. She never addressed bar association events, spoke at law schools, or appeared on discussion panels, and never gave interviews. Those who needed to know, knew; those who didn't were of no concern.

Shortly after joining BMU, Patisse married the CEO of a Wall Street hedge fund. The marriage lasted four years and produced no kids but yielded her a lump sum divorce settlement rumored to be north of $400 million. The logical conclusion was that Patisse must have known some really damaging things about her husband to leverage that kind of money.

Paine enjoyed what was happening with the Manifesto movement but had no illusions. The insurgency had moved into what he called the "popular myth period," marked by the appearance of progress using traditional means, and a corresponding decrease in attacks. Reality would set in later, after proponents of peaceful reform realized that the power structure would make its stand in the eastern states that didn't allow initiatives. The establishment was not about to go down without a fight. First would come demonstrations, followed by suppression, and finally, insurrection. Until then, Paine was content to bide his time and prepare.

And why not? Things continued to go his way. In Oregon,

which historically put more measures on the ballot than any other state, leaders of the legislature announced that a CCR referendum would be on the next ballot. Nineteen states, over half of the thirty-four needed to call a Constitutional Convention, had now either passed resolutions or were in play.

Chapter 31: Nerds

History having demonstrated that there was simply no limit to American entrepreneurial ingenuity, the debut of The Ultimate Insurgent video game should have come as no surprise. Yet it caught everyone flatfooted. Surprise, however, did not keep it from being an instant success. In the first ten hours orders topped $40 million. For a brand new game with no advance marketing push, the response was unprecedented. On the other hand, the game benefitted greatly from a pre-sold market created by the real insurgency.

Players were given the option to create and name their own villains. The faces of real people, including politicians and business leaders, could be photo-shopped on to avatars ranging from grotesque sci-fi creatures to people wearing normal business attire. For male villains, that meant expensive suits, power ties and extravagant watches. Female villains accessorized with pretentious high-fashion handbags, shoes, and jewelry.

Gamers also had a choice of where to pursue their targets. Attacks could be set in trendy restaurant and theater districts or well-guarded private communities, but the favorite locations were Capitol Hill and Company Headquarters. Something about hunting these virtual crooks and "Scumdog Politicians" on their own turf resonated with the gaming community. At the premier level, Outsource Pursuit, targets were forced to flee to foreign countries to be pursued through dangerous slums, polluted rivers, toxic waste dumps, and finally through their own out-source factories. If a player succeeded in killing off enough company execs, all of the company's stock and assets were awarded to its employees.

By its third day on the market, Ultimate Insurgent had racked up $176 million in sales, and showed no signs of slowing.

Government was helpless to stop it. It's creators had followed Paine's example and made it difficult for the government to interfere with on-line versions by using servers in Venezuela for the company's website. Game CD's were produced in three different offshore locations. A duplicate set of masters and one-third of the initial production run was kept offshore so that U.S. authorities could not impound the entire inventory.

Paine wasn't sure what to think about his crusade being transformed into a video game. It could trivialize the movement and even divert attention away from the AI website. On the other hand, the game might act as a powerful promotional tool. In the end, Paine decided that since the ruling elite made real life a game, one in which they made all the rules and played with people's lives as if they were toys, *Why not a game to go along with a real thing?*

The ruling class certainly knew why not. The military used video game simulations to condition soldiers to kill the enemy. The Ultimate Insurgent might inspire more people to try doing just that.

One of the Manifesto Amendments required the use of unbiased computer programs to create fair, equal, and compact election districts completely devoid of partisan bias. It was a perfect tie-in topic and Crystal jumped on it. Traditionally a majority of the public had a low opinion of Congress but liked their particular representative. Not anymore. Now many voters wanted to throw all the bums out.

Doc suspected that questions about the redistricting amendment, coupled with the furor swirling around the new video game, might induce Paine to call and perhaps stay on the line long enough for an effective sequential trace. He was right. Paine was forced to call and reiterate the simple essence of his plan: "The program would use certain specific natural and man-made terrain features such as mountains, canyons, bodies of water, highways, and major streets, along with the boundaries of airports, school campuses, military bases, parks, and so forth to draw compact districts that are as uniform in size and shape as possible."

Crystal turned the conversation to the issue that bothered her the most: "Wouldn't this wipe out many existing districts that were specifically created to help elect minority candidates to Congress and state legislatures?"

"Yeah. So what?"

"Whattya mean, so what? Don't minorities deserve protection against discrimination?"

"That depends on how you define minority. Unless there's some radical, unexpected change, in fifteen or twenty years there will be no racial majority. Hispanics will be the largest, outnumbering whites, among a plurality of racial and ethnic groups. Besides, some districts that are drawn specifically to elect whites will also be eliminated. Candidates in the new districts will have to appeal to a greater diversity of voters."

"Still seems like an over-reaction," she argued.

"Hey, it's reform. Reform requires change. You can't have change without, you know, *change*. You need to give this some more thought." With that he hung up and yet another trace effort went for naught.

Doc waited after the show and opened the van's sliding door when Crystal came out of the studio. Once the van cleared the parking lot, he passed her a glass of wine. "Got to you tonight, didn't he?"

Crystal looked over and asked, "Does this mean we're entering a new phase, the off-the-record free exchange of ideas and opinions?"

"Call it a test drive."

She shrugged.

Doc pounced on it. "Whattsa matter? Is it that on this issue, Paine happens to be right?"

Crystal was stunned. *Jeez, what is it with men? First, Doc won't talk to me about the issues, then when he does, he takes the side of the bad guy?* "I can't believe you think he's right. About anything."

"He's right about almost everything. It's just that his methods are wrong."

All she could say was, "Wow."

"Hey, you wanted insight, I'm giving you insight. Personal, unofficial, off-the-record, never-to-be-repeated insight."

This wasn't the kind of insight she expected, and she stalled, shifting in the seat, re-crossing her legs, and taking a sip from her glass.

"What's the matter? Suddenly reform is not so great when it changes something you're comfortable with?"

"I'm just not sure that this change is actually a reform. It feels more like a retreat into the past, or a leap into some utopian future that doesn't exist."

"Utopian future? Aren't we already past the point where minorities need special treatment in drawing districts? We've elected a black president, an Austrian-born governor of California, and a Canadian-born governor of Michigan. We have minorities on the Supreme Court. We've got minority governors, senators, congress members, Cabinet secretaries, state legislators, mayors, and military leaders. Instead of electing extremists from gerrymandered districts, wouldn't we be better served by electing more moderate representatives from diverse constituencies?"

For a man who had been reserved and close-mouthed, Doc was suddenly a fountain of eloquence, and it took Crystal by surprise. "Sounds good in theory. I'm just afraid that in practice we'd lose a lot of those minorities."

"Okay, let's look at the issue in reverse. Paine's right about demographic trends. Pretty soon, whites are going to be a minority. Do you think we should then draw districts specifically to insure the election of whites?"

Doc was getting under her skin. "My, aren't you being intellectually rigorous tonight?"

"Hey, I'm always intellectually rigorous. I thought you were, too. Isn't that why you named your show Crystal Clear Nights? Wasn't the idea to be absolutely clear, rigorously honest and consistent on issues? Maybe you should rename the show. Crystal Murky Nights has a nice ring to it."

"You know, nobody likes a wiseass."

"Yeah, but what have I got to lose? I'm not gonna get laid anyway."

Crystal rode the rest of the way in silence. Doc's thinking wasn't anything like she'd expected. But what really bothered her was the realization of how reform would bring a new, unpredictable era in politics. Now for the first time she understood how the politicians felt; *unpredictable was scary.*

Paine broke his previous pattern of scattered, intermittent calls by phoning Crystal two nights in a row. Doc's whiz-techs traced the first night's call to a townhouse development outside Tulsa, Oklahoma. Built at the height of the subprime housing bubble, it was a virtual ghost town. Spliced into the electrical circuit and the phone lines for two of the few remaining occupied units, the call-forwarding device was hidden in an upstairs closet of a vacant unit in an eight-unit cluster. Forced to clear each vacant unit one a room at a time, it took FBI agents and the Tulsa P.D. SWAT team fifteen minutes to finally locate it. Connecting the RFT unit took only a few seconds.

The whiz-techs were halfway through the secondary trace when Paine told Crystal, "I'd like to stay and chat a while longer, but I have to go now," and hung up.

The next night Doc's whiz techs again traced Paine's call, but there was another twist; it came from a different eight-unit cluster of the same Tulsa townhouse development. This totally unexpected development threw off the field response. After weeks of working the Main Core Suspect Pool and then responding to the previous night's trace, the best agents from the Tulsa FBI office were off-duty. The back-up team was late rolling, but still arrived at the location ahead of Tulsa SWAT, which was redirected from a planned drug bust.

Unwilling to wait for SWAT, the FBI agents took the initiative, found the forwarding device, and hooked up the RFT unit. Again, Paine hung up before the trace could be completed. To make matters worse, the Tulsa PD drug bust went ahead minus the SWAT backup but turned out to be an attempted rip-off that left one officer dead and another wounded. The drug dealers escaped and became the focus of an intense manhunt. The Tulsa Police Chief called it, "a triple F operation. That stands for federal freakin' fiasco."

Friday morning Doc assembled the key members of Bravo to discuss how Crystal might keep Paine on the phone long enough to complete a sequential trace.

Scott asked, "How does he know when to hang up? Is he operating on a clock?"

Scanning the trace logs, Gretchen Polamalu noted that the calls had gotten longer over time, but still not long enough.

Everyone thought for a moment, then Kenny announced, "He knows when to hang up because we're stupid. He's using cameras again. He's got the locations under video surveillance."

Sure enough, Paine had once again turned surveillance technology to his own ends, hacking into the condo development's security system.

July

Chapter 32: Purchasing Power

Paine's crusade changed the mood of Fourth of July, which this year fell on a Monday. Celebrating the first American Revolution clashed with the fact that a second one was underway. Commemorating the greatness of America ran head-on into discontent over the problems of America. Security concerns prompted most politicians not to attend traditional festivities. In Wisconsin and Indiana, key politicians used the long weekend to huddle in secret meetings.

The mood on Madison Avenue also changed. The advertising community returned from the long weekend with the realization that it could no longer ignore Crystal's rising popularity. Even though her show was accessible in most markets only over the Internet it was now a bona fide cultural phenomenon, and its small cadre of loyal advertisers was reaping huge rewards. By Tuesday afternoon, not long after Wisconsin and Indiana announced special legislative sessions to pass convention resolutions, the sponsor boycott crumbled.

And Madison Avenue got a big surprise.

At Crystal's insistence, the station refused to accept ads from financial institutions and health insurance companies. All new sponsors also had to pay markedly higher rates and settle for less advantageous positions in the ad rotation behind advertisers who had been with the show from the outset.

After boycotting Crystal Clear Nights failed, the issue for the advertising community became how best to profit from her popularity. On Wednesday Liz Fielding received two proposals for a Crystal Dickerson TV show. Liz called and outlined the key elements of each proposal. Crystal was intrigued but still unsure about appearing to exploit what was at least a national crisis, if not a national crime wave.

On the other hand, the situation with Paine was dragging on far longer than she had ever imagined. Maybe it was time to seize the moment. They decided to have Liz Fed Ex copies to Crystal to review and pass on to WHYY owner Charles McTige. She was contractually required to do so, but Crystal liked "the old man," and felt indebted to him for giving her a chance when no one else would. More to the point, she trusted the crusty old guy, who felt more like an uncle than a boss, and was pretty sure he'd help her get the best deal, while naturally securing a piece for himself, which was only fair. Paine may have put her on the political and media map, but only after McTige put her on the air.

Crystal's subject for the week was the extremely controversial amendment requiring public financing of all elections. Liberal callers loved eliminating the ability of corporations and lobbyists to buy political influence with massive campaign contributions. But preventing labor unions, civil liberties groups, and independent organizations from influencing campaigns with contributions and ads was a whole nother matter. On an emotional level, eliminating private campaign ads just felt un-American, a limitation on freedom of speech, and made many across the political spectrum uneasy. Eliminating private campaign contributions sparked fears that voters would not feel invested in the outcome of elections. On the other hand, a caller pointed out that eliminating the need to raise funds would double or even triple the time politicians had to do their jobs, to actually work for the people. To those opposing the amendment, a politician working for the people rather than the elite was an alien concept.

Paine knew that it was important for him to maintain a leadership role on the operational front. Waiting until after an attack was reported to claim responsibility could look like he was trying to take credit for one of his disciple's work. So he called that night just after 8:30 local Los Angeles time to report his most daring attack yet. "I just blew up a fundraiser for Senator Littleman in Beverly Hills."

In the control booth, Doc jumped out of his seat. Paine had never called immediately after an attack.

Crystal was taken by surprise. "You're kidding."

"Would I kid about the best government money can buy, up for sale to the highest bidder, government of the rich, by the rich, for the rich?" and hung up.

Two minutes later a text message arrived on Doc's phone:

MODEL AIRPLANE BOMB. LITTLEMAN
FUNDRAISER IN BH.

TWO DEAD. SEN AND 2 DOZ INJ. GLORIA
WORKING W/LLE.

LLE was Bureau shorthand for Local Law Enforcement.

By the time Crystal's show ended, Doc had a preliminary report from Jack Rose and his Gloria personnel on the scene, a gated mansion on Hazen Drive with a spectacular view of the city. Paine's weapon of choice was another radio-controlled model airplane carrying two pounds of finishing nails packed around a half-pound of Flex-X. The dead man was a high-level movie studio executive who was standing near the explosion. The dead woman, the wife of a local real estate developer, was seventy feet from the blast and caught one stray nail in her left eye. She collapsed straight down like a bag of sand and bled so little that it was hard to tell where she'd been hit. Senator Littleman escaped life-threatening injury but lost his right hand after instinctively raising it to shield his face as the plane approached.

Police found the plane's remote control and detonator in a mansion under construction on Mulholland Drive. As with previous attacks, everything had been cleansed of all fingerprints, DNA, and other forensic evidence. There was nothing useable from the DAS video, which had a lot of dead spots along the hillside canyons. Once again Paine had struck and then vanished like a ghost.

Charles McTige rarely came into the station, particularly in the summer, preferring to spend his time at his home on the Maryland shore where he kept in touch with the station's General Manager by phone, email, and the occasional videoconference. So when he suddenly showed up on Thursday morning, everybody knew something was up.

Crystal arrived a few minutes later and went straight to McTige's office. He came out from behind his desk as soon as she entered. "Hi, Crissy, nice to see you."

"Hi, Charlie, nice to see you," she said as they hugged. Everyone else addressed him as sir, or Mr. McTige, or if they were in his inner circle, Charles. She alone was allowed to call him Charlie. With three sons, she was the daughter he never had, and he was the father figure missing from her childhood.

"You're looking radiant. More beautiful and confident with every passing day."

"Thanks. You're looking good yourself."

"Eh, I'm in pretty good shape...for the shape I'm in." It was one of his favorite lines, but true. At 79, the Marine Corps Korean War combat vet with a Purple Heart and a Bronze Star was in better shape than most men in their forties or fifties. He'd grown up working summers in the copper mines around Crested Butte, Colorado, where Friday nights were spent arm-wrestling grown men twice his age. He didn't smoke or drink, and he worked out running, swimming, and lifting weights four times a week. Shaking hands with him was like grabbing the business end of a backhoe. Eight years earlier, at the age of 71, he still had enough punch to knock a would-be mugger out cold on a Baltimore sidewalk. "Please," he said, gesturing toward a chair.

She sat down and crossed her legs. McTige settled into an identical chair across the small side table. "And just be thankful I'm not closer to your age, or I'd be chasing you around the room," he added playfully as he picked up the Fed-Ex envelope from Liz.

Crystal chuckled and leaned forward slightly. "What do you think?"

"I think there is both great opportunity and great danger in these proposals. I assume you know what the dangers are?"

"They'll want to change what I do."

"Precisely. They love you because you're new and different, but they'll try to make you conform to their preconceived notions of what new and different should be, which will be another shade of white. You know the paint story: there's plain white, polar white, arctic white, eggshell white, soft white, evening white, but it's all still white. Right now, you're one of those Astrobright paper colors, sunburst orange or brilliant yellow or electric blue. And you should stay that way."

The first proposal was for a one-hour show where Crystal would devote about four to eight minutes on each of five segment topics. McTige dismissed it as "formulaic, heavily dependent on your personal popularity and on finding hot, hook topics. They'll tell you it's all going to be classy and issue-driven, but the first time ratings dip they'll wanna doll it up with tabloid crap and tell you that the issue is the latest misadventure of some errant starlet or rock star drug addict. They think personality trumps issues. The truth is, issues make and define the personality. Look at all the people who've failed with this kind of show. Hot one day, gone the next."

Crystal nodded. "That's what I'm worried about."

"On the other hand, this one," he said, holding up the second proposal, "isn't there yet, but it has potential. The concept is okay but the format and execution need work."

"So, you think I should do it?"

"No, I think you should own it."

See looked at him quizzically.

"You remember Johnny Carson, right? He was before your time but you've seen clips of his shows, right?"

"Yeah, sure. Of course."

"Funniest guy ever. And as serious as a heart attack when it came to business. You think Carson got richer than God by working for NBC? Not a chance. When his first contract was up, his lawyer told NBC, 'you want him back, from now on, he owns and produces The Tonight Show'. David Letterman, same story. CBS doesn't own and produce his show, Letterman's company does."

All Crystal could think was, *wow*. "So how do we do that?"

"Let me handle things. I understand that you have to use a voice scrambler now to talk to your lawyer?"

"Yes."

"Damn eavesdropping government bastards. Lemme borrow it long enough to confer with your attorney, what's her name?"

"Liz Fielding."

"Right, Fielding. Okay, let us strategize, then we'll see how these folks like negotiating in a tiger's den."

Crystal giggled. She'd momentarily forgotten that Charlie's nickname, a holdover from his Marine Corps days, was Mc*Tiger*.

Two hours later Liz called and announced, "Surprise. We're coming to you." Saturday was Crystal's birthday. Liz had invited her up to New York to celebrate with two of their college girlfriends. "Hope you don't mind."

"No, not at all." And she didn't, not really. It's just that with a woman's home there has always been personal clean and guest clean. "Why the change?"

"Because Monday morning we're meeting with two producers and a lawyer from the company that's going to make you a television star."

"But their offices are in New York."

"Crissy, darling, we're not going to meet on their home field. A guy asks you out on a date, you don't drive to his place. At least, I hope you don't."

Monday? "Things are moving pretty fast."

"They always do when you're hot."

The idea of being hot, in the business sense, felt strange. "When do you arrive?"

"Tomorrow night, 10:35. We'll listen to your show on the way. Can you leave a key in the usual place?"

"Sure. But I feel bad about you taking a cab."

"Who said anything about a cab? Your boss reserved a limo. Yours for the weekend. Said it was a birthday present."

"Great. See you tomorrow night." Crystal hung up and immediately called her half-day once-a-week housekeeper. After a little polite pleading the woman agreed to make a second visit Friday afternoon to spruce up the place.

Before the Friday show the station staff surprised Crystal with a birthday cake and a champagne toast. Besides the card from the station staff, the agents on her protective detail gave Crystal a bouquet of flowers and a card endorsed, "To our favorite assignment."

Crystal wondered if Doc had anything to do with it, but decided probably not.

After a week of debating public financing of political campaigns,

Crystal was still unsure about the idea. Intellectually she understood the arguments for it, but emotionally, it was just like the reapportionment amendment. Something about a completely neutral level playing field was scary. On the way home she asked Doc if it scared him, too.

"Yes, but not for the same reason it scares you. It's the other section of the amendment, the one that makes it easier for third parties to develop, that's the problem. Put that into effect and you'll see the eventual demise of the two-party system."

"You mean the one-party system, don't you?"

"You really think there's no fundamental difference between Republicans and Democrats?"

"Not in terms of influence by banks and big corporations."

Once again they finished the last leg of the trip to her condo in silence. When the van rolled to a stop in the parking lot, Doc reached under his seat and handed her a box of Godiva chocolates and a card. "Happy birthday," he said,

"Well, this is a surprise. Thank you."

Doc shrugged, trying to be nonchalant, but they both knew better.

Crystal put the box and the card with the earlier bouquet of flowers she'd received from the protective detail.

When Crystal stepped out of the van Kelli noticed the box and the card. She filed the matter under "things I didn't see."

Liz and Crystal's two friends from college, Tiffany and Carol, stood up when they heard the door open. And sat right back down when Gretchen entered, her Glock cupped in both hands, arms fully extended, elbows locked. The procedure had become such a routine that Crystal had forgotten to warn Liz. Gretchen conducted a quick sweep of the condo, announced, "Clear," and holstered her weapon. Only then did Crystal and Kelli enter.

"Sorry, guys, forgot to warn you about that," Crystal said as she deposited her purse and gifts on the kitchen island. "Liz, Tiffany, Carol, say hello to Gretchen."

"Hi, Gretchen," came the chorus.

"And Kelli."

"Hi, Kelli."

"Hi, nice to meet you," Kelli replied. "I'm off this weekend, but Gretchen and the rest of the team will see you tomorrow."

After Kelli and Gretchen left, Carol asked, "Are they going everywhere with us, all weekend?"

"Yes, but they'll be in other vehicles, in front and behind us."

"Big, black Suburbans, probably," said Liz.

"White Tahoes more likely," replied Crystal. "Supposedly less conspicuous."

Carole shuddered and said, "Weird. A little scary."

"I think it's kinda cool," announced Tiffany.

"Weird, scary, cool, whatever. You get used to it after a while," Crystal replied, with a sideways glance at Liz that told her that, *no, you don't really get used to it.* "And you can stand up, now."

Only then did the three women realize they were still seated. They stood up and took turns hugging Crystal. Off to the side she noticed a pair of designer shopping bags holding gift-wrapped presents. "And what have we over here?"

"No, no, no, little Miss Inquisitive," teased Liz. "Not until tomorrow."

Crystal pretended to pout, then carefully put aside the unopened card from the Godiva box and sat down on the couch. She untied the ribbon and passed the box around. Each of them took one chocolate square and nursed it daintily over the next hour as they caught up on girl-talk.

When it was time for bed, Tiffany won the coin flip and got the twin bed in the tiny guest room, with its own bath just off the living room. Carol got the sofa, and Liz doubled up with Crystal in her queen-size bed.

As Liz unpacked, Crystal read the card that came with the candy. Noticing Liz' inquisitive look, Crystal passed her the card. "Happy Birthday, and many more to come." No signature, just a capital D.

"An admirer? Anyone I should know about? Strictly as your lawyer," she added.

"No." Crystal didn't really believe that.

Neither did Liz.

Saturday morning the four women piled into the limo for breakfast at a famous Baltimore waterfront restaurant that catered to the fishing fleet. Then they took off down to D.C. to sightsee.

Carol insisted on one stop in particular, at the Vietnam Memorial. She purchased a single white rose from a flower vendor and placed it on the ground at Panel 16 right, which bore the name of her father's brother. She knew him only from family pictures and one old faded home movie. All these years later her father still couldn't get through a Memorial Day without crying about the big brother who didn't survive a battle in the Iron Triangle. Carol traced his name from the wall on a piece of paper that she tucked away carefully in the side pocket of her purse. It was for her father, who had never been able to afford a trip from Oregon to visit The Wall.

In the late afternoon they went back to Crystal's and opened her presents. After a brief nap they got decked out in their best cocktail dresses and rode back down to enemy territory for dinner at Brandywine, one of D.C's most prestigious eateries. The maitre' d was surprised when Gretchen flashed her I.D. and insisted that Crystal's party be seated in a corner booth away from the windows. Two male agents took seats at the bar near the front door with a clear view of the entire room and, through the windows, at the street outside. Gretchen positioned herself near the booth with a view of anyone coming from the kitchen or the back door. The group did not go unnoticed by other diners. As some people gradually realized who Crystal was, more than a few venomous stares came her way.

After a hearty Sunday morning brunch Liz and Crystal saw Carol and Tiffany off at the Amtrak station then headed back to Crystal's place. On the way, Liz asked her, "So who's D?"

"Who?"

"D, from the birthday card."

"Oh, he's leading the hunt for Tom Paine."

"Any reason he didn't sign his name?"

"He's very...circumspect."

"And?" Liz shot Crystal the, *Okay, give it up* look.

"He's bright, very analytical. Confident. Determined, possibly to the point of obsession."

"And?" Liz wanted the good stuff.

"Well, he's tall, seems to be in great shape, with thick dark hair and penetrating deep blue eyes."

"I'll bet that's not all that's penetrating about him. Are you pumping him for information?"

"That would be pumping a dry hole. He keeps his cards so close to his vest that even he doesn't know what's he's holding." Crystal decided to steer the conversation in a different direction. "So, what's on the agenda for tonight and tomorrow?"

"Tonight we'll go over your goals and concerns. Tomorrow, you pop in, tell them how thrilled and flattered you are by their offer, then disappear. If something important comes up that we haven't prepared for, I'll step out to confer with you. Otherwise, you leave the trench warfare to the ground troops. You want me to do something to earn my extravagant fee, don't you?"

That night Crystal and Liz spent hours brainstorming over a couple of Lean Cuisines and white wine, then turned in early. With Tiffany and Carol gone, this time Liz took the guest room.

Chapter 33: Money, Money, Money

The WHYY receptionist showed the three guests from All Spectrum Media Inc., into the conference room where refreshments were set out on a side table. None of them noticed the surveillance cam in the ceiling or the vintage microphone sitting like a decor prop on a table across from the hospitality spread. This made them three-for-three; they had also failed to note the sign by the front entrance: Premises Under Video and Audio Surveillance.

Charles McTige waited until everyone was relaxed and settled in before he and Liz entered the conference room together. McTige took his place at the head of the table with Liz on his right. The positioning wasn't just symbolic; it allowed them to glance at each other's notes. On cue, Crystal entered exactly two minutes later and stayed just long enough to tell the folks from ASMI how excited she was about their proposal. As soon as the door closed behind her McTige asked, "Okay, let's get down to business, shall we?"

The turning point came three hours later. Responding to proposed format changes laid out by McTige, one of the All Spectrum Media producers, Tracey Bonnero declared, "That's not the show we've proposed."

McTige promptly replied, "Well, I'm glad we've got that on the record. Now we can focus on the show you're going to get."

The reference to being on the record hit ASMI lawyer Kendrick Taylor like a lightning bolt. Instinctively he leaned back and glanced discreetly around. That's when he noticed the ceiling camera and the cable connected to the vintage mic, a cable that was only necessary if the mic was in use. Taylor leaned forward casually and said, "It's almost one. How about we break for lunch and reconvene in, say, ninety minutes?"

"See you at two-thirty, sharp," McTige replied, as he turned to Liz and added, "My treat."

McTige took Liz to his favorite French cafe but they left Crystal at the station. She was talent, and it was always best to keep talent away from negotiations. McTige did, however, bring Crystal a French peasant lunch of salad, brie, warm French bread, and Perrier with a lime.

At an upscale coffee shop a half-mile away, the trio from ASMI had a considerably less enjoyable meal. Taylor explained to Bonnero and her producing partner, Colin Livesay, how their entire negotiating position had been compromised by Bonnero's "that's not our proposal" comment. It was an established element of plagiarism law that an idea couldn't be protected, only a specific format or expression of that idea. Now that McTige had them on tape denying that the show McTige proposed was their concept, they were virtually dead in the water, legally and leverage-wise. If they didn't agree to the new format, and whatever financial terms McTige was about to propose, he could just go ahead and do the show without them.

"But isn't it illegal to tape someone without their consent?" asked Livesay.

Taylor told them about the sign by the front door that he had deliberately looked for on their way out. "It's called implied consent. They posted clear notice that the facilities were monitored, and we didn't object. End of story."

Negotiations resumed on time and continued non-stop until just before six p.m. ASMI did still have one negotiating strength: their sales and syndication infrastructure could package the show with national advertisers and mount the kind of major promotional push that made it an attractive buy for independent stations across the country. The question was, *how much value was each side willing to put on that infrastructure?*

When the trio from ASMI walked in that morning they owned one-hundred percent of a proposed one-hour show that would have paid Crystal about $450,000 a year. When they walked out, Crystal owned one-hundred percent of a proposed two-hour show that would pay her a base salary of more than two million dollars plus ten percent of ASMI's gross national syndication revenue and twenty percent of the ad revenues WHYY made for carrying the show in the Greater Baltimore Demographic Marketing Area. For producing Crystal Clear With Crystal Dickerson using WHYY's television studio, McTige Broadcasting Inc., got the other eighty percent of the local DMA revenue and another ten percent of ASMI's national syndication money.

For McTige, the deal was a win-win-win. The TV show would be simulcast over the radio, meaning he'd keep raking in the money the station currently made, and he could charge higher ad rates for her new show than he presently got for the old reruns that presently aired in that time slot. And to top it off, there was that ten percent of the national syndication loot.

Formal contracts would take weeks to finalize but Liz memorialized the key points in a Deal Memo. For Crystal, the potentially life-changing document seemed faintly unreal, but McTige cautioned, "Remember, right now it's only a deal. A lot has to happen before it becomes a show."

She nodded. One thing levelheaded Crystal Renee Dickerson learned long ago was not to count chickens until they hatched.

After McTige left, Liz gave him most of the credit for the deal. "Watching him was better than any law school or B-school negotiating class, ever." It was clear that the Mc*Tiger* still had sharp claws and big teeth.

Crystal gave Liz a big hug and walked her out to the limo for the ride to Baltimore's Amtrak station.

Watching TV in the Amtrak lounge while waiting for her train, Liz learned that the Minnesota legislature would convene in special session to pass a convention resolution. The number of states with resolutions in play was now twenty-two.

Liz was back home in her New York co-op when Crystal's show began discussing the Manifesto's Economic Bill of Rights. The subject reminded Crystal of the deal memo locked in her desk. If the TV show became a reality and lasted even a couple of years, and if she invested the money she made wisely, she would be assured a minimum level of economic security for the rest of her life. Young, smart, educated, beautiful and talented, Crystal had opportunities that most people could never even dream about. It made her think about all those regular people who were not as fortunate. They needed and deserved these simple protections:

Section 1: Congress shall enact and the President shall sign all legislation necessary to create, protect, and insure a robust, diverse, and self-sufficient economy producing all goods and services required for the security of the nation and the comfort, prosperity, and well being of its people.

Aimed at ending out-sourcing of domestic manufacturing capacity, and thereby driving a stake in the heart of corporate oppression by globalization, Section 1 revolved around the idea that government had a responsibility to protect domestic jobs, just like every other nation did. This would diminish the influence of the financial industry and return a great deal of clout, as well as financial security, to those in the manufacturing sector. Of course, those whose obscene profits came from exporting jobs and importing cheap products didn't see any advantage to that, which made for a lively discussion.

On Tuesday the West Virginia legislature placed a convention resolution referendum on the next ballot. The recent theft of explosives from a coal mining operation reportedly influenced the decision. Crystal spent that night and Wednesday discussing the amendment to replace the Federal Reserve with a true national bank that was:

> *"...operated and controlled solely by the Treasury Department and vested with all powers necessary to protect the value of the national currency and properly regulate the amount of money in circulation to insure the lasting strength of the national economy."*

Although its Chairman was nominated by the President and confirmed by Congress, the Fed was a for-profit private entity owned by a cartel of national and international banks, and was not even incorporated in the U.S. As one expert noted "the Federal Reserve is no more a government agency than Federal Express." The astounding thing was that the Fed had been given the power -- which, according to Article 1, Section 8.5 of the Constitution was supposed to reside with the U.S. Treasury Department -- to determine how much money the U.S. prints. The banner across the top of U.S. currency that used to say "Treasury Note" now read "Federal Reserve Note."

In theory, the Fed used its power to increase or decrease the supply of money in public circulation to match the growth or decline in the economy, thus avoiding inflation. In reality, the Fed used its power not to create money, but to create debt, which was then characterized as money to the people and companies that borrowed it. The Fed manipulated the supply of this debt-money to create economic bubbles that banks then exploited for their own gain. Abolishing the Fed and putting control of U.S. currency back in the hands of the Treasury Department struck directly at the people who really determined everyone's economic wellbeing.

Crystal usually dismissed callers who predicted that the political and economic elite would never allow the Manifesto Amendments to be enacted through peaceful means. This week she was struck by the number of callers who were obviously quite knowledgeable about the Fed, and who supported replacing it with a true central bank, yet also still predicted that Paine's Economic Bill of Rights would be enacted only through violent insurrection. It wasn't their arguments that bothered her; it was the tone of acceptance and resignation in their voices.

Redistricting and public campaign financing had made Crystal uneasy on an emotional level, but they were aimed at government and politicians. Paine's Economic Bill of Rights rattled her on a deeper level because it took on the giant sinister corporations and the seemingly untouchable people who ran them. Crystal now realized that corporate interests did more than just influence government actions and policies. They had become the government. As economist Simon Johnson claimed, the U.S. had become an oligarchy, where a small group of ultra-wealthy well-connected people pulled the levers of power, and elections were largely a public relations con designed to perpetuate the myth of democracy.

As one caller put it, "The United States has four branches government, the legislative, the judicial, the executive, and the corporate. The first three are subordinate to the last. The corporations give the orders, and the other three branches do the marching."

Watching Crystal stare out the van window on the way home, Doc sensed that she felt burdened. "Depressing, isn't it?"

"What?" She swiveled her chair to face him.

"Depressing -- the realization that this is all for naught, that Paine's utopian fantasy is never gonna happen."

"That's what you think it is, a utopian fantasy?"

"It is if you define utopian as an unrealistic, unachievable perfect world."

"Unachievable? Why? Because special interests will go to any length and use any force necessary to continue in power?"

"No, because the vast majority of Americans don't really want major, transformational change. It's a comfort thing. Life may be rough on some people, but not on enough. Real change scares people; they think they might lose what little they have. That's why most Americans, that great mass in the middle, want incremental change, reforms that nibble around the edges of familiar policies and institutions. That's why certain special interests have accumulated so much influence over the last thirty years. They've done it incrementally, a little piece here, a little more there, and so forth. The only way anyone will reverse that trend is the same way, a little bit at a time."

"But what if the pendulum has swung too far, what if the oligarchs..."

"Oligarchs? That's a loaded word."

"Not if it's true'" Crystal replied. "What if the oligarchs have such a grip on power that they can block any reform, no matter how incremental, and can force the government to put down any form of protest?"

"Society must have law and order," Doc replied, "or it ceases to become a society, and then nobody has any rights. If necessary, government will use the appropriate level of force to stop riots or demonstrations that get out of control. But despite all those lunatic, conspiracy-nut predictions floating around the Internet, the United States government is not going to trample our civil liberties. We are not going to sweep people up and disappear them off into secret prisons. It's just not gonna happen."

"Hypothetically," she asked, "If that did happen, would you be part of it?"

"I catch lawbreakers. That's what I signed up for, and that's what I do."

"And if at some future point, the laws being broken were wrong?"

"Then I'd quit."

"And do what? Stand on the sidelines?"

"Well, I sure as hell wouldn't go around assassinating people and blowing up buildings."

"Not even if that's what it took to restore democracy?"

"I see no evidence that democracy has been lost. Therefore, it doesn't need to be restored. We have a functioning representative form of government, and as long as we do -- which I believe will be forever -- reform must come from within, using legal methods and procedures. It can't, and it shouldn't, be imposed externally."

"I'm glad our Founding Fathers didn't share that attitude."

"That was a different circumstance, with an entirely different political structure."

"Yeah. Then we had a king surrounded by powerful, favored aristocrats. Now we have a president surrounded by powerful, favored aristocrats."

Doc let her have the last word. They were both shocked at how much she was beginning to sound like Paine.

On Thursday morning Kentucky followed West Virginia's lead and put a convention resolution referendum on the next ballot. Friday afternoon Wyoming and Kansas announced plans to pass convention resolutions. The number of states now in play was twenty-six.

Only eight to go.

Chapter 34: Town And Gown

Crystal was amazed at how fast things moved on the television show front. On Monday, ASMI producer Stacey Bonnero called and said that Crystal needed to come up to New York Friday afternoon for the Advertising, Media, & Marketing Awards on Saturday night. "You'll be at one of our front row tables. We've also scheduled a press conference and cocktail party Friday evening to introduce your new show to the world."

Crystal couldn't help but notice the inference that New York was the center of the world.

Bonnero added, "We've reserved a suite for you at the Ritz Carlton Central Park, and we'll get you a ticket on the shuttle. Will you be bringing a guest?"

A quick thought -- *Doc?* -- flashed through Crystal's mind. She resented the fact that ASMI had scheduled these appearances without consulting her, but decided to let Liz handle it. "I'm not sure. Look, I'm in the middle of preparing for my show. Liz Fielding will get back to you about the details."

"That's fine. I'll wait for her call."

Crystal got Doc on the phone. "They wanted to know if I was bringing a guest."

"You tell 'em, yeah, four of 'em?"

"That's not what they meant."

Doc needed a plausible reason to go along. "These events open to the public?"

"Why? You think Paine might show up, maybe try to contact me?"

"It's possible. I can't imagine that he doesn't want to meet you at some point."

"Anybody can buy a ticket to the awards dinner. Of course,

he'd have to know about it, know I was going to be there, so forth and so on. That's pretty much of a long shot."

"Well, so far he's managed to find out where a half-dozen very important targets were going to be at specific times, so I think he can probably locate you if he wants to."

"Yeah, you're probably right." Crystal twiddled the phone cord around her finger. "So, does that mean I won't get to see you in a rented penguin suit?"

"What makes you think I need to rent one?"

"So, I get to see you in it?"

"Not sure yet." Doc hung up and asked Grace to bring him the local yellow pages. He needed to buy a tux, hopefully from a store that gave federal employees a discount.

Next Crystal dialed Liz in New York. After conferring with Kelli about security issues, Liz called Stacey Bonnero. "Hi, Stacey, Liz Fielding. About Crystal's trip this weekend."

"Yes, yes, what can I do for you?"

"Well, first of all, you can never, ever schedule any public function for my client without checking with her first. Are we clear on that?"

Not used to being read the riot act, Bonnero blurted, "Well, things were moving pretty fast --"

Liz interrupted. "I don't care if things are moving at warp speed, you check with Crystal first before making plans, announcements, or commitments. If you can't reach her, you call me. Got it?"

"Yes."

"Good. Now, about this weekend: shuttle tickets won't be necessary. My client has her own transportation. She will, however, need two more hotel rooms, adjoining hers on either side. And six extra tickets to the awards show." Liz wasn't sure if "D" was coming, but better to get a ticket for him, just in case.

Stunned, Bonnero got as far as, "I don't think --" before Liz interrupted again. "You're aware that my client is under 'round the clock FBI protection?"

Bonnero had no idea that Crystal had an FBI security detail, but rather than admit her ignorance, she defaulted to the standard modus operandi of the advertising industry: lying. "Yes, of course. It just slipped my mind...so many things going on."

"Yes, I'm sure you've got a full plate," Liz said, condescendingly. "Her party will arrive between four-thirty and five o'clock on Friday. Please put the rooms under the name K. Randleman."

Stacey stifled the urge to ask who "K. Randleman" was and instead inquired, "When will we know if she's bringing a guest?"

"When she gets there, I would imagine. Is there anything else?"

Bonnero, feeling like an alligator had taken a bite out of her ass, assured Liz there wasn't, and hung up.

Liz immediately called Crystal and they shared a laugh over ASMI footing the bill for two more adjoining suites at the Ritz Carlton. Including city sales and bed taxes, those two extra suites would cost fifteen hundred to two grand each, per night, for two nights. Throw in the cost of six more tickets to the awards dinner, and ASMI was going to spend a bundle more than they'd planned, which was fine. As Liz said, "You make plans without checking first, you pay a penalty, an arrogance tax." Next time Stacey Bonnero would know better.

Doc took Kelli along to help him pick out a tux, which proved to be difficult for a variety of reasons, not the least of which was fit. Size 48-Long tux jackets don't usually come with thirty-four inch waist pants. Finally they found a "big and tall" chain store that catered to, among others, members of the Washington Redskins. Doc tried to shop by looking at price tags while Kelli kept dragging him to designs with better fabric.

"Why bother with something that isn't going to have the desired effect?" she asked.

Finally they agreed on a Calvin Klein model at a price remotely close to what he could afford. Kelli pronounced the choice, "Stylish. Very classy. Crystal will approve."

At the register, Kelli saw Doc blanch a little as the clerk added on the price of the shirt, studs, cufflinks, bowtie, and shoes. "Ah, the lengths men go to impress us."

"I didn't know men still tried to impress you."

"I don't encourage it, but sometimes the poor souls just can't help themselves."

As they left the store, Doc told Kelli not to mention anything to Crystal. "So, you don't want her to know you just bought a tux that's way above your pay grade. You want her to think you just keep this one hanging in your closet for those weekly invitations to social events with heads of state, right?"

"Something like that."

"Fine. But just remember, this isn't a prom, so don't bring her a corsage."

Ever since the Economic Bill of Rights appeared on the AI website, Doc had been certain that Paine or a member of his family had somehow been screwed, one way or another, out of a pension. This made Doc equally certain that Paine couldn't resist calling the show during this week while Crystal discussed the pension protection amendment. He was right.

Paine stayed on the phone for thirty-five minutes. Doc's whiz-techs traced the call to an almost deserted condo tower in Miami. The FBI's Miami Swat team quickly connected the RFT device to Paine's Remote Call Forwarding machine. The incoming call traced back through the Vonage Internet phone service to a vacant former Circuit City store in New Jersey where the FBI's

Newark SWAT team found a computer connected to yet another Remote Call Forwarding device. The incoming call to that device finally traced back to a prepaid cell calling from Toledo, Ohio. By the time agents got to that location the phone was still there but Paine was long gone.

To save money, the bankruptcy trustees for the Miami condo tower had eliminated building security, so there was no surveillance camera footage of Paine entering or leaving. The same was true for the abandoned Circuit City store in New Jersey, where Paine had tapped into the alarm system for electrical power. The Vonage Internet phone account linked to a prepaid cell that had been paid for with a money order from the same New Mexico check cashing store Paine had used to pay for AI's Venezuelan website host. Once again, since checks and money orders were imaged and then shredded, there was no way to check for fingerprints.

Meanwhile, another event was about to occur, right in Doc's backyard.

It took retired nurse Doreen Basilinkus three weeks of following Rick Lindemann, Chair of the Senate Health, Education, Labor, and Pensions Committee, to get his pattern down. Usually the senator left the Russell Senate Office Building, went up Massachusetts Ave NW and then diagonally northwest past DuPont Circle and on to his luxurious home in the exclusive Kalorama Hills section of D.C. But on Wednesdays, he cut back south off DuPont Circle on 19th Street. The first week she lost him in traffic but eventually she tailed him to a mid-rise condo on 20th Street NW and saw him take the elevator up to the ninth floor condo of his mistress.

On this Wednesday, Basilinkus waited in the parking structure and timed her walk to arrive at the elevator lobby simultaneously with Lindemann, whose Capitol Police bodyguard held up his badge to stop her from entering the elevator.

Since Chris Bennett's murder in Oregon, VIP security teams were on the lookout for femme fatales, but Lindemann couldn't imagine that this slightly chubby gray haired woman was a threat. "It's okay, Mike," said the senator.

Having learned long ago not to argue with Capitol Hill types, Officer Mike stepped aside.

"Thank you," Doreen said with a half-smile to the senator.

"What floor, ma'am?" Mike asked.

"Seven, please." After Mike hit seven, then nine, Doreen said, "Thank you," pushed her purse strap over her shoulder, and put her hands together.

As the elevator car slowed for the seventh floor, Doreen reached in her purse and fumbled for her keys. Still fumbling as the door opened, she stepped halfway out of the elevator before turning back to give the senator another half-smile, and say "Thank you" a second time. Lindemann got as far as "That's quite all..." before a bullet from the little five shot .32 caliber revolver in her purse shattered Officer Mike's right kneecap. As he screamed and grabbed his knee, Basilinkus turned slightly and shot Lindemann in the abdomen about midway between his dick and his bellybutton.

Then Basilinkus pulled the little gun from her purse and calmly shot Lindemann twice in the head. Like several of Paine's personal victims, he died with a strange look of amazement on his face. With his gun pinned in its holster under his hip as he lay crumpled in the corner, there was nothing Officer Mike could do to stop her from firing the last round into his forehead.

The attack took less than three seconds. Basilinkus left an old newspaper clipping on Lindemann's body, quoting his vow not to vote for any health care reform bill that did not include a public option. Having watched too many decent people die because they couldn't afford adequate health care, it was her way of delivering a message about his failure to keep that vow.

Despite the gun's small caliber, in the confined space of the elevator car each shot sent a loud report echoing down the hallway. The sound didn't bother Basilinkus. Following AI's Operational Doctrine she had cotton in her ears. But it did terrify those residents who were home at the time. By the time a few brave souls ventured out to investigate, Basilinkus was down the fire stairs to the parking garage. Before she swung her legs behind the wheel her low-heeled business shoes went into a plastic bag and she drove off north on 20th Street wearing a pair of comfy slip-on flats.

Basilinkus wondered as she drove past the Commission on Collegiate Nursing building what the nursing community would think of her committing murder in the name of improving health care. By the time she turned left on P Street NW, sirens filled the air. Twice she had to pull over to let black Suburbans with flashing lights pass.

Unlike Jenny Carnes, Basilinkus had not been aroused by the act of killing. In fact, she felt surprisingly detached. Nothing like the anguish she'd experienced many times in the ER, trying to save people who'd waited too long before seeking treatment. *Maybe I'll feel bad later. Maybe I'll have guilt pangs, and develop PTSD. Or maybe I'll just feel sorry that I didn't kill one of those sonsabitches sooner.*

Scott coordinated with the D.C. and Capitol Police on the Lindemann investigation. DAS footage identified the getaway car but the trail quickly went cold. Following instructions on the AI website, Basilinkus had purchased the old clunker for a modest amount of cash and never changed the title. In another example of the serendipity that characterized the insurgency, in this case the seller was an illegal immigrant who had also not reregistered the car when he acquired it.

Trace analysis at the scene of the shooting showed GSR on tiny strands of leather, most likely from a woman's handbag. The insurgency now included at least two female assassins working on opposite coasts, and that worried Doc. It was beginning to look like everyone was a potential threat. *What's next, babies in strollers popping a cap in someone's ass?*

Crystal had a different concern. For her it signaled that public anger was reaching the boiling point. Although fiction often portrayed women as assassins, Crystal knew that in real life it took a great deal to provoke a woman into an act of violent political terrorism.

Doc was still seething over the previous night's fruitless pursuit of Paine's phone call daisy chain when he called again to gloat over the Lindemann hit. This time the trace started in a repossessed townhouse in Spring Hill, Florida, a suburban community devastated by foreclosures about thirty-five miles north of Tampa, then to another former Circuit City location, this time in Phoenix, and finally to the parking lot behind a deserted warehouse in an industrial park in Willowick, Ohio, just west of Cleveland. Doc was getting increasingly pissed off, but there didn't seem to be anything he could do except keep on trying until Paine made a mistake somewhere along the way.

On the drive back to Buffalo, Basilinkus dumped her shoes and coat into a river. She hid the gun in a waterproof container under some rocks in the woods behind a highway rest stop. Purchased by her great grandfather in the early 1900's, it was a family heirloom and she just couldn't bear to throw it away, especially now that there was some real history attached to it. If the law didn't catch up to her in a year or so she'd retrieve the gun and put it back in the old cigar box where it had rested for nearly a century. She planned to leave it with the family lawyer along with a letter explaining everything, to be delivered to her daughter after Doreen died. It would be her contribution to the family's legacy.

As progress on convention resolutions and initiative drives in surrounding states put those states off limits, legislators in Texas and Tennessee faced the problem of target intensification. Their rugged Second Amendment image notwithstanding, most legislators in these states had little stomach for confronting the relentless violence of the insurgency. Lindemann's murder pushed them over the edge. *If authorities can't protect a high-ranking Senator in the nation's capitol, why should we run around with a target on our backs?* Both legislatures only needed abbreviated half-day sessions to pass convention resolutions. Later Thursday afternoon the Alaska legislature also put a convention referendum on its next ballot.

Crystal's caravan to New York left on Friday afternoon at one o'clock. Kelli Randleman and a male agent from Crystal's regular protective detail led in a white Chevy Tahoe with tinted windows. Gretchen Polamalu followed at the wheel of Doc's van with Doc and Crystal in the back. Melody Ganz and another male agent followed in another Tahoe. Crystal spent the first half of the trip on her iPad, studying bios of VIPS she was scheduled to meet over the weekend.

Doc used the time to read the latest summary reports on the investigation of the Suspect Pool, which had finally been narrowed down to just over 3,800 suspects, people that couldn't be positively linked to any of the Crusader's attacks, but also couldn't be cleared. About 2,000 people on the list could not be found. According to records, they existed, but they were off the grid, some deliberately in hiding, others starting new lives (for whatever reason) under aliases, or had just dropped out, scraping by on the street or in homeless camps. Of the 1,800 suspects they had current location data for, the question was, "Now what?" Keep them all under surveillance? Doc did the math in his head: Factoring in days off, it would take a minimum of more than 20,000 cops and FBI agents. *Im-fucking-possible.* Doc put the report aside and let himself fantasize about what it would be like to be alone on a trip with Crystal, just the two of them. It was a dangerous dream to indulge, but he just couldn't help himself.

Crystal eventually tired of staring at the screen and shut off her iPad. A few minutes later they crossed the Ben Franklin Bridge over the Delaware River between Philadelphia and Camden, New Jersey. "Well, there's irony for you," she said. "On one side you've got the birthplace of the country, Independence Hall, the writing of the Declaration of Independence and the Constitution, home of the Liberty Bell. And just across the river you've got Camden, with the lowest per-capita income in the country, the highest crime rate, forty percent unemployment, and four tent cities full of homeless people who can't get a job because we're too busy making sure that the Masters of the Universe on Wall Street get even richer."

"Like they say, life is not fair."

"Unfair is one thing, rigged is something else again. One side holds all the cards and they get to deal from the bottom of the deck. You think this is what our Founding Fathers had in mind? You think they'd do it all again if they knew it would come to this?"

Doc ignored the question and went to the heart of what was really bothering her. "It's not your fault."

She shot him a *how dare you?* look.

He chuckled. "Hey, it's what you were thinking. You think the strain of the last two weeks hasn't showed? Discussing political reform is abstract, theoretical. But economic reform?

That's personal. Here you are, talking about radical reforms like abolishing the Fed, guaranteeing the right to join unions, eliminating corporate welfare, and so forth, things intended to help the average person, and at the same time you're about to become a zillionaire TV personality. The contrast between where you're going financially and where most of the country is bothers you. You feel guilty, like it's somehow your fault."

The idea hadn't occurred to her, but even if it did hit close to home she wasn't about to let on. "Oh, is that right?"

"Yeah, that's right. You wanted my insight. Remember?"

"Into Paine, not me."

The Friday night cocktail party went off without a hitch. Crystal wore a dazzling Armani business suit cut about three inches above the knee, and matching heels. A pair of Balenciaga earrings highlighted her fuscia-colored silk blouse by Von Hiemel.

Doc wore a lightweight summer suit, his best tie, and maroon tassel loafers.

Only one person, a young advertising sales rep, inquired about Doc's cover story, that he managed station operations for WHYY. "So what is it exactly that you do?"

"I make sure that our limited number of employees use their limited resources to do unlimited amounts of work," Doc replied. It was a line FBI agents frequently used to describe their own jobs.

"Hey, that's pretty good," responded the young man, a brief spark interrupting his bored look.

Doc and Crystal spent Saturday morning conferring, but not with each other. Doc met with Bill Ramundo at Alpha's offices to discuss the fruitless search for The Crusader. Doc hoped a fresh perspective might spot something he'd missed. Unfortunately, Ramundo didn't have any more answers than Doc did, and all he could do was offer consolation.

Farther uptown, Crystal and Liz Fielding met with ASMI to go over the lineup of station clearances and sponsor commitments for the show. Given the economy, the numbers were not spectacular but the show was cleared in enough markets and had sufficient primary sponsors to be a firm go.

"Congratulations, you're going to be a star," producer Colin Livesay announced at the end of the meeting.

"I'll settle for being a success," replied Crystal, truthfully.

"Don't worry, that's assured. This show can't miss. It's one hundred percent fail-safe," he proclaimed.

She didn't believe him for a second.

Crystal emerged from her suite at the Ritz for the AMMA awards wearing a dazzling emerald green Valentino gown slit halfway up each thigh with matching shoes and a gold clutch purse from Oscar de la Renta. The neckline revealed a tantalizing but discreet bit of cleavage, just a hint of firm, uplifted, milky white skin. Her hair was pulled back to accentuate the gold earrings and matching Tiffany necklace resting just below the hollow of her neck. Like her outfit from the night before, everything was on loan, part of promotional trade-out deals ASMI had arranged with various fashion houses and jewelers.

Doc had been apprehensive about seeing Crystal all dressed up, afraid his eyes would betray him, and they almost did. He didn't know exactly what to say, and was running various adjectives through his mind when Kelli got him off the hook.

"Doesn't she look stunning?" Kelli asked.

"Yes, she does," he answered.

"You look mighty dashing, yourself," Crystal replied, running her hand down the arm of his tux.

"Of course he does," said Kelli, motioning toward the elevator. "Didn't you know? He's the FBI's James Bond."

The group was halfway down the hall before Doc remembered

to compliment Kelli and Gretchen on their outfits. They didn't mind the tardy compliments. Both recognized a man in love.

Throughout the evening Doc couldn't stop thinking about how beautiful Crystal looked, and how much he wanted to touch her, to slip his arm around her waist, to just make contact. It felt ridiculous, like he was sixteen again. At one point, Crystal turned to a woman on her right. The top of her gown bloused out, accidentally giving him a full view of her right breast. Instead of aroused, he felt guilty, like he was spying on her, and immediately looked away. Scanning the celebrities, high-powered media moguls and Fortune 500 business types in attendance he thought to himself, *Gotta stop torturing myself. Gotta get away from her before it's too late.*

But deep inside, he knew that he just wasn't that strong.

Chapter 35: Backstory

Ron O'Leary left a good white-collar job with a large air cargo company to join the Army after 9-11. He survived two deployments to Iraq with only minor shrapnel wounds to one arm and no apparent damage to his psyche. With twelve days left in his third tour, it looked like the thirty-one year-old Sergeant from Indiana would again make it home with at least his body intact. Then came the Stop-Loss notice, indefinitely extending his tour. It was a bitter pill for a man desperately longing to restart life as a civilian. It wasn't just the heavy losses his unit suffered in fierce fighting that ate at his mind. It was the unrelenting threat from Improvised Explosives Devices, which seemed to be everywhere. Defying all logic, as the IEDs grew bigger and more deadly, they also became harder to detect. O'Leary hid his fears well. None of his family and friends back home noticed anything different in his phone calls and webcam chats.

One person who did notice was O'Leary's mentor, the company's ranking noncom, Sgt. Major Mike Horvath. Despite a fifteen-year difference in age, O'Leary and the grizzled lifer became best friends. Dubbed Starsky & Hutch by the young troops in their command, O'Leary and Horvath returned the favor by christening their unit The Bad Boys. Every sortie in search of insurgents was accompanied by singing of a bastardized version of the theme from the long-running TV show, COPS. "Rag-heads, rag-heads. Whatcha gonna do...when we come for you?"

What endeared Horvath and O'Leary to the men and women under their command most was their commitment to hillbilly armor. After the Army failed to learn the lesson of Somalia and put armor on its Humvees, Horvath and O'Leary improvised. O'Leary knew how to weld from helping out in his father's shop back in Indiana. Horvath commandeered the hulks of damaged Iraqi APCs. O'Leary scavenged useable sections and welded them to the doors, roofs, hoods, and floors of the company's Humvee fleet. But even with the hillbilly armor, the platoon didn't do much singing on convoy duty. In the long lines snaking along the highway, everyone felt like a tin duck in a shooting gallery.

The Army failed to get much benefit from Sgt. O'Leary's stop-loss order. Just twenty-two days into the extension of his tour, on what would have been his original date for Separation From Service, O'Leary was riding shotgun in a Humvee when an IED took out the convoy's lead truck. The second truck in line swerved past the burning wreck but was immediately turned into flaming junk by an RPG. Another IED took out the bridge behind them, trapping the convoy in a kill zone a hundred yards long. By the time O'Leary got his seat belt off and opened the door the familiar flat whack-whack-whack of AK-47's was ripping into the convoy from somewhere up on the left. On the right flank came a more disturbing sound, the steady chug-chug-chug of at least two American-made M-60 light machine guns. It occurred to O'Leary that at the moment, "light" was not the best way to describe being on the receiving end of the M-60's .30 caliber slug.

A barricade ambush only offers three possible outcomes: Call in enough help to make the attackers withdraw; attack into the ambush and kill or drive off the enemy yourself; wait to die or be taken prisoner. Staying alive long enough for air support and reinforcements to arrive meant finding cover. Judging by the direction of the fire up front, the enemy was set up to pour fire straight down the ditch on the left like a river of death.

Horvath should have realized that the other option, the ditch on the right, was too good to be true. For some reason, he didn't. Calling out, "Right flank defilade." Horvath led his squad in a race across the hot tarmac and flung himself headlong into the ditch. The Sergeant Major -- all 240 pounds of muscle and another forty pounds of gear -- landed directly on an anti-tank mine.

O'Leary was lucky. Just as Horvath took flight into the ditch, O'Leary frantically called out, "Nooooo!" His open mouth equalized the pressure in his ears while the door of the Humvee diverted the shock waves, preventing the concussion from turning his internal organs into jelly. Unfortunately, the door didn't protect his legs. The right one was peppered by shrapnel and the left, closest to the hinged side, shattered just below the knee when the blast smashed his leg between the door and the rocker panel. Despite excruciating pain, O'Leary never lost consciousness, or his presence of mind. He spit out whatever it was he was choking on, then barked an order over the radio for a squad at the rear of the convoy to clear the ditch with Mine Clearing Line Cord, a long, rope-like explosive shot out of a mortar and detonated electronically after it lands. Only after two of his men dragged him into the ditch did O'Leary realize how badly he was injured and descend into shock.

Surgeons at the Ramstein Military Hospital in Germany tried their best but eventually had to amputate O'Leary's left leg just below the knee. When he had healed sufficiently, Army medical personnel back in the States fitted him with a prosthetic lower leg. A captain from the Office of Commendations stopped by one afternoon, read a short citation lauding O'Leary's leadership in saving the convoy, and pinned a Bronze Star on his chest. After months of physical therapy and a promotion to Staff Sergeant, doctors mustered him out with a thirty percent disability rating, the minimum needed to qualify for monthly disability benefits.

Ron O'Leary's body may have healed but his mind sure hadn't. Family and friends described the man who came home as "hollowed out." The family hoped talking might help. O'Leary appreciated their efforts but declined. He wasn't any different from most vets with PTSD. The VA simply didn't have the resources to deal with the tidal wave of men and women who needed help. Unable to get professional care, O'Leary turned to self-help solutions: alcohol and drugs. When those didn't enable him to cope with civilian life, he simply withdrew. He fashioned a sleeping loft in the barn on his grandfather's farm, bought a construction site Porta-Potty that was emptied every other week by a sanitation service, and took to bathing, even in the winter, in an old claw foot bathtub using water heated in buckets over an open fire. Every Thursday he left money and a grocery list in an envelope on a workbench just inside the barn door. His mother and sister took turns going to the store, returning to leave the groceries and his change on the same workbench. Anything he couldn't microwave or eat right out the container O'Leary cooked over an open fire. It reminded him of good times camping with his father.

As long he kept the taste of something in his mouth, O'Leary was somewhat functional. Since the taste of food only lingered so long, he turned to sugarless chewing gum and beer, both in quantity. By day O'Leary chewed gum and welded scrap metal into abstract art that went on sale in the front yard next to the highway. Every time he fired up his acetylene torch the flame reminded him of the brilliant daylight flash from the mine set off by Mike Horvath. But the bluish-yellow flame also generated a fascination, a magnetic pull.

Every evening O'Leary bathed, fixed dinner, and drank himself to sleep, sometimes getting four or five hours of peace before the nightmares hit. After really bad ones, when he vomited out the little window by his bed, he rinsed the taste out of his mouth with a room temperature beer from the nightstand, then fell back to sleep for a few more hours.

At first, stories of the AI attacks just brought O'Leary more nightmares. It was easy for him to understand how a small-scale insurgency could wreck such havoc. "It's hard when you can't tell the bad guys from the civilians, isn't it?" he wondered aloud. But O'Leary liked what he read in the Manifesto Amendments. The more he read them, the more he believed *it shouldn't take an insurgency to get them enacted.* But evidently it did.

Then an ad on Craigslist caught his attention.

August

Chapter 36: Participatory Democracy

Special Observations Group Director Tony Gilman knew that for SOG to succeed it had to achieve its goal and also be untraceable. Any trail from operatives he put in the field had to hit a dead end before it got to him. JGod may have had faith in Gilman's loyalty, but Gilman felt no great compulsion to justify that faith. This led him to set up several phony identities for himself, and create a maze of shell corporations in places like Belize, the Isle of Mann, and Estonia. Each offshore entity was further hidden behind phony domestic organizations set up as LLCs.

With his fronts in place, Gilman recruited four key operatives, his Four Aces. All had experience in domestic and offshore covert ops. Each could be counted on to keep secrets and, if necessary, flee to places like Paraguay rather than roll over on the boss. Of course, such loyalty would be handsomely rewarded on a lifetime basis.

Gilman and his Aces in turn recruited eight Field Organizers, two working under each Ace. None of the Field Organizers ever met Gilman or knew his identify. The Four Aces and eight FO's then sorted through thousands of personnel records of people who had applied for positions in law enforcement but either flunked out during physical training or failed their psych evaluation. Within that population SOG looked for a subset of candidates who fit a specific profile: strict religious upbringing and a strong authoritarian predisposition. Each had to be stuck in a mundane job that provided no status or sense of accomplishment. They also had to be single, and free to relocate on short notice.

Each prospect underwent a quick investigation, including review of all their electronic communications, from IMs and emails to posts on social networking sites, looking for evidence of personal frustration and resentment over the direction of the country. Gilman finally zeroed in on forty-eight primary prospects.

The Special Observations Group's first contact with Larry Jessup in Topeka, Kansas, was typical. Field Organizer Dick Bahner approached him in the parking lot outside a supermarket and called out, "Hey, Larry Jessup." Bahner immediately introduced himself under the alias Todd Barnes and said, "You are the Larry Jessup who applied for a job with the Topeka PD, right?"

Jessup wondered, *How the hell does he know that?* "Yeah, that's me."

Bahner immediately planted the hook. "Good. I work for a special government task force. We're interviewing a small number of people for an undercover operation. If you're interested, be here tonight at 8:30." Bahner handed Jessup the address and room number of a condo-style chain motel.

Only one prospect failed to jump at the bait. The others, including Jessup, all showed up at their designated motel at the appointed time. In each case, one FO maintained counter-surveillance outside to insure the prospect hadn't brought along the local cops or FBI. Once inside the room, the prospect was checked to make sure they weren't wired. Then the Field Organizer made a show of going through a thick dossier of information about the prospect, designed to both intimidate and convince them that this was, indeed, a government operation. Then came the signing of an official looking but completely phony Government Confidentiality Agreement. After two hours answering a long multi-phasic psychological profile, the prospect was told that he or she would be contacted within a few days if they had been selected for the job.

From the forty-seven final prospects, Gilman selected ten men, representing a cross-section of ages, looks, and employment skills, plus six women, including three fetching enough for seduction missions. Gilman knew from experience that certain strict religious types would happily sleep with someone in the name of patriotism.

Only after making the final cut did the operatives learn that the position paid $6,000 a month plus expenses, with a three-month probationary period leading to permanent employment. Since each currently made little more than minimum wage they were elated. Being part of an elite, covert government agency and making this kind of money was the stuff of dreams.

Training took ten days. Each Field Organizer trained only the two recruits who made up his team. Nobody outside one team knew about the others. Each recruit was given a cover identity and personal history. Not the kind of in-depth identity package given to real spies and deep cover agents, but sufficient to pass basic scrutiny and hold up in casual conversation. Playing off the Sweet Sixteen theme, each got a codename; Suite A through Suite R. Suite made the code name look and sound like part of a business address. Gilman skipped the letter "P." The alliteration to "Sweet Pea" did not appeal to his humorless demeanor. The three attractive female recruits became Suite A, B, and C. Gilman used "Ass," " Babe," and "Cunt" to mentally separate them from the other thirteen, whom he derisively referred to as "the muppets."

With access to NSA intercepts of phone and e-mail communications between Manifesto Party chapters it was easy for Gilman to identify his targets. Like all true grassroots movements, the Manifesto Party had to make up in volunteers what it lacked in hard dollar resources. Gilman knew that when his operatives showed up with enthusiasm and abundant free time to donate to the cause, they would have no problem infiltrating party chapters.

Just as the Suites were settling into their assignments, Massachusetts announced that it would put a convention resolution referendum on the ballot. By then, every convention initiative drive had turned in at least fifty percent more signatures than needed to qualify in that state. The number of states that had either passed convention resolutions or would decide some form of convention measure in the next election was now thirty-one.

Only three to go.

Chapter 37: Counterinsurgency 101

One way to wage a counterinsurgency has always been official direct repression, using the police and military. Another tactic was to discredit the insurgency, undercutting the popular support it needed to survive. Even when this approach didn't end the problem outright, it often set the stage for the kind of official government force that the public would otherwise have found unacceptable. The third method was the application of unofficial direct force in the form of mercenaries and private death squads.

In theory, civil authorities were supposed to provide the force necessary to suppress all non-violent expressions of Manifesto support. However, Benjamin Nasitir's cabal of twenty-first century robber barons wasn't about to sit back and leave their fate to bumbling government types. Project Backfire would be their version of the last century's Pinkerton goon squads and the coalmine owners' private armies.

Like some who claw their way up from humble beginnings, Michelle Patisse had a searing hostility toward the working class. Her blue-collar parents, her less successful siblings, and her modest suburban roots were stains on her status that she would go to any lengths to deny and obliterate. That world and the people in it were not just beneath her; they were lesser beings, an inferior species which had to be kept in its place.

While Tony Gilman's Special Observations Group targeted the Manifesto movement using subtlety and guile, Patisse had a different game plan. Her first target was its foot soldiers, and her weapon of choice was deadly force. Scorched earth was okay; scorched bodies were even better. Project Backfire gave her a chance to wield power she'd never had before and she was determined to cut a wide swath. Patisse would measure success the same way the military does, by territory conquered and a body count of casualties inflicted on the enemy. To achieve those goals she needed an army, and a veil of legitimate authority to use it. She knew where and how to get both.

In the initiative states, Paineville camps had been a key source of manpower for petition drives. It didn't take a genius to know that in the crucial non-initiative states, the Manifesto party would mine these camps for protest marchers. Chronically unable to find work, Paineville residents had the time, and as long as protest organizers provided transportation and a sack lunch, these folks had nothing to lose and everything to gain. Their individual sad tales of economic woe also made heart-rending media narratives.

Patisse's plan was elegant in its simplicity. First, she formed Land Value Investments, LLC to acquire the properties on which Paineville camps stood, either buying from the owners at fire-sale prices or from the states by paying off the past-due tax liens. Next, teams of architects threw together phony development proposals for the properties LVI acquired. Then a PR firm coordinated presentation of these plans to the appropriate city councils and county boards. The bankers behind Project Backfire promised financing. Local officials, enthused over the prospect of community investment and badly needed jobs, not to mention the resulting tax revenue, opted to overlook the escape clauses attached to those financing commitments. Of course, each project was contingent on the owner exercising, "full and exclusive occupancy and control of the site."

LVI was only half the equation. The other half was PIPS, Property Investment Protection Services, another LLC. LVI gave Patisse the veil of legitimacy; PIPS provided the muscle. To run it, Patisse recruited Ricardo Lehner, a retired Green Beret Major with a sordid résumé. An instructor at the Army's notorious School of the Americas at Fort Benning, Georgia, Lehner had trained officers from Latin American countries in brutal strategies to suppress democratic movements. More recently he had been Vice President of Operations for a private security contractor working for the American occupation government in Iraq.

Patisse and Lehner selected their targets carefully. Squatting in abandoned buildings gave homeless people shelter from the elements and provided them with amenities not easily found in outdoor tent camps. Out-of-work construction workers rigged bootleg connections to water and electrical lines. In many cases, old sewer connections were still in place. Citing potential danger to their employees, most utility companies gave up trying to disconnect the illegal hookups.

Armed with an eviction notice, Lehner's Property Investment Protection Services mercenaries descended on the first camp just outside Pittsburgh at dawn. Accompanied by black helicopters circling overhead, they arrived in a massive convoy of Suburbans and surplus military trucks with bullet-resistant hard sides. Most carried AR-15's. Announcing the eviction order over a bullhorn, Lehner gave the surprised residents a half-hour to pack up and leave.

As soon as the deadline passed, PIPS forces swept through the grounds carting out everything that hadn't already been carried away by fleeing squatters. Disputes between PIPS personnel and squatters were settled with physical force. Even the huskiest of the dispossessed were no match for the muscular, well-trained PIPS agents carrying truncheons and pepper spray in addition to their firearms. The building that had shielded the squatters from the weather now provided PIPS with cover from the prying eyes of the media and authorities.

Beleaguered local police could only watch as PIPS shoved five hundred people out onto the passing highway. Some got out with their cars and other meager possessions. Many were not as fortunate. A fleet of waiting tow trucks hauled away the remaining cars to an impound lot where it was unlikely that the owners could afford the towing and impound fees. Mini-bulldozers known as bobcats scooped up anything that was left and dumped it into waiting trucks headed to the public dump. Just after ten a.m. a TV crew captured the final note, sounded by a middle-aged man sitting on an embankment across the road. The man shook hands with a couple of friends, then pulled a small revolver from his coat pocket and shot himself in the head.

Watching video with Doc back at Operations Center D, it reminded Kenny of two searing images from his Vietnam days: a Buddhist monk setting himself on fire outside the Presidential palace to protest the corrupt South Vietnamese regime, and the famous photo of a South Vietnamese Army officer shooting a suspected Viet Cong in the head at high noon on a main street in Saigon. Kenny got up and went out for a walk. He needed some air.

For Patisse the first PIPS eviction produced the desired effect, dominating news programs and talk radio. Squatters at other camps, even on properties not owned by LVI front companies, were put on notice: move, be forced out at any moment, or prepare to make a futile Alamo-type stand against superior private security forces. Local governments with pending proposals from LVI front companies also got the message: if you don't get the homeless off our property, we will. Either way there was sure to be more confrontations, and more bloodshed.

The question of how high the body count might go was of no consequence to Patisse. She also knew that waging war on Paineville camps would drive some desperate homeless Manifesto supporters to embrace the violence of Paine's insurgency, but that didn't bother her, either. The homeless didn't have the patience, the resources, or the skill set to plot and execute the kind of anonymous precision attacks advocated by Paine, especially not on well-protected high-value targets. People driven over the edge by eviction were much more likely to explode in haphazard, unfocused violence that terrified the general public, which would play right into her hands, and those of government at all levels.

Satisfied with the launch of Phase One, Patisse implemented Phase Two of her strategy: stiffening the resolve of political figureheads. For decades corporate and financial elite had paid good money to buy elected representatives and government officials. *Now, when the going got tough, these sniveling wimps thought they could change sides, or turn tail and run for cover? Not in her world.* Patisse wanted to make sure they feared her more than they feared any insurgency. As she told the Senate Majority Leader, "Paine or one of his followers might kill you. But if you cross us, we *will* kill you. And the great thing is, we can blame it on the insurgency."

Not one politician to whom Patisse delivered this message doubted for a moment that she meant it.

Meanwhile, the American Insurgency just kept growing. Paine thought of each insurgent as a sole proprietor engaged in the business of reform. In Indiana, Ron O'Leary prepared to change the way business was conducted.

Chapter 38: The Cure

Hailey Hill and Ron O'Leary represented two different Americas. Hill had always been soft and flabby. O'Leary on the other hand, even in his diminished semi-alcoholic state, still maintained a vestige of fitness. O'Leary enlisted knowing full well he would be sent into harm's way. A classic chickenhawk, Hill loudly supported the use of American military power but during the Vietnam War, after his student deferment expired, his father had the family doctor phony up documents showing that sonny-boy had a chronic kidney problem.

During his years in Congress, Hill maneuvered his way into being chairman of both the House Ways and Means Committee and the Armed Forces Appropriations Subcommittee. Because so much government spending goes to the military, and because what the government collects in taxes is affected by legislation drafted by the Ways and Means Committee, the combined power and influence of the two chairmanships under one man was unprecedented. It gave Hill enormous power to advance or derail appropriations and legislation. He made sure all that power translated into money: money for his campaign, his relatives, his high-priced call girls and serial mistresses, and for offshore corporations and LLCs in which he had a hidden interest. Not to mention millions in just plain old cash.

Hill took care of his backers in the financial industry on the legislation side, making sure they paid as little as possible in taxes and faced the absolute minimum in regulatory oversight. He took care of the defense contractors on the appropriations side. But that was as far as his patriotism went. While Sergeant O'Leary waited months for an appointment with the VA, Hill voted against increased VA funding. For him it was more important to funnel money to the people who profit from wars than to those who are injured and maimed fighting them.

As cautious as he was evil, Hill took steps to make sure that his life was as safe as his Congressional seat. He had pushed through plenty of spending bills funneling lucrative contracts to private security contractors like Overlord and Praetorian, who were now more than happy to return the favor by providing free 24/7 protection for the Congressman, his family, his mistress, his D.C. home in Georgetown, and his farm back in Alabama. Included in the freebies was the use of an armored limo. As the American Insurgency grew, so did the congressman's protection. His farm became a virtual fortress. The surrounding forest was cut back to reduce cover for snipers. Guards with dogs and night vision equipment patrolled the perimeter around the clock. Concrete barriers were installed on three sides of the compound, including a zigzag pattern on the long private driveway. After the model airplane attacks in California and Texas, screens were erected to thwart any miniature dive-bombers sent his way.

On the east side, geography provided the main defense. Anyone approaching from the nearest road had to navigate two miles of dense forest and thick brambles, including three steep creek gullies. Then there was an open field of rolling grassland nearly a quarter of a mile wide where Hill's prized Angus beef grazed. Any attacker who got across that field still had to weave through a maze of barns, sheds, and other support buildings. After dark, floodlights triggered by hidden motion sensors bathed the field and the edge of the tree line in light.

To the high-tech hot dogs from Overlord, who spent most of their time in Iraq dealing with urban warfare, this seemed like more than enough protection.

For Ron O'Leary, whose unit had fought its way across Iraq, it would be just another day at the office.

O'Leary left a note on the workbench where he usually put the weekly grocery list and set out in a rented bobtail truck for

Clinton, the town nearest Hill's farm. This time he left the beer and gum behind. Every minute on the road he wanted to remember that other road, the one from Fallujah to Baghdad.

Arriving around noon, O'Leary checked into a discount chain motel. He unloaded a 500cc motorcycle from the truck, slipped on a backpack, and a few minutes later turned down a dirt road used by the farm adjoining Hill's to park trucks and farm machinery overnight during harvest and planting season. At the end of the short road O'Leary hid the bike and went to work.

The abundance of poison oak in the forest behind Hill's farm worked in O'Leary's favor. It encouraged the Overlord patrols to stay along the perimeter of the pasture and only venture into the brush just far enough to replace burned-out floodlights. Having grown up around poison oak, O'Leary knew how to protect himself. He wore coveralls, a long-sleeved Lycra-cotton shirt, leather gloves with latex inner-liners, a Lycra-cotton head sock, a plastic facemask, and boots. One pair of calf-length socks ran under the overall legs, a second set over. The extra clothing made him sweaty and uncomfortable, but no more so than the body armor and combat gear he'd worn in Iraq where temperatures sometimes reached a hundred-and-twenty degrees.

Two hours later O'Leary returned, soaking wet with perspiration, ditched his protective clothing, and rode back to town for a meal and a nap.

After dinner Hill and his guests, two hedge fund lobbyists, retired to the library to discuss the price of derailing legislation that would impose a version of the Alternative Minimum Tax on hedge funds. They settled on a $750,000 pay-off to Hill, with another $55,000 to Chet Berler, Hill's chief of staff, then sat back to watch the Falcons-Dolphins exhibition game on Hill's 72-inch top-of-the-line flat-screen. Two miles to the east, O'Leary backed the "Bad Boys Special" out of the rental truck on to the dirt road he'd used earlier.

Between the hillbilly armor and 300 pounds of SLX in the back, the modified Hummer weighed fifteen hundred pounds more than when it rolled off the assembly line. Wary of straining the drive train or suspension, O'Leary spent an hour easing the Hummer through the trees and underbrush. The quarter moon gave off just enough light to find his way along the route staked out on his earlier recon by small dots of paint on trees. Against the quiet of the forest, the engine sounded like a siren as it labored to pull the Hummer out of the creek gullies, but O'Leary knew it wasn't really that loud. His heightened perception was just normal mission anxiety.

Three minutes into the fourth quarter of the football game, Hill and his guests heard a commotion outside. Several Overlord guards ran past the window and opened fire at something across the pasture. Hill and his guests quickly dropped to the floor, but couldn't resist peeking over the windowsill.

Outside, Hill's guards couldn't understand why the pasture floodlights didn't come on automatically as they were supposed to, but the answer was simple: on his morning scouting mission, O'Leary zapped the motion sensors with an infrared laser. Just before busting out of the forest, O'Leary used a telescoping extension rod to tilt the lights up. When the guards turned them on manually, instead of illuminating the pasture they blinded themselves with the brilliant white glare from several dozen two thousand watt bulbs. Disoriented, they lost track of the Bad Boys Special and fired blindly, hitting spooked cows more often than the Hummer. Rounds that did find the target pinged harmlessly off its hillbilly armor. The Hummer's tires sustained a few hits but its military surplus tire inflation system pumped air in faster than it leaked out.

Eventually a lucky round came through the small driver's eye-slit in the steel plate and hit O'Leary in the throat. But it was too late to stop him from crashing into the house. The last thing O'Leary noticed before he hit the detonator switch was the taste of blood trickling into his mouth. He'd finally found a cure for the taste that had stuck with him ever since that day on the road from Fallujah.

The taste of Sergeant Major Mike Horvath's brains.

The explosion obliterated the house, vaporized the occupants, tossed pieces of concrete foundation a hundred yards, and left a hole eighteen feet deep and one hundred feet across. Flaming debris set fire to several out buildings. Everyone inside the house and nine security guards died.

The story of O'Leary's battle with PTSD immediately appeared in the media. Paine was sympathetic. Watching some of his Vietnam buddies finally find peace in death, he understood how a suicide mission could feel like a win-win solution. But that didn't mean he was happy. Despite the increased fear it would generate among potential targets, Paine objected to suicide attacks on a fundamental philosophical basis, and called Crystal Clear Nights to make his point.

"Hello, Tom, calling to gloat?" Crystal asked.

"Am I glad another public enemy is dead? Yes. Do I agree with the method? No."

"The method? What difference does the method make?"

"People like Sgt. O'Leary have already sacrificed far too much. Too many good guys have already died. The idea isn't to die for our country; it's to make the bad guys die for our country. This is about killing people who deserve killing. They brought this wrath down upon themselves."

Crystal pounced. "So it's blame the victim? That's your argument?"

"Hill wasn't the victim, O'Leary was. Look at the facts. We're not some Third World country. We have no history of widespread political violence. Our insurgency is growing for only one reason. It's the only choice left, the only way to end the corrupt politicians' control of our government. It's the one tool that the politicians and the bankers and the corporate plutocracy don't control, and can't stop."

Crystal paused. She would never admit it on the air, but Paine was right.

He picked up on the pause and before she could formulate a response he said, "Good night," and hung up. The call was far too short to trace.

Whatever problems Paine had with O'Leary's methods didn't prevent him from adding tombstones for Hill and the two lobbyists on AI's virtual Boot Hill. Like Larry Speakes' wife, Mrs. Hill didn't rate a tombstone. Paine considered the failure of wives to demand integrity and honest, ethical behavior from their husbands greatly responsible for the decline in accountability all across American society.

This was the moment Doc had feared most. Suicide missions were a hallmark of holy war. Since by definition, suicide missions didn't need an escape plan, they required a lot less recon and intel gathering, which reduced the chance that the attacker would be detected by counter-surveillance, or make some other mistake during the planning stage. Doc now began to doubt his hypothesis that if he took down Paine the air would go out of the insurgency. Every day it became more evident that two new forces were operating on the political landscape. On one hand, AI was functioning exactly as Paine hoped, as a highly focused and disciplined yet completely decentralized fellowship of individuals committed to violence as a tool of reform. Simultaneously, an entirely separate movement, using legitimate traditional political methods, had coalesced to promote passage of the Manifesto Amendments.

Crystal picked up on Doc's unease. Both sensed pressure building up on two mammoth tectonic plates, one representing the public, the other the special interest political establishment. An earthquake was inevitable. Neither one was quite sure exactly who and what would be left standing, or what the country would look like afterwards.

Chapter 39: R & R

O'Leary's suicide attack notwithstanding, Paine saw the waning days of summer as a delusional lull before "the Storm of Reform." He firmly believed that a Manifesto movement committed to using traditional legal political methods would not succeed. It might get close to the finish line, but not over it. Only after polite attempts at reform failed would enough people willingly engage in the violence necessary to restore democracy. And that wouldn't occur until later, in the fall. It would take that long for the game of protest and repression to play out. Until then, Paine was content to rest and observe. Even a patriot needs a vacation.

He wasn't the only one.

Crystal, too, needed some time off. With her TV show scheduled to launch the first week of September she wanted to relax and enjoy Mom's home cooking before undertaking the biggest step of her young career. Doc arranged for SAS Delta in Dallas to provide a protective detail.

She wondered if that was really necessary.

"Absolutely. Letting you go off unprotected would be an invitation for Paine to make direct contact, and I'm not going to let that opportunity slip by. Not to mention the threats from anti-insurgency types or some garden variety stalker."

"What makes you think I have a stalker?"

"What makes you think you don't? Because nobody's sent you a note saying that the two of you are destined to be together for eternity?"

The idea had never occurred to her.

"And if you don't have one now," Doc added, "You certainly will once you're on TV."

Crystal loved coming back to visit Garland, a community of about 200,000 northeast of Dallas. Consistently ranked as one of the Top 100 Places to Live by various magazines and polls, she liked the city's quiet pace, and its mix of old and new, the Patty Granville Arts Center with its elegant soaring glass atrium just a few blocks from hundred year-old Garland High School, which Crystal attended. She especially liked her mother Laura's Chandler Heights neighborhood of modest, middle-class homes and tall mature trees. Although they talked several times a week, Crystal missed her mother and decided that if the TV show was a success, she would buy a house but keep her condo so that mom could use it for long visits.

On her second day home Crystal took Laura shopping in Dallas. Laura found Crystal's FBI protection detail a little unnerving, and wondered if her daughter was really in any danger. After the sun went down, they sat in the backyard lawn swing sipping margaritas. When Crystal mentioned how much she would make if the television show became a success, Laura spit her margarita and almost fell out of the lawn swing.

While Crystal relaxed in Texas, Michelle Patisse, the overlord of Project Backfire, had to do something to distract the media from O'Leary's suicide attack, which still dominated the news cycle. She sent Property Investment Protective Services operatives to clear out another Paineville camp, in New Jersey. This time the squatters were better prepared, not to resist, but to evacuate, their belongings organized and their vehicles pointed toward the exits. The efficiency of the evacuation and the lack of confrontation destroyed its TV news value.

Patisse was furious. If she couldn't provoke bloodshed between Paineville squatters and PIPS forces, she'd simply orchestrate it. She found the perfect setting at a camp in Rochester, New York.

When PIPS forces swept through the building, designated PIPS members fired throwaway weapons over the heads of fellow PIPS agents coming the other direction. The sound of the gunfire and the muzzle flashes showed up on outside video shot by the media, but the shooters themselves did not. Even if a later investigation determined their identities, it could all be blamed on friendly fire in a fog of war environment. In a sense, this was true; they were in a war, one waged against the poor and middle class by Wall Street. Having manufactured a pretense to justify the use of lethal force, PIPS operatives shot seven people dead, including a fourteen year-old girl and a twelve year-old boy. Six others were wounded.

Crystal and her mother watched coverage of the Rochester bloodbath over their morning coffee. Eventually a spokesman for the LVI front company that owned the Rochester property issued a statement decrying the bloodshed while noting that PIPS guards "had no option but to defend themselves."

At Operations Center D, Doc had other concerns. He didn't like the idea of goon squads substituting for regular law enforcement any more than he liked criminals and terrorists. It also struck him that a private security contractor like PIPS had the expertise and capability to carry out the two nearly simultaneous sniper attacks that convinced everyone AI was a movement and not just an individual. *Could the insurgency be a charade to justify greater government power and a suspension of civil liberties?* The idea was extreme, but not unthinkable. Similar methods had been used to bring the Nazis to power in Germany, and later copied in other countries. For years some political observers had worried that if anti-government civil disobedience in the U.S. ever reached a certain level, a false-flag operation might be staged to give the government cover to employ repressive measures.

Doc didn't believe that would ever happen, but others might

feel it was worth a try. A conspiracy involving a private security company raised another intriguing possibility, the use of foreign nationals. All this time Doc had been looking for American suspects. Security companies regularly employed personnel with service in foreign armies and national security agencies from Latin America to the old Eastern bloc. *Maybe I've been looking in the wrong haystack?*

In addition, this kind of conspiracy would certainly have the technical capacity to hack video in order to track targets. At this point, he was grasping at straws, so *might as well grasp at this one.*

Doc outlined his thoughts to his Blessed Trinity and told them, "Let's find out more about these companies. Look for employee travel that might indicate target recon leading up to any of the AI attacks. Check employees coming into the country just prior to any of the attacks, or going out soon after. But keep it on the down low."

Crystal waited until late that night to call Doc. With the NSA listening, both knew they had to keep it short and businesslike.

He greeted her with, "Hey, I thought you were on vacation."

"I am, but I saw the Rochester incident and wondered if you know anything." It was the kind of question she knew he couldn't answer, but she just wanted to connect with him.

"Only what I see on TV."

"Maybe you'll know more by the time I get back?"

"Tell your mother the FBI says hi."

Crystal stifled a giggle and said, "Yeah, right. Bye."

"Bye."

Patisse knew that the Paineville evictions would inspire more people to support the Manifesto Party, so at the same time she formed LVI and PIPS, she established PAV, Patriots for American Values, a high-sounding name that implied grass roots origins. Paid operatives set up small storefront offices in heavily conservative districts, then recruited Local Organizers who were put on a modest salary. Using e-mail lists from various rightwing political groups these LO's recruited more followers.

Now Patisse turned PAV loose against Manifesto Party offices and supporters using tactics borrowed from the pro-life playbook. Locks on office doors were super-glued. Phone and utility cables were sabotaged. Protestors carrying signs branding Manifesto supporters as traitors harassed local Manifesto Party officials coming and going from work, the grocery store, even church. Their homes were picketed and their children taunted. The overt goal was to make every Manifesto party operation as difficult and time-consuming as possible. The more sinister covert goal was to create an environment that encouraged individuals to take more extreme action.

By the end of the week PAV started to produce its desired unofficial effects. Manifesto supporters had their homes, cars, and offices vandalized, ransacked, and splashed with paint. Death threats came by phone, in notes left on windshields, and on signs that showed up overnight in front yards. With quintessential irony, in two cases the people harassed were undercover SOG Suites and the harassment enhanced their credibility within the Manifesto movement.

Just as Patisse intended, Manifesto Party fundraising appeals, local demonstrations, and voter registration drives all suffered. Efforts to help victims of the Paineville evictions were particularly hamstrung. Some Manifesto party volunteers either threw in the towel on their own or were forced to quit by worried family members. Public identification as a Manifesto supporter caused some people to lose their jobs. Kids of local Manifesto Party leaders suddenly got cut from high school sports teams preparing for the coming fall season.

It was ugly, and that was exactly how Patisse wanted it. For her it was recreation.

Chapter 40: Domestic Jihad

Having anticipated that LVI and PIPS might come under scrutiny, Patisse set up an early warning system to let her know if anyone began nosing around for data on the companies. When Bravo's initial inquiries set off alarm bells, Patisse reached out to have the dog put back in the cage. On Monday morning White House Chief of Staff Zak Wooten talked to A.G. Godfrey, who talked to FBI Director Bartholomew, who delivered the message to Doc in the Chapel. "I hear you're looking into these Paineville evictions."

"Yes."

"Why?"

"If Paine wants to provoke more unrest, these squatter evictions would be one helluva good way to do it. We still don't know how Paine finances his operations. I thought maybe tracing the money behind these private mercenaries might lead us to a common source."

"This seems at best, a very tenuous strategy, so henceforth concentrate your resources exclusively on direct methods of finding this damned Tom Paine. Are we clear?"

"Yes, sir."

The Director signaled that the conversation was over. As Doc reached for the door the Director asked, "You still running an airtight ship down there?"

"Far as I know."

"Good."

The implication was clear. Any leaks to the press would be presumed to have come from Doc.

On the way back to his office Doc decided that the order to back off must have come from very high up in the chain of command, at least the Attorney General, probably the White House.

Hoping that Crystal's return from vacation and the recent Paineville bloodshed might prompt Paine to call, Doc arrived at WHYY a half-hour into her show and stayed until the end. When they met in the hallway, they instinctively hugged. It was brief and spontaneous, but still not the thing agents normally do with civilians involved in a national security investigation. Both immediately felt awkward, a feeling heightened by shock at how good the fleeting contact felt. The feel of her hands on his back registered as much as the press of her breasts against his chest. The width of his lat muscles made her realize how tapered he was, but she immediately turned the conversation to business. "Think these Paineville evictions are designed to send a message?"

"You tell me."

"Know who's behind them?"

"No."

"But you're trying to find out?"

"Not my job."

Crystal looked at him for a second. She knew then that somebody had put a very big foot down.

Given the violence that was about to erupt, FBI Director Bartholomew's order for Doc to focus on the hunt for Paine was for the best. In the end, Tony Gilman, not Michelle Patisse, would provide the key to the case.

Tuesday morning Crystal started rehearsals for her TV show. Not having been in front of a studio camera since her college days as a broadcasting major, she needed practice reading copy off the teleprompter, and learning to shift smoothly from one camera to another. The set-desk for her TV show was only a counter top and Crystal suggested putting a modesty panel on the front.

Colin Livesay ruled that out. "You've got the best legs since Mary Hart and we're not going to hide them."

Crystal reminded him, "This isn't an entertainment show."

"All television is entertainment. If it helps, think of it as serious entertainment."

"Look at it this way," Stacey Bonnero offered. "Above the table will appeal to the half of the audience interested in the content of the show. Below the table will appeal to the half that wants to fuck your brains out. When they tabulate ratings, they count both halves."

While Crystal rehearsed, those on both sides of the Manifesto issue stepped up their activities.

The easiest place for a woman to kill a man has always been in the bedroom. The easiest place for a woman to kill another woman was in the ladies' room. Midway during the lunch rush at Delmonico's in the New York financial district, Jessica Wychek, head of securitization at Silverstein-Goetz, got up from her table to visit the sandbox. A woman in a blonde wig and stylish Oakley sunglasses picked up her vodka martini and followed.

In the restroom, while Wychek answered nature's call, the woman, later dubbed Madame X by the media, wiped her martini glass free of fingerprints and DNA with an alcohol towelette. When she heard the toilet flush, Madame X pulled a cheap .22 out of her purse and covered it with a folded newspaper to muffle the sound. Wychek opened the stall door, saw the newspaper pointed at her, and started to say something. Madame X shot her right in the mouth. Wychek collapsed between the toilet and the stall divider. Following the instructions on the AI website, "Two in the head, make sure they're dead," Madame X plugged Wychek a second time.

Madame X calmly exited the ladies' room and made her way out a side door to the alley. She was half a block away before the body was discovered. A block after that she took a cab to the Bronx. Despite claims that the city's DAS network would help fight crime, the only borough where the network was incomplete also just happened to always have the highest crime rate. Protecting the poor from crime was less of a priority than protecting the financial and social elite from angry protestors. It also explained why no surveillance drones were operating over that part of the city.

After exiting the cab in a surveillance dead zone, Madame X retrieved a small gym bag hidden behind a bodega, changed into a different outfit, and vanished. Wychek's murder inspired a week of increased violence, beyond the mayhem that had already been underway for months.

As the expanded use of drones plugged holes in Domain Awareness System networks nationwide, and major office buildings became security fortresses, attacks in the heart of a city, like that on Wychek, became increasingly rare. So naturally insurgents turned to hitting the royals as they came and went. Commuting became a gauntlet as assailants stalked commuters to and from train stations and Park-'n-Ride lots serving upscale suburban communities. Using a limo or a chauffeured town car to and from work meant becoming a target. Any Master or Mistress of the Universe coming or going from New York's financial district was fair game. Those in or around D.C. who appeared to be more than just a secretary ran the same risk. And for insurgents unwilling to commit murder, kneecapping became great sport.

Dining al fresco on vacation in Palm Beach, Heidi Scanlon, a lobbyist for several health insurance companies and wife of Senator Max Scanlon, found out the hard way that crossing her legs made the top knee an inviting target. A man wearing sunglasses, a baseball cap, and a fake beard strolled up and shattered her knee with a single round from a .357 Magnum, then escaped on a motor scooter and finally vanished in a DAS dead zone between Palm Beach and Miami. The nasty scar from the knee replacement operation was a permanent reminder to Mrs. Scanlon that it's not nice to fuck over the public to line your own pockets.

Insurgents unwilling to kill or maim people also made a sport out of targeting the toys and palaces of the elite. Someone burned down the lavish home of the chairman of the House Rules Committee, where bills were sent to die so that House members never had to make uncomfortable votes. An insurgent on a motorcycle firebombed the home of the Chairman of the Senate Commerce committee. In Maryland a bankrupt contractor leveled a dozen homes of the rich-and-infamous with a homemade tank before a nimble police officer leapt on the back of the modified bulldozer and shot him through an eye-slit. Despite armed security guards patrolling marina docks, a number of yachts went up in flames, or sank after divers drilled holes in their hulls. Luxury cars were church-keyed, doused with paint, and set on fire. Tires were slashed. Windshields and windows were smashed, and interiors doused with cat urine.

Bank branches in smaller communities not able to afford the Domain Awareness System became easy targets for Molotov cocktails. Even branches with armed night security guards weren't exempt. Confronted by masked attackers armed with assault rifles, guards usually opted to flee rather than resist. Amazingly, they were somehow just never able to get license numbers or provide accurate descriptions of their attackers' vehicles.

In Darien, Connecticut, billionaire Morris Braverman hosted one of his famous charity fundraisers, where financial elites gathered to congratulate each other for donating tiny portions of the vast fortunes they'd swindled, conned, and stolen. Just as Braverman began the obligatory round of laudatory toasts, a stolen

Beechcraft loaded with three hundred extra gallons of gasoline slammed directly into the lavish great room. The attack killed twenty-seven people including Braverman, injured dozens more, and turned the mansion, including his collection of exotic cars in the subterranean garage, into cinders.

Later that same night in posh Bergen County, New Jersey, a laid-off tool-and-die maker plowed his explosives-laden SUV into a country club charity banquet, killing eighteen people plus himself. The message in both attacks was simple: charity begins with secure jobs, fair wages, and safe working conditions. Like political fundraisers, charity showcases for predatory tycoons and their pretentious trophy wives were now clearly high value targets.

Pro-Manifesto insurgents weren't the only ones busy as summer rolled to an end. Inspired by the stepped up actions of PAV, freelance opponents of reform took the fight to new levels. Manifesto Party Interim Chairman Ellis Brown's home was aired out by assailants firing AK-47s. Fortunately, his wife was out of town and Brown was in the basement practicing his legendary pool-shooting skills. In Brooklyn, New York state Manifesto Party chairman Darnell Davis escaped death when a bomb under his car fizzled and burned instead of exploding. Other party leaders weren't so lucky.

The Nashville chapter coordinator was shot dead walking to her car. The Kansas party chairman was killed by a sniper on a lonely side road leading to his farm. The treasurer of the California Manifesto Party was shot and killed while driving through the Central Valley on Interstate 5. In neighboring Nevada, the chapter treasurer vanished, prompting speculation that, just as in the movie Casino, there was another freshly filled hole somewhere in the desert.

Manifesto Party offices in both Philadelphia and the state capitol of Harrisburg were firebombed. In Colorado, a Special Observations Group Field Organizer paid a biker gang $20,000 to firebomb the hardware store owned by the Denver area Manifesto Party chapter president. The Baltimore chapter president barely survived a savage beating by three bikers in ski masks wielding axe handles and baseball bats. Businesses operated by party leaders were vandalized or aired out in midnight drive-by shootings. All across the country, major party donors were the targets of death threats, vandalism, and harassment. In the most provocative attack, one of Gilman's Field Organizers tossed two grenades into Missouri Governor Doug Brand's home outside St. Louis. The damage was extensive but the family was away at the time and there were no injuries. Conveniently, no DAS drones were operating in that neighborhood at the time of the attack.

While Patisse's PAV operation and those inspired by it went for overt action, Gilman's SOG operation used more subtle methods. Acting on an anonymous tip, police found child porn on the computer of the Minnesota chapter chairman, who swore that it was planted, which it was, by Gilman's female agent dubbed Suite A. In Delaware, Suite C seduced the married state party president. Then her SOG Field Operator leaked proof of the affair to the media.

Chapter 41: Practice Makes Perfect

The most prominent victim of the week was not, however, a bankster, lobbyist, corporate titan, or government official. Just as Crystal's television career was set to launch, Jonathan Bender's ended. In media circles where conflicts of interest were taken for granted, Bender scaled new heights. Whenever he appeared as a guest on a news show he was identified as the senior editor of a prominent Beltway blog and a regular columnist for various news publications. Nobody ever mentioned that he also raked in millions as a consultant for a prominent lobbying firm and was getting paid to advocate his journalistic positions. Vain and unprincipled, Bender appeared nightly on various programs to criticize, condemn, and mischaracterize the Manifesto Party. Coming home from one such appearance, Bender turned off River Road into the posh Somerset section of Chevy Chase, Maryland. He was a block away from his house overlooking the Kenwood Country Club when an IED triggered by a prepaid cellphone killed him instantly.

The man responsible, an electrician whose unemployment benefits had expired, left an anonymous typewritten warning to the media stapled to a nearby tree. "If you don't start telling the truth, more of you will follow Mr. Bender to Hell."

Doc's whiz-techs scoured the note but there were no fingerprints or DNA. The paper was generic white multiuse paper sold by the case at big box office supply stores.

The typewriter, a forty year-old IBM Wheelwriter inherited by the bomber from his dead mother, was at the bottom of Chesapeake Bay, its removable font disc now a melted gob of plastic in a Maryland landfill.

Although they worked hand-in-hand with the elite to perpetuate the oligarchy, the lords of mainstream media were genuinely shocked at being targeted. Until now they had always felt above the fray. For most, courage was something they'd only read about in books, and they were petrified. Targeting the press was something that happened in dictatorships and Third World narco-states, not in the U.S. The idea of being held accountable for what they wrote or said, as well as for what they didn't write or say, had never occurred to these faux-journalists. Suddenly, failing to do real, hard-hitting reporting could have fatal consequences.

One immediate reaction was phony outrage and the suggestion that attacking the media was not the best way to encourage more positive coverage. The steno-journalism corps also argued that they couldn't possibly be expected to provide favorable coverage to a movement rooted in violence against the government.

To the insurgents, mainstream -- or as they called it, lamestream -- media coverage couldn't get much worse, so what did they have to lose?

Paine called Crystal to offer the comment, "Those who make peaceful revolution impossible make violent revolution inevitable. You know who said that? President Kennedy. The press has played a huge role in making peaceful reform impossible."

"You really think Kennedy was talking about America? You really think he would approve of what you're doing, that he would have turned against our form of government?"

"Why not? Jefferson and Franklin and Washington turned against King George."

Michelle Patisse wasn't about to let the threat that Bender's murder represented to the captive media go unchallenged. She sent PIPS minions to warn prominent reporters and pundits not to change the way they covered the insurgency and the Manifesto movement.

Suddenly, whichever path those in the media took put them in somebody's crosshairs. Even reporters who had faced danger in countries torn by civil war found themselves in a new predicament. This time the danger wasn't thousands of miles from home. Now they had to consider possible threats to their families as well.

The escalating violence between pro and anti Manifesto forces reminded Doc that the end result of insurrection is often civil war. He feared the country was coming dangerously close to the day when violence between opposing sides was an ingrained part of the political process. The violence between rival factions also created much more work. With no way of knowing which attacks might be Paine's own personal handiwork, Doc had to supervise the investigation of every attack, which meant mountains of reports, physical evidence, background checks on the victims, and so forth. So far, none of it was paying off.

September

September

Chapter 42: Capitol Ideas

Crystal insisted on debuting her TV show on Labor Day Monday. ASMI wanted to wait until Tuesday, but Crystal liked the idea of talking about the circumstances of working class people in a modern society on the day dedicated to them. She also knew that her competition would opt to take Monday off and have a three-day weekend.

Old Man McTige chuckled listening to Crystal tell Livesay and Bonnero, "Opening on a holiday against substitute hosts is a great way to boost the first night's ratings and get more people to sample the show." *Girl's got a good head on her shoulders.*

"Hello, everyone, I'm Crystal Dickerson and welcome to the first edition of *Crystal Clear.*" She'd practiced the line a dozen times, but it still felt strange knowing that this time viewers in homes across the nation were watching on live broadcast television rather than an Internet webcast.

"I hope you've all had a wonderful, enjoyable holiday. But many Americans did not. They couldn't celebrate Labor Day because they are no longer labor. Their job no longer exists. It has been shipped overseas where workers toil for pennies doing the work that once housed, fed, educated, and sustained us as a nation. For others, the job they do have is not secure. They never have a day off from anxiety and despair. They wrestle nightly with the terror of getting laid off, of not being able to pay the mortgage, of keeping up with insurmountable credit card bills, or covering the medical costs if, God forbid, someone in their family gets sick or injured. What happened? How did America get into this position? What can be done -- what must be done -- to fix it? We're going to look for answers tonight with my guests, Manifesto Party founder and Chairman Ellis Brown, and the former Chairman of the President's Council of Economic Advisors, Michael Rose."

Ellis Brown was the ideal leader of the Manifesto Party. Not many workers on the GM production line had the determination to attend night school for nine years to earn both a B.A. and a Masters. Nor would they have seen the wisdom of getting an MBA just to understand the tactics, principles, and mindset of the bosses across the negotiating table at contract time. Brown might have become something far greater than just a mid-level UAW official but the very thing that limited his advancement in the internal politics of the union -- refusal to compromise on key principles -- made him the ideal surrogate for Paine, and the perfect public face of the Manifesto movement. In fact, Brown was such a perfect surrogate that Doc initially wondered if Brown *was* Paine. However, Brown had ironclad alibis for the time of several attacks, and had been in the hospital on one occasion when Paine called Crystal's show. Still, the fact remained that Brown was Paine without the violence, and the Manifesto movement gave him a chance to achieve his own destiny. Typically, Brown never thought of it as destiny, but merely an opportunity.

Economist Michael Rose, on the other hand, epitomized the revolving door between Wall Street, academia and Washington. Rose rotated between corporate jobs, government posts, and academic positions. Dips in his salary during his government and academic gigs were made up for many times over by lucrative consulting fees for multinational conglomerates and corporate-funded so-called think tanks that were really belief tanks established to produce support for predetermined policy positions. Rose shouldn't have agreed to be on the show, but an insatiable lust to be on TV was his undoing, and he badly underestimated Brown. For every claim Rose made about the benefits of free trade and globalization, Brown had facts and statistics to prove the opposite. For every defense of the status quo, Brown had twice as many arguments for reform.

Near the end of the show Crystal asked Brown about the claim that Manifesto supporters were being unreasonable in demanding such rapid and extraordinary changes.

"Let me quote George Bernard Shaw: 'The reasonable man adapts himself to the world; the unreasonable one persists in trying to adapt the world to himself. Therefore all progress depends on the unreasonable man.' He wrote that in Maxims For Revolutionists. We need a Constitutional revolution, and we're going to achieve one. Starting next week, we're staging protests in the capitols of five key states that have not yet passed Constitutional Convention resolutions. We only have to get three of those five." Brown identified the five as New York, New Jersey, Rhode Island, Pennsylvania, and Maryland.

"How long are these demonstrations going to last?" Crystal asked.

"As long as it takes."

Brown's plan to apply what he called "big pressure in small places" was brilliant. Capitol police departments were not well prepared to deal with long occupation rallies on a massive scale. Already stretched to the limit after months of providing increased security for elected officials and capitol offices, they were in no condition to face the challenges these rallies presented. The first thing officials in each capitol did was meet to discuss options.

New York and Pennsylvania decided to try using the recent counter-Manifesto attacks as an excuse for courts to ban the demonstrations. Instead of taking precautions to prevent violence against protestors, New York and Pennsylvania argued that the demonstrations should to be banned to protect the participants, for their own good. Concerned about being nominated for Name

That Target, judges in both the state and federal courts found this argument unpersuasive.

After New York and Pennsylvania failed to get outright bans on the judicial front, all five states fell back on their favorite tactic of confining demonstrators to protest zones far enough away from the capitol itself to render the protests invisible and thus ineffective. Out of sight, out of mind. And generally, out of the press as well. Although Brown preferred non-violent civil disobedience, he was determined to move from the protest zones to the capitol buildings where the demonstrators could not be easily ignored. Brown knew that the inevitable pushback from establishment and anti-reform groups would result in violent confrontations.

Tony Gilman was determined to turn those confrontations into full-blown street warfare. For him it was a numbers game; he only had to win in three states, with Pennsylvania, New York, and Rhode Island being the most likely. Just as important as winning the state capitol showdowns, Gilman had to preempt a major protest in D.C. The only way to accomplish that was through martial law, and the only way for the President to justify invoking preemptive martial law prior to a D.C. protest was to insure that the battles in the state capitols were so ugly and violent that risking anything similar in Washington was simply unthinkable. Gilman knew that the Manifesto Party would claim to be the victim of sabotage by covert agents. To make that claim difficult to prove, he planned to use different tactics at each location. The trick would be knowing which tactics to use in each situation, and when to strike.

Apart from the Naval Academy across the bay, Annapolis was just an old fishing village, its small cluster of capitol buildings accessible only by a maze of cobblestone streets. Much to Tony

Gilman's distress, Maryland Governor Ryan Vallely presented a simple, low risk strategy to top city and state officials: Do nothing. Welcome the protestors' participation in the political system. As he put it, "They're looking for confrontation, don't give it to them. Just because they're outside waving signs and chanting doesn't mean that we can't go on conducting business as usual. Eventually they'll get tired and go home. In the meantime, it's the best of all worlds. The extra security will discourage individual acts of terrorism." The Governor left unsaid the part about letting pitched battles and anarchy reign at the other capitols under siege by demonstrators.

Minorities made up two-thirds of the population of Providence and the city, a maze of over a thousand streets laid out in haphazard fashion, consistently ranked near the top in the poverty index, with as many as thirty percent of residents living below the poverty line. Violent crime was a constant problem, and the city's per capita rate for property crimes was fifty percent above the national average. The only place for protestors to demonstrate was a large grass field across from the capitol, but it was catty-corner from the city's largest retail center, the Providence Place mall. The last thing Governor Thomas McKnight and Mayor Orlando Jefferson wanted was a surly crowd of the downtrodden milling around casting covetous looks at the mall and all those material goodies inside. Nor did they want protestors anywhere near the Rhode Island Convention Center, just across Memorial Boulevard from Providence Place. Conventions and trade shows were too difficult to attract to risk having one disrupted.

Thus the decision was made to exile the Manifesto Party demonstration to Prospect Terrace Park, five blocks east of the capitol grounds. This was like telling people who wanted to picket the Vatican that they'd have to do so from Sicily. To avoid blame if the move backfired, McKnight convinced Jefferson that it should be announced as a city policy decision. It might be more palatable to the city's minority community coming from the African-American mayor rather than from the white Irish governor.

From the day Ellis Brown announced formation of the Manifesto Party, he'd been building a strike fund designed to finance actions at the final recalcitrant centers of power standing in the way of enacting the Manifesto Amendments. Building this strike fund was a major reason that the Manifesto Party By-Laws prohibited contributions to any candidate's campaign.

Brown now put part of this strike fund war chest to use financing legal challenges to the restrictions placed on demonstrators. Led by attorney Niles Goldstein, more commonly known in East Coast legal circles as "Nails" Goldstein, the party's legal eagles went after the regulations and restrictions state authorities intended to impose on the protest rallies. Nails started with the most egregious case, Trenton, New Jersey, where officials conspired to designate as the protest zone a piece of vacant land eight blocks from the capitol complex. According to lawyers for the city and state, this unnamed patch of bare dirt and weeds was the only place large enough to accommodate the rally. There was only one problem with that argument: a much larger and more accessible area, Stacy Park, was just across the street from the State House. Federal district judge Calvin Berryhill quickly issued an injunction requiring the city to make Stacy Park available for the protestors. The judge threw in an order for the city to provide "all such water, sanitation, and police protection as required to insure the health and safety of protestors, government employees, and bystanders alike."

Like Berryhill, the justices of the Federal Appeals Court for the Second District saw no reason to make themselves targets of the insurgency and refused to hear the city's appeal.

Fresh from victory in the so-called Second Battle of Trenton, Goldstein set his sights on Providence. The Providence City Attorney argued that Prospect Terrace Park was the only suitable protest location. Nails countered with a poster-sized aerial photo of the huge grass concourse bordering the entire south and east sides of the State House grounds. Nails produced charts showing that it had more than twice the acreage of the park. Like his judicial brethren, the judge in this case didn't see any reason to paint a target on his back: Verdict for the plaintiff.

However, in this case, the decision went exactly as Tony Gilman wanted. The Manifesto party got its forum in front of the Rhode Island State House, but the Special Observations Group got a perfect stage for the riot the governor and mayor feared.

The expansive concourse on the back of the capitol complex in Harrisburg, Pennsylvania, was a perfect location for a political rally, but state officials could usually count on the state courts to shuttle a protest of this magnitude off to some other site. Now, however, judges had to think about how anti-democratic bias in their rulings might put themselves in danger. Nails didn't even have to file suit. The state Supreme Court let it be known through back channels that it would not come down on the city's side.

One place Tony Gilman didn't have to worry about was Albany, where the Manifesto party's bid for a perfect game came to an end. The judge assigned to the case ruled that confining the protest to Lincoln Park would not infringe on the demonstrator's First Amendment rights. Albany Police Chief Tony Mulroney welcomed the judge's ruling. Mulroney viewed the Manifesto Amendments as a dangerous restriction on the powers of government, and considered a pro-Manifesto demonstration in his town as a personal affront. Denouncing the Manifesto party as, "people who are not willing to work within the system," he conveniently forgot that demonstrators would be working within the system established by that portion of the First Amendment granting the people the right to peaceably assemble and petition the government for redress of grievances. The chief also decided to take the judge's order confining the protestors to the park literally. He vowed that, "anyone who doesn't follow orders or who fails to disperse when told to do so is a criminal and will be dealt with as we do all other criminals -- swiftly and harshly."

Mulroney's plan was simple: keep the demonstrators in an area too far from the capitol to have any effect, harass and intimidate them in every way possible, and then stage mass arrests to show them who's boss.

Brown's attitude was, *We'll start there, but we're not going to stay there.*

And thus the stage was set for the first round of the endgame to determine whether America got reform or just more repression. Regardless of how easily or difficult things went, Ellis Brown planned to win.

But before that, another question had to be answered: Despite spectacular initial ratings, would Crystal Clear survive past its first week on the air?

Chapter 43: Special Effects

Michelle Patisse's hatred for Crystal Dickerson was both wide-ranging and pathological. Patisse hated Crystal's concern for common folk even more than she hated her support of the Manifesto Amendments. From a strategic perspective, someone promoting the Manifesto cause on the radio was annoying, but not critical. Radio was full of personalities that reached audiences of varying size. On the other hand, by virtue of simply being *on television*, even second or third tier TV shows conveyed an aura of legitimacy. Letting a pro-reform message into American homes five nights a week was just not acceptable. There was also another factor: Patisse was attractive, but nearing fifty. Crystal was under thirty and gorgeous. That made it personal.

For Patisse, the war on Crystal Dickerson was going to be bitch on bitch.

Patisse's IT techs grabbed every second of the satellite feed from the first three days of Crystal's show. That gave them more than enough shots of her face, neck, and hands for what Patisse wanted. Swapping a celebrity's head onto the body of a nude model had been a staple of the Internet since Photoshop was first introduced. Yet with former Playmates working as TV show hosts and newscasters, the stigma of just appearing nude no longer had any significant political impact. But porn was another story. Thanks to advances in computer technology, not only could a person's face be morphed onto another's body, that face itself could be animated and changed to look younger or older. If you had the money, that is, and Patisse had more than enough money for the most sophisticated special effects computer software available.

Patisse couldn't just paste Crystal's face onto the body of a model in an existing sex tape. Too many people would recognize the staging and the actors. The solution was an entirely new tape that looked like it had been made back in Crystal's college days. PIPS located and recruited two willing young male actors, both with drug problems and no close relatives. Finding a body double for Crystal didn't take long either. For more than a few girls, twenty grand in cash was hard to resist.

Given that the purpose of the tape was to ruin Crystal's reputation and career, just showing her having sex, even with two guys, was not sufficient. The Internet was full of videos of young women who had made a similar one-time lapse in judgment. This tape had to show conduct that couldn't be rationalized or explained away, conduct far enough outside the norm that it was guaranteed to offend the morals and sensibilities of society in general. To this end the video featured a painful simultaneous double penetration and ended with the guys spraying the woman with semen.

Anonymous tips about the tape, which was leaked onto the web via an overseas server on Saturday morning, were sent to several tabloid radio and TV shows. By noon the story went viral. That many of those who claimed to be the most outraged by this tape's existence also raced to see it for themselves was a predictable example of the hypocrisy behind the purported morality of American politics.

Everyone at ASMI panicked, but Crystal felt only anger. She knew it wasn't her on the tape, and arranged a special Sunday night edition of Crystal Clear to prove it. To eliminate any possible voice print comparison the video did not contain a single word spoken by the girl. But Patisse, despite all her attention to detail, hadn't realized that ears were as individual and unique as fingerprints, no two alike. When one of the guys pulled the coed's hair aside to show her sucking him off, he inadvertently exposed a perfect side view of the girl's right ear. Since Crystal wore her hair shoulder length, even if Patisse's techs had known about the uniqueness of ears, there wasn't any TV footage of Crystal's ear to morph onto the model. A computer scan comparison of Crystal's ear with the ear in the porno tape proved conclusively that they didn't match.Unfortunately, by then all tracks back to Patisse had been eradicated. The performers and the director had been taken out on a cruise in the Caribbean and fed to the sharks. Even the two hit men who performed the job didn't know who hired them. They did, however, take the liberty of giving the girl another double penetration before they killed her.

Chapter 44: Redress of Grievances

In addition to his other talents, Ellis Brown paid careful attention to detail and had spent the summer preparing Manifesto Party chapters across the country to participate in the capitol demonstrations now set to begin. Members from chapters all across the country had been organized into travel brigades. Aware that the FBI would infiltrate party ranks, Brown put only trusted associates, men and women he knew from his UAW days, in charge of these travel brigades. To minimize the damage that a leak in one chapter could inflict on the overall operation, Brown kept his plans compartmentalized as much as possible and treated each travel brigade as a separate cell. Only he and Sofia Lofgren, his key aide, knew all the details. To make it harder for both of them to become victims of pre-emptive arrest under the Patriot Act or the NDAA, Lofgren and Brown never traveled together and most of their contact involved scrambled phones or encrypted emails routed through proxy servers, anonomizers, and the Tor network. Now it was time to put their plans into action.

In Annapolis the entire week went by without anything to see except people clogging the streets in every direction. Local merchants quickly saw a bright side as protestors drifted in and out buying snacks and even the occasional souvenir. Every day around noon Gov. Vallely thanked the crowd for their peaceful participation in the political process, and assured everyone that the legislature was paying attention to their concerns. It was a lie, but if the rally dragged on long enough it might become true.

In New Jersey, where Judge Berryhill had ordered the city of Trenton to provide water for the protestors, someone left the park's sprinklers on over the weekend, turning the field into a muddy bog. But Brown's troops had the site under surveillance and early Monday the busloads of protestors were accompanied by delivery trucks loaded with plywood.

By eleven, the grass was covered and the park filled with protestors. By noon, Nails Goldstein had city and state officials back in front of Berryhill, who ordered the sprinkler system disconnected and directed the city to reimburse the cost of the plywood. The judge made it plain that if protestors met with any more dirty tricks, Mayor Cox was going to jail, and just in case that might become necessary, he ordered federal marshals to join the mayor's security detail forthwith. When Cox complained, Berryhill gave him the option of immediate residence in a holding cell. The mayor opted for the marshals. After that the rest of the week went uneventfully.

In Albany, the trouble started immediately on Monday morning. Arriving protestors were searched and when protest staffers tried to distribute box lunches the meals were seized on the grounds that the party lacked a license to provide on-site food service. In a strict interpretation of the court order limiting protestors to the park, police would not let them leave until the official ending time for the rally at seven p.m. On Tuesday the Albany strike captain, Darnell Davis, solved the lunch problem by distributing the lunches to demonstrators as they boarded their buses, but the situation remained tense.

Back at Operations Center D, Doc watched all of the capitol protests using a combination of DAS and other video sources. He also got regular reports from local FBI agents on scene at each location. Except for the unnecessary tension created by the police chief in Albany, "So far, so good," he told Kenny. "But anything could set things off."

"Anything, or anyone."

"You're thinking Paine?"

"Violence is his weapon of choice."

"Be taking quite a chance."

"Come on, Doc. This guy is the definition of carefully planned daring action. My bet is, if he starts something, he'll be outta there before the noose tightens."

"Yeah, outta there...and on to the next location. Let's get Ed running facial recognition scans of all the crowd video looking for people who show up in more than one place."

Doc didn't know it but he had just made a decision that would change the future.

After proving the porno tape phony, Crystal went back on the air riding a new wave of popularity. Patisse had badly underestimated how many women would be outraged by the attempt to smear another woman. Even women who didn't agree with Crystal politically, or hadn't previously been interested in the Manifesto movement, flocked to support her.

Patisse was furious. She immediately sent PAV protestors to picket WHHY and Crystal's condo continuously until further notice. She instructed PIPS to start a campaign of anonymous death threats against her, and bomb threats against the station.

Additional pushback against the Manifesto movement came in the form of a massive media disinformation campaign whose underlying goal was to encourage a violent unofficial response. There was a definite symmetry to the equation: the violent tactics of Paine's insurgency fostered legitimate public protests on the left. Now, careful manipulation of the media fostered violence against those protests from people on the right. It was a perfect formula for civil war. And everybody knew it.

In the meantime, Tony Gilman remained content to sit tight and let the pressure build. But then again, he could afford to wait.

Although SOG was a covert op, since the American Insurgency had the potential to inflict damage to the economy, and thus affect the strength of the dollar and the stability of financial markets, Tony Gilman also had a legitimate cover identity as a Domestic Terrorism Consultant for the Treasury Department, which gave him the opportunity to advise local and state authorities on their response plans and tactical decisions. This wasn't a case of the fox in the henhouse. Coupled with SOG's infiltration of Manifesto Party chapters, Gilman was the fox in *both* hen houses. While his left hand advised government officials on how to deal with the demonstrations, his right stood poised to instigate acts of lawless violence. All he had to do was wait for the right moment in each location. And with tensions in Harrisburg and Albany escalating, Tony Gilman decided that now was a good time to choreograph violent confrontation between Manifesto supporters and counter-protestors.

It was not in jest that Pennsylvania had long been described by pundits as "Philadelphia on the east, Pittsburgh on the west, and Alabama in between." The heartland of the state was home to dozens of white supremacist organizations including several klaverns of the KKK. Gilman's FO's recruited these groups as provos, a provisional army of shock troops.

Manifesto supporters arriving at the state house Thursday morning found hundreds of hostile counter-protestors already occupying the prime real estate on the plaza facing the capitol concourse. The police belatedly established a buffer zone between the two groups, but tensions built throughout the day as Gilman's provos kept up a constant stream of invective using multiple bullhorns that drowned out the Manifesto party's p.a. system. Finally, two fed-up burly ex-Marines flanked the police lines and charged the provos from behind.

Other Manifesto supporters surged through the police lines to join the struggle for control of the bullhorns. The Harrisburg cops hadn't searched the provos, so the violence wasn't limited to swinging fists and picket signs. Rolls of coins, chain belts, and padlocks tied to bandanas came into play.

Watching a link to a closed circuit police feed, Gilman quickly ordered Suites D and H into action. As D hurled rocks through the capitol building windows, H set a police car on fire, then hurled rocks through the windows of the State Library that faced the concourse on the east.

The Harrisburg police reacted by firing tear gas into the crowd, but the gas was quickly sucked through the broken windows into the ventilation systems. Some officers had to be diverted to provide security for those evacuating both the capitol building and the library.

In Albany, Gilman used a clever ruse to get some New York Neo-Nazi provos into the park where the police would find it difficult to separate them from Manifesto supporters. He chartered buses from the same company used by the Manifesto Party and outfitted his New York goons with baseball caps to hide their shaved heads and Nazi skull tattoos. To keep police from noticing the inflammatory wording of their signs, Gilman's FO's instructed the provos to carry them off the bus two at a time, face-to-face. The strategy worked brilliantly. When the provos suddenly unveiled the signs, the police were as surprised as the Manifesto supporters. Chief Mulroney, however, was happy to let the situation percolate and hope that a riot broke out.

He got his wish.

Shortly after one p.m. SOG Suite M, acting on a text message from his Field Organizer, tried to yank the bullhorn away from an anti-Manifesto speaker. Suites F and K immediately lobbed rocks at the counter-demonstrators. This was the signal the provos had been waiting for, and they eagerly charged headlong into the crowd.

Manifesto supporters trying to flee the melee were stopped at the park exits by police barricades and officers on horseback. Chief Mulroney decreed by bullhorn that, "no one will leave this park until order has been restored and those responsible for violence taken in custody." This ran counter to good police procedure and made it harder to regain control, but control wasn't Mulroney's goal, chaos was. He wanted an excuse to let his men clamp down.

Following a massive barrage of tear gas, officers in helmets and gas masks rushed into the park from every entrance. Anyone who couldn't get out of the way was pushed to the ground, kicked or hit with batons, and then arrested. Choking and blinded by the gas, caught between anti-Manifesto goons on one side and the charging police on the other, Manifesto supporters had no choice but to try breaking out of the park through the police barricades. It was exactly what Mulroney wanted. He unleashed five hundred officers he had been keeping in reserve, and also impounded the Manifesto Party buses. People who made it past the barricades were arrested, bound with flex cuffs, and herded into the buses for transport to a college gym Mulroney had commandeered to use as a massive temporary holding cell.

By the time the park finally closed, eleven hundred Manifesto Party supporters and sixty SOG hate group provos were in custody. Ninety of those arrested were treated by paramedics or at local hospitals before being booked. The park was a mess as the pungent odor of tear gas and pepper spray clung to the trees. Mulroney announced that the park would be closed on Friday and through the weekend for cleanup, and to allow the courts to process the arrested. The Chief added that if anyone tried to protest before Monday, he was, "empowered to proclaim martial law to keep this city safe and functioning."

In Providence, there were no confrontations between police and protestors, who covered every inch of ground from the capitol to the Providence Place mall, but as the week wore on temperatures on both sides kept going up. Casualties of the War on the Working Class, many protestors were long-term unemployed who had been angry well before Paine and his Manifesto came along. It wouldn't take much to set them off. Over at the mall, the food court did a land office business from the protestors, but the other stores were largely empty as shoppers, wary of the protest crowd and accompanying traffic congestion, stayed away in droves.

A delegation of merchants from the mall pleaded with Mayor Jefferson and Governor McKnight to do something. Gilman laid the groundwork for mayhem by offering what appeared to be a perfect solution: that the merchants seek a court order limiting protestors to the northern half of the capitol grounds, away from the mall entrance. Everyone agreed it was a great way to put potential shoppers more at ease. The judge heard the case Friday afternoon and ruled in favor of the mall, with the new restrictions set to go into effect on Monday.

On Saturday morning, Providence rally coordinator Chuck Holochek awoke to the aroma of breakfast, courtesy of his new girlfriend, Jolene Starkweather. When they finished eating Jolene announced that she had a great idea: "Why don't we also picket the mall?"

At first, Chuck wasn't quite sure what she meant.

"Look," she said, "Let's make up signs about how the mall is only concerned about profits. You know, Profits over People, Commerce over Democracy, that sorta thing. The people marching around outside wouldn't be violating the judge's order. They'd be protesting the mall, not the legislature."

Chuck loved it. "It's brilliant."

Jolene flipped open her laptop. "No, " she giggled, "*This* is brilliant. Come here, look."

Chuck got up and peeked over her shoulder.

"I knew I remembered something about this," she said, "and there it is."

On the screen was an article about a court ruling that people could not be prevented from handing out political literature inside malls because malls were the modern equivalent of the old public square in the middle of town, an area traditionally protected as a free speech site.

"Wow," Chuck admitted, "that is brilliant."

It certainly was. Unfortunately for Holochek and the Manifesto Party, it was the brilliant idea of Tony Gilman, supplied to Jolene, aka Suite Babe, earlier that morning through a secret email account.

Later Holochek decided he should give Ellis Brown a heads-up, but Jolene talked him out of it. "Ellis delegated responsibility to you to run things here. We should concentrate on doing what we have to do to be successful without bothering him over every little detail."

Her argument made sense, but it didn't hurt that when she made it she put her hands together on her knees, which caused her upper arms to push her breasts together, and made her scooped-neckline blouse billow out. Chuck had only been sleeping with her for a month and was still in the hormonal phase when simply a glance at her cleavage was enough to make him harder than Chinese arithmetic.

Chapter 45: Road Work

In the second week of the capitol protests, things got ugly from the get-go.

Protestors housed in motels surrounding Harrisburg awoke Monday morning to find every tire on every bus slashed. Most protestors spent the day watching TV and playing cards while replacement tires were trucked in from Philadelphia and Pittsburgh. The mainstream media made no mention of the sabotage, preferring instead to cite the day's small turnout at the capitol as evidence that the protest had run out of steam.

Brown's Pennsylvania rally coordinator responded by hiring armed security to guard the buses, but on Tuesday morning they were ambushed en route to the capitol by motorcycle riders who threw Molotov cocktails on the rear tires. All the protestors got off safely, but by the time local fire departments responded every bus was fully engulfed in flames.

The bus attacks weren't the end of SOG's dirty work. On Wednesday, Gilman sent two former Chilean death squad mercenaries, more recently employed by the State Department as private contractors in Iraq, to Carlisle and Lancaster. Members of the Pennsylvania House from those areas commuted to the General Assembly when it was in session. As the rep from Carlisle turned off the highway, a sniper's bullet drilled him squarely in the head. Minutes later another sniper shot killed the rep from Lancaster as she waited for traffic to clear at an intersection. An anonymous caller to a Harrisburg radio station claimed responsibility for the attacks on behalf of the insurgency.

Nobody, including Paine, knew if it was true, and it had to be taken at face value.

On Monday in Albany, Chief Mulroney was treated to a sight no one had ever seen before: eleven hundred protestors released on bail the previous week were back carrying picket signs with the slogan "So Arrest Me -- Again" The signs were a red flag, and Mulroney was happy to be the bull. It never occurred to him to wonder what they hoped to accomplish by being arrested again.

When brought before Judge Mortensen, each protestor plead not guilty but refused to post bail or sign the Pledge To Appear for Trial required for Release on their Own Recognizance. In effect, they demanded to be jailed until trial. Since Albany didn't have nearly enough jail cells to handle that many prisoners, a furious Mortensen had to remand them back into custody at the temporary holding facility. If he dismissed the charges and turned them loose they were simply going to come back and protest the next day, which would have made a mockery of his authority.

As far as the judge could tell, the only upside was that if enough protestors went to jail, the Manifesto rally might peter out.

No such luck.

The next morning Darnell Davis announced to the protestors that they would no longer remain in Lincoln Park, too far away to have any impact on the legislators in session at the capitol. With Davis leading, the crowd marched to the park entrance where they were beaten, gassed, and arrested. Despite the massive police effort, several thousand protestors managed to escape the park and march to the capitol where legislators and staff watched from the upstairs windows as officers on horseback charged into the crowd swinging batons with enthusiastic abandon.

By late afternoon, Albany had another fourteen hundred prisoners on its hands. Like those arrested the day before, these protestors also demanded to be jailed, which really meant that they demanded to be housed and fed. Many, including a large number who had been evicted from Paineville camps by Michelle Patisse, also demanded medical attention, which Nails Goldstein reminded the court the state was required by law to provide. Cheerfully quoting chapter and verse from the statutes and implementing court decisions, Nails made the case that Mortensen really only had one option: take control of local hospitals under the legal concept of exigent circumstances, and order those hospitals to provide the necessary medical care.

Governor Scharkanzky was appalled at Mortenson's order, but even though the state was on the hook to reimburse the hospitals, he didn't really have a voice in the matter. He asked the head of the state's Health Services office how much it was likely to cost. The advisor did a little quick math in his head and guesstimated that it would run the state between two and four million dollars a day, for God knew how long.

Brown's plan was now clear: overwhelm the system, just as the system had overwhelmed the people. The system caused the problems of unemployment and outsourced jobs and unaffordable healthcare, so make the system pay the price.

On Wednesday in Albany it was déjà vu all over again. Manifesto supporters again tried to march on the capitol building. Again there were mass arrests, and again nobody agreed to pay the fine or post bail. With no place to put them, Judge Mortensen had to dismiss the charges. The defendants left the courtroom chanting "Nah-nah-nah-nah, hey-hey-hey, to-mor-row."

At the capitol, Governor Scharkanzky huddled with key officials and advisors, including Tony Gilman, who suggested letting future rallies take place across from the capitol, allowing the police to concentrate all their forces in one place. By taking

Gilman's advice the Governor set in motion the very riot he wanted to prevent.

Concentrating almost all of the Albany PD around the capitol left the rest of the city with only token police protection. On Thursday morning Gilman's provos fanned out across the city's major retail areas wearing bandana masks and carrying pro-Manifesto signs. A staged fight by two SOG Suites was their cue to set cars on fire and throw rocks through windows. Soon both gangbangers and alienated, disenfranchised citizens joined the melee and within an hour full-scale looting was underway. The governor and state officials had no choice but to adjourn the legislature to allow law enforcement to focus on quelling the rioting.

The events in Harrisburg and Albany were nothing compared to what happened in Providence, where Jolene Starkweather convinced Chuck Holochek to let her run the protest inside the Providence Place Mall. She assigned two other SOG infiltrators, Suite E and Suite I, to the mall squad. Mall management dismissed a printout of the court ruling allowing political activity inside malls, branding the document an Internet fake. When security moved to confiscate the demonstrators' pamphlets and picket signs, E and I provoked a scuffle that quickly turned into a brawl.

Responding to Jolene's tweet, "We're under attack by police and security," demonstrators on the capitol grounds turned and surged toward the mall. The police were quickly overrun, and then it became a stampede.

Mayor Jefferson immediately directed police to use whatever force necessary. A barrage of tear gas, beanbag projectiles, and rubber bullets drove many protestors to seek safety in the business district on the east side of the civic center complex, where a young, pregnant Hispanic woman coming out of thrift store was hit by a tear gas projectile that fractured her sternum and drove it back into her heart. She went into full arrest, dropped like a stone, and fractured her skull on the sidewalk. The incident was caught on a protestor's phone and the video immediately started to circulate among other protestors.

That was all it took. Somebody pried a chunk of asphalt out of a pothole and hurled it through a window. As police rallied to the scene, an officer was shot just below the brim of his riot helmet. Dragging their dead comrade, the remaining cops retreated.

Looting and fires quickly spread to other areas of the city. With the police tied up around the civic center complex, street gangs seized the opportunity to hold up four local banks. Knowing that police response would be slow in coming, they took their time and got away with big hauls, hitting one bank for $452,000.

Meanwhile, Suites E and I removed the digital recorders from the mall's security office. Normally the mall uploaded its video to the DAS network after the close of business each night. No one had thought to switch over to real-time delivery. Now all visual record of the Suites' part in the initial altercation with mall security was gone forever.

In the rest of the city, the rioting and looting escalated. Street gangs divided themselves up into shifts in order to pillage diligently around the clock. Gov. McKnight had no choice but to declare martial law, and order out the Rhode Island National Guard. The legislature adjourned and the Governor retreated to the temporary crisis headquarters set up at the Convention Center.

Thanks to years of personnel and equipment attrition during tours in the Middle East, the tiny RI National Guard unit that finally deployed in Providence on Tuesday was hardly more than an armed troop of Boy Scouts. Conversely, the gangs in the streets were a potent force. To reach minimum manpower levels, since the early 90's the Army had steadily lowered recruiting standards. Major gangs like the Bloods, Crips, and MS-13 responded by sending gang members into the military to get training in tactics, weapons, explosives, and communications technology. Providence immediately experienced the downside of having that knowledge back on the street. The guardsmen weren't prepared for the coordinated level of resistance they encountered.

At a shopping center north of the capitol, gang crossfire forced guardsmen to barricade themselves inside a store until they could be evacuated in a Bradley Fighting Vehicle. In other areas, gang ambush squads in upper floor windows held back cops, guard units, and free-lance looters until fellow gangbangers finished methodically looting prime merchandise from the stores along the streets below. By nightfall the number of confirmed dead in Providence stood at twenty-two, including five police officers, two firemen, one paramedic, and seven guardsmen.

Rather than risk having riots break out in Trenton and Harrisburg, the New Jersey and Pennsylvania legislatures decided to adjourn until the unrest passed. Gilman had successfully thwarted passage of convention resolutions in four states, and although Annapolis had avoided the mayhem and remained in session, so far Maryland showed no signs of drifting into the Manifesto Party win column.

Then Ellis Brown upped the ante.

Halfway through Crystal's Friday night show, Ellis Brown called to announce that the following Wednesday the Manifesto Party would begin mass demonstrations in New York City and continue those demonstrations until the New York legislature reconvened and passed a Convention Resolution. He also added the cheery news that if the Maryland legislature "didn't get on the stick and pass a Convention Resolution," Baltimore would also be hit with massive sustained demonstrations. It didn't take a clairvoyant to know that if the Pennsylvania legislature didn't act, at some point Philadelphia would also be targeted.

Chapter 46: Broadway Kabuki

The First Amendment granted the people the right to "assemble peaceably and petition the government for a redress of grievances." Government, anxious to maintain and exercise power, considered that right to be not without limitations. Thus people couldn't just show up and protest, not in great numbers, anyway, without complying with certain regulations. Ostensibly meant to insure that things remained orderly and didn't threaten the rights or safety of others, the real purpose of these regulations was to minimize, or preferably eliminate, the effectiveness of the demonstrations. To achieve that goal, authorities devised a series of games. If a handful of protestors wanted to pace back-and-forth with picket signs in front of a building or outside an event, it was no big deal. But if organizers planned on attracting a larger crowd, or using an amplified public address system, that involved getting a permit, and a kabuki performance with local authorities.

With his New York State Coordinator Darnell Davis still in jail in Albany, Brown sent Sofia Lofgren to NYC to help Wilbur Pike deal with the obstructionist NYPD. A mere five feet tall and barely a hundred pounds, Sofia Lofgren was Tinker Bell without the wings. Even at fifty-eight, a good bra still held up a pair of imposing tits that she downplayed with high neckline blouses and loose fitting jackets. Her rack wasn't the only thing imposing about Lofgren. Below short black hair flecked with gray were dark penetrating eyes and the greatest voice ever to come out of such a small, feminine body. It wasn't masculine or booming, just full and fearless. If she'd held different political views, Sofia Lofgren would have made a great spy because she honestly did not know fear. She understood it in the intellectual, abstract sense, but had never actually felt it. Maybe it was genetic, a chromosomal abnormality inherited from her war hero father. But as a result, nobody intimidated her. Usually, it was the other way around.

The meeting should have been posted on YouTube. On one side sat Lofgren, Wilbur Pike, and Nails Goldstein. Across the conference table were Deputy Mayor Lisa Mingino, NYPD Assistant Deputy Chief Roosevelt Lewis, and two Battalion Chiefs from the NYFD, who were generally content to observe. Unless the demonstrations erupted into acts of arson, or fire hoses were needed to break up an unruly crowd, the NYFD's only real concern involved the number and positioning of paramedics. Nails and Mingino were also there mostly for show, Mingino to signal that the Mayor had the NYPD's back, and Nails to demonstrate that if the city was unreasonable, the Manifesto Party was ready to drop a big, heavy litigation hammer.

Since the 1980's a number of able and qualified minority officers had risen to high levels within the NYPD, but Roosevelt Lewis was not one of them. A stooge of the first magnitude, his role in the establishment's kabuki theater was to put a racially benign face on otherwise blatantly discriminatory and fascist policies. Lewis opened the meeting by announcing that he assumed the Manifesto Party wanted to stage their demonstration in Central Park and that the city had no objection to use of that venue.

Lofgren replied that he assumed wrong. The party intended to start in Central Park then march down Seventh Avenue to Broadway, and follow it all the way to the heart of Wall Street to surround the Federal Reserve Bank building at Broadway and Cedar Street.

The city had already modeled this possibility, but kabuki demanded that officials appear taken by surprise. Lewis begged Lofgren's indulgence while he and Mingino conferred with their respective superiors. Lewis and Mingino then spent the next twenty minutes in a side office taking care of other business. While Mingino chatted with her caterer about a dinner party she was hosting later in the week, Lewis put down a couple of bets with his bookie and called the manager at Barney's to get the credit limit raised on his daughter's account.

Lofgren staged a little performance of her own. When Lewis and Mingino returned to the conference room she was busily highlighting passages in a book with an arresting title: The Leadership Secrets of Attila The Hun. The message: forget Sun Tzu's The Art of War, the Manifesto Party was going to take New York the same way the Huns sacked the Roman Empire.

"So, how many people are you expecting?" asked Lewis.

"Two hundred and fifty thousand," replied Lofgren. "On the first day. More after that."

Completely ignoring the fact that Ellis Brown had already promised that the protests would be open-ended, Mingino asked, "After that?"

Lofgren smiled pleasantly and said, "Yes. Every day until we get what we want."

There was something unnerving about Lofgren's calm gaze, and Mingino quickly glanced over at Lewis.

This was his cue to deliver the city's counteroffer. "Demonstrations in the financial district are out of the question. We simply can't allow demonstrators to clog the streets of the financial district which are, as you know, small and narrow to start with."

"I'll tell you what I know," responded Lofgren. "I know that Wednesday we are going to march down Broadway and picket the Federal Reserve. On Thursday we're gonna picket Goldman Sachs. On Friday, Silverstein-Goetz. We'll start the following week with JPMorgan Chase, then Wells Fargo and so on and so on. We can do it with a permit and the assistance of the city, or we can do it without. But we will do it, over and over every damn day until the state legislature meets our demands."

As the Manifesto Party delegation headed for the door, Lewis announced, "I hope you like jail."

Lofgren smiled and said, "I've been there before. It's a merit badge."

After Lofgren and her group left the conference room, Lewis asked Mingino what she thought. "I think that Nails Goldstein never said a word."

"And that means?"

"I wish I knew."

So did Nails. He had remained silent on orders from Brown. Nails had no knowledge of exactly what Brown and Lofgren planned, and Brown had kept it that way on purpose. Attorney-client privilege did not exempt attorneys from responsibility to notify authorities if they became aware of a client's plans to commit a future crime, large or small.

Nails had been present because, predictably, the city reacted to Lofgren's vow by asking for a Temporary Restraining Order against the march. Thoroughly rehearsed for his role in the kabuki, the judge ruled for the city. Nails appealed to the state Appeals Court, and then the Federal Circuit Court.

After the appeals were denied, a reporter asked Lofgren about the prospect of being arrested.

"I hear Riker's Island is lovely this time of year," she replied, referring to the city's infamous floating corrections facility.

The courts having sided with the city, it was now time for Mayor Rothenberg to play his trump card, the real reason for all the kabuki in the first place. After recounting the city's efforts to reach a compromise, and the Manifesto Party's promise of prolonged illegal protests in the face of an adverse court decision, the mayor branded leaders of the Manifesto Party as "nothing more than political terrorists, intent on defying the law to impose their rule on the people of New York City, New York state, an indeed, if possible, the entire country using the tools of violence, arson, intimidation, and anarchy. We will simply not allow these tactics to disrupt the lives of everyday New Yorkers and the functioning of the world's financial system."

Rothenberg then unveiled a plan that would disrupt the lives of several million New Yorkers as nothing since 9-11. "I hereby declare a state of emergency in the area of Manhattan south of Canal Street. Pursuant to powers granted to me to deal with such emergency situations, this area will become a security zone. Checkpoints will be erected at every intersection leading into the zone and remain manned around the clock indefinitely as long as the threat persists. Entry into the zone will be limited to people who live, work or attend school there, and business men and women who can demonstrate a valid reason for visiting companies in the zone. All inbound traffic from the Brooklyn Battery Tunnel and the Brooklyn Bridge will be detoured onto West Street, FDR Drive, or the S Street Viaduct. From five a.m. to four p.m. only certain Zone Express Trains will be permitted to stop within the zone. These trains will be limited to passengers who are authorized to enter the zone. People will be screened at all stops outside the zone for the proper credentials or documentation before boarding. Any demonstrators who attempt to infiltrate or camp inside the security zone will be arrested and dealt with accordingly."

Rothenberg paused for a moment. "I realize this will be a hardship on many people, but it is necessary to insure public safety." He could have added, "and private profit," but didn't. "It will also take an enormous amount of manpower. Therefore, by arrangement with the White House, several brigades of the Army's Fifth Infantry Division are in transit from Georgia and will deploy to assist the city's existing force of sworn personnel."

For a moment the room went completely silent. Then someone asked, "Are these soldiers going to be authorized to use deadly force?"

"Yes." The thought of troops armed with machines guns not only didn't faze the mayor, he looked forward to it. *Time to give those rat bastard protestors what they deserve.*

A reporter asked, "How long have plans for something like this been in existence?"

The mayor replied, "Ever since 9-11 the city has constantly revised and updated plans designed to deal with all foreseeable contingencies."

In truth, it was only after public outrage over the 2008 financial meltdown that city officials, leaders of the financial community, and the White House had begun to prepare for the day when the robber class would need protection from the rabble.

October

Chapter 47: Bite Of The Apple

It immediately became clear that the NYPD and the U.S. Army did not share a similar definition of checkpoints and barricades. To the city, a barricade was a cop car parked sideways, flanked by long blue sawhorses and officers in riot gear. The barricades set up on the south side of every intersection along Canal Street by the men of the U.S. 5th Division under Major General Logan Bristow consisted of a six-wheel 2-1/2 ton truck parked sideways behind a double row of concrete K-wall barriers topped with razor wire, supported by an armored Humvee with a .50 cal MII machine gun.

Uniformed NYPD officers at sandbagged checkpoints across Canal Street on the north side of each intersection were supported by a four-man army Fire Team with an M240 SAW light machine gun. Lookout teams equipped with sniper rifles occupied rooftops at each intersection.

All pedestrian and vehicular access to the security zone was straight in across Canal Street after going through a checkpoint. Vehicles not cleared for entry were diverted down Canal Street, which was otherwise closed except for official and military vehicles. New Yorkers normally jaywalked with impunity but now even the most arrogant and self-absorbed waited obediently for the green light. Maybe it was all the military hardware on display. Or perhaps it was the body language of GI's whose bodies were in Manhattan but whose minds were already back in Fallujah or Kandahar.

Similar barricades and checkpoints controlled traffic at all the tunnels and bridge exits into the Security Zone. To billet his 6,000 troops Gen. Bristow commandeered every square inch of park space in and around the Security Zone including Battery Park, the greenbelt areas along the Hudson River, and the

Brooklyn Bridge approach ramps.

The media described the preparations as "pro-active, precautionary measures" and "a prudent deterrence to the violence and rioting that has characterized previous Manifesto Party demonstrations in other cities."

Watching raw video feeds from the various network news satellites Crystal dubbed the southern tip of Manhattan the Green Zone, after the bunkered complex set up by U.S. forces in Baghdad. Much to the chagrin of the White House, the rest of the media picked it up, which was fitting because, after all, green was the color of money.

For Doc and Kenny back at Operations Center D, the images were also very disturbing. It was one thing to mobilize the National Guard in response to an emergency, but deploying regular army units as a primary defense against non-violent domestic protest was unprecedented and struck at the heart of the concept of civilian authority. Doing so to protect private financial institutions struck them as particularly ominous. Nevertheless, by Tuesday night the stage was set in lower Manhattan for an epic confrontation between the power of people and the people of power. All that remained was to see how Manifesto Party leaders and protestors reacted.

And Ellis Brown had some surprises in store.

Brown had known that some state legislatures, especially New York, would adjourn rather than face pressure from demonstrators. This meant that New York City could be the key to the fate of the entire movement. If pressure in the Big Apple caused the New York legislature to cave in and approve a convention resolution, other states would also break and push the total over the magic number of thirty-four. If New York held, the other states would probably also hold and all would be lost.

To win "The Battle of New York" Brown needed new tactics. He found inspiration in a subsidy program the government created in the early days of the Second Great Depression to help the auto industry. Dubbed "Cash for Clunkers," the program paid people who traded in older vehicles rebates of up to $4,500. For a month Brown had run his own stealth Cash for Clunkers program, stockpiling hundreds of old, cheap vehicles, many of which barely ran.

Very few people who worked in the financial district lived in the vicinity. Some resided uptown in Manhattan and took the subway, cabs, or car services to and from work. Others lived across the Hudson River in New Jersey, on Staten Island, or to the north in Westchester County and the posh suburbs and estate communities of Connecticut. Except for a few very high-level execs who could helicopter in and out, there were only five ways for these workers to get off the lower end of Manhattan by vehicle: the Holland Tunnel on the west, the Williamsburg Bridge on the east, and either the Brooklyn Bridge, the Brooklyn Battery Tunnel, or ferries to Brooklyn and Staten Island on the south. The Army and police had done a thorough job of preparing to prevent demonstrators from getting into the Green Zone. It never occurred to them that perhaps Brown intended to keep the financial wizards who worked there from getting *out.*

Precisely at 3:15 p.m. Wednesday afternoon in a coordinated, rehearsed operation, rows of clunkers eight deep slowed and came to halt, packed tightly, bumper-to-bumper, on all the streets, bridges, and tunnel entrances serving the Green Zone. Some drove up over curbs to block the sidewalk. All the drivers got out, locked the doors, and walked away. Brown called it a "clunkercade." In only eight minutes, every street, tunnel and bridge leading in or out of lower Manhattan was blockaded by abandoned cars.

This wasn't the only trick Brown had up his sleeve.

The authorities had gone to great lengths to control what people could get off the Zone Express Trains at subway stops in lower Manhattan. They had given little thought to the evening exodus, where the plan was simply to allow people only to board, but not get off, the regular evening commuter trains. It never occurred to them that there might not be any room on those trains. Subway rides were inexpensive. It took a lot of manpower but not much money for huge swarms of Manifesto protestors to board at stops outside the Green zone and fill the evening trains to capacity. Hordes of Wall Street warriors hustled down to the subway platforms only to be greeted by train after train, every car overflowing with angry protestors unfurling signs with ominous messages. Once the trains passed out of the security zone, the protestors got off, dropped another token in the turnstile, and hopped on another train headed back through the Green Zone.

By five o'clock sidewalks inside the Green Zone were clogged with frustrated financial types pouring back out of the subways. Normally, they would hail a cab, but thanks to the clunkercade, cabs couldn't get in or out. Neither could the massive fleet of town cars and limos that usually serviced the Masters of the Universe. The ferries could only handle a small fraction of the increased demand. On 9-11 tugboats and fishing craft helped ferry people off the island. Now, in the Second Great Depression, the banksters weren't nearly as popular. This time many captains decided to knock off and go home early, or suddenly had mysterious engine problems. Lower Manhattan became complete chaos. It took police until midnight to re-establish normal traffic flow. Meanwhile, along the streets just outside the Green Zone, protestors settled in for the night.

A few of Crystal's callers thought the clunkercade strategy would backfire because it disrupted the lives of too many regular folks. The majority, however, thought it was brilliant and innovative.

Doc and Kenny agreed. They marveled at how Brown was able to plan and pull off the clunkercade without the Army or civil authorities getting wind of it. Knowing Gen. Bristow, they also worried about how he would react.

Their concerns were well founded.

Thursday morning Gen. Bristow ordered his forces to disperse the protestors gathered north of Canal Street and arrest anyone who resisted. His troops were equipped with an array of non-lethal weapons, but once again Brown had put his strike fund to good use.

When the troops fired tear gas, demonstrators reached into backpacks and donned gas masks. When the Army fired beanbags and rubber bullets, protestors countered with plywood shields. When the troops resorted to sonic cannons, demonstrators went into their backpacks again and pulled out motorcycle helmets, sound cancelling headphones, and the kind of industrial headsets worn by airport workers.

Gradually a combination of fire hoses, water cannons, and overwhelming troop strength forced the protestors farther and farther back up Broadway and the adjacent avenues. But it was slow going. Bristow had planned on having the streets opened by noon, and predicted that the farthest he would have to drive the protestors back before the crowd dispersed would be 23rd Street, the main east-west thoroughfare in the trendy, gentrified Chelsea district. He was wrong on both counts. His troops didn't make it to 23rd Street until after two o'clock, and those protestors who hadn't already been arrested and trucked away to the temporary detention center at Citi Field remained massed and defiant.

Bristow had no choice but to order his troops to continue pushing the demonstrators north until they broke up. "To Central Park if you have to."

The bloodshed started when troops pushed the protestors back to 27th Street where the Fashion Institute of Technology occupies the entire north side of the block between Seventh and Eighth Avenues. Brown ordered his strike captains to funnel protestors down that block, where they could mingle with students getting out of class. He saw it as a perfect opportunity to further slow down the advance of Bristow's troops.

Tony Gilman, keeping tabs on the situation via the same DAS images and encrypted satellite video being sent back to the Army's CENTCOM headquarters in Tampa, saw a chance for something better. He had Suites L and N take up positions near the middle of the block and fire at the soldiers advancing from each direction. Three soldiers went down, one with a fatal head wound. The Suites then dashed into FIT, a complex of buildings connected by hallways, aerial pedestrian bridges, and basement tunnels. Confronted by masked men waving guns, FIT's unarmed security staff ducked behind their desks. The shooters re-emerged from new positions and fired another volley at the soldiers.

Predictably, fire discipline among the troops broke down and several fired into the crowd. Soldiers at the other end of the block interpreted this as more hostile fire and shot back. Five protestors and thirteen students were killed, with six protestors and eight students wounded. Two soldiers were also fatally hit by friendly fire. During the chaos the Suites escaped through FIT emergency exits out onto 28th Street and disappeared into the crowd.

At OCD, Doc immediately ordered a review of all surveillance video from FIT's internal security cameras. Doc hoped desperately that Paine was one of the shooters, and that at some point he'd removed his bandana in view of an FIT security cam.

Meanwhile, back on the streets of Manhattan, the sound of the gunfire carried over to 6th Avenue where many protestors became enraged and began pelting advancing troops with rocks and bits of asphalt from a street repair project. Others looted snack shops and delis for cans and bottles to throw. This just provoked more gunfire from the troops. Nobody was killed, but six people were wounded.

One block over the news was grimmer.

Madison Square Garden sat just behind Penn Station on Seventh Avenue between 31st and 33rd Streets. By the time troops forced the protestors this far back, the evening commuter rush was well underway. To cap things off, the Knicks had a game that night against the Nets. The mayor and the league should have postponed it but didn't, because cancelling the game might make it appear that things were not under control in the Big Apple. As if 6,000 armed troops patrolling the streets was the normal state of affairs.

While hordes of protestors jostled with fans and commuters, Gilman's Field Organizer in the area capitalized by having Suite O fire at advancing troops. Weary from the daylong clash with protestors, soldiers operating on raw frayed nerves opened fire again. The body count was eleven killed, including three teenagers on their way to watch the game, and eighteen more wounded.

As protestors fell further back their anger tuned into indiscriminate rage. Stores and shops were trashed and set afire. The upper floors of some of these buildings contained apartments and condos. The potential for mass casualties demanded that fire crews helping the troops quickly switch to knocking down these ground level fires before they flared out of control. Without the fire hoses and water cannons, the troops were left with only two ways to battle the remaining protestors: hand-to-hand combat, or more live fire.

The final confrontation came in Times Square, where five more civilians were killed in the last free-fire episode of the day. After that, the remaining protestors melted away and the exhausted troops saw no reason to follow. They also had other work to do. Over seven thousand arrested protestors remained to be transported to Citi Field in Queens.

Stadiums have always made great temporary detention facilities. Accessible from major roads, they had restrooms and concession facilities to handle large numbers. Luxury boxes could be commandeered as temporary offices and housing for officers. Detainees could be left out in the open while guards took shelter from the elements under the stands. High walls shielded against the prying eyes of the public, as did the wide parking lots that could also be used to billet troops, store vehicles, or set up processing and support operations. Yankee Stadium was closer and would have made more sense, but it was in the Bronx, where some still referred to one police precinct house as Fort Apache. Parts of Queens were pretty rough neighborhoods, but chances of the natives getting restless there were still much less than in the Bronx.

There was no little irony in using a stadium named after one of the financial institutions that many blamed for the Great Recession to imprison citizens protesting the oppressive power of financial institutions over their lives.

Despite her willingness to be arrested, Sofia Lofgren was not among those in custody. Neither was Wilbur Pike. Both were too valuable for Brown to let be taken out of the game this soon. The time for he, and them, to lead from the front was still a ways off.

The White House characterized the deaths in New York as unfortunate and blamed the protestors for "using tactics clearly designed to provoke violent confrontation and needless bloodshed, which have been the hallmark of this movement since its inception."

Crystal called Doc to ask what he thought. "This is why the military is not meant to be used as a civilian police force."

She asked if he was coming by later, but he replied that he was too busy. She suppressed the urge to ask what he was working on.

Crystal hosted a very somber show that night. The loss of life was shocking, but thirty-eight dead in a single day was only part of the story. The larger issue was who the dead were, and why they were killed. In previous civil disturbances the victims were almost entirely poor and minorities, some of which had engaged in looting. This time there had been no riot or looting until after the shooting started, and most of the victims were middle and working class whites or college students. To some people, the Army's reaction was entirely justified; the protestors were "un-American" and "deserved what they got." But to most people, and especially Crystal's audience, the Army had over-reacted in an oppressive and frightening manner.

Halfway through the show word came from the White House that after discussions with Mayor Rothenberg and Gen. Bristow, President Welch had declared federal martial law in the borough of Manhattan. The order included a seven p.m. to six a.m. curfew. Besides military and civilian law enforcement, the only people exempt from the curfew were government employees, medical personnel, and bicycle messengers delivering emergency prescriptions. All tunnels and bridges in and out of Manhattan were immediately closed until the curfew lifted at six a.m. the next morning. To prevent a repetition of the previous clunkercade, tow trucks from as far away as Pennsylvania and New Hampshire were stationed along all bridges and tunnels in and out of Manhattan.

Never had the heart of New York City been subjected to such measures. The impact on the city's economy and the lifestyle of many in the tri-state area was nearly beyond comprehension. Even worse, nobody had any idea how long it would last.

On Friday morning Brown again demonstrated how prepared he was for the government's response. While the government concentrated on yesterday's battlefield, Brown moved the action to two new locations in Queens. Massive clunkercades shut down all traffic lanes on the four expressways that fed traffic in and out of JFK. The resulting chaos affected not just the country, but world travel. People couldn't make departing flights. Arriving passengers could not get to their ultimate destination. Crews couldn't get in to man aircraft. Incoming flights had to be diverted to Newark, Philadelphia, Hartford, and Boston. The LaGuardia clunkercade also played havoc with traffic around the Citi Field detention facility.

Brown's strategy was a calculated gamble, designed to bait the government into imposing increasingly harsh restrictions until the public at large got fed up. Brown knew that if enough of the public eventually joined the demonstrations, the government would be forced to back down. The flip side of that belief was the gamble that Welch wouldn't take the ultimate step, that there was a line the President would not cross.

At 2:30 p.m. Brown lost that bet.

Instead of an incrementally tougher response to the Manifesto protests, the White House went to the civilian equivalent of

Defense Condition Four: Welch designated the Manifesto Party a terrorist organization "whose leaders have shown a willingness to condone murder and other acts of terrorism. My administration cannot and will not sit by and let these anti-democratic fringe elements paralyze our nation's economy and transportation infrastructure, or threaten the financial capitol of the world. Their tactics do not adhere to the principles of representative government and a civil discussion of issues on which this country was founded."

Welch announced that arrest warrants were being served by the FBI on Brown, Lofgren, all Board members, chapter officials, protest coordinators, and strike captains, as well as big-money donors including Cece Rayfield as "threats to national security." Welch also ordered all Manifesto Party offices and assets seized.

Asked by a reporter if this meant that rank-and-file members of the Manifesto Party were also now considered terrorists, Welch responded, "In difficult economic times, some people are more easily taken in by populist propaganda from those who would seek to overthrow our form of government. We are not going to pursue action against people who have been duped and misled by the Manifesto Party in the past. However, going forward, anyone who supports the party or participates in any activities on its behalf will be subject to arrest and appropriate punishment."

To make sure the message got through to everyone, Welch announced the deployment of additional Army brigades and martial law in Baltimore, Philadelphia, and D.C.

Brown, Lofgren, and the other Manifesto Party leaders weren't just arrested; they were classified as enemy combatants and immediately confined without arraignment or a chance to call an attorney. When Nails Goldstein filed habeas corpus petitions on their behalf, he was charged with "providing material support to a terrorist organization" and also jailed at an undisclosed site.

Designating the Manifesto Party a terrorist organization was unprecedented. Never before had a bona-fide political party been outlawed. Even the old Communist Worker's Party had been allowed to exist. The implications for democracy were frightening. For decades, government at the state and federal level had pursued policies designed to marginalize protest. Out of sight was out of mind, for the government, politicians, the political elite, the press and, unfortunately, for the public at large. Banning the Manifesto Party as a terrorist organization was the ultimate extension of this policy.

Doc and Crystal were aghast. It struck at the heart of everything they believed.

Chapter 48: Double Trouble

Form And Image Recognition software applied the principles of facial recognition to design elements. Facial recognition software worked best with images captured clearly, head-on, with adequate lighting and focus, which wasn't always possible. When dealing with patterns and shapes a mere outline could be enough to pull up potential matches. With luck, a FAIR search would lead to a photo with a clear view of the person's face that could be run though the facial recognition database. Even if that didn't link the photo directly to a name, a subsequent photo might capture the person's car and license plate. Of course, FAIR has its own limitation: any change thwarts the process.

Doc's attempt to find a lead to Paine's identity from video of the demonstrations hinged on finding someone who appeared to instigate or direct violence at more than one demonstration. Ideally, he hoped to find a match between that person and images from Domain Awareness System and other sources taken near Paine's previous attacks. The break Doc was looking for finally occurred because in covert field operations agents had to travel light and a limited wardrobe also led to one of the less glamorous aspects of field ops: doing laundry, often at coin laundromats that had security cameras to protect against theft, vandalism, and assaults on female customers. This is where Suite K made a small but fatal mistake. He wore the same plaid jacket to both the Albany protest and to a later meeting with a SOG FO using the alias Todd Barnes. It was typical of someone without sufficient training, and it would eventually rock the country.

The FAIR software used by Doc's whiz-techs picked up Suite K instigating an attack on Albany police lines. A DAS networked security camera in a mini-mart parking lot caught him hailing a cab. The driver's trip sheet tracked Suite K to a discount chain motel where another security camera showed him leaving a few minutes later with a bag of laundry. Since motels like this one had coin-op washers and dryers on-site for guests, the whiz-tech running this particular scan search immediately made "Mr. Plaid" a person of interest. It didn't take long for the whiz-tech to identify the laundromat closest to the hotel and pull up the relevant security video.

To a casual observer, Suite K's visit looked perfectly normal. He came in, sorted loads of white and colored items, loaded the machines, and then sat down on one of several cheap plastic chairs to wait. Ten minutes later a burly man around fifty packed up his laundry and left, leaving behind a USA Today newspaper. Suite K retrieved the paper and began reading it. When his own laundry was done Suite K exited, taking the newspaper with him.

Professionals in the intelligence community traditionally operated on the premise that "There are no coincidences." The possibility that this was a carefully orchestrated exchange between an agent and his handler, and the newspaper concealed instructions, briefing materials, operating cash, or a new identity packet was too great to ignore. The chance that the Burly Man might be the illusive Tom Paine made follow-up imperative.

Doc's whiz-techs now had good, clear straight ahead headshots of both men to run against all available databases. And that's when things got interesting. Suite K, aka Mr. Plaid, had a Nebraska driver's license in the name Reed Patterson, and a recent Iowa license issued in the name Michael Anderson. The Burly Man from the laundromat also had two driver's licenses: a Virginia license under the name Dick Bahner and a recently issued Florida license under the name Todd Barnes. The whiz-techs also found two other pictures for Bahner: a military ID from his days as an

Army Ranger, and a work ID from his last job before he retired, as a Secret Service agent assigned to the Domestic VIP Protection Unit.

The excitement among the key staff in Doc's office was palpable, but restrained. After so many months of fruitless dead-ends, the prospect of finally having a possible lead on Paine's identity gave everyone a rush, but nobody dared celebrate prematurely. Dick Bahner had escaped scrutiny in the Main Core Suspect Pool because phone and credit card records placed him well away from Palm Springs when Navarro and Trammello were shot. If Bahner was Paine, this contradicted the hypothesis that Paine started out as a lone wolf. On the other hand, it explained where AI got its operational and tactical know-how. Bahner certainly had the background to train others to carry out attacks and escape detection.

Bahner's former Secret Service employment, however, raised the disturbing possibility that the Manifesto movement was somehow government connected, possibly a rogue effort at reform from within, but more probably a nefarious officially sanctioned covert op designed to provoke civil unrest that would serve as an excuse to justify the imposition of martial law and the suspension of civil liberties. If Bahner had co-conspirators inside key government agencies, Doc couldn't risk the chance that a deep background check might trigger hidden trip wires and tip him off, as had happened with the inquiry into Michelle Patisse's LVI and PIPS operations. For the same reason, an investigation of Mr. Plaid/Reed Patterson/Michael Anderson was equally delicate. If Patterson's whereabouts at the time of Paine's early attacks could be verified, then Bahner's organization had to have more members.

Doc set the tone going forward. "Everything about this aspect of the case is now on a purely need-to-know basis. All research, phones calls, and conversations are conducted behind closed doors. For the time being, let's stick with their early descriptors, Mr. Plaid and The Burly Man. Where are they, now, at this minute? What are they doing? Who are they calling or meeting with? Is Burly Man the top of the food chain, or is he reporting to someone higher-up?"

Doc turned to Agents John Price and Manny Castaldo. "John, you take the Burly Man. Manny, you've got Mr. Plaid. Tap and tail 24/7. Use as few agents as possible, but as many as necessary. Report directly to me first, then Grace." Doc swiveled back to his Administrative Supervisor Grace McCallister on the other side of the table. "Write up the status reports on one of our off-line computers. Make a copy for me and put the original in your security safe. No distribution without my personal authorization."

Grace nodded. She and everyone else understood the possible government connections Doc was worried about, and it worried them as well.

After the meeting, Ed Bridges set up facial recognition and FAIR searches for Bahner and Patterson in all the cities where protest activity had taken place. Doc assigned Gretchen to do a very cautious, discreet background search on both men. The address on Bahner's Todd Barnes Florida license turned out to be one of those private mailbox places and unlikely to be used again in the near future. However, Bahner's Virginia address was real and John Price's team set up surveillance on it. They picked up Bahner when he returned home that evening and sat on him all night.

A well-trained covert operative could shake most tails, but not all. Even without relying on a GPS tracker or cellphone tracking, a tail team with enough agents, cars, and air support can become unshakeable. Wherever the target went, the tail followed.

However, even with a large surveillance team, some agents were so afraid of losing a target that installing a GPS tracker on the suspect's vehicle became irresistible. Fortunately, Agent Price was smart enough not to do so, because first thing the next morning Bahner checked his car, including the undercarriage with a mirror, looking for just such a device.

Watching from a safe distance, Price knew that even if Bahner wasn't Tom Paine, he was worth tailing for some reason.

Linking a person to a specific prepaid cellphone wasn't easy, but with enough resources it was possible; the person just had to use the phone while on the move, and travel far enough. Bahner did exactly that, taking a long, circuitous drive through DC, over into Maryland, back into Virginia, over into Maryland again, and finally back home. Fortunately Bahner stayed on his cell phone the entire time. Doc's whiz-techs compared his route to all cell traffic passing along each successive cell tower. Eventually, only one number showed up in each tower service area. Another prepaid cell that Bahner called, and received several calls from, also stood out. The mystery phone went dead after Bahner's last call, but Doc's whiz-techs put an alarm on the number to alert them the next time it went active. In the meantime, Kelli assembled an additional tail team, complete with air support, ready to track and identify the user of that phone.

The next morning the mystery cellphone went active again. Like Bahner, the person using it drove in a seemingly random, circuitous manner. At first Kelli's air support pilot and observer had no idea which car they were looking for, but as fewer and fewer cars in the traffic pattern matched the changing cell tower input they finally picked the right one out of the mix and guided the tail team into position. Eventually the car parked in the lot outside a suburban office building in Arlington, Virginia. Agents traced the registration to a Conrad Rubio, a naturalized citizen of

Chilean descent who had shadowy connections to the late Chilean dictator Pinochet's secret police.

Unwilling to take a chance that agents following Rubio into the building might be noticed and arouse suspicion, Kelli instead sent the license numbers of every car in the parking lot and surrounding street parking spots over an encrypted computer link back to Ed Bridges at OCD. As Ed ran DMV and background checks on the registered owners, one name sent a chill down his spine.

Doc and Kenny were spit-balling ideas about how the insurgency might be linked to the demonstrations when Bridges burst in. "You'll never guess who has offices in that building."

"I don't have to guess, you're gonna tell me," replied Doc.

Bridges passed Doc a sheet of paper with Tony Gilman's name and brief rundown of his previous job as head of the Secret Service Presidential Protection Unit. There was also a notation that the building itself was federally owned, and assigned to the Treasury Department.

Doc passed the paper to Kenny, who muttered, "Holy shit."

Doc leaned back in his chair, thought for a minute, and said, "Thanks, Ed, good work."

It was Ed's signal to leave. He closed the door on his way out.

Doc invited Kenny to join him on a walk around the block, which they spent mulling various possibilities. They now had direct links from a riot provocateur in Albany to a high-ranking former Secret Service agent with past connections to the White House. Three of the men identified so far had the expertise required to orchestrate and execute all of the insurgency's attacks. But they still faced the same questions: *Was one of them the elusive Tom Paine? Or were they part of some covert government op? If so, was it officially sanctioned or an off-the-books black bag job? Did the trail stop with Gilman, or did it go higher? And if so, how high?*

Finally Doc told Kenny, "Give Larry O'Neil a team and let him tail Rubio. Have Kelli take Gilman. Let's call him Spooky for the time being. And give her a backup team in case anybody else interesting suddenly shows up in the mix. And warn her, no pillow talk with Ganz." It wasn't that Doc didn't trust Melody, but at this point, information containment was the name of the game; the fewer people who knew what was happening, the better. In fact, given Gilman's previous government connections, now that his name had surfaced in the investigation, Doc felt the need to take certain future conversations with his inner circle off-campus. Even in an environment as secure as OCD, Doc couldn't be sure the walls didn't have ears.

Over the years Doc had tooled around looking for quaint local mom-and-pop coffee shops where he could unwind, overhear what folks were talking about, and take the temperature of the average citizen. One of his favorite spots was Rebecca's in Baliston, a small town west of D.C. He took a dozen key agents there for a lunch briefing on the new developments. The thirty-five minute drive had a surreal feeling. The reality of D.C. as an occupied zone, complete with Army troops on every major corner and checkpoints on all travel arteries, was something the agents never thought they'd see. The farther out they got the more the military presence diminished. By the time they reached Baliston the atmosphere was different, almost idyllic.

Originally a small bakery and coffee shop, Rebecca's had expanded over the years into a rambling warren of rooms. At Doc's request the manager opened a windowless room in the back for Doc and his party. The room's entrance at a right angle off a long hallway made line of sight visual or laser acoustic observation impossible. Doc hadn't taken his key people out of the office just for conversational security. A change of scenery and a relaxed environment could stimulate the kind of fresh thinking that connected old pieces of information into new theories and leads.

Operating on the theory that there were no coincidences was not the same as saying there was no such thing as serendipity. As the group was leaving for the ride back, 78 year-old Lucille Widen came out of the nearby fabric store and flicked the car alarm for her white 4-door Camry. The alarm chirped and the locks released, but when Lucille pulled the door handle, the alarm went off and lights flashed. Lucille hit the alarm button again and again, but the door remained locked and all the bells and whistles went off like New Year's Eve.

Finally Scott walked over and pointed out to Lucille that *her* white 4-door Camry was three parking spots over from the identical one she was trying unsuccessfully to open.

In Doc's van, Kenny observed, "People get to a certain age they shouldn't be allowed to drive anymore." He expected some kind of return comment but Doc was staring off into space, lost in deep thought.

All the way back to the office, Doc kept tossing things around in his mind. *What was bothering him? What pieces of the puzzle was he looking for?* He went back to the mysterious fatal car crash of Arlen Stowe, and worked his way forward, incident-by-incident, attack-by-attack. Finally the pieces came together and he sat up straight in the seat.

"Got it?" asked Kenny.

"Maybe," replied Doc.

The minute they walked back into OCD Doc convened the group in the conference room. "The thing that always bugged us about the K Street bombings was, how did Paine get a stolen rental truck through the highway checkpoints? Every commercial vehicle and RV entering the city had to stop, have its paperwork checked, and get the once-over from a bomb-sniffing dog, right? Now let's admit it, there are ways to beat the dogs, but combining the dogs with the paperwork check is supposed to eliminate truck-bomb threats. That's the theory, right?"

Scott tapped his pen on the table and said, "'Cept the theory didn't work out in practice."

"What if it didn't work because there were two trucks, one stolen and one rented? What if he steals one truck, builds the bomb, conceals the odor with some combination of other scents, then uses the license plates, VIN tags, and paperwork from the legit truck to get the stolen truck through the checkpoints?"

Kenny finished the hypothesis. "He parks the truck, swaps back the stolen plates and VIN tags, leaves in the getaway car he had planted nearby, puts the VIN tag and the plates back on the legit truck, drops it off at the rental place, and walks away scot-free, nobody the wiser."

"Exactly."

"Except," Scott noted, "We checked all the rentals for a couple hundred miles in every direction. Even the renters who were about the same height and build as the guy we caught on tape had verifiable alibis. They were seen moving this or that from here or there."

Doc leaned on the table. "But that doesn't mean they didn't make two runs. And we checked for duplicate trucks, but not for duplicate ID on the drivers." He turned to Ed Bridges. "Check all the truck rental places we looked before. Run the driver's license photos of every renter against all driver's licenses nationwide."

"You think we'll find the same face on more than one license?"

"And probably under several different names. How long you think that'll take?"

Ed thought for a minute, mumbled something about, "two hundred million licenses...two simultaneous searches," and finally announced, "Not sure. The key is how quickly we find the first match. Once we've got that, we can drop all the other renters out of the search group and just concentrate on more matches to that one face."

"Get on it." As Bridges turned to leave, Doc added, "Keep the circle tight." Bridges nodded. Enthusiasm and lust for the kill could cause even veteran agents to make unguarded comments, and after all these months, nobody wanted anything about Paine's possible identity to leak out prematurely.

Bridges could have raced to Doc's office as soon as the first match came up, but instead he did what Doc expected: finish the search and pull together background on all the matches. When Bridges announced that he had something, Doc gave those who were leading stakeout teams an hour to get back to the office for show-and-tell in the Control Room.

Once everyone settled in Bridges put up eight driver's licenses around the perimeter of the main video screen. "As you can see, we have one face with eight different identities, eight driver's licenses under eight different names in eight different states. They have different hair and eye colors -- which could be dye jobs and contacts -- and different birthdays, but the same face and height/weight dimensions. The men all have something else in common." Ed paused for effect. "They're all officially dead."

Doc flashed back to the feeling he'd had for months that he was chasing a ghost. "So how dead is officially dead?"

"Social Security has them down as deceased, and so does the IRS. The heirs or estates of four of them have already filed final tax returns and the IRS has closed out those files. The other four are pending final IRS disposition. Now here's where it gets interesting: one license was issued four years ago in Oregon. The other seven were all issued in the last year, and involved a lost license from a different state."

Kenny interrupted. "So in seven of these eight cases somebody walked into a DMV office, said 'Hey, I moved here from such-and-such, lost my old license, yada-yada-yada, gimme a new one'?"

"Basically. But there's more. It just so happens that the VA shows the same person with the Oregon license from four years ago as still alive and eligible for VA medical care." Bridges put one license at center screen. "Victor Nolan Truex. DOB 06-04-49. Five feet-ten-and-a-half inches tall, one hundred and seventy-five pounds, brown hair, blue eyes. I requested his service file from DOD. Guess what? It's classified. All they would tell me is that he was honorably discharged on 4 August 1972."

Doc turned to Kenny. "Classified? Still? What the fuck?"

"Could be he was involved with something outside normal channels, like the CIA Phoenix program. Maybe military intelligence, or some off the books Special Ops shit in Cambodia or Laos."

"The CIA?" Scott tossed his pen on the table. "Hey, maybe he knows who killed Kennedy."

Doc smirked and wheeled his chair around toward Grace. "Call the Under Secretary of Defense for Anti-Terrorism. Tell him to notify the Army Records Depository in Maryland that I'm sending an agent to pick up a copy of this guy's full, un-redacted file, and I don't want him coming back empty-handed."

Grace nodded and immediately left to get that ball rolling.

Doc turned back to Ed Bridges. "So, to recap, this guy Truex faked his own death?"

"Not necessarily faked, more likely just reported."

"Reported?"

"Yeah. I did a little checking. Seems the Social Security Administration has an incurably bad habit of listing people as dead who aren't. Happens over ten thousand times a year. Mostly simple input errors. Some schmuck transposes two numbers or spells 'Frances' with an "i" instead of an "e" and, presto, someone alive and kicking becomes bureaucratically dead. That info then goes to the IRS. Lately there's been another twist. Seems death certificates are expensive. With the economy in the dumpster, instead of getting a whole bunch of certified copies at $15, $20, $25 a pop, folks are getting one certificate and running off color copies. Technically, Social Security and other government agencies aren't supposed to accept death certificates without the official state or county clerk's embossed seal, but in real life, well, we all know how that goes."

Kelli leaned forward and asked, "So, somebody gets a legitimate death certificate, scans it into their computer, and then just swaps their name, address, and other info, and that's it, they go off the grid?"

"It's not quite *that* simple. You'd need to learn to use an airbrush tool well enough to airbrush out the original data -- name, description, and so forth. Then you'd have to re-enter the new info in the right typeface. It would take time and practice. It's not something you could master overnight."

"But not something that would stop somebody who is determined to wage war on the United States government."

Bridges shrugged and nodded.

Scott broke into a broad grin. "Ain't technology wonderful?"

Doc shot him a look of mock reproach and then announced, "Okay, let's find out everything we can about this guy, especially things that might tell us where he is. Don't mention his name any more than you absolutely have to. Otherwise identify him only as Suspect One. Let me know if you find anything that requires immediate action. Otherwise, all reports go through Grace."

The key members of Bravo reassembled in the conference room again just before seven that night to bring each other up to speed. Doc had Dr. Herren from Behavioral Sciences sit in as well. Doc asked, "Okay, what do we know now that we didn't know this morning?"

Scott started the briefing. "Victor Truex was born at St. Vincent's Hospital, Portland, Oregon. Only child of Eugene and Edna Truex. Father was a welder. Mother taught school, later became a secretary. Straight arrow, blue collar, Catholic family. Lifelong registered Democrats, with no known affiliations or connections to any leftist or commie groups. Paid their taxes, voted in every election, probably mowed the grass every other Sunday. Our boy Victor went to Sacred Heart elementary and St. Ignatius High. Played football and ran track. Chief Justice of the Student Court his senior year. Graduated fifth in a class of two-hundred-and-two students, then got a BS in aeronautical engineering from the University of Washington."

"Aeronautical engineering? That explains the model airplane bombs."

"Explains more than that. In engineering school, you take one semester of every other engineering discipline besides your specialty. In his case, that means one semester chemical engineering, one electrical, one mechanical, one structural."

"Perfect training for the well-rounded terrorist of tomorrow."

"Exactly." Scott glanced back at his notes to pick up where he left off. "While at UW young Victor enrolled in ROTC, and also got his fixed wing pilot's license."

Kenny flipped open a thick, dark brown military service folder and took over the briefing. "After college Truex reported for duty at Fort Rucker, Alabama, where he was commissioned a Lieutenant 2nd Grade and graduated first in his class from helicopter flight school. He spent six months in 'Nam, then came back for three months of advanced training at the Special Operations School at Fort Benning, Georgia." Kenny paused for a moment, "Now, get this: he returned to 'Nam as part of the Ghost Riders, a unit that ferried Special Ops teams, CIA Phoenix program guys, Recondo units, and so forth deep into enemy territory. Also flew White Star missions to rescue fliers down behind enemy lines. Survived being shot down twice, including once where it took him and the Ops team six days to make it back to one of our forward fire bases. Finally separated out as a Captain with a Purple Heart, a Bronze Star, and a Distinguished Flying Cross. Went to civilian flight school, got certified for all ratings on multi-engine craft, and became a pilot for...wait for it...BlueStar Airlines."

Everyone immediately flashed back to the assassination of former BlueStar CEO Tim Brantley and CFO Aaron Goodman in Michigan.

Doc was not happy. "But when we ran former employees of BlueStar against our suspect base, he didn't show up because he was, quote, officially, unquote, dead. Just great. Just fuckin' great." Doc let out a deep breath. "So what else?"

That was Kelli's cue. "Two years after joining BlueStar, Truex married a stewardess named Lori Lynn Rossmore. Two kids, Michael, a mid-level district exec with a big box office supply store, lives in Torrance, California. Daughter Leslie married Kyle Morrison, a financial manager for a plastics manufacturing company. She's a stay-at-home soccer mom. They live in Fountain Valley."

Gretchen raised her pen and caught Kelli's attention. "The California connection makes sense. Torrance is only a few miles from the old Hawthorne Mall where we found Paine's first remote computer setup. Fountain Valley is not very far from the Brea redevelopment project where we found one of those remote calling devices, and it's relatively close to Anaheim Hills where that bomb took out what's his name, the ex-VA guy...John Ronda. If Truex spent much time visiting his grandkids, he could have easily become familiar with these areas."

Doc scanned the group. "Anything to suggest that the family is involved?"

"Not so far," answered Scott. "No travel or communication patterns tied to any of the attacks, no suspicious website visits. Michael and his wife are registered Democrats. Mr. Morrison is registered as 'Declined to State' and his wife as a member of the Green Party."

Grace laughed. "The Green Party? In the OC? That's hard-core conservative turf. Mrs. Morrison better watch out or she'll get drummed right out of the soccer van pool."

"What about his wife?"

Bridges answered that one. "Be pretty hard for her to be involved, seeing as she's dead. Really, truly dead. Killed in a traffic accident two years ago. Car went off a cliff along the Oregon coast. Got a copy of the autopsy, state death certificate, insurance claims. It's all legit."

Things were finally starting to fall into place, but Doc still had plenty of questions. "Okay, so far, so good. Now, a) do we have any idea where Paine is; b) do we know how he's financing his operations; and c) does anything link him to Spooky?"

Kenny addressed the last question first. "So far, no crossed paths or common links that we know of. Doesn't mean there aren't any, just maybe we haven't found them yet."

Bridges said, "We may have something on financing. I had our techs scan surveillance tapes from unsolved bank and credit union holdups over the past two years committed by white males of the same approximate height, weight, and age. Many, of course, wore sunglasses, fake beards, etc., but we've already isolated three bank robberies where the perp is a solid preliminary match for Truex. One each in Oklahoma, Nebraska, and Tennessee. I'm betting we'll find more before we're done. He also collected on his wife's life insurance policy -- not much, $60K -- but cleared a cool $528,000 after taxes on the sale of their house."

Doc tossed the math around in his head: *The insurance and house sale finance a new home somewhere else and a normal retirement life, so the kid's don't suspect a thing. The bank robbery loot finances his terrorism hobby.* "Any idea where he moved to?"

"We traced numerous calls from his kids to a cell number in Boulder, Colorado. The billing address is a private mailbox, but through cell site tracking we've narrowed down the general area. We're running database checks but so far no record of any house or condo on the tax rolls in his name or any of his aliases. We're checking the credit bureaus to see if anyone ran a credit check on him as part of a rental application."

"Check for properties registered under the name of a trust or a corporation."

Bridges nodded and scribbled a reminder on a Post-It note.

Doc put his hands on the table and said, "Good work, everybody. Go home and get some rest. You've earned it."

"What he means," Scott teased, "Is that you're gonna need it."

As everyone stood up, Doc motioned to Kelli to stay. Dr. Herren also hung back to examine Lori Truex' autopsy file. Doc asked Kelli how things were going on the Spooky investigation. She assured him the probe was expanding and they were putting pieces together right and left.

When Kelli left Doc asked Herren, "You got something for me?"

The Professor nodded and showed Doc the autopsy file, "Page two, down at the bottom, under Additional Unrelated Findings."

"Stage Four cervical cancer, metastasized to the liver and the pancreas?"

"I'd say you've found Mr. Paine's motivation."

Doc was annoyed that the Professor still referred to Truex by his *nom de guerre*, but skipped directly to the most likely scenario. "Okay, let's see: BlueStar goes belly up, takes its health care plan down with it. Vic, he's past mandatory retirement age for commercial pilots, but he's still got the VA. Wife's a different story. She loses her medical coverage just when she needs it the most. Maybe she even delays going to the doctor until things are too far along. Now the choice is spend everything they have, everything they've planned to live on in retirement or leave to their kids, in an attempt -- probably futile -- to extend her life. Or she can go out on her own, before things get too rough. Think that's how it went?"

"It's certainly a plausible scenario."

"You think he was in on it?"

"Her death? No," Herren replied. "I think that particular morning she probably kissed him goodbye, told him she was going to visit a friend, and then drove off that cliff on one last flight. With a big crash landing." Herren thought for a moment, then added, "Maybe she did it to save him from himself. If he's robbed banks to finance his terrorist crusade, certainly the idea of doing so to pay for her care must have crossed his mind. He wouldn't necessarily have even had to say anything. Sometimes wives really do have extra sensory perception."

Chapter 49: Dragnet

Doc sat down with Kenny to discuss his next move. There was no question that Doc had to inform Director Bartholomew that they now had a strong lead on Paine's true identity. There was also no question that the Director would have to advise everyone up the line, all the way to the President himself. The issue became: what was the best tactical use of the new information? Doc had to figure out the right action to recommend, get the Director to sign on to that strategy, and then get the White House to cooperate.

The choices were simple, and each had advantages. Plan A was an ambush strategy: stake out the homes of his son and daughter, identify and track his cellphone, locate his new home or current safe house location, then swoop in the first time he shows up. Plan B was hold a press conference, plaster his picture all over the news, and enlist the help of the public. Doc and Kenny strongly favored Plan A, but Director Bartholomew would only agree to present both options to the White House and let President Welch make the call.

Although Plan A was clearly the best in terms of public safety, and presented the greatest opportunity to take down Truex without deadly fireworks, for purely political reasons Welch went with Plan B. The President was certain that the manhunt announcement would be a huge psychological blow to the Manifesto Party, would push the demonstrations and martial law out of the headlines, and would mobilize the public. With a $10 million reward on his head and his picture everywhere, Truex would have nowhere to run or hide.

Thomas Paine had tormented Welch and put a permanent stain on the President's place in history. Now the President took pleasure in personally making the announcement of Paine's true identity. Welch's heart warmed with the knowledge that *we know who you are. We're gonna catch you, and then we're gonna kill you, you cocksucking terrorist bastard.*

Director Bartholomew got the press conference delayed long enough for agents to place all members of Truex' family in protective custody. Ed Bridges' research team also finally identified Truex' new home address on the outskirts of Boulder. Just as Doc suspected, it was recorded in the name of a trust. Boulder police SWAT and an FBI bomb squad received the okay to enter, defuse any explosive devices, and secure the premises.

Paine missed the press conference. At the time he was blissfully cruising Interstate 70 in Kansas headed toward his safe house outside Pittsburgh. With Ellis Brown in jail and the Manifesto Party banned, it was time to reassume the mantle of leadership. On long drives Paine often listened to local talk radio, trying to get a sense of what callers thought about the state of the country. This time, however, he was in the mood for music. Brooks & Dunn. Jackson Browne. Bob Seger. On old CD's.

Midway between Hays and Salina he pulled into a rest stop. Several vans and campers were clustered together at the far end, part of the great homeless plague afflicting the nation. Parked sideways across the back of the lot was a semi. Lettering on the door said Danielson Trucking, and under that, Evansville, Indiana. Just below the window was the name *Gordy* in a nice, flowing script.

Gordy Danielson was washing his hands when Paine entered the men's room. Unlike Paine, Danielson had watched the President's press conference over lunch at a truck stop cafe. With the photo from the press conference still fresh in his mind, Gordy was positive that the man at the urinal was Victor Truex.

Paine emerged from the men's room to find Gordy leaning

against the fender of his Blazer. His first thought was that maybe the trucker was gay, cruising the rest stop.

"You've got a problem," Gordy announced.

"I do?" answered Paine, warily.

"If you're Victor Truex, you do."

The sound of his real name hit Paine like a sledgehammer, but he fought the urge to show any reaction. "Victor who? Never heard of the guy."

"That's interesting, since an hour ago, the *en*-tire world has heard of Victor Truex. The President went on the tee-vee, sayin' this Truex fella is The Crusader, aka -- that means also known as -- Tom Paine. And if you ain't him, you're sure as hell his *eye*-dentical twin, so either way, you've got a problem. In fact, seein' as there's a ten million dollar bounty on your head -- dead or alive -- I'd allow that what you got is prolly the biggest problem I've ever seen."

"And the solution you've got in mind leaves you rich and retired?"

"Me? Hell, no. I don't mind workin', bein' out on the open road. And I certainly ain't one for blood money." Gordy stood up straight. "What I suggest is, first we gotta get you off the highway, out of the public eye before other folks recognize you."

Paine didn't know what to think. *Was this guy genuine, or was this a scam to get him someplace where he could be safely subdued and turned in for the reward?* Paine, who always traveled unarmed except when en route to a specific mission, didn't have a gun with him. The trucker appeared to be about the same age, but was a good four inches taller, thirty solid pounds heavier, had a Marine Corp tattoo on one forearm, and just generally looked like he could still handle himself pretty well. The trucker was also definitely right about one thing: Paine had to get out of the public eye while he considered his options. "So, what's the plan?"

"Well," Gordy said, nodding south along the turn-off road,

"I've been stoppin' here off-and-on for the better part of twenty years and I don't believe I've ever seen any sign of that old gray barn bein' in use. If'n the door still works, I figure we stash this SUV and I'll give you a ride as far as I can."

"How far is that?"

"How far you headed?"

"Buffalo." *No sense letting this trucker know too much too soon.*

"Well, I can take you to Evansville. Prolly can find somebody else to take you on a piece further from there."

Gordy led the way down a back road to the old gray barn. The door was a struggle but they muscled it open far enough to pull in the Blazer. Paine grabbed a large gym bag out of the back, then they manhandled the barn door closed again. Paine climbed into the truck and settled on the sleeper couch in the spacious compartment behind the cab.

"Welcome aboard. If you wanna catch up on your fame and notoriety, just flip on the radio back there. The only stations not talkin' 'bout you are the ones that play gospel music."

Sure enough, every station Paine turned to was all over the Victor Truex story. They had all his aliases along with the license numbers and descriptions of his work cars registered under those names. The Feds had already discovered and raided two of his safe houses. It felt strange to hear himself referred to in the media by his real name. Over the past year he had come to think of himself as Tom Paine, and except around his family he'd felt like his old identity was really dead.

The trucker must have been reading his mind because he said, "I'm Gordy. What you prefer bein' called? Victor? Vic? Tom? Mr. Paine?"

He thought about it for a moment. "Tom." The government could chase Victor Truex, but he as going to continue to live as long as he could as Thomas Paine.

After about ninety minutes the news accounts became repetitive and Paine switched off the radio. Up in the cab, Gordy tooled down the highway at a steady pace listening to an iPod. When they reached Gordy's destination in St. Louis, he pulled the curtain behind the cab closed. Paine sat quietly while Gordy unhitched the trailer and had his paperwork signed by the dock master.

By the time they passed the outskirts of St. Louis it was dark enough for Paine to move up into the cab. He was so accustomed to driving long stretches by himself that despite the dire circumstances it felt strangely comforting to watch the faint scenery go by on the fringes of the truck's powerful headlights. *America may not be the country it once was, but even at night it's still a beautiful sight to behold.* It also occurred to him that this might be the last time he'd get to see any wide-open spaces. Gordy hadn't said much the entire ride. It felt strange. *Shouldn't he have a million questions?* "You always this quiet?"

"Me? Hell, no. I can talk your ear off. Just figured you needed time to think, plan out your next move." He paused, then added, "So, you got some super-duper escape kit in that bag of yours?"

"I wish."

"You mean to tell me, you turned the powers-that-be inside out with all those perfectly planned attacks, but didn't have an escape plan all set up if'n you had to go on the lam?"

"Had plenty of contingency plans. Just never figured to be in quite this situation." It was true. Paine always thought the odds were greatest that the Feds would show up at his door in Boulder, surround him in one of his safe houses, or catch him in the process of an attack. He never considered that he'd be caught out in the open without weapons, supplies, or effective transport.

"Guess you're just not the criminal type."

"And what type are you, Gordy? You coulda just drove on, left me on my own."

"I'm German on my mother's side. Germans have a word, flict. Doesn't really translate to English. Means a situation where an opportunity creates an obligation. In this particular situation, the opportunity to help created the obligation to help."

"I'm sorry, I still don't understand."

"Democracy, man. They told me I was fightin' for it over in 'Nam. But somehow I ain't seen much of it in the last thirty years or so. Not 'til you come along, anyway. Let's just say that you've raised the level of concern for the democratic process and the wellbein' of the common man."

Paine was surprised by Gordy's eloquence. "You wax awfully philosophical for a truck driver."

"That's because I read."

"You read?"

"Yeah. Always take a book with me on the road. If I have to wait for a load that ain't ready, or for a warehouse crew to unload, instead of muchin' donuts and jackin' my cholesterol up another notch I read. Or I listen to a book on tape. Sometimes my wife dictates a book and I play it back. Helps give us something more in common, you know, strengthen the marriage bond."

"Impressive."

"Hell, you wanna be impressed, I even graduated college. Just can't stand the bullshit-and-tie world."

Paine chuckled. He never ceased to be amazed at how uncommon so many everyday Americans were. "So, Gordy, where are we headed?"

"My ex-girlfriend's house."

"From before you were married."

"Well, not exactly."

"Oh, from back before you decided to strengthen those marriage bonds."

"Yeah. Before that."

Annette Duckett lived in a well-maintained white clapboard one-story house set well back from the road on the outskirts of Evansville. Gordy parked midway down the long gravel driveway.

"You sure I can stay here?" asked Paine.

"No, but I'm hopeful. And it ain't like we got a lotta other options."

Paine watched as Gordy walked up to the house and knocked on the door. A moment later Annette stepped out on the porch. She looked surprised to see Gordy. A short question-and-answer session ensued. Annette asked and Gordy answered. Finally Annette nodded her assent.

As Paine got closer to the porch, he saw that Annette was more than a little attractive. In fact, she was downright hot. Older Hollywood star hot, like a Sela Ward or a Heather Locklear. Paine didn't know how much Annette weighed in high school, but was willing to bet she hadn't put on many pounds since. He wondered what a woman like her was doing in place like Evansville. It had been a long time since he's felt the stirrings of lust, and for it to happen under the present circumstances struck him as strange, even bizarre. *Last wish of a condemned man?*

Gordy handled the introductions.

Annette said, "Hello, Tom. Come in. You're just in time for supper." Then she turned to Gordy. "Now run along, before you get all of us in real trouble."

Paine couldn't tell if she meant trouble with the law, or with Gordy's wife. *Probably both.*

Annette followed Paine into the house, locked the door, and closed the blinds. "Make your self at home," she said as she continued into the kitchen, where she retrieved some pork chops from the freezer and stuck them in the microwave to defrost. "You want a beer?" she called out.

"Thanks, that would be great."

Annette returned to the living room with a bottle of Bud Light and said, "We're having pork chops with apple sauce and green beans. If that's not good enough, your other options are a peanut butter-and-jelly sandwich or a Lean Cuisine."

"Ms. Duckett --"

"Annette."

"Okay, Annette, I've already eaten a lifetime supply of Lean Cuisines, so I'm very much looking forward to those pork chops." He gestured around the living room. "If you cook half as well as you decorate, it'll be a feast fit for a king."

"Well, I don't know about that. I don't entertain kings much."

"Just wayward truckers?"

"Trucker. Singular. And that was a long time ago."

With that she turned and went back to kitchen, leaving Paine to sip his beer and look around the living room again. He hadn't lied. The place really was decorated with style. "You have a TV?" he called out. "I sorta need to catch up on current events."

"Remote's on the end table. Just point it toward the window and press the button," came the reply from the kitchen.

He did as instructed and a flat screen TV slowly rose from inside a stylish cabinet in front of the big bay window.

Paine watched a rerun of the President's news conference and an up-to-the-minute recap of the story, including remotes from outside the homes of his children. For his family, the worst-case scenario had come to pass. They were now paying the price for his actions. The sins of the father would be visited on them. It pained him to watch the family photo albums and computers removed from the two homes referred to by the media as "possible evidence."

There were also the obligatory vacuous interviews with neighbors. "We had no idea. They seemed like such a normal family." *That's because they are a normal family, you moron.* "The boys are really good athletes." *What does that have to do with anything? They're kids, for Chrissakes.* Paine could only shake his head when reporters breathlessly announced that several firearms had been removed from the homes. As if owning a gun was somehow conclusive evidence of treason or terrorism. The worst part was watching his daughter, Leslie, plead for him to surrender. Her brother Michael was also there but didn't speak. Paine wondered why. *Too mad to say anything? Or too likely to say, "Fuck that, stay on the run, Dad"?*

Paine's kids knew nothing of his activities, so unless the government planted evidence and fabricated a case, eventually they would be exonerated, but whether their lives would ever return to normal was unlikely. Maybe they could sell their story to the media for enough money to make up for the turmoil. Then suddenly his mind switched gears and he wondered how things were now going to change for Crystal Dickerson.

Paine waited patiently until Annette summoned him to the table. He didn't want to just dig in without checking so he asked, "Do you say grace?"

"Do you?"

"No, not usually."

"Me neither. My experience is, most people who bless their food spend the rest of their time damning others for their sins, real or imagined."

Paine didn't know quite how to respond, so he just nodded, and looked down on the feast in front of him. *This is one helluva an interesting woman.* Paine was an okay cook and fixed meals from scratch when he was home but his last good, sit-down meal fixed by a woman was several months back, when he'd last visited his kids. The dinner in front of him looked and smelled great. It tasted even better. The pork chops were cooked all the way through but still soft and juicy, not dried out, and the green beans were fresh from Annette's garden out back. Halfway through eating, Paine asked the big question. "How long can I stay here?"

"Gordy said he'd have you out by the time I get home from work tomorrow. I'll go shop at the mall, have dinner, make it as late as I can. But you need to be gone before I get back."

"So I just wait for someone to show up?"

"Don't answer the front door. Anybody Gordy sends will come around to the kitchen."

Paine nodded. "Your work. What do you do?"

"I'm the head of library services for the city."

That explained the connection with Gordy, the well-read trucker. It also sparked another thought. "So, the fantasy of the sexy librarian isn't entirely a myth."

Annette looked at him for a moment.

Fearing he'd said the wrong thing, Paine apologized. "I'm sorry. I guess librarian jokes get a little old after a while."

Annette paused to chew and swallow another piece of pork chop. "They said on TV that you're a widower."

"Yes."

"That's good. I no longer sleep with married men." She said it with such a deadpan delivery that Paine almost snorted his coffee.

After dinner was over and Paine had helped clear the table, Annette pointed him toward the guest bath, stroked the side of his face, and said, "I can't go to work tomorrow with whisker burns." She waited until Paine was out of the shower to start the dishwasher.

They came face to face again in the hallway when he emerged from the bathroom with a towel wrapped around his waist. They looked at each other for a moment, then shared a soft kiss. "You need to know, I haven't done this in about three years," he said.

"No need to worry. I'm lucky. I climax really easily."

And she did. Again, and again, and again. Paradoxically, that made it easier for him to maintain control. He became invested in seeing how many times she climaxed. And they weren't little ones. The first, produced by his tongue, felt like her thighs were going to break his neck. Each succeeding orgasm was just as strong.

After having endured a long dry spell, Annette felt good having a man inside her. But sex with Paine had an added dimension. She genuinely admired the man and what he had done for the country. She also wondered if she would ever reveal it to her children, maybe much later in life, or in a letter left behind to be read after she was gone.

Finally, after at least a half-dozen orgasms, she encouraged him to "come with me."

He did, with more intensity than he expected. For the next several minutes they laid there, still connected, and every time his cock twitched, she jerked with another spasm.

Just before they went to sleep she set the alarm back a half-hour, to leave time for round two in the morning.

While Tom Paine blew his rocks in Evansville, back in Baltimore Crystal hosted a very unusual show. Every guest and caller wanted to know how she was reacting to the news about Paine's true identity. Could she add anything and did it make any more sense to her now? Her response was mostly, "No, not yet."

The next morning, Annette climaxed three more times, fixed Paine breakfast, kissed him goodbye, and left for work a little before eight. Gordy showed up two hours later at the kitchen door.

When Paine answered the knock, Gordy grinned and said, "For Public Enemy Number One you look mighty rested."

Unwilling to encourage a discussion about the previous night, Paine just shrugged and locked the door behind him.

Once back in the truck, Gordy laid out the plan. "You got anything against wetbacks, greasers?"

"No."

"Good, 'cuz the guy takin' you the next leg was born and raised here but according to the Census Bureau he's still part of the Hiss-panic demographic. Name's Ray Otania. Went to high school with him, served with him in 'Nam. Lucky for you, he's on his way back to Pittsburgh from Memphis and stopped here to visit his folks."

Pittsburgh? Should he take a chance on going to his safe house there, or should he assume that it, like the others, had been compromised and was staked out, crawling with Feds ready to pounce?

"The bad news is, Pittsburgh's as far as we can get you. Don't know anybody that we trust who's headed up to Buffalo from there. The good news is, we know a car you can steal. If'n you don't object to that sort of law breakin', of course."

"Why not? They can only hang me once."

"Tom, they ain't a-gonna hang you. That implies some kind of due process and such. Man, they're a-gonna lynch you. You got about as much chance of going to trial as I do to get religion."

Gordy wasn't telling Paine anything he didn't already know. The likelihood of being murdered while in custody had factored into his decision from the very beginning.

They met up with Ray Otania at a wide spot on a side road east of Evansville. Gordy pulled in facing Otania's White Freightliner, passenger door to passenger door. "Good luck, Tom."

"Thanks. Too bad I never had the chance to meet you."

Gordy grinned and nodded.

It only took seconds for Paine to hop out of Gordy's rig and into Otania's. By the time he settled into the sleeper compartment, Ray had the rig underway. Behind them, Gordy was also headed back toward the highway.

Chapter 50: Ultimatum

Halfway to Pittsburgh Paine asked Ray Otania the same question he'd asked Gordy: "Why are you helping me?"

"Nam," came the reply.

"Nam?"

"Yeah. Didn't Gordy tell you?"

"Just said you guys were over there."

"Said on the news that you were one of the Ghost Riders. You saved our asses a coupla times. Fire Base 12, over in II Corps."

Paine shook his head. *Sometimes, what goes around really does come around.*

"Also said you flew some White Star missions."

"Yeah."

"Really? True shit?"

"True shit."

"Well, if'n you can fly a hunert clicks beyond the DMZ rescuing downed pilots, the least I can do is get you to Pittsburgh."

The White Star missions weren't a hundred kilometers, more like eighty at the most, but Paine wasn't about to argue. The more he thought about it, the more amazed he was. Judas sold out Christ for thirty pieces of silver, yet two truckers and a librarian wouldn't sell him out for $10 million. It made him wonder, *What is the present day inflation-adjusted value of thirty pieces of silver? Evidently, not enough for some people.* Still, there was no denying the irony of his situation: after two years of meticulous planning and totally independent, anonymous operation, now he had no anonymity, was still free only by accidental good fortune, and was completely dependent on the grace of others for temporary help that did nothing to solve his permanent problems.

It was nine p.m. when Otania turned off the interstate into an older, blue-collar residential neighborhood on the outskirts of Pittsburgh. Peeking out the sleeper compartment window, Paine noticed that about half the houses were dark, with no lights on and no cars in the driveways. *Probably vacant. The economic downturn at work.*

Otania pulled over to the curb at an intersection and pointed down the cross street. "Fourth house on the left. Gray with a red door and white trim. Go around back, break in through the kitchen. You'll find a set of keys in a dish on the kitchen table. In the garage there's a Dodge Ram pickup. Guy what owns it is off on a long haul, won't be back for three days. Be sure to close the garage door after you leave. Neighbors see it open they'll know he's been ripped off and call the cops."

"Think he cares what happens to the truck?"

"He's three months behind on the payments."

"So if it disappears and the insurance pays off he'd be happy."

"Expect so."

"Thanks." Paine grabbed his gym bag. "And don't forget to wipe my fingerprints off."

"Wipe your fingerprints off? Hell, I'm gonna stick a fire hose in here."

Paine chuckled, slipped out of the cab, and started down the dark street, the silence broken only by the sound of Otania's truck lumbering off into the night.

Paine decided to hide out and wait until the following night before hitting the road again. He needed time to think. He broke a small pane of glass in the back door, found the keys with no problem, grabbed a few snacks, and let himself into the garage through the side door. On a shelf filled with camping gear he found a musty sleeping bag that he laid out on the floor behind the truck where it would be shielded from sight. Within minutes he drifted off into a fitful sleep. A sleeping bag on a cold hard floor didn't come close to a nice warm bed with the sexy Annette Duckett.

Paine spent the next day going over his options again, as he had ever since Gordy approached him at the rest stop. Everything boiled down to *What's best for the movement? What advances the cause the most, or sets it back the least?* He could try fleeing, but where? Just because a country didn't have to extradite him didn't mean it wouldn't. Enormous diplomatic and economic pressure would certainly be brought to bear. Not to mention the probability of a drone missile strike on wherever he was hiding.

He considered the pros and cons of suicide, but what purpose would that serve? Many would consider it cowardly. None of the Founding Fathers had off'd themselves. *What about a Kamikaze mission, going out in a blaze of glory?* Intriguing, but impractical. He had to assume that all of his safe houses were compromised, which meant that he had no weapons or resources. He also couldn't think of any great, worthy, game-changing target, and even if there was one, with his face splashed all over the news 24/7 the possibility of getting close enough to it was zero.

Or maybe there was one final mission he could pull off. One that might advance the cause on many fronts.

Paine's trip from Pittsburgh to Baltimore took four-and-a-half hours. He drove carefully, not too slow but not too fast. Either one might invite unwanted scrutiny by a state trooper. He'd gained lots of practice at this type of controlled driving on his way to various missions, but unlike those occasions, this time fake I.D. would be of no help, and he couldn't shoot his way out of trouble. If a cop tried to pull him over, his only options would be surrender, or one of those futile chases that ends up on Amazing Police Videos.

The Dodge Ram pickup had a comfortably throaty rumble,

but the tank was only half-full. Fortunately, before embarking on his crusade Paine had stashed hundreds of gallons of gas along highways and back roads all across the country. The sites varied from abandoned barns and under rusting hulks of old farm machinery along rural side roads to derelict buildings in decaying metropolitan areas and thick brush near highway rest stops. The ability to refuel without coming under the scrutiny of security cameras had played a key role in avoiding DAS identification when the FBI cross-referenced footage from gas stations around different attack sites. On this trip he refilled from a cache outside Frederick, Maryland. Just after four a.m. Paine reached his destination, an abandoned industrial building in a section of Baltimore. He made himself as comfortable as possible in the back seat and dozed off. He had eight hours to kill.

Crystal and her staff had just started the daily noon production meeting when Melody Ganz burst into the conference room, ordered everyone else out, and told Crystal, "Line 5. Put it on the speakerphone."

Crystal did as she was instructed.

"Hi, Crystal, this is Victor Truex. I'm willing to surrender to you tonight." He paused a moment. "Under certain conditions."

Twenty minutes later Doc and Director Bartholomew arrived at the White House to brief President Welch and his key advisors including Attorney General Godfrey, White House Chief of Staff Zak Wooten, Department of Homeland Security Secretary Hoover, Treasury Secretary Gesner, and Secretary of Defense Don Blaney.

Doc related Paine's five demands. "One, the designation of the Manifesto Party as a terrorist group must be rescinded and all of its leaders released from jail. Two, he'll surrender only to Ellis Brown. Three, Brown escorts him to WHYY where a government representative will give Brown a check made out to the Manifesto

Party for the $10 million reward. Fourth, he will be allowed to appear live and uncensored for the full two hours of Dickerson's show. Fifth, he wants you, Mr. President, to personally announce acceptance of these terms."

Presidents never liked being on the receiving end of an ultimatum, and they really didn't like being given a three-hour deadline.

"That arrogant prick," muttered Wooten.

"And if I refuse?" The President asked.

"He sets off an unspecified number of explosive devices at locations around the country that will cause massive civilian casualties."

"What's to stop us from grabbing him when he gets to the station, before he set off the devices?" asked DHS Secretary Hoover.

At times like these Doc marveled at how dumb Hoover really was. "Passive detonation," he answered. "Devices on timers or set to go off if inadvertently triggered by a third party. Some teacher opens up the wrong drawer in her desk and blows up a classroom full of kids, that sort of thing."

"Is that what he's threatening, to blow up schools?" asked the President.

"Not specifically, but the term innocent civilians is telling."

"Isn't this the guy who took great pains to minimize collateral damage?"

"The situation's changed. His entire game plan was to escape identification. Now that's out the window and he's a cornered animal with no good choices."

Director Bartholomew added his two cents. "We should also consider the possibility that going on live TV for two hours is his definition of a blaze of glory, and makes surrender worthwhile."

"So, Agent Medlin, what do you suggest?" asked the President.

"I think we have to look at this from the perspective of

capability. If Truex has taught us anything it's that he's versatile and highly skilled. He's killed with sniper shots, static pre-planted IEDs, target-specific vehicle bombs, truck bombs, even small aerial bombs. He's shown the ability to execute nearly simultaneous attacks on opposite sides of the country. Hell, we still don't know how he killed Senator Stowe and Admiral Copeland. He's also managed to stay one step ahead of our wiretapping and electronic trace technology. And the wild card in the equation is that he's a skilled pilot in both fixed wing aircraft and helicopters. Purely from an operational standpoint, I have no doubt that he can do what he's threatened to do."

Director Bartholomew added, "With his demonstrated ability to plan ahead, we have to consider that he may have game-planned this scenario a long time ago and put things in place, ready to go if necessary."

Doc nodded his assent and then continued. "That brings us to the second question: will he follow through on the threat? On the one hand, he's a serial killer. But given his prior aversion to mass casualties, this could just be a bluff. But what if it isn't? Let's say you refuse his offer and he starts blowing up schools, movie theaters, churches, whatever. What kind of blowback are you going to get?"

Bartholomew then added that given the huge pool of potential targets, there was no way that law enforcement officials, public agencies, and private security companies could conduct effective searches before Paine's deadline. "If you believe that he's willing to make good on his threats, then you must be prepared to accept that there will be lots and lots of casualties."

Secretary of Defense Blaney concurred. "There are just too many potential targets. It isn't a question of performing physical eyeball searches. You have to know what you're looking for; you need bombing detection devices or bomb-sniffing dogs. You need people who know how to inspect suspicious items without setting off an anti-tampering trigger."

The President looked around the table. "Thank you,

gentlemen." As everyone started to leave, Welch asked Godfrey to stick around for a minute.

Forty minutes before Paine's deadline, Welch addressed the media in the White House Briefing Room. "Today terrorist Victor Truex offered to surrender to Crystal Dickerson, a talk show host in Baltimore."

A murmur swept the room.

"His surrender is contingent on the government meeting certain conditions, one of which is that the government rescind the designation of the Manifesto Party as a terrorist organization and release its leaders from custody. Mr. Truex also demanded that he be allowed to appear on Dickerson's show."

A stunned hush fell over the room. *Was the President really going to agree to this?*

"If these conditions are not met, Mr. Truex has vowed to set off what he claims are numerous explosive devices planted in locations where they will cause hundreds, perhaps thousands, of civilian casualties. Therefore, as distasteful as it is to me personally -- and as I'm sure it is to most Americans -- based on his proven ability to carry out attacks, for the safety of my fellow Americans I agree to those terms."

The room erupted in a sea of waving hands and calls of "Mr. President."

Welch motioned for everyone to settle down. "I also want to make clear that we have no evidence to suggest that either Mr. Brown or any other leaders of the Manifesto Party have any previous connection to, or involvement with, Mr. Truex or any of his acts of terrorism."

Doc was too busy coordinating surrender logistics to watch Welch's press conference. There were five hours between the President's announcement and the start of Crystal's show. Allowing for the time necessary to rendezvous with Brown and get back to the studio, Truex must be somewhere within two hours of Baltimore. It was imperative that local law enforcement agencies within that radius issued stand-down orders. The last thing Doc needed was for some ambitious street cop to recognize Paine and attempt to take him into custody. Actually, that was the second worst thing that could happen. The worst would be Paine ending up dead or in a coma from a wreck caused by some teenager texting their BFF.

There was also the problem of Ellis Brown, who was as surprised as anyone by the turn of events. Brown had only agreed to participate if Welch exonerated the Manifesto party of any involvement with Paine's vigilante violence. But Brown still had to be transported from his place of custody to WHHY in time to get word from Paine about where to pick him up.

Last, Doc had to handle Crystal, who was adamant about not having anything to do with any kind of government double-cross. She didn't want to be a party to anything that might cause Paine to blow things up, and threatened not to do the show. In the end, their long attraction to each other made the difference. She didn't think Doc could lie to her, not face-to-face. It was only after he looked directly into her eyes, swore that he knew of no plans to double cross Paine, and would not participate in any such plan, that she finally agreed to go along. Doc could see her point, but also thought she was having a big league case of stage fright. The enormity of what was about to happen was scary. He didn't blame her. He was as nervous as a cat in a room full of rocking chairs.

Two hours after Welch's press conference, Paine called WHYY and left instructions for Brown to pick him up at the southeast corner of the White Marsh Mall. Paine then drove to a deserted section along the banks of Back River Bay where he wedged a pebble in the truck's carburetor linkage, threw the shift lever into drive, and jumped back as the truck sailed off into the murky water. With the windows down to hasten sinking, in less than a minute there was nothing left except a few bubbles and gentle, dissipating ripples. From the time it took for the waters to settle the truck was at least fifteen feet underwater, where it would likely remain for many years, if not forever. For a moment Paine wondered which insurance company would have to pay off on it.

Paine then walked to the intersection where Pulaski Highway crossed Interstate 695 and called a cab to take him the rest of the way to the White Marsh Mall. He hoped his baseball cap and sunglasses would be sufficient to escape recognition long enough to make his rendezvous with Brown.

While Doc prepared for Paine's surrender, Kelli's surveillance team watched another drama play out. Normally, Tony Gilman left his office only for lunch. Today, however, he suddenly hustled out to his car and took off. Twenty-five minutes later he parked on a residential side street, slipped down an alley, and ducked through a back gate. Kelli ran the address and gasped when she saw that it was the home of Attorney General Joe Godfrey. She immediately called Doc on an encrypted phone. He dispatched additional agents to reinforce her surveillance team.

Gilman stayed for about forty minutes, then left the same way he came. Half of Kelli's newly expanded team under Ed Obrador remained behind to keep tabs on Godfrey while she and the other half stayed with Gilman.

Chapter 51: Primetime

Brown was nervous about picking up Paine and delivering him to WHYY. He wasn't sure how much stock the public would put in Welch's pronouncement that the Manifesto Party was not linked to Paine by anything other than its support of the Manifesto Amendments. Beyond that, it wasn't everyday that a private citizen was asked to assist in the surrender of perhaps the greatest murderer in American history.

Paine was sitting in the shade on the southeast corner of the White Marsh Mall, right where he'd said he'd be. For a moment the two men measured each other. Finally Paine walked around to the passenger's side of Brown's rented Chevy Impala and dropped his gym bag on the back seat.

"Mind if I have a look?" Brown asked.

Paine unzipped the bag and pulled it wide open.

Brown ruffled through it, finding only a few clothes, a toiletries bag, and a couple of cell phones. No guns, no bombs, no canisters of poison gas.

Paine climbed in the front seat. "I need you to do me a favor. Here's five hundred dollars. Buy me a decent suit, a white shirt and tie, some dress shoes." Paine handed over a note with his sizes and color preferences.

For Brown it was almost surreal. "So, what, now I'm your personal shopper?"

"Hey, it pays well. You gotta do something for your ten million."

Brown chuckled. *He has a point.*

A half hour later Brown emerged from the mall, hung a suit in the back seat, and handed Paine two shopping bags containing a white dress shirt, a nice blue-gray-and-red striped tie, and a pair of black loafers. Paine changed in the car on the way to WHYY. Dressed up he looked like any normal businessman.

"Goin' off to jail in style, like John Gotti, I see," said Brown.

"Just making sure they have something decent to bury me in."

On Doc's order, all spectators and media were kept well away from WHHY. Scott was ready and waiting in the parking lot. While he frisked Paine, other agents checked Paine's bag, the trunk and engine compartment of the car, and the underside using mirrors. Satisfied that there were no dangerous devices, Paine was led inside, where he and Brown were separated.

After thanking Brown for his cooperation, Doc and Kenny went into the conference room to meet Paine face-to-face for the first time.

"Ah, we finally meet. Prey and pursuer."

"Cop and criminal," replied Doc.

"In that case, I prefer fascist and patriot."

"I don't give a rat's ass what you prefer," Doc said as he stepped forward and performed another, more thorough frisking, checking Paine's collars, the lining and hems of Paine's coat and pants, and his shoes.

When Doc finished, Paine said, "See, nothing. No razor blades, no hat pins, no suicide capsules."

Doc stepped back and sized up Paine. There were so many things he wanted to ask him, about motivation, target selection, and mission execution. For now, all that would have to wait.

Paine announced that he wanted to meet Crystal before the show. "I think that would make both of us more comfortable."

Doc nodded to Kenny, who left and returned moments later with her in tow.

Paine immediately extended his hand. "Ms. Dickerson. Pleased to meet you."

Instinctively, Crystal reached out and shook hands. His handshake was firm but friendly, and he had a slightly rueful, disarming smile, not at all what she'd expected. "Mr. Truex."

"Tom, or Mr. Paine, if you don't mind. Victor Truex died with his wife."

She nodded. Briefed about the circumstances of Lori Truex' death, she now knew that speculation about his motives was true. "I'm sorry for your loss."

Paine nodded and for a fleeing moment another rueful half-smile crossed his face. Then he went right back to business. "Let's discuss how I'd like this to go."

It only took a few minutes for them to agree on the sequence of topics, how much time they'd leave for any listener questions, and other format issues.

In her opening remarks, Crystal admitted that it felt strange seeing Paine sitting calmly across the desk. The country felt the same way. It was bizarre, bordering on the surreal, yet hypnotically compelling to watch possibly the biggest criminal in American history interviewed on live television like a movie star promoting their latest film.

Crystal sensed that Paine's dry, clipped explanation of his wife's death was an emotional defense mechanism. After he recounted his ancestor's role in the Revolutionary War and his decision at Point Pleasant, Crystal asked if Lori would have approved of his actions.

"No, but if we'd had insurance to fight her cancer, none of this would have happened. I don't know if that's a good thing or a bad thing, but it is what it is, and speculation about what might have been serves no purpose." For Paine, it was important not to spend his final minutes as a free man dwelling on a past that felt increasingly distant. How and why things got to where they did was far less important than where they might go from here.

Crystal quickly moved on to the question that most fascinated her: "Why me? Why my show?"

"Your stated philosophy of calling out both parties equally. I wanted to test your sincerity, see if you'd sellout under pressure or temptation. Plus, your voice reminds me of my wife's. So there you have it, rigorous pragmatism married to rank sentimentality."

"And if I had, as you say, sold out, what then? Would I have become a target?"

"You were too well guarded for that. I would have just stopped calling. But you were either smart enough or principled enough not to fold, and it seems to have paid off handsomely."

Crystal looked him straight in the eye and said, "Changing never crossed my mind."

Paine sensed that she was telling the truth.

"And so now that you're here, in person, what do you want to talk about?"

Paine pulled a handwritten outline from his coat pocket and smoothed the pages on the desk. The transcript of his statement read:

> "My parents were always very adamant about the responsibility of every citizen to be informed about issues, to vote, and to support candidates who shared their views. In a democracy, the people are supposed to control the government, and the government is supposed to regulate business for the common good of all. As I looked at the situation the country is in, the lack of real health care reform, the subservience of government to Wall Street, the ability of wealthy individuals and huge corporations to buy politicians, the excessive power of the Military-Industrial-Congressional complex, the shafting of the middle class, the destruction of the social safety net, I realized that we were fast becoming a fascist state, where the roles are

reversed and corporations, not the people, control government.

We have an illusion of democracy, a façade of elected representation, but it's all fake, a charade designed to soothe and deceive the public. We have one corporate party, wearing two masks, one labeled Democrat, the other Republican. But there is no essential difference. Government and business are merging into one giant criminal enterprise. The biggest threat Americans face isn't from other countries or foreign terrorists, it's from our own banks and corporations. The President isn't the President of the United States, he's the President of the United Corporations of America, It's Robin Hood in reverse, stealing from the poor and giving to the rich. It's government of the rich, by the rich, for the rich. The grip these oligarchs have on government grows stronger every day. Pretty soon we will not be able to stop them, no matter how hard we try.

So I asked myself, "'Who's going to do something about this? And I realized the answer was, "When am I going to do something about this?" I once read where a movie producer said that he made the kind of movies he wanted to see. So I asked myself, "What kind of reforms would I like to see? What kind of reforms would bring us back to the kind of democracy my ancestors fought for?" That led me to create the Manifesto Amendments. In doing so I realized that the Constitution isn't just a framework for our government and our society, and it's not just an enumeration of our rights and liberties. The Constitution is a fence, a protective barrier between the people and the predatory tendencies of those with legal or economic power.

But how could I make the amendments a reality? Create another blog, become one more person shouting truth into a howling wind? And then I realized that the establishment -- the elite, the oligarchs or plutocrats, whatever you want to call them -- don't fear words. They commit financial terrorism, economic homicide, and industrial manslaughter without any fear of the law, because they control the government that is supposed to enforce the law. The system is rigged against justice, against reform, against real, meaningful change. Those who benefit from having power never surrender it willingly. The only weapon they fear and understand is violence. It is the one form of power they can't control, co-opt or buy off. They use it against us, so we have to use it against them. Until the insurgency, only good people were dying.

We're told that anger is wrong, that anger is uncivilized, that we need to be polite, as if those on the other side are good people who just have a different opinion. That's not true. They're not good people, they're criminals, enemies of the public. We have to recognize that politicians are what they do, not what they say. We have to stop being seduced by bright smiles and gleaming rhetoric and carefully crafted sound bites. This is a battle of good versus evil, and we need to be angry, to be outraged. We need to hate them as much as they hate us. We have to fight fire with fire."

Crystal asked Paine what he thought his chances were in the beginning, if he believed that his ideas would get as much support as they did.

"To tell the truth, I was skeptical. In the end I just decided that it was either time for real reform or it wasn't, in which case that would be the end of it."

"So if the public hadn't responded, at some point you would have quit?"

"Yes. Governor Brand's decision to back the amendments and Ellis Brown's formation of the Manifesto Party were the turning points. Not sure how long I would have carried on if those two things hadn't happened."

Paine spent the last hour of the show connecting the Industrial Policy section of the Economic Bill of Rights to the amendment requiring universal military service, a no-exemptions draft. "After the civil rights and anti-war protests of the 60's and 70's, the establishment realized that a healthy middle class had too much free time to meddle in the affairs of government and business. At the same time, the Pentagon wanted an all-volunteer army so that future wars would not face widespread public resistance like Vietnam did. You have to remember, the U.S. military has always served the dual purpose of defending us, as in World War II, and as muscle for American businesses. We've used the military and the CIA to insure that our companies have priority access to the natural resources of weaker countries, and in some cases, access to their markets. That's why we have over seven hundred military bases in other countries."

Crystal was incredulous. "Seven hundred foreign military bases?"

"At least. Counting military missions, secret installations, and what the military now calls 'lily pad' bases spread around the world, some experts say the total is closer to one thousand."

"How do the people in those countries feel about our military presence there?"

"It's certainly ironic. We think of the U.S. as a democracy, but many people abroad view the United States as an imperialist empire. We don't actually colonize and tax these countries, but we might as well. The effect is the same."

Paine then returned to the other half of his argument. "Corporations have always wanted to break the labor unions and cut wages. Finally they settled on the myth of globalization and free trade so that they could outsource manufacturing, and later customer service and other support functions, to slave-wage foreign countries. However, some of the jobs lost over here had to be replaced or the economy would completely tank. So, many non-combat functions that had previously been carried out by soldiers were privatized, contracted out to companies like KBR and Halliburton."

Crystal asked, "So not only the troops but also their support personnel became dependent on the military for their livelihood?"

"Exactly. And with globalization slowly cutting back on wages and reducing the number of jobs, more and more people no longer had the time or the economic security it takes to be politically active, or to protest government actions. More importantly," he added, "this paradigm is unsustainable. After decades of shortchanging domestic spending to over-support the military, we now need to spend huge amounts on infrastructure repairs and upgrades. But on the other hand, government simply cannot be the long-term employer of both first and last resort. Both government and business have been looking for an alternate reality that simply doesn't exist. To be economically viable, we have to make things here, both for domestic consumption and export to other countries."

Paine's two-part solution consisted of a return to traditional industrial economic policy and universal military service, where everyone received six months of military training and then served eighteen months, either in a combat unit or performing public service work. Paine argued that an all-volunteer army "is fundamentally immoral because it rests on the premise that the privileged and fortunate don't have to make any contribution to the country that provides them with so many benefits and opportunities. The benefits of citizenship should not be free to some and costly to others simply by accident of circumstance. Two years of service is a small sacrifice given the benefits of being an American. It would also insure that people from all parts of the country and all cultural backgrounds met and interacted with folks from other races, regions, and backgrounds."

According to Paine, universal national service would breed a broad sense of fairness, equality, and shared sacrifice among Americans, not to mention making the military less able to get into risky, misguided, and immoral interventionist wars to benefit corporate interests.

Crystal couldn't help but notice the irony of a terrorist serial killer talking about other people's immorality. She asked Paine if he thought the Manifesto reform movement would eventually succeed.

"That depends. For justice and reform to be achieved, people inside the institutions of government must change. The public can only do so much. At some point, the people who make the institutions function must either change or be replaced. We'll see if that happens."

Paine closed with a statement to his kids: "Three things I have always loved are you, your mother, and my country. After your mother died I had a choice to make. But it wasn't a choice between you and my country; it was a choice to do something for both you and my country, or do nothing for either. I hope you can understand."

The show was two hours of the most extraordinary television ever, the highest-rated, most-watched program in history. It was certain to be the most memorable show of her career, and Crystal didn't quite know how best to sign off. "Normally I thank people for being my guests," she said. "In this case, I guess I should thank you for surrendering."

"There were no good options, so I picked the least worst of the bad ones." He looked at her and said, "Keep the faith. If you don't, no one will."

Doc had to admit that he was impressed by Paine's performance.

The White House had a different view.

Chapter 52: Circle Of Betrayal

Doc and Kenny led Paine directly from the studio into the conference room, where Gretchen waited with a video recorder and a voice stress analyzer.

Doc motioned for Paine to take a seat. "Okay, we kept our end of the bargain, now it's your turn. Give us the details on all the IEDs you've got planted."

Paine smiled and said, "There aren't any. It was all a bluff."

"Why should we believe you?"

"What purpose would it serve to lie? The good I've done in the past, and all of tonight's good PR, would be wiped out. I'd be just another murderous psychopath, no less evil than the government. No value in that." He leaned back in his chair. "The truth is, I was on the road when the shit hit the fan. Didn't have a thing with me. No weapons, no supplies, nothing. With most of my safe houses splashed all over the news I hadda assume the others were compromised as well. An empty threat was the only bargaining chip I had."

Doc believed him, but glanced over at the voice stress analyzer anyway. The light stayed green, indicating that Paine was telling the truth. "Well, I hope you enjoyed yourself. Tonight was your show. From here on, it's my turn. I'm going to enjoy interrogating you and testifying against you at trial."

Paine scoffed. "You haven't got any intention of letting me go to trial. You're not going to let some media-savvy defense attorney keep me in the news for years, attack the evidence or try for jury nullification. I'll be murdered long before that. They'll claim it was suicide or a heart attack."

Doc was indignant. "That's not the way we do things."

Paine suddenly realized that Doc was being truthful and shook his head. "You actually believe your own shit. Man, you're in denial."

Doc and Kenny cuffed Paine's hands behind his back and escorted him toward a side door.

In the parking lot, Doc and Kenny were surprised to see a military green Suburban with dark tinted windows, two military Humvees, and a squad of Marine MPs with M-4 assault rifles and MP-4 submachine guns. The officer in command, Colonel Keslowski, stepped forward and handed Doc an Executive Order signed by President Welch designating Paine as an enemy combatant and ordering him transferred into military custody.

"You mind if I check this with my boss?" Doc asked.

"Be my guest."

While Doc hit Bartholomew's number on speed dial, Gretchen came out to announce that Secret Service agents had just arrested Brown in the station lobby and confiscated the $10 million reward check.

Kenny looked at Doc and said, "What the fuck?"

The Director told Doc that both decisions were out of his hands. "I made them use Secret Service agents to arrest Brown because at least that way, the Bureau doesn't have to take the blame for the double-cross."

Doc didn't know which made him feel worse: what was happening or the "I told you so" look on Paine's face as he was muscled into the back of the Suburban.

While everyone's focus was on Paine, Kenny surreptitiously shot cellphone pictures of Col. Keslowski and the two sergeants in the MP detachment.

"Where are you taking him?" Doc asked Keslowski.

"To a secure military facility."

"Okay, what facility?"

Keslowski shot Doc a dismissive glance and pulled the Suburban door closed behind him.

As the Suburban and its Humvee escorts left the parking lot,

Kenny snapped pictures of the government license plates and the military ID numbers stenciled on the vehicles. "Maybe we should follow them?" Kenny asked.

"Nah. They'll just block us off with the Humvees. Might even put us in custody."

For Kelli's tail team, nighttime surveillance of Tony Gilman was usually a yawning bore. He and his wife ate dinner alone and hardly ever went out. Tonight was different. Not only did Gilman go out, a mile from home he changed to another car. The license plate came back to Mortimer Enterprises, LLC, which was probably a front company of some sort. Kelli called Doc. "Hey, we've got an interesting development here."

"You're not the only one."

Kelli updated Doc on the situation, and requested more cars to rotate into the tail mix.

"You have air, right?"

"Yeah, but I hate to have it get too close."

"Do your best, stay as far back as you can without losing contact. We'll join up A-SAP."

At that moment Crystal came out of the station and shot Doc a questioning look. He said, "Sorry, we'll talk later," then jumped in his van and took off.

When Kelli reported that Gilman had turned off onto Three Notch Road, Kenny said, "I know where he's going. Patuxent Naval Air Station."

Just about that time the chopper assigned to Kelli's team announced that they had to break contact because of restricted airspace around the base. Doc ordered the chopper to set down at nearby St. Mary's County Regional Airport and await further instructions.

Following Gilman right up to the base gate was dicey, but Kenny supplied a solution. He had Kelli and another tail car driven by Ron White race ahead along an alternate route, pull over fifty yards from the main gate, get in one car together, and pretend to make out. It was the kind of behavior that young servicemen and their lady friends had been doing outside military bases since cars were invented.

During his days on the Secret Service Presidential Protection Unit, Tony Gilman would have paid close attention to the two lovers parked by the side of the road. But he was no longer in the protection business, and with his mind focused on the task ahead he paid them no mind.

As Gilman's car approached the guard shack, Kelli rested a Nikon motor-drive camera with a mammoth 2,000 mm zoom lens on the steering wheel. The lens had an infrared night vision option but in this case it wasn't necessary. After 9-11, entrances to military bases were lit up brighter than Vegas on New Year's Eve.

According to standard military procedure, Gilman should have been asked for ID, had his name checked on the Pass List, and his car inspected for contraband. Instead, Colonel Keslowski emerged from the guard shack, got into Gilman's car, and the two rode off into the base.

In the tail car, White, an ex-Marine, said, "Wow, ain't never seen that before."

Fortunately, Kelli got photos of the entire sequence, including a clear, sharp close-up of Keslowski's face as he entered Gilman's car.

Kelli left her tail team where they could photograph any vehicles entering or leaving the base, then met up with Doc and Kenny in the parking lot behind a nearby cafe. While Doc brought her up to speed on developments regarding Paine, Kenny ran a check and discovered that Keslowski was the Deputy Chief Training

Officer for the Marine Corps Security Guard Battalion at the Marine base in Quantico. Officially, this unit trained Marines for duty guarding U.S. embassies, consulates, and trade missions overseas. However, there were rumors about Guard Battalion personnel occasionally being involved in blacks ops. Kenny was certain that if he dug deep enough into Gilman's Marine Corp service file he'd find a connection to Keslowski.

Doc and Kenny were still conferring with Kelli when a unit watching the gate reported that Gilman and the colonel were leaving in separate cars. Doc looked at his watch: only eighteen minutes since Gilman entered the base. *A helluva long late night drive for something that only takes a few minutes.* Doc ordered one tail team to follow Col. Keslowski, who was probably heading to off-base housing in one of the nearby residential tracks. The rest of the tail squad and Air 16 reacquired Gilman on Three Notch Road and followed him home for the night.

The number of pieces kept growing, but Doc still didn't know what the puzzle was supposed to look like. Things became clear the next morning when Doc's phone rang and the Director said, "Turn on the TV."

White House Press Secretary Jason Barrymore was at the podium. No relation to the famed acting family, this Barrymore was nevertheless a talented actor in his own right. Every day he gave a masterful performance imitating a human being. "The White House regrets to announce that at approximately 1:23 a.m. this morning Victor Nolan Truex committed suicide while being processed into custody. While undressing prior to being strip-searched, Mr. Truex swallowed a cyanide capsule hidden in the collar of his shirt. Medics attempted to save him but were unsuccessful. His body has been transferred to the Pathology Unit at the Bethesda Naval Hospital for a full autopsy. The President is disappointed that Mr. Truex chose the coward's way out rather than stand trial for his heinous crimes. The government looked forward to prosecuting him with great vigor."

For a moment, Doc thought he might hyperventilate. The image that flashed across his mind was the look on Paine's face as he was hustled away by Keslowski. Paine's words echoed in his head: "They'll claim it was suicide, or a heart attack." There were only two possibilities: Paine's death was an execution staged to look like a suicide, or Doc himself had failed to detect the cyanide capsule. *Scott searched him once in the parking lot, and I searched him again, and we both missed a suicide capsule?*

As soon as he reached OCD, Doc summoned Ginger Bridges to his office. "We still have Paine's gym bag, the stuff he had with him when he surrendered? We haven't sent that along to forensics yet?"

"Nope. I mean, yeah," Ginger replied. "I mean, yes, we've got it and no, we haven't transferred it from intake to processing yet."

"Good. " Doc got up and marched to the door so fast that Ginger had to scamper to avoid being trampled.

As they hurried through the OCD bullpen Doc barked for Kenny, Scott, and Gretchen to join them. After the long night, Kelli was home sleeping. He'd bring her up to speed later.

Ginger retrieved the gym bag, still sealed in a large plastic evidence container, from the evidence intake locker and took it to the Trace Evidence Analysis Unit. Doc hardly ever ventured down to the Trace lab, so his presence was enough to turn the heads of every whiz-tech on duty. The day shift lab boss, Mike Naren, immediately dropped what he was doing.

Doc's orders were simple: "Check every inch of this bag and every inch of everything in it for traces of cyanide."

"Yes, sir."

As soon as Naren signed the Chain of Custody form Doc released Ginger back to her office, then pulled up a stool and announced, "We'll wait."

Naren waved several of his staffers over to document the careful opening and unpacking of the gym bag.

The casual clothes Paine had worn the day before were still on top of the pile in the bag. In a pants pocket Naren found receipts from the stores where Brown had purchased Paine's new outfit. Naren carefully sealed the receipts in separate plastic bags and handed them to Doc for inspection.

As Doc noted the date and time of the purchases, he suddenly recalled the brand new, never-been-laundered feel of Paine's clothes when he searched him. Doc slumped on the stool. Everything he believed, everything he'd stood for in his career, had been smashed. Demolished. Crushed and pissed on. Paine hadn't killed himself. Someone, most likely Tony Gilman, had forced that cyanide capsule down his throat.

Scott and Gretchen gathered around as Doc passed the evidence bags to Kenny. In a moment the air went out of them as well.

Once he had photocopies of the receipts in hand, Doc led his team to a quiet spot down the hall and handed one set of copies to Scott. "Take a team out to these stores. Show photos of Paine and Brown to the sales clerks, the managers, anybody who was involved with these sales. If they're off duty, track 'em down. See if they can ID either Paine or Brown. If not, get a description of the buyer. Get any store or mall surveillance video of the transactions, customers entering or leaving the stores. Check other sales at about the same time. Track down the purchasers, see what they remember."

Gretchen piped up with a suggestion. "I think we should get Q&A statements from every witness on video."

Doc nodded.

Scott asked, "And if they identify Paine or Brown, then what?"

"For the customers, the video statements will be enough, but take the store clerks and managers into protective custody."

"And bring them where, here?"

"Fuck, no way." Doc thought for a moment. "We still have custody of that safe house Paine had outside Pittsburgh, right?"

Kenny nodded yes.

"Good. Take them there. Be sure they don't take their phones."

Kenny quietly added, "Make several copies of all tapes, from the stores and the Q&A's. Give the originals to Ginger, then stash the copies in various safe locations."

"And don't tell us where they are," Doc added.

Doc told Gretchen he'd see her back in the office in a few minutes. He and Kenny stood silently until Gretchen and Scott entered the elevator. Then Kenny said, "Using one of Paine's safe houses adds a nice touch of irony to the situation, expediency crossed with poetic justice."

Doc smiled ruefully.

Kenny didn't have to ask what Doc was going to do. He already had a general idea. "You know this is probably not going to end well."

Doc nodded. "Maybe you should put in for retirement this afternoon. End you career in a blaze of glory and ride off into the sunset with your pension."

"And miss all the fun? Fuck that."

"Okay, first assignment, find out where they're holding Ellis Brown." Doc didn't have to tell him to do it quietly, under the radar.

The federal justice system did not have its own jail or holding facility in the immediate D.C. area so federal prisoners were held in whatever space was available at city and county jails spread across several counties. Using discreet back channels, Kenny finally located Brown at the tiny local jail in Eldersburg, Maryland, northwest of Baltimore.

Doc recognized the irony that to get there he would have to use the bridge across Liberty Lake. *Yeah, that's where our liberty is, at the bottom of a lake.*

The DOJ had Brown confined under a Patriot Act "No Outside Contact" order, but it never occurred to the Eldersburg officers on duty that night that "No Contact" included FBI agents.

Doc interviewed Brown in his cell rather than an interrogation room, where it would have been taped and observed by every officer on duty.

The first words out of Brown's mouth were, "I'm not talking without my attorney present."

"That's gonna be a little hard, since he's in jail, too, and both of you are being held under a no-contact order." Doc waited a moment to let Brown digest the information, then asked him about his shopping spree at the White Marsh Mall. "At any time from when you left the store to when you delivered Paine to the station, was he out of your sight?"

"No. Not for a second. We were together all the way."

When Doc revealed that Paine had supposedly sewn a suicide capsule in the collar of his shirt, everything suddenly made sense to Brown. "So, what happens now? I hang myself in my cell?"

"Not if I can help it."

Chapter 53: Wet Work

Doc could only hold the store personnel for forty-eight hours just on his own authority. Anything longer required a material witness warrant from an Assistant U.S. Attorney and approved by a federal judge. If things went as planned, within that forty-eight hour window the situation would be resolved to a point where the witnesses could be released. However, Doc still needed an Assistant U.S. Attorney to issue some warrants.

A lot of warrants.

Under the legal concept of universal execution and custody, as long as an Assistant U.S. Attorney had original jurisdiction over some aspect of a case, any warrant he or she issued could be served by federal agents anywhere in the U.S. or its territories and possessions, and the defendant moved wherever that Assistant United States Attorney wanted without a state extradition hearing. Fortunately, two of the warrants Doc needed were for Special Observations Group Suites originally recruited from Texas, and Doc knew right where to go: Angela Boone. Her case against former President Lyman was stalled, inching ahead under a blizzard of appeals and motions filed by attorneys for Lyman and his co-defendants. With her career already at risk, she might be willing to double down and go after yet another administration.

With all communications compromised by NSA eavesdropping, Doc needed to present his evidence to Boone face to face. Doc covered his absence with an email to the Director saying he was in the field, tying up some loose ends involving Paine's safe houses. Given the witnesses stashed at Paine's former Pittsburgh safe house, it was technically true. It was also normal for agents to feel drained at the end of a long, arduous case, so Bartholomew translated it into Doc taking a little R&R outside the office and gave the matter no further thought.

Doc's plane landed in Dallas at nine-forty a.m. By the time he grabbed a Dodge Charger rental car and reached the Federal Building in downtown Dallas it was after eleven.

Boone was in the middle of a deposition on another case when the receptionist let her know that Doc was there. Startled, Boone turned the deposition over to an assistant and met Doc in her office. "Well, this is a surprise. Congratulations on finally catching the elusive Mr. Paine."

Doc noticed how almost no one, even in government, referred to Truex by his real name. "Thanks, but I think that finally is the operative word."

"So what brings you to my corner of the world?"

"I need to buy you lunch."

Angela Boone looked at Doc, and Doc looked around at the walls of her office. She knew then that *whatever he wants to discuss is far too sensitive to talk about here.* "Great. I know just the place."

They rode together to a rambling old cafe off the Stemmons Freeway about ten miles from the office. The place reminded Doc of Rebecca's, where he had broken the case, thanks to Lucille Widen's inability to remember exactly where she'd parked her car. They found a quiet table in a secluded corner. Both ordered the chicken and shrimp fajitas plate. Doc asked for a tall Sprite, easy ice. Boone ordered a margarita. "I have a feeling I'm gonna need it."

Once a government agency targeted a specific phone number, other numbers to and from that phone became a Circle of Contacts, CirCon for short. CirCons were a two-edge sword; they could be an enormous boon to law enforcement, and an equally enormous infringement on civil liberties. Using a CirCon to identify and break a terrorist cell was a great patriotic service. Using a CirCon to identify a reporter's confidential sources or infiltrate and harass political opponents and protest movements was a threat to democracy.

Even if all the numbers called by a particular phone were prepaid cells, using the same tailing process used to link Conrad Rubio to Bahner and Bahner to Gilman, with enough time and manpower an agency could tie each individual anonymous prepaid cell to a particular car, residence, or office. Agents would then photograph the people who came and went or operated that vehicle. Grab fingerprints and DNA off things left in the trash, cross-reference car registration, property title records, utility bills, run all that through the government's massive databases, and Voila! a dossier on each suspect. Or in this case, on every SOG operative.

For the next hour Doc laid out everything for Boone: the entire Special Observations Group false flag operation to sabotage the Manifesto party, the connections from Tony Gilman to AG Godfrey, Colonel Keslowski, and Paine's death. When Doc finished, Boone immediately thought about ordering another margarita, but realized that she needed to stay sharp. "Okay, so whattya want from me?"

Doc gave Boone a list of thirty-three warrants. The names on three warrants, to be served after Doc interrogated those arrested in the first sweep, made her wince. "Shouldn't we wait to see what kind of corroborating evidence we get from the first arrests before I issue warrants for two sitting Cabinet secretaries and the White House Chief of Staff?"

"Can't. Once the ball starts rolling, we won't be able to keep a lid on things. I'm gonna need to act fast. You'll have to trust me not to execute those warrants unless I get what we need."

Boone took a deep breath. Doc was right. *Everything had to happen lightning fast, or it wouldn't happen at all.* Ironically, she now pondered exactly the same questions that Paine considered on the bluffs of Point Pleasant after killing Arlen Stowe: *How did our Founding Fathers feel when they made their momentous decisions? What would they do in her position?* With Paine dead, and the Manifesto movement apparently dead in the water as well, her future was very much a murky crystal ball. The decision came down to, *either this is the right thing to do --and might put me a step closer on the road to the White House -- or it's the biggest mistake of all time and it's gonna put me on an express bus to a federal penitentiary.* Finally she agreed. "On one condition."

"What's that?"

"Marry me. Then, if this doesn't pan out, maybe we'll be able to have conjugal visits after they toss both of us in jail and throw away the key."

Doc laughed. "Deal."

After they got back to the car Doc realized that what he was about to do could keep him separated from Crystal forever. At times like this he wondered why he hadn't become a cabinetmaker or a building contractor. On the other hand, then he would never have met Crystal in the first place. *What the hell, if I'm screwed, I'm screwed. Can't worry about what I can't control.*

Boone called ahead and cleared her afternoon calendar. When they got back to the office, she sat down and created the warrants herself. There was no way she was going to bring anyone in her office into the loop. The warrants were issued in each arrestee's real name and aliases, but Boone logged all of them into the Justice Department computer system as John Does 1 through 33. She put the actual text of the warrants in an encrypted file to which only she and Doc had the password and encryption key. Each warrant had to have sufficient specifics -- "particularity" -- and that dragged the process out. It was after nine p.m. when they finally left the office. For whatever reason, Doc found himself suddenly feeling at ease. Maybe it was relief at having taken the steps to forge ahead. Maybe it was just fatigue catching up to him. Whatever the reason, he slept the entire return flight.

The next morning Doc convened his most trusted agents for a sunrise breakfast at Rebecca's. Up until then nobody outside Doc's tight inner circle knew anything about the connection between Paine's death and Gilman, SOG, or the AG. No one except Kenny knew about his visit to Dallas, or what he was planning. Doc was struck by the fact that in order to fulfill their oath to defend the Constitution his team had to meet secretly, in a backroom, like some anti-government terrorist group. *Hell, maybe we are anti-government. At least this particular government.*

Doc set up his arrest teams and distributed the warrants accordingly. He would personally arrest Tony Gilman. Agents under Scott's supervision would arrest Rubio, Bahner, and other SOG personnel in the greater D.C. area. Kelli was given command of two arrest teams. One, under her direct supervision, to handle arrests in Philadelphia, and a second, smaller unit headed by Manny Castaldo to execute the Harrisburg warrants. Gretchen Polamalu was dispatched to New York to coordinate takedowns in New York City, with Larry O'Neill along to supervise in Albany and John Price in Providence. Manpower for the New York, Albany, and Providence raids would be supplied by Bill Ramundo's New York SAS Alpha team.

The meeting ended at seven a.m. Scott and Ed Obrador headed back to OCD to pick up their support teams. Kelli, Gretchen, O'Neill, Price, and Castaldo went directly to Reagan National Airport where FBI jets and the rest of their teams waited. While Doc set off to ruin Tony Gilman's day, Kenny went to a nearby big box home improvement store to pick up a few supplies.

Thanks to good surveillance, the arrests went off without a hitch. All the suspects were taken completely by surprise. To avoid jurisdictional issues, Col. Keslowski was picked up before he arrived on base. The colonel tried to pull rank and invoke his military status but Ed Obrador gave him the choice: "Shut the fuck up," or be gagged. In Providence, Chuck Holochek was shocked when the arresting agents read the charges against his girlfriend, Jolene Starkweather. He felt worse after she gave him the "you stupid fool" look.

Gilman and Conrad Rubio were picked up at the SOG office. Both were disciplined enough not to say anything except, "I want my lawyer." While other agents whisked Rubio away for booking, Doc took off in his van with Gilman. Scott stayed to secure the site until the whiz-techs arrived to dust for prints and check for traces of cyanide.

At first Gilman thought he was being taken to a jail in Baltimore area. It wasn't until Doc's van turned off into a deserted factory area that he began to worry. The idea crossed his mind that maybe the AG and others higher up the food chain had decided to sever links to Paine's murder, permanently. When Doc pulled into an old warehouse, the table, chairs and video camera suggested interrogation. On the other hand, the sight of Kenny, clad in black from head to toe with a hood over his head to protect his identity, portended something more extreme. *Maybe it's all stagecraft, designed to intimidate.* Then again, he couldn't stop trying to figure out what was under that new blue tarp in the corner.

Kenny escorted Gilman out of the van and cuffed him to an eyebolt screwed into the top of the table. Doc sat down across the table with some files and his laptop. Over the next forty minutes, Doc laid out his case: phone records, background on the Suites, surveillance logs, video and still photos, including Gilman arriving and departing from Patuxent NAS on the night of Paine's murder. "So, that's what I already know," said Doc. "Now, in case you haven't figured it out yet, you're going to tell me all the things I don't know. I'm gonna ask questions, and you're gonna give me answers. Clear, honest, one-hundred percent complete answers."

"I'm not gonna tell you jack shit."

"Oh, but you will. You will tell me anything I want to know. And this is why," he said, holding up a bottle of water. "And that," he said, pointing.

On cue, Kenny lifted the tarp to reveal a wooden bench tilted downward on one end.

"You can't do that to me. Waterboarding is illegal. It's torture. You can't use evidence obtained by torture at trial."

"Boy, for a guy with all your experience, you're either pretty stupid or not up on current events." Doc shoved a manual across the table. "See this? Says right here on the cover: United States Department of Justice: Guidelines and Regulations Regarding Interrogation Of Persons In Custody. This says what I can and can't do. And you know what? It's fulla loopholes carefully written to let agents -- me -- get away with all kinds of shit that used to be torture but is no longer torture, simply because we decided to call it something else." Doc paused for a sip of water. He'd just fed Gilman a total line of bullshit. CIA and DOD interrogation manuals allowed for torture, but not the DOJ manual, and Doc counted on Gilman not knowing that.

Doc got up and began strolling back and forth. "But, just for the sake of argument, let's say you're right, this is torture, and I can't use what you tell me against you. That still doesn't mean shit. Why? Because I've already got enough evidence to put you away for a thousand years. Or maybe you weren't paying attention when the warrant was read to you this morning. Let me refresh your memory."

Doc read from the warrant. "Acts of Terrorism. Conspiracy to commit acts of terrorism. Acts in furtherance of terrorism. Conspiracy to deprive others of their civil rights. Inciting acts of violence against the government. Money laundering. Possession of counterfeit government documents. Manufacture and distribution of counterfeit instruments of identification."

Doc paused to explain that these charges related to the creation of the phony IDs and fake driver's licenses. After another sip of water he continued. "Use of false documents in furtherance of crimes involving interstate commerce -- that's your stooges using those phony driver's licenses to rent cars. Turns out a couple of those cars were registered in states other than where they were rented."

Doc stopped for another sip. "And then we got the good stuff: Murder. Conspiracy to commit murder. Murder of a civilian on a U.S. military installation. Accessory to murder of a person in government custody under color of authority. Interstate travel to commit murder -- you drove from your home in Virginia into Maryland when you killed Paine."

Doc tossed the warrant aside and tapped the cover of the DOJ manual again. "See here, where it says Department of Justice? Well, justice is what we're gonna have."

Kenny helped Doc manhandle Gilman over to the board, As they strapped him down, Kenny asked, "You were a Marine, right?"

Gilman nodded.

"Well," Kenny continued, "I went you one better. I was a SEAL. That means I went to SERE school. You know what SERE is, right? Survival, Evasion, Resistance, Escape. You know what they do at SERE school? Among other things, they waterboard you. Show you what it's like. Guess what? It's a lot more fun being the waterboard*er* than the waterboard*ee*."

Again, this was all theater, designed to soften up Gilman. Kenny had never been a SEAL and had never been waterboarded, although he had seen training films on how it's done.

While Doc unscrewed the cap on the water bottle, Kenny held

Gilman's head between his knees and clamped a rag over his mouth.

"You ready?" Doc asked Gilman.

Gilman evidently didn't believe that Doc would actually waterboard him, and stared back defiantly, but his defiance was short-lived. Like most people who advocate government torture, it never occurred to Gilman that it would ever happen to him. One bottle was all it took. After he finished gagging and spitting and puking water back up Gilman gasped, "Okay, okay."

Kenny was appalled. "You fucking pussy. You sack of shit, you're not only a disgrace to this country, you're a disgrace to the United States Marine Corps."

The rest of the interrogation went smoothly. They wiped off Gilman, sat him back at the table in a fresh, dry shirt, turned on the video camera and watched as he outlined the entire plot, spelling out in detail the roles of the Attorney General, Secretary of the Treasury, Vice President, and White House Chief of Staff Zak Wooten. Names, dates, places, times, amounts. Just when Doc and Kenny thought they'd heard everything, Gilman offered to trade something even better.

For immunity, of course.

Ten minutes later Doc called Boone using a private encrypted cellphone. She answered an identical phone Doc had given her on his Dallas trip. After he repeated Gilman's offer, Boone took a CD with templates for her office letterhead and several Department of Justice documents to a local FedEx Office location where she drafted Gilman's immunity deal, a Material Witness Warrant so they could hold him in protective custody, and just in case it became necessary at some future date, a WITSEC Witness Protection agreement. She faxed the package to Kenny waiting at another FedEx office store in Baltimore. If Gilman produced what he promised, the political ground was going to open up and swallow a whole bunch of people.

Chapter 54: Rendition

If there was ever a time that Doc wanted to be alone with Crystal, it was now. And if there was ever a time he didn't trust himself to be alone with her, it was now. So he took Kelli along. Crystal was surprised to see them at her door so early in the morning. Fresh out of the shower, she was wearing only a short terry cloth robe. If it were only Kelli or only Doc, she wouldn't have felt uneasy. But no matter how you sliced it, three people was one too many for what she was wearing. She was also angry. After Paine's surrender she thought things between her and Doc would move forward. Instead, she hadn't seen or heard from him for two very tough, tense days and she was irritated. She also had strong suspicions about Paine's alleged suicide, and desperately needed Doc to put her at ease. "What do you want?"

"Sorry. Didn't mean to catch you by surprise. I have to talk to you."

"For two days you don't call, and now suddenly we need to talk?" she asked, testily.

"Actually, no, I couldn't." Sensing her unease, he quickly added, "Maybe you'd like to take a minute to change."

Crystal retreated into the bedroom and came back a few moments later wearing a pair of jeans and a sweatshirt. She fluffed her hair out and sat down at the small dining table with a cup of coffee. Pointedly, she didn't offer him one.

Doc nodded to Kelli, who strolled out onto the little patio terrace and closed the sliding glass door. Until now, only Kenny knew what Doc was planning. Putting Kelli out on the terrace protected both her deniability and Crystal's confidentiality.

"I'm going to tell you something that almost no one else in the world knows. And then you're going to have to make a decision."

Crystal took a wary sip of coffee. *Whatever he was going to disclose must be damn important.*

Doc then revealed everything, and laid out his plan going forward.

During the whole time she never said a word, just sat there in progressive stages of shock. By the end she was almost breathless. The magnitude of what he told her was staggering. After building a career on challenging political power, she was scared, more scared than she'd ever been before in her entire life. She desperately needed reassurance, to be held, to feel his strength transferred to her. "You're asking a lot. If I agree, after that, then what? What do I do? What do you do?"

"I'm not sure, but I hope we do it together."

When Doc and Crystal arrived at WHHY the station was surrounded by an angry mob holding signs accusing her of betraying Paine and being responsible for his death. It was the kind of irrational reaction that angry protest often sparks. Both she and Doc noted the irony that her greatest need for protection came after Paine was not only apprehended, but dead.

"Hi, and welcome to Crystal Clear. My guest tonight is the man who led the hunt for Thomas Paine, FBI Senior Special Agent Darren Medlin. Until now, Agent Medlin has rigorously avoided the spotlight. His focus was always on the job and his oath as an FBI agent, not personal fame or celebrity. Now he will reveal some shocking new developments in this story. Good evening, Agent Medlin, welcome to the show."

"Thank you. Good to be here."

Doc began by taking the audience through the hunt for Paine, starting with the mysterious deaths of Arlen Stowe and Admiral Copeland, a time Doc described as, "Before we even knew there was a Tom Paine out there."

"And once Paine announced himself and posted his

Manifesto, what did you think then?"

"I thought the reforms expressed in the Manifesto Amendments were valid, but that his choice to use violence was completely wrong."

"And after his capture did something happen to change your mind?"

Doc took a deep breath. "No, I still believe that non-violent action is the proper strategy, but now I'm not sure that either violent or non-violent action will be effective."

"And why is that?"

At that point, there was no turning back. For the next hour Doc explained in full step-by-step detail the SOG false flag sabotage operation, replete with photos, copies of telephone and bank records, and videotaped statements.

When he finished, Crystal summarized: "So you're saying that officials at the highest levels, up to and including the White House, deliberately engaged in illegal, covert actions to undermine a legitimate political party, and to sabotage the fair, legal political process. And that these actions led directly to the deaths of police officers, soldiers, peaceful protestors, and innocent bystanders. Is that correct?"

"It goes farther than that, to the President himself." Doc reached into his briefcase and pulled out a piece of paper. "This is Executive Order number 44-1105NS/C. It is on official White House stationery. The letters "NS" stand for National Security, and the "C" is for Classified."

"So this is a classified document, and you're risking prison by revealing its contents."

"Forget the contents. I'm risking prison for just revealing its existence." A copy appeared on the TV screen in a box, with Doc and Crystal in a smaller box off to the upper left. "It's dated 25 October of this year and reads, By Order of the President: Having determined that Victor Nolan Truex, also known by the alias

Thomas Paine and the pseudonym The Crusader, is an enemy combatant who presents a clear and present danger to the safety and security of the United States, the Attorney General is hereby ordered and authorized to execute Victor Nolan Truex, using such person or persons as may be necessary. The existence and contents of this order shall remain Top Secret until fifty years after my death." Doc set the paper down on the desk. "It's signed by President Welch and witnessed by his Chief of Staff, Zak Wooten."

"So this Executive Order authorizes the murder of an American citizen without trial or due process of any kind."

"It's more than that. This document describes Truex as a 'clear and present danger' but it was created after Truex had agreed to surrender. More importantly, even though Presidents have claimed authority to kill citizens without trial or even indictment, you can see that the President and the Attorney General didn't really believe they had this authority, at least in this case, because the execution of Nolan Truex was falsely depicted as a suicide."

"And how do you know it wasn't a suicide, an attempt by Truex to make himself a martyr for his cause?"

Doc explained how Paine could not have concealed the cyanide capsule in his shirt collar. "But that's not all. I interrogated the man who did the killing. He's the one who provided this letter. He wouldn't carry out the hit without this 'get-out-of-jail-free card. Here, listen for yourself."

In the control booth Sam pushed a button and part of Gilman's videotaped statement went out to millions of Americans. While the tape played, Doc got a text from Kenny confirming that Operation Torch was a success. When the video ended, Doc announced that Attorney General Godfrey, Treasury Secretary Gesner, and White House Chief of Staff Wooten had just been taken into custody.

Crystal signed off the show by saying, "Despite the ability of politicians and corrupt institutions to get away with actions that strike at the very foundations of our democracy, I have always had faith in our political system to cure itself. After tonight, I no longer have that faith. All I can say is, good luck. The country is going to need it."

Doc and Crystal took off their headphones and just sat enveloped by an eerie silence. Despite the surreal quality of what they had just done, there was no going back now. Finally Crystal pursed her lips in a half smile. *Might as well get on with things.*

The surreal atmosphere Doc and Crystal felt in the booth also hovered over the entire station. Normally, after a blockbuster show like this, phones rang off the hook with calls from other news outlets wanting interviews, background information, and confirmation of various points. Instead, there was silence. All over the country, news directors and network execs wondered, *Do we run with this story?* It was one thing to cover terrorism and insurrection, or public protest and civil disobedience, but a story about Presidential treason, a clearly unconstitutional White House program to sabotage and subvert the entire political process?

Oligarchies always depended on the invincibility of the lead oligarch. As long as the big dog remained safe, unchallengeable and all-powerful the only remaining issue was, *How far down the line did that safety and protection extend?* But if the big dog became vulnerable, then everybody was vulnerable. Paine's insurgency and amendments had been a bad enough threat to the elite from the outside. Now, a senior FBI agent had challenged the oligarchy with damming evidence from the inside. That was even more dangerous.

White House Press Secretary Barrymore hastily issued a statement categorically denying all of Doc's claims and dismissing the idea that the AG, Treasury Secretary, and White House Chief of Staff were under arrest. Pressed by reporters to produce the three men for interviews, Barrymore went out on a limb and promised that all three men would be available for the Sunday morning news talk shows. In truth, the White House had no idea where the men were, and their promised appearance on Sunday was more prayer than certainty.

Doc, on the other hand, knew exactly where the men were. After being arrested by Scott and Kelli, three of the most powerful men in America now sat helpless, hands cuffed behind their backs, in his van in the WHHY parking lot. Accustomed to barking out orders, now they dared not even speak to each other for fear that the van was bugged, which it was.

In the station hallway Doc told Scott and Kelli, "Remember, you were only following my orders, and executing valid warrants issued by an Assistant U.S. Attorney. Then, as ordered, you delivered the prisoners into my custody. You had no forehand knowledge that I was going to appear on this show tonight. Given Ms. Dickerson's involvement with this case and the threats recently made against her, my presence at the station was not unusual. You had no forehand knowledge of the White House Executive Order relating to the assassination of Victor Truex."

They nodded. Everything he said was true. Doc had deliberately kept them in the dark to shield them from repercussions. Both could now answer any polygraph exam truthfully.

Kenny was a different story. He had been privy to Doc's plans, and a participant in key elements. That morning he had filled out his retirement papers, effective at the end of shift. All that remained was for him to hand over his service weapon, badge, and ID. At a ceremony in the station conference room he cut a cake recognizing his forty years of service to the bureau and the country. The small group toasted Kenny with some thirty year-old bourbon Crystal borrowed from Charlie McTige's private liquor cabinet. She knew he wouldn't mind.

After the cake and the toasts came the good-byes. Nobody knew exactly what was going to happen next, but Bravo wouldn't be the same without Kenny. Or Doc, but nobody wanted to talk about that. For a bunch of hard-core, tough-as-nails FBI agents, there were a lot of damp eyes in the room when Kenny walked away into his new life.

While Melody Ganz and the protective detail escorted Crystal back to her condo, Doc drove his prisoners to Eldersburg where he deposited them in the same jail where Ellis Brown had been held. He even made sure that Godfrey got the same cell Brown had occupied right up to the moment when Doc presented a Release from Custody order signed by Angela Boone. Doc also explained to the Watch Commander that, barring a court order to the contrary, a "No Outside Contact" order meant that no one, not even federal agents or members of Congress could receive any information about a prisoner without prior written authorization from the Assistant US Attorney issuing the arrest warrants, which in this case was Angela Boone in Dallas. Revealing or confirming the location or identity of a prisoner under "No Outside Contact" status was a federal felony under the Patriot Act.

As soon as Doc got back to D.C. he dropped the van at the office and drove his silver Dodge hemi Challenger over to Crystal's.

Melody Ganz wasn't surprised when Doc showed up and announced that he was taking over her security. *About time these two hooked up.* Melody felt a tinge of jealousy. Rubber and plastic only went so far. Walking to her car for the drive back to the condo she shared with Kelli, Melody made the decision to start looking around for her own apartment. And some real meat.

Once they saw Melody leave the parking lot, Doc led Crystal toward the elevator. On the short ride down, she asked where they were going.

"You'll see."

Chapter 55: Shockwaves

For Crystal, something about finally being alone with Doc in the muscular, throaty Challenger made the long, roundabout drive to Doc's country house simultaneously relaxing and exhilarating. As they got father out into the country, the bright moon that illuminated the changing scenery made it seem like being in a movie.

To convey how he had felt about Crystal for all the past months, Doc plugged his iPod into the radio and played the Vince Gill song that always summed up his feelings for her, *Whenever You Come Around*.

The lyrics gave Crystal insight into an emotional side of Doc that up to now she'd only guessed at, and it made her feel even more in love with him. Fittingly, she also fell in love with his house the moment they pulled into the driveway. Too far outside the city for an everyday home, it would be an ideal weekend hideaway. It was solid, traditional, and spacious but not pretentious. *The kind of place real people live.*

Doc unlocked the door, flicked on the light, and held the door for her. Crystal entered, surveyed the living room and then took a couple of steps into the partially remodeled kitchen. She heard him close the door and set down her bag, followed by the beep of the alarm system being reset. She was admiring the improvements to the kitchen when he suddenly switched the lights off, leaving her bathed only in moonlight from the kitchen skylight. Sensing him moving toward her, she turned back for the kiss that was coming. As she leaned into him he took her head gently in his hands and let his lips glide over her cheek, the side of her neck, and her throat. Only then did he let his lips touch hers, in soft little pecks. Finally their heads tilted to just the right angle and their lips gently fused. He waited until her lips opened before letting his tongue delicately mingle with hers.

At just the right moment, when any longer would have seemed forced, he broke off the kiss. Their eyes met briefly, then he pulled her to him, gently guiding her hips so that his thigh rested between her legs, against her pubic mound. It was exactly the kind of preliminary contact she needed to relieve some of the yearning. Her body melted to his. Immediately all the tension went out of her hands as they rested comfortably on his shoulders. They stood locked in this silent embrace for several minutes, like two dancers not dancing. Finally he kissed her again, and led her gently to the master bedroom.

They undressed each other slowly, as if both knew there would be plenty of time for their passion to explode. Finally, when she had nothing on except panties, he gently laid her on the bed. Something about the look in his eyes was asking her to take the initiative, to reveal herself to him. For women, revealing themselves to a new lover has always been a profoundly significant moment. If Crystal was right, he wasn't just asking her to do something sexy, he was asking -- and also giving permission -- for an act of brazen overt sexuality and wanton sexual aggressiveness that also signaled surrender to passion, the proffering of the ultimate prize, and permission to, "Take me. Have your way with me." Gambling that her instinct was correct, Crystal raised her legs, rotated them back over her head and slowly slid her panties off.

He pronounced her beautiful, and when he tasted her, she shuddered and emitted a long, deep moan.

She was surprised at how little time it took for Doc's tongue and fingers to induce an earth-shaking climax that left her huddled in a semi-fetal position, a quivering mass of orgasmic Jello. She had never climaxed that hard for that long in her entire life. *And he hasn't even fucked me yet!*

Doc spent the next ten minutes gently caressing her while the endorphins racing through her body gradually dissipated. When she recovered and was once again ready he entered her with gentle, tantalizing slowness.

As they settled into a comfortable rhythm, one word kept

creeping into Crystal's thoughts: perfect. His body felt perfect. The way he fit inside her felt perfect. His combination of aggressiveness and tenderness was perfect.

Something must have given her away, because Doc raised up slightly to look into her eyes and said, "Talk to me. Tell me what you're thinking, what you're feeling. Tell me what you want."

Crystal had never felt so sexually safe, so able to trust and totally be herself, with anyone. Now, at the ultimate intersection of love and lust, his encouragement unlocked a vault of passion. For the rest of the night -- for the rest of the weekend -- her thoughts and emotions and descriptions of the sensations she felt came pouring out. Sometimes it was a torrent of Babel, short exclamations and expletives mixed with grateful moans and involuntary gasps. Other times it was coherent sentences containing terms and an explicitness that she would have never ever used with anyone else. After each orgasm she kept thinking, *Thank God we're not home in my condo with its paper-thin walls.*

While Doc and Crystal enjoyed orgasmic bliss, the White House went through living hell. Normally President Welch relied on Chief of Staff Wooten and the Attorney General to do his dirty work. Now they were unreachable, nowhere to be found. All anybody knew was that they had been taken into custody by agents from Bravo armed with valid DOJ arrest warrants. Until Godfrey and Wooten were located, Welch was stuck with the White House Deputy Chief of Staff, John Shaar, and the Chief Deputy Attorney General, Willis Moseley.

Shaar was used to operating in Wooten's shadow, carrying out orders, not conceiving and executing strategy. Moseley was a complete fish out of water, caught up in events for which there was no playbook. He described the AG's status, and his own, as "nebulous and uncertain." Godfrey hadn't died, resigned, or temporarily transferred authority to Moseley. No previous AG had ever been indicted, much less arrested, while still in office. Moseley had no idea what kind of real power or legal authority he had. Welch didn't give a shit what Moseley thought he could or couldn't do. All that mattered was what he *would* do. Judging from Moseley's hesitancy, Welch deduced that the answer to that question was *not much*.

Everyone agreed that Moseley had the authority to order Justice Department personnel to search for Godfrey's whereabouts. Hopefully, if they located JGod they would also find Wooten at the same place. DOJ attorneys all over D.C., Virginia, and Maryland were rousted out of bed and set to work calling every local, state, and federal jail, prison, honor farm, and military stockade up and down the eastern seaboard. Thanks to the Doc's lecture to the Eldersburg Watch Captain, and the "No Outside Contact" warning taped to the glass above the duty desk switchboard, when a sleepy DOJ attorney called he was told that the only people in custody at the time were a suspected burglar and a woman sleeping off a DUI.

FBI Director Bartholomew's situation was complicated by the fact that one of his own senior agents had gone off the reservation by arresting Godfrey and Wooten. Welch couldn't be sure that The Director wasn't in on the plan. Keeping him at arm's length was the best solution, one that Bartholomew happily agreed with wholeheartedly.

When reached in Dallas, Angela Boone told Welch only that, "the accused are being held until their arraignment on Monday." She declined to reveal their location, citing the President's status as an unindicted co-conspirator.

Welch vowed to fire her.

Boone pointed out that technically only Godfrey could do that, and after his arraignment, there would be questions about whether he still had that authority or if a court would intervene on her behalf. She said "Good night, Mr. President," and hung up.

DHS Secretary Hoover also felt it best to remain at arm's length from the White House. Doc's revelations were like a fire in an ammunition dump. Explosions would continue until the fire burned itself out. Until then, anybody who got too close could become a casualty.

The Vice President, Art Lundegaard, was no help to the President, either. Like Welch, the VP was constitutionally immune from arrest while in office. But he, too, had been named as an unindicted co-conspirator, and was now looking at probable impeachment. On one hand, they could all escape punishment with a Presidential pardon; on the other hand, the VP didn't trust Welch to give him one. He decided that later, if it became necessary for him to act, he would demand an undated blanket pardon from the President as the price of his cooperation. In the meantime he was content to stay out of the line of fire and avoid giving answers or making suggestions.

WHYY normally ran pre-recorded programs from midnight to five a.m. This time the station ran Crystal's Friday show on a continuous loop. Furious, Welch ordered the NSA to block the transmission.

Even for a rabid government control freak like Director of the NSA Chad Seeley, this was a startling order. Blocking the broadcast of a licensed TV station was unheard of, and had Orwellian implications. "Are you sure this is what you want?" Seeley asked.

"Goddamn fucking right it's what I want! Now do it!" Welch bellowed, completely abandoning his legendary unflappable cool. Welch also ordered both the WHYY website and the separate Crystal Clear website blocked, and the station's phone lines disabled.

Unfortunately for Welch, Paine left a note in his bag with the password for the American Insurgency website. Anticipating the censorship instincts of the White House, Doc had posted the show video and copies of his evidence on the AI site. As with previous AI postings, devoted fans and followers created links, cloned sites, and workarounds to insure that it remained available.

Other than occasionally checking the news to see what was going on with the story of the century, over the weekend Doc and Crystal did little more than sleep, snack, and screw each other's brains out. After breakfast Saturday morning Doc took her on the dining room table, pulling her hips against him as he pounded into her until they were both bathed in sweat and the hair around her neck was wet and matted. When she came she grabbed the edges of the table for more leverage. Later that night he took her from behind in the spoon position on the couch, and then she tasted him just as he had tasted her the night before. Sunday, after he installed some door casing and baseboard molding in the kitchen while she lined the new cabinets, they showered together where he took her from behind. She felt so wonderful with him inside her, his body pressed against hers, warm water raining down from the overhead shower while the cool granite tile pressed against her tits and stomach. Eventually she sensed that this time Doc, who had previously demonstrated flawless performance stamina, might be having trouble holding back. "Come for me, baby," she told him. "It's okay." When he mumbled something about "not fair to you" she reached back, grabbed his hair, and commanded him: "Goddammit, I said come for me."

At that point no man could have held out any longer. This time he was the one who emitted a groan of surrender, and as he pulsed inside her Crystal felt satisfaction in finally having driven the great FBI super-agent beyond the limits of his self-control. The shockwaves convulsing through Crystal and Doc rivaled those rippling through the body politic.

Sunday was panic day at the White House. When the

administration couldn't produce Godfrey or Wooten as promised for the regular Sunday morning mock news shows, the media finally gave the story the coverage it deserved. Primetime news anchors and political talk show hosts cut short their weekend getaways to headline "Special Reports." One huge question was, "Where is Agent Medlin?"

The simple answer was, "on vacation." Late Friday afternoon Doc had notified Human Resources that he was taking a couple of vacation days. Taking vacation time over a weekend was unusual, but it had one unique advantage: while on vacation Doc was legally exempt from being on call and was not required to be reachable by the Bureau. To prevent being traced by their cellphone signals, he and Crystal left theirs at her condo. Doc's official residential address was his D.C. condo. His country house was still carried on the tax rolls in the name of a trust set up by his maternal grandmother. Nobody at the Bureau had the slightest clue where he was or how to find him. His circuitous route had taken them well out of the greater D.C. DAS coverage area, and now they could fly all over looking for his Challenger, but it was in the garage. For forty-eight hours Doc was as much of a ghost as Paine had been for all those months.

Everything suggested that Godfrey, Gesner, and Wooten would be arraigned in Federal Court in Dallas on Monday. Welch was desperate to prevent that arraignment. After having struck out in their search of East Coast jails and prisons, DOJ lawyers and FBI investigators checked all of Texas, Louisiana, Oklahoma, and Arkansas as well as every private charter flight into Dallas-Fort Worth that left, or was scheduled to leave, the Baltimore-Washington area between Friday night and early Monday morning. Welch was so desperate to head off an arraignment that he activated Seal Team Six to rescue the defendants using force if necessary.

The administration wasn't the only group operating in crisis mode. All day Saturday and Sunday lawyers for WHYY, the ACLU, and the National Association of Broadcasters scurried around filing emergency briefs and petitions with various courts demanding that the NSA be ordered to unblock WHYY's signal. Lawyers from the Solicitor General's office first tried to get the petitions dismissed. Failing that, they tried to extract an agreement from WHYY not to rebroadcast Crystal's Friday night show. Charlie McTige personally told them to piss up a rope. In the end, the Federal Appeals Court issued orders to the NSA, and the Supreme Court refused to hear an appeal. Nobody knew for sure, but thousands of phone calls threatening violence if the jamming wasn't stopped probably had something to do with the outcome.

Welch's first instinct was to order NSA to ignore the court decrees, but cooler heads convinced him that he had a big enough constitutional crisis on his hands without provoking another one, especially without a functioning Attorney General and Chief of Staff to help carry the ball. There were also rumors that networks and reporters were threatening not to interview any members of the administration if the signal jamming didn't stop. By Sunday afternoon WHYY was back on the air.

Sunday night Doc fixed Crystal a candlelight dinner. Halfway through, he looked across the table, and said, "I love you."

She came over, sat on his lap, and let her arms encircle his neck. "I love you, too."

For several minutes they rocked gently while he stroked her hair. "This may be a little bit of the cart before the horse, but I was just wondering, how many kids do you think we should have?"

She thought for a minute and answered, "Two. How about two?"

"Sounds good to me. I guess we can fight over names later."

She chuckled, kissed his lips, and settled back into his embrace as tears of happiness rolled down her cheeks.

It was a storybook ending to the greatest week of their lives.

Chapter 56: Repercussions

Unlike Doc and his Bravo team, the agents assigned to locate Godfrey, Gesner, and Wooten weren't used to real out-of-the-box thinking. It was pretty obvious that Angela Boone wasn't going to send the three primary defendants to Dallas on a commercial airliner or a DOJ plane. So naturally the agents assigned to track down the three defendants went hunting for charter flights originating on the East Coast. It never occurred to them that Boone would charter a private jet from Oklahoma City, transport her prisoners back on the return leg, and have them driven from Oklahoma City to Dallas. Boone further obscured the transaction by putting the charter fee on her aunt's credit card. To prevent interference by other federal agents or even the military at the Dallas courthouse, Boone brought the judge, his court reporter, and three federal Public Defenders to a banquet room at a downtown Dallas hotel.

Doc escorted his prisoners into the makeshift courtroom through a side door. The arraignment took less than ten minutes. All three pleaded not guilty. As much as Boone wanted to slap them in solitary confinement at some undisclosed location, there were practical limits to how far she could go. She allowed the defendants to be released on their own recognizance, which required them to sign statements acknowledging the court's jurisdiction and agreeing to return to Dallas for further court proceedings.

Immediately after the arraignment Doc hopped a flight back to Baltimore. While he was somewhere over Tennessee, Boone held a press conference on the steps of the Dallas Federal Building where she announced that, "due to safety concerns, defendants Godfrey, Gesner, and Wooten were arraigned in a closed courtroom proceeding. All three are now en route back to Washington aboard a DOJ plane which is scheduled to arrive at approximately 4:45 this afternoon at Reagan National Airport."

Giving out the destination and arrival time guaranteed that the media would flood Reagan National. Boone suspected they would be disappointed. The government would likely re-route the flight, probably to Andrews Air Force Base. Which is exactly what happened. There was no way the President was going to allow the three men to face the media.

The President greeted Godfrey, Gesner, and Wooten in the Oval Office where he handed them letters of resignation to sign. The letters were the usual political spin: "innocent of all charges...looking forward to vindication in court...resigning to avoid being a distraction." Godfrey and Gesner took it in stride.

Not so Wooten. Used to thinking and acting as if he was Co-President, at first the White House Chief of Staff couldn't believe what was happening. He had expected Welch to issue a statement expressing support for him as "vital to the administration." Once he realized he was really, truly being thrown under the bus, the egomaniacal sawed-off little prick became livid and refused to sign. Welch wasn't surprised. He simply dialed his secretary and said, "Ask Mike to step in, please." Mike Runyon, head of the President's Secret Service detail, entered with two burly agents who escorted Wooten out of the building.

Government officials weren't the only ones who had spent the weekend trying to locate Doc. Exactly as Crystal had predicted, movie producers, literary agents, publishing houses, and shows like Dateline and 60 Minutes flooded his FBI message box. When it filled up, they flooded hers as well. Finally they turned to calling Liz Fielding. Returning Liz' call using the phone scrambler was Crystal's first order of business when she got to her condo.

"Where the fuck have you been?" Liz asked. Crystal couldn't help but laugh. Liz was caught off guard. "Did I say something funny?"

"Yes, very much so," Crystal replied, between giggles.

For a moment Liz, still didn't understand. Then it hit her. "Oh my God! Finally?"

"Un-huh."

"Well, don't keep me in suspense, how was it?"

"Spectacular. And he said he loved me, and we agreed on how many kids to have. But no ring, yet. Don't think he's had time to shop for one."

"So, the sex was spectacular, he's the fuck of the century..."

"The millennium," she corrected.

"Okay, the millennium, and he said he loves you, and wants to have children with you?"

"Yes!" Crystal replied, dancing around the small patio deck like a little girl pretending to be a ballerina.

Liz suddenly felt a stirring south of the border, a reminder that she needed a good boning. "Does he have any brothers?"

"Sorry, 'fraid you're outta luck on that one."

Liz forced her mind back to business. "Well, in that case, do you know if he has an agent? Because he's gonna need one and if not, I volunteer."

While Crystal and Liz discussed Doc's future, several people in the Bureau's D.C. Human Resources office nearly got whiplash when he strolled in, seemingly unconcerned, to hand over Kenny Johnson's badge, gun, ID, and retirement papers. The consensus was that he should have turned in his own at the same time. *Save yourself a second trip.* Doc, however, had no intention of resigning. Fired or suspended? In that he had no choice. But give up without a fight? *No fucking way.* Not only was it a matter of principles, there loomed the issue of damages for the wrongful termination suit that he would almost certainly have to file.

The case of Tom Paine and the American Insurgency ended for Doc the same way it started, with a phone call. Director Bartholomew summoned him to a meeting in The Chapel.

"You just hadda do it, didn't you?" asked the Director.

"I told you at the very beginning not to put me on the case if you were afraid where it might lead."

"You know that by not getting my authorization you broke regulations."

"There's an exception in those regulations when an agent has a reasonable belief that the supervisor to whom they answer might be involved in the activity under investigation."

Bartholomew bristled. "You accusing me of being part of this?"

"Do I personally believe so? No. Is it possible? Yes. Was there any way to be sure? No. Until this thing is all said and done we won't know exactly who is or isn't involved." He paused a moment, then added, "Might not even know then."

"Might? You really think the government is gonna let the Attorney General and the White House Chief of Staff be dragged through a trial? This ain't the 70's. Hell, if John Mitchell was Attorney General today, they'd give him a pardon and the Medal of Freedom."

Doc shrugged. "I can always dream."

Bartholomew rocked in his chair. "I don't guess you're gonna do this the easy way?"

"Not a chance."

The Director leaned forward. "You know there will be an OPR investigation?" he said, referring to the Office of Professional Responsibility that investigates violations of laws and DOJ or Bureau regulations by agents. "You know that even if by some miracle you manage to wiggle around everything on this case, they're gonna go back and turn over every rock in every case you ever worked until they find something, or invent something, they can hang you with. You do know that, right?"

"Good luck with that. I'm looking forward to it."

Bartholomew didn't doubt Doc for a minute. *Smart, fearless, righteous, straight arrow prick, probably looks forward to being a martyr.* The Director picked up a form and read aloud: "Agent Medlin you are hereby informed that you are being placed on suspension without pay pending an OPR investigation into your actions relating to the arrests of Attorney General Joseph Godfrey, Treasury Secretary Patrick Gesner, and White House Chief of Staff Zak Wooten. You are ordered to surrender, forthwith, your badge, identification, and all Bureau-issued weapons and equipment. Your office, locker, and any Bureau-issued vehicles have been secured. They will be inventoried and any personal items returned to you within fourteen days. You are advised to retain counsel, and notified that any statements you make from this time forward can and will be used against you in civil, criminal, or administrative proceedings. Please sign in the box at the bottom of this page indicating that you have received this warning and notification."

Bartholomew shoved the paper across the table. Doc signed it, then placed his badge and ID on the table. He removed his .40 cal Glock from its holster, ejected the magazine, and racked out the round in the chamber. He loaded the loose round back into the magazine, and placed it on the desk next to the gun.

The Director logged the weapon's serial number in the appropriate inventory box on the form. "I'm gonna miss you around here. Sorta."

"Maybe you'll still be here when I return."

Not fucking likely, thought the Director. "Agents are waiting at the elevator to escort you from the building. I trust you drove your own vehicle?"

"Yep."

Bartholomew stood up but didn't extend his hand.

Doc nodded and closed the door behind him when he left.

Kelli and Scott were waiting grim-faced in the hallway. Instead of taking Doc directly down to the parking garage, they stopped on the third floor where agents and staff still assigned to Bravo filled the hallway and gave Doc a round of applause that could be heard throughout the building. He wanted to shake hands, hug people, and say goodbye, but knew that would put Kelli and Scott in a tough position so he just nodded and said, "Thank you. Always do the best you're capable of. Remember, your oath is to the Constitution, not to the President or the government."

Just as the door started to close Gretchen jumped into the elevator. "What the hell, why not?" she said, and rode down with them.

In the parking garage Doc hugged his escorts. "You know you're all probably gonna get suspended pending an OPR review."

"Hell, after this I need a vacation," Scott joked.

Everybody laughed, and then watched Doc's Challenger reach the top of the exit ramp and turn left on Pennsylvania Ave.

Crystal started Monday night's show with a cheerful, "Hello out there. I hope you all had as enjoyable a weekend as I did." *If they only knew!* "Tonight our very special guest is the Interim Chairman of the Manifesto Party, Ellis Brown, and I promise it will be worth watching." Crystal hoped her audience didn't expect the kind of fireworks that had gone off the previous week. *Sorry folks, those kinds of events just don't happen every day.* She was wrong. This was another one of those days, or, to be precise, nights.

After the usual opening pleasantries, Crystal asked the big question, "Where do you go from here?"

"Back to the streets," Brown responded. "Tomorrow we resume demonstrations in New York and we start new protests in

Washington. We need everyone to come out and join us. Getting the Manifesto Amendments on the ballot in all fifty states is an obligation that we all share, for the good of our country and our future as a democracy."

"So, just to be clear, you're asking your supporters to defy the President's declaration of martial law in New York and D.C.?"

"Yes. We believe that it is unlawful and we will defy it."

"And if violence erupts?"

"Without government infiltrators to incite violence, I'm confident that we'll be able to protest in a peaceful manner. If the government chooses to respond with violence, the blood will be on the President's hands."

Crystal was flooded with calls and emails from people in other parts of the country asking what they could do. She had spent the day thinking about Paine's contention that too many women had abdicated their position as the moral backbone of the country, and his assessment that if reform was going to be achieved, it was now or never. She decided it was time to step up. "Everyone needs to get out and show solidarity," she said, knowing full well that solidarity was a politically loaded word. "Protest on your own. Everybody must unite to stop the tyranny of the elite. Go down to the corner and stand there with a sign that says, *Stop the Tyranny*."

Recognizing a good idea when he heard it, on the next commercial break Brown texted orders to his subordinates to get their printers in New York and D.C. started making *Stop the Tyranny* signs.

Getting ready to leave the station after the show, Crystal felt strange and uneasy. She'd become friends with Kelli and Melody and Gretchen. Now she wondered what it would feel like to walk outside in the dark and drive home by herself, without a security detail.

She needn't have worried. To her surprise, Doc was sitting on the fender of his car in the parking lot.

"Hi, what are you doin' here?" she asked, as they hugged.

"Came to follow you home."

"You could have just let yourself in and waited for me there."

"Now how would I do that? You can't shim open a deadbolt with a credit card, and I wasn't about to pick the lock."

Crystal was surprised. "I thought you kept a key," she said, referring to the spare keys used by her protective detail.

"Nope. The only way I'm gonna have a key is if you give it to me."

God I love this man! "We can arrange that."

"Okay, but tomorrow I'll get the locks changed. Just to be safe."

As Doc opened the car door for her he said, "And don't drive too fast," he said. "I don't have my junior G-man get-out-of-speeding-tickets badge anymore."

She smiled at the joke, but knew how much it must be eating at him.

At Crystal's condo Doc surprised her by filling the tub with bubble bath. He sat on the lid of the toilet while she luxuriated in the tub and related her conversation with Liz about representing him.

He teasingly asked her if they had discussed more than just his economic prospects.

She coyly invoked "attorney-client privilege." Half a glass of wine later she pulled the plug, stood up and washed her hair under the shower. She felt comfortable with his gaze traveling over her body. It felt both sexy and natural.

"You're beautiful," he said, " In fact, you're so out of this world that Fox Mulder was right. There are alien life forms among us."

She giggled and said, "Funny, I was thinking pretty much the same thing about you."

It felt so good to snuggle together. Crystal would have been happy to have sex, but Doc wanted to establish some ground rules; just because she was naked didn't mean that he had a right to expect it. He promised to have her for breakfast, though. The last thing he remembered before he fell asleep was how wonderful she smelled, the scent of the bubble bath on her skin and the shampoo in her hair.

The next morning, after breakfast in bed and sex in the kitchen they turned on the TV to discover a different world.

Chapter 57: Shock And Awe

This time Ellis Brown had greatly underestimated the public's fury. Just as Paine hoped, his murder created exactly what the movement needed: a martyr. And martyrs always had a tendency to inspire. Combined with the revelations of the White House's secret Special Observations Group campaign, Paine's murder set a match to pent-up anger in everyone who was not part of the plutocracy. Three hours before the scheduled start of the demonstrations, crowds outside Army checkpoints on the outskirts of D.C. numbered in the hundreds of thousands and were climbing by the minute.

Brown wasn't the only one surprised by the turnout. Reports from the checkpoints flooded the White House and the Field CP of General Warren Stanfield, commander of the 2nd Brigade. And it wasn't just the size of the crowd; it was the mood. A young lieutenant at a checkpoint described it as, "an air of surly determination." One sign seemed to capture public sentiment:

Tom Paine
Rest In Anger

On President Welch's orders, NSA shut down local D.C. and New York cellphone and Internet access. This came as no surprise to Brown and Lofgren who had drafted a contingency manual. Now, orders were signaled the old fashion way: two yellow flares shot into the sky.

One of Gen. Stanfield's aides wondered, "What the hell do you think that means?"

Stanfield sarcastically responded, "It means that any minute now, dispatch riders will be galloping through town on horseback like the War of 1812."

The use of loudspeakers was illegal under the martial law decree, but Brown needed them, both to direct crowd movement and test the army's resolve. Reacting to the flares, Brown's strike captains at each checkpoint stepped forward with a bullhorn and proclaimed: "I am in violation of Martial Law Edict Number 7, prohibiting the use of amplified sound systems. Either arrest me, shoot me, or get out of our way."

It was a cold day and the Army commanders had no way of knowing that each protest leader wore a five-layer Kevlar vest with a ceramic trauma plate under his jacket. On the other hand, the protest leaders had no way of knowing if any shots they provoked would be aimed at their heads. Surprised by the massive turnout, checkpoint commanders either asked permission not to arrest protest organizers, or requested heavy reinforcements before doing so. Given the fluid, still-unfolding conditions, General Stanfield ordered everyone to hold their positions and ready their fire hoses.

A few minutes later, two green flares went up. At each rally point, big burly protestors equipped with homemade blast barriers rushed to the front. On command, the crowds surged forward at a steady, measured pace. The army units responded with streams of water from the fire hoses. It had worked before, and it worked again now.

For about a minute.

Then the hoses went limp. At the same time, in buildings all over town faucets went dry and toilets stopped working.

Brown had spent his time in jail thinking of how to improve his tactics and overcome the military's response to the earlier demonstrations. This time he organized special brigades in both New York and D.C. to take over key municipal water pumping stations and underground sector control valves. Each brigade included unemployed construction workers and former municipal employees who knew how to shut off the valves that supplied hydrants around the key protest areas. Two critical D.C. pumping stations were guarded only by a few cops with sidearms, who did what cops always do when confronted by superior numbers: haul ass for safety. Getting to the various sector control valves was even easier. Many of the manhole covers over these valve stations weren't even welded down. It didn't take long for protestors armed with cordless saws to free the few that were spot-welded in place.

Once the flow of water stopped, unease set in among officers manning the checkpoints. The earlier New York City demonstration had proven that homemade blast barriers and head protection effectively neutralized rubber bullets, beanbag rounds, and even sonic cannons. Like a giant fist slowly closing, all across D.C. the crowds moved forward, not running or charging, but in a controlled manner that was all the more ominous simply because it was so disciplined.

Gen. Stanfield now faced a choice: order his men to fire or fall back. It wasn't just the prospect of wholesale slaughter that gave him pause. He didn't know how extensive the loss of water pressure was, or when it might be back in service. Firing into the crowd might provoke acts of arson. Without water pressure, the result could be uncontrollable firestorms. The British burned half of Washington to the ground in the War of 1812. Stanfield wasn't anxious to go down in history as the man who caused it to go up in flames a second time. Like any commander charged with defending a position, Stanfield had established pre-determined fallback positions, smaller and smaller defensive rings. He ordered his units back to the intermediate ring.

As the soldiers retreated, most of the protestors converged on the National Mall. A large contingent led by Sofia Lofgren split off and besieged Capitol Hill. Under orders from Stanfield, the troops there retreated until the only real estate they held was the Capitol building, the plaza steps out in front, and the adjacent House and Senate office buildings, which were connected to the capitol building by a network of underground tunnels. Other groups spontaneously broke off to surround the headquarters of the IRS, the Federal Reserve, and the two primary American instruments of worldwide financial exploitation, the World Bank and the International Monetary Fund.

In New York the number of protestors also far exceeded expectations, and there was a twist in the age demographic. Demonstrating the power of social networks, hordes of teenagers throughout the city and the Tri-State area went truant to join the demonstration. Motivated by an irrational blend of youthful idealism, rebellion against authority, and feelings of invincibility, they seemed to sense what the moment meant to their future. Surprised by the high turnout of white kids, many minority teens in the crowd decided to test the mettle of the Wonder Bread crowd. A cry went up, "White chicks to the front!" Within minutes, the frontlines were filled with young white girls. Half were afraid the soldiers would shoot. The other half was sure they wouldn't. But with the crowd behind them and the soldiers in front, they had no place to go.

Initially things played out as they had in D.C. When dropping water pressure rendered the fire hoses useless, General Bristow's troops retreated to intermediate defensive positions. But he had a bigger area to defend than Stanfield did in Washington. Bristow was also a different kind of man, one selected to head the 5th Division because he was authoritarian enough to enforce the will of the government without being distracted by the age and skin color or nationality of the enemy. He proved it by announcing over the Army's powerful field address speakers, "This is an illegal assembly. If you do not disperse we will use deadly force. You have one minute to begin dispersing or we will open fire."

Darnell Davis, now free on bail from his arrest in Albany, led the massive crowd on Broadway at 14th Street in counting down Bristow's deadline: "Sixty ...fifty-nine...fifty-eight." By "fifty," crowds at nearby intersections joined in.

At his Command Post, Bristow heard the chant over the comm lines to his junior officers along the perimeter. The taunt chafed at his very soul.

After "zero," there was a momentary silence, an eerie quiet New York hadn't experienced since before the White Man arrived. Then Bristow's voice boomed over the loudspeakers. "Attention Broadway detachment...Ready."

As they had been trained to do, the soldiers raised their weapons.

"Aim."

M-4s snapped into firing position.

And finally, "Fire."

At that moment the concept of the all-volunteer army came back to haunt the oligarchs. Too many of the troops came from poor backgrounds and had only joined the military because there were no other jobs. Too many already had PTSD from shooting civilians in Afghanistan or Iraq, and knew they couldn't handle the nightmares from shooting fellow Americans. They hadn't signed on to kill cute young white chicks. The girls across the street were ones they wanted to fuck, and perhaps marry, but not shoot.

After a moment of silence that seemed to drag out forever, a single shot rang out. But it wasn't fired at the protestors. Corporal Richard Grant, 25, of Edina, Minnesota, stuck the muzzle of his M-4 under his chin and blew his brains out. Like Sgt. O'Leary, Grant had finally put an end to his nightmares, in his case ones born in the small mountain villages of Afghanistan. Watching video from Army choppers circling overhead, the furious Bristow repeated his order to fire. And then the breakdown became complete.

Many officers in the junior ranks believed that their patriotism and their morality had been betrayed by the actions of President Welch and SOG. It ran counter to what they had been brought up to believe as kids. This was not the government of the country they had sworn to protect. The people massed across the street were not the enemies they had sworn to defeat. One such officer, Lt. Prudhomme, in command of the Broadway detachment, made the most serious decision an officer can make, to refuse an order in the face of the enemy. Prudhomme ordered his men to "Secure weapons. Fall back, by squads, double time."

Everyone listening on the communications net heard the order: Bristow, Prudhomme's fellow unit commanders, General Stanfield in D.C., the head of the military's Joint Operations Command in Tampa, Florida, and even the President's advisors in the White House Situation Room.

Darnell Davis and Wilbur Pike could hardly believe it. Both had believed their lives were about to end. Behind them, teenage white girls cried and shook and tried not to wet themselves with relief. Davis quickly recovered and ordered the crowd to advance in an orderly fashion. He couldn't help adding, "Just because the Army ran, doesn't mean we have to." He got one of the biggest ovations ever given on Broadway.

Once the Broadway checkpoint collapsed, officers at the remaining checkpoints up and down the line also lacked the motivation to spill American blood and ordered their troops to fall back, allowing the protestors unimpeded access to the Financial District.

Unfortunately for the demonstrators, the army wasn't the last line of defense for the Masters of the Universe. The handpicked Overlord security guards guarding the headquarters of Silverstein

Goetz had experience snuffing out protests on behalf of despotic regimes in foreign countries. When the surging crowd of buoyant protestors closed in, they had no qualms about firing. In a bitter twist of irony so befitting the hypocrisy of the elites, New York City, known for its draconian laws against private citizens owning guns, was now the city where officials looked the other way as Overlord personnel carrying fully-automatic M-16's spewed high-velocity rounds into the crowd. The firing continued even after the protestors scrambled into horrified, panicked retreat.

Darnell Davis and Wilbur Pike had been right all along. They did die that day, taken out by shots to the head. Leadership of the protests fell to Chuck Holochek, who had been sent down from Providence to help out. Holochek regrouped his stunned and anguished protestors two blocks from the Silverstein building. He made sure, however, that all the other major financial buildings in the district, as well as the Civic Center, remained surrounded. Neither the Army nor Overlord moved to occupy the bloody ground around the Silverstein building. Eventually, city EMT's entered this no-man's land to tend the wounded. Officials from the Coroner's office followed to document the scene and remove the dead. The immediate death toll was forty-seven. Eleven more died later at nearby hospitals. Nearly half the dead were teenagers.

Despite the shutdown of the web and cell service in the area, images of the Manhattan Massacre quickly appeared on the Internet, posted by couriers on motorcycles who rushed across the bridges into outlying communities. Holochek also dispatched protestors to the headquarters of the major corporate news networks where incessant chants of "Coverage now! Coverage Now!" convinced the bosses that they had no choice except to cover the story in depth.

Meanwhile, back in Washington, Stanfield's troops and

protestors gazed at each other across intersections like armies in the first Revolutionary War. Only this time the Red Coats wore green fatigues. Then, to the surprise of everyone, a Humvee stopped in the middle of the street and General Stanfield stepped out.

Stunned, Ellis Brown realized that in the parlance of old cowboy movies, Stanfield wanted to parlay. He walked to the Humvee where he and Stanfield shook hands.

Stanfield asked, "Don't suppose I could get you to call this whole thing off?"

"No."

Stanfield shrugged and said, "Hadda ask. Suppose you heard about what happened in New York?"

Brown nodded. "I assume it's worse than I've been told."

"Probably is," Stanfield replied. "I don't want anything like that to happen here."

"Good. Then all you have to do is pull back."

"See the problem with that is, we've got to insure the safety of the President."

"We're not out to harm the President, just force the government to do the right thing."

"Then we can compromise?"

Brown replied, "That depends on your definition of compromise."

Stanfield signaled to an aide who quickly spread out a map on the hood of the Humvee. The General outlined a plan for a reduced perimeter, allowing protestors to approach as close to the White House as a three-block wide area, from 15th to 17th streets, and from Lafayette Park on the north to Constitution Avenue on the south. This area included the Eisenhower Executive Office Building on the west side of the White House and an even more significant building on the east, the U.S. Treasury. Just as with corporate politics, where the closer your office to the boss the more power you had, locating the Treasury Building next to the White House was no accident. Aside from Roosevelt's declaration of war against Japan in 1941, no President in the last hundred years had made any significant decision about foreign or domestic policy without first seeking the counsel, if not the approval, of the Secretary of the Treasury.

In return, Brown had to guarantee that protestors would not attempt to advance further. For Brown the east and west lines were okay, but north and south weren't close enough. He wanted to occupy the Eclipse, a large oval field just across the street from the south lawn of the White House. On the north, Brown wanted to occupy Pennsylvania Avenue itself, not just Lafayette Park across the street. Stanfield balked, but Brown played his trump card. "Well, it's either that or we try things the New York way."

Stanfield thought about it a minute and reluctantly agreed, but only after extracting a promise that protestors would not engage in any action that posed a physical threat to the White House, the Executive Office Building, or the Treasury Building.

"Now here's the other thing," said the General. "We've got to maintain open vehicular and pedestrian access to the White House and these two other buildings. That's non-negotiable." He proposed two entrance corridors on E Street leading up to West and East Executive Avenue, respectively, and wanted three hours to get everything set up.

"Two hours," Brown countered.

"Hell, I got a lotta manpower and materiel to get re-positioned."

"They're soldiers. They're used to double-timing it."

Stanfield grunted. Two hours was all he needed, and he knew it.

Brown had one final request. "General, it'll be a lot easier for me to communicate this deal and keep everyone under control if

I can send out a Twitter message. Much better than shouting over a bullhorn and hoping that the message gets passed to the folks in the back. Plus it would be good to let my people in other parts of the city know that we've reached an accommodation here."

Stanfield reached into the Humvee for a scrambled field phone. For the next few minutes Brown lounged against the vehicle as Stanfield repeated his request several times to people up the line. Finally he roared, "Goddamnit, turn the fucking Twitter thing on!" Stanfield fumed for another few moments, then said, "Thank you," about as sarcastically as he could and turned to Brown with a grin. "Be up and running in a matter of minutes." They shook hands again and Stanfield said, "Nice doin' business with you," as he climbed back in Humvee.

Two hours later Stanfield's entire green line of troops and vehicles fell back to their new perimeters like rolling up a carpet. Brown waited ten more minutes, then led the huge crowd in an orderly march diagonally across the mall to the Ellipse across from the White House. With protestors also filling Pennsylvania Avenue it was impossible for the President to avoid seeing and hearing the massive crowds.

By mid-morning all across the country, crowds inspired by Crystal's plea the previous night showed up carrying homemade "Stop the Tyranny" signs at intersections in cities big and small. Mass transit stops, subway cars and buses were clogged with more protestors carrying similar signs, which also suddenly appeared in the side windows of cars. High school kids in virtually every city ditched classes to join protests. Some were just out to skip school, but others were serious about the chance to change the country.

When lunchtime arrived in New York, people who tried to leave the television network buildings realized they were being held hostage by the protestors out front. One of Davis' strike captains told a network PR director, "The only people who get to leave this building are reporters and camera crews going out to cover the protests. Nobody else out, no food in."

"But we'll go hungry," he harried PR man complained.

"So what?" came the reply. "A lot of us have been going hungry for years."

Not about to give up any hard-won ground, protestors in Washington and New York were well prepared to stay where they were overnight. Brown's quartermaster logistical operation included tents, sleeping bags, gas space heaters, and commissary units to feed the protestors in rotating groups. The money saved by not supporting candidates had once again paid off in a big way. In spite of the Manhattan Massacre, for protestors in both cities it was beginning to smell like victory.

Crystal devoted her show that night to calling for more nationwide solidarity protests. Buoyed by the day's national turnout, she urged her audience to "get out in the streets of your city or town tomorrow. Get your neighbors to join you. It doesn't matter how small your community, even one person standing on a corner can make a difference if that one person is replicated in enough communities." She then went one step further and called for a nationwide general strike. "Don't just hold up a sign for an hour or two in the morning. Hold it up all day. Don't go to work. If you really want change you have to be willing to do some of the work and take some of the risk." She closed by suggesting new, simpler signs. "Just make a sign that says, 'Stop'. That's all, just one word: Stop. Let's all join together and bring the country to a halt until we get back the government we were promised by our Founding Fathers."

A caller asked Crystal if she was going to go to work and collect *her* paycheck. On the spur of the moment she answered, "Yes, I'm going to be here so that you'll have a place for your voice to be heard. But I'm donating my entire salary for the month to the Manifesto Party."

Watching in the control booth, Doc did some quick math. At the rate she was earning ad revenue bonuses, a month's pay totaled around $300K. Her willingness to put herself on the line, not only with the general strike call but financially made Doc love and admire her all the more. Still, after living off his FBI paycheck, he hadn't yet come to grips with what it was like to have the kind of money she made. Hopefully, those deals Liz Fielding was working on would pan out, and he could feel like he was making an equal contribution.

Chapter 58: Endgame

A little after three a.m. on Wednesday morning the National Park Service Rangers and National Guardsmen on Statue of Liberty Island were surprised by a flotilla of commercial fishing boats, cabin cruisers, sailboats, and tugs. Using grappling hooks and cargo nets, protestors swarmed the island from all sides. The Rangers were stripped of their keys and put ashore in Jersey. The guardsmen were put in rubber boats and told to row to shore.

When President Welch awoke later that morning, the three universal symbols of America -- the White House, the Capitol Building, and the Statute of Liberty -- were all under siege, held hostage by Manifesto Party supporters.

The next shoe dropped when the New York Stock Exchange opened, only to freeze three minutes later after stocks fell twenty percent and automatic computerized trading stops took effect. Two hours later the stops released and the process repeated itself. The turmoil in New York and Washington was enough for foreign investors to flee U.S. stocks and bonds. Rumors of a plan by Russia, China, and India to start a new international reserve currency to replace the dollar sent a dire message to Welch and his corporate bosses: fix your problems or America will be replaced as the financial big dog on the block. This naturally triggered emergency meetings at the White House. For those who attended, getting there wasn't much fun as the two access corridors on E Street became gauntlets of furious protestors shouting taunts and epithets.

Outside the White House along Pennsylvania Avenue, Brown filled the front lines with students.

Press Secretary Jason Barrymore accused Brown of hiding behind kids.

Brown replied, "The President is the one who's hiding, behind fences and gates and guns and raw military power. Hey, Mr. President, come out, come out, wherever you are."

The crowd picked up the chant.

Inside the White House, the Secret Service urged the President not to come out, but to get out, to evacuate by helicopter to Camp David. Welch was incensed at the suggestion. It wasn't a question of courage; he was scared shitless. And it wasn't a matter of principle, or of trying to maintain a steadfast image for public relations purposes. It all boiled down to the fact that he had been legitimately elected President of the United States and this was, at least for the time being, still *his* house. He wasn't about to forsake the symbol of his imperial supremacy, no matter what.

About noon, Kenny called Doc, who had just arrived at WHHY with Crystal for her noon production meeting. "Hey," Kenny asked, "Wanna go on a field trip?"

"Where to?"

"Thought I'd go down and take in the crowd. Kinda historic, you know?"

"Sure, I'm up for it." They decided to meet halfway and take one car into the city.

As he and Kenny walked the final mile to the White House, Doc had trouble adjusting to the recognition resulting from his appearance on Crystal Clear. All along the way, he was met with waves and applause and requests for his autograph. One buxom young woman asked him to sign her blouse. By the time they reached the White House, word raced ahead and the crowd opened to let them through.

"You feel like Moses parting the Red Sea?" teased Kenny.

"No. But it does remind me of something we've both seen before. 30 April 75." He was referring to the huge crowd massed around the U.S. embassy during the fall of Saigon. Doc had only seen news footage of the event, but Kenny had been one of the Marines on the last chopper off the embassy roof.

Brown invited Doc and Kenny to a portable stage set up on Pennsylvania Avenue across from the White House. Brown thanked Doc for all he had done, and asked if he wanted to address the crowd. Doc declined, but he and Kenny hung around to take in the scene.

The previous evening a nephew of Cece Rayfield, the heiress who financed the first Manifesto Amendment initiative campaigns, had rented two replica guillotines from Hollywood prop shops and shipped them overnight on charter flights to D.C. and New York. One had been set up in front of the famous charging bull sculpture on Wall Street. By mid-afternoon the other arrived in front of the White House. Demonstrators responded by hitting local markets for melons and cantaloupes. Soon "Public Enemy" wanted posters of the President, Congressional leaders, banksters, and corporate CEOs were taped to the melons. The crowds cheered the characteristic "Shussh-WHOMP!" as falling blades sliced effigy melons in mock executions.

That night Crystal broadcast from directly in front of the White House. Her call for an historic general strike had been a resounding success. Absenteeism at work skyrocketed as an estimated sixty million people participated. Some stayed home out of fear of the protestors, but the effect was the same. What really made her strike call a success was how it manifested itself in smaller cities, little towns, and even wide-spot-in-the-road villages. Word rapidly spread up the political grapevine to members of Congress, White House staffers, and the obsequious suckups in the punditocracy. The response to her call hadn't reached the grass roots level, it had reached the grass *seed* level. The White House and Congress had to take notice.

It also made her a hero. The massive crowd chanted "Cry-stal! Crys-tal! Crys-tal!" so much at the beginning of her show that Brown had to get on a bullhorn and tell them to quiet down. Engineer Sam fed the show to the sound system so that everyone could hear. As callers reported results from protests around the country, cheers went up.

Through a Herculean effort, her show staff in Baltimore and assistants at All Spectrum Media in New York had assembled pictures of every victim of the Manhattan Massacre. Crystal displayed every photo and read the name of every victim, now known as the Manhattan Martyrs. For each of the teenagers, she read off the name of their school and their grade. Except for the sounds of crying, the crowds everywhere fell eerily quiet during the reading. The last picture she put was that of Victor Truex, aka Tom Paine. "Most of all," she said, "let us not forget the first martyr in the battle to reclaim the liberties and freedoms on which this country was founded."

Crystal closed the show by calling for continuation and expansion of the general strike. She stayed and signed autographs for two hours, until Doc finally dragged her way. Again the crowd parted, although this time many reached out as she went by, just to say they had touched her, or perhaps to confirm for themselves that she was real.

As historian Howard Zinn noted, "Democracy is not what the government does, it's what the people do." For any government that pretends to be democratic but really isn't, a moment comes when that government must either bend to the will of the people, crush popular dissent with massive murderous force, or disintegrate. For the Welch regime, that moment arrived at mid-morning Thursday. By then it was clear that the general strike was going to be even bigger than it had been on Wednesday. Although President Welch was the immediate focus of anger, Congress wasn't off the hook, and it held the solution to the problem.

Just before noon Brown was invited to the White House for a meeting with leaders from both parties. The President did not attend. Senate Majority Leader David Ardmore and House Speaker Leon Rembert had a solution: Congress would adopt the Manifesto Amendments and send them to the states for ratification. "Of course, we'd like to make a few small tweaks and adjustments," Ardmore added.

Brown looked across the table and said, "Well, I guess we could shuffle the sequence of the Amendments around, you know, change the numbers." While Ardmore exchanged glances with the other officials present, Brown looked down at his watch. "I've got people waiting. What's it gonna be?"

Twenty minutes later Ellis Brown stood on a platform on the Ellipse lawn before an estimated one million people and a worldwide television audience to announce that Congress had caved.

At nine a.m. the next morning, the House passed the Manifesto Amendments, word for word as they appeared on the American Insurgency website. The Clerk of the House hand carried the bill to the Senate where it was approved unanimously.

Afterword

A week after Congress sent the Manifesto Amendments to the states for ratification, Liz Fielding finalized spectacular book and movie deals for Doc and Crystal. Doc's totaled over $13 million, and her's another $8 million.

The following April, on a perfectly beautiful Saturday afternoon, Darren Robert Medlin and Crystal Renee Dickerson were married in a beautiful ceremony at St. Michael the Archangel Catholic Church in Dallas. Kenny Johnson was Best Man. Scott was one of the ushers. Kelli Randleman, Gretchen Polamalu, and Liz Fielding were among the bridesmaids.

Mr. and Mrs. Medlin returned from their honeymoon to a new home in the Baltimore suburb of Columbia.

On the last day of August, the FBI's Office of Professional Review reluctantly exonerated Doc of all charges related to his arrest of Godfrey, Gesner, and Wooten. Just to prove a point, Doc returned to work for a month, then resigned and opened a custom woodworking business. Kenny Johnson became his partner.

That November, for the first time in a half-century, voters went to the polls with a real choice in how the country should be governed.

Thanks for reading. If you enjoyed Public Enemies, please feel free to:

Write a review on Amazon.com.

Like Finchville Publishing and Fans of Public Enemies on Facebook.

Visit PublicEnemiesBook.com for info about personal appearances by the author, blog discussions about Public Enemies, and new releases.

Mention Public Enemies to friends and on blogs you visit.

www.ingramcontent.com/pod-product-compliance
Lightning Source LLC
Chambersburg PA
CBHW051541250626
47157CB00001B/134